SHAKE THE DREAMLAND TREE

Sleep, baby, sleep.
Your father tends the sheep.
Your mother shakes the dreamland tree,
Down falls a little dream for thee.
Sleep, baby, sleep.

SHAKE THE DREAMLAND TREE

Susan Moore

MICHAEL JOSEPH

LONDON

MICHAEL JOSEPH LTD

Published by the Penguin Group
27 Wrights Lane, London W8 5TZ, England
Viking Penguin Inc., 375 Hudson Street, New York, New York 10014, USA
Penguin Books Australia Ltd, Ringwood, Victoria, Australia
Penguin Books Canada Ltd, 2801 John Street, Markham, Ontario, Canada L3R 1B4
Penguin Books (NZ) Ltd, 182–190 Wairu Road, Auckland 10, New Zealand

Penguin Books Ltd, Registered Offices: Harmondsworth, Middlesex, England

First Published in Great Britain 1991
Copyright © Susan Moore 1991

Typeset in 12/15pt Photina

This book proof printed by Antony Rowe Ltd., Chippenham

A CIP catalogue record for this book is available from the British Library
ISBN 0718133994

Part I

CHAPTER
ONE

The child, aged seven, lifted the dustbin in search of
something to eat. As she did so, the interest on her
mother's holdings in sterling went up another de-
cimal point.

Inside the dustbin was a slush of soiled paper
napkins, bottle tops, and discoloured rice drying in
a crust at the edges. A broken wine glass had been
dropped into the remains of an omelette filled with
shiny unheated mushrooms from a tin. Someone
had stubbed out a cigarette in a banana fritter.

The child put down the lid beside the bin. At an
address on Waverley Place in SoHo her mother's
income jumped an unexpected eighty thousand
dollars, courtesy of a Florida realtor passing by on
his way from a good lunch at the Café Iguana.

She handled soggy chips and a couple of undamaged lychees into a discarded hamburger
carton. A Korean steelman in Toronto moved some

3

equity into futures: her mother's holdings inched up half a million dollars.

The safest place to eat was by a bus stop near the local McDonald's, where people might think she was just a school kid squandering her pocket money on the way home. The child had been brought up to be wary of attracting notice, especially from anyone in authority. She wore pink vinyl sneakers, a filthy anorak, and a party skirt that was too short. Her wrists stuck way out beyond her sleeves. In the creases of her elbows and behind her knees, eczema had left a line of weeping sores. She had no socks. Under her soiled woollen hat, clumps of hair stood up amid scaly grey patches of ringworm.

Standing on the crowded pavement, the child was watchful as she ate. Her cough was worse today and she found it hard to breathe. She felt hot.

In a shop window behind her, the image of her grandfather spoke to nobody from a bank of ten television screens; one of his series was being re-run. As he mouthed inaudibly, his locations changed, with bewildering speed. First he had his back to a football match being cheered, down below by Liverpool supporters. From a succession of high places he looked down on other crowd scenes: From a succession of high places he looked down on other crowd scenes: a horse race with the riders in Renaissance dress, over earth-strewn cobbles in the city of Siena; white-painted Australian Aborigines dancing among huge boulders on a mountaintop; and a Voortrekker commemoration full of women wearing sunglasses with their calico bonnets; clearly he was discussing tribalism in its various forms. Lastly, as if to suggest self-mockery, he addressed the viewers wearing ceremonial robes of his own. In the gown and motarboard that went with one of his many honorary degrees, he was commenting on a procession of people garbed like himself far beneath him in an Oxford quadrangle.

The child coughed again wiith the sensation of a small explosive going off in her chest. Before it got properly dark would she recognize the way to the house she was looking for? The home she'd fled from was in a place she knew only as 'the village'. Before her money ran out it had been partly by luck that she'd got a bus ride all the way here into Birmingham.

Since she'd woken up that day, the trust fund established at her birth had grown by another one hundred and seven dollars and twenty-two cents.

Among the terminals of an Office on the top floor of a house in Chelsea, her father was dictating his answer to a letter from the National Society for the Prevention of Cruelty to Children. Outside were the treetops of Cheyne Walk and a huge view of river and sky. The Society had written to him in tones of respect borderning on awe. It was how he was addressed by most organizations to do with protecting children in danger. As he spoke into the dictaphone, he wore the businesslike frown of someone regularly confronted with the worst of life; this correspondence touched on a rumour to do with snuff videos.

5

The child finished eating and wandered off into a subteranean walkway beneath one of the city's traffic-stricken roads. At the same moment her mother nodded again at the auctioneer from Sotheby's. Like several dozen of the usual people, all careful to bid with bold gestures, Maria Dolores de Rapu Adams was sitting on a rickety gilded chair amid the marble wastes of an unheated country mansion in Wiltshire. The house's first owner had built it in 1730, on the profits of his transatlantic slaving fleet. Now his heirs were selling up and going to live in an ugly new villa above a Portuguese fishing village.

It was colder indoors than out. Beyond the great cedar by the circular drive, fog hid everything. Several bidders, their sheepskin collars turned up, were dressed as if for a point-to-point. Others were huddled in furs damp with condensed breath.

A cloud of sable covered Maria up to the tiny sapphires in her ears. Its wintry gleam contrasted with the South Sea islander in her looks. She'd been born on an atoll in Micronesia and her face had the strong elegance of a pagan idol. Her expressive amber eyes and her drift of blue-black hair, worn today in a chignon, put people in mind of perfect limbs clad only in ritual garlands and a hot ocean wind. In Maria, every sea-going race on earth had left some genes. Her ancestry included Lowland Scots missionaries, Portuguese explorers, a crewman from a Siberian whaler, an imperial Chinese child prostitute, German copra-growers, and a Japanese naval lieutentant killed at Guadalcanal. A Tahitian relative, eight generations distant, had sailed with the Bounty mutineers. The seed spilled over from so many harsh or sordid lives had bred in her a beauty of great originality.

Many people thought they understood Maria. It was her bad luck, she always supposed, that those who knew the least had most to say about her. The popular press, second-guessing their readers, had made her into a fashionably dressed icon. The glossies and the quality papers were more ambiguous; their public expected a twist to what they read. Some articles hinted that her sophisticated exterior hid a generous heart, desperately wounded. Others made the expected reference to her unlikely origins and went on to suggest that she was some kind of tropical Snow Queen. Maria was still astonished at her own indifference to such lies. She had found that almost no one could humiliate her any more, and nothing at all could make her afraid.

Unknown to Maria, the strongest clue to her was one that almost no one saw. It lay hidden in an old snapshot owned by her husband – one that he couldn't bear to look at very often. In it, Maria was shown soon after leaving the fly-blown shanty town where she'd been born. She was standing in the garden of Stinscombe Old Rectory, Gloucestershire, dressed in the brand new uniform of an English private school and looking anxious to please.

Even now, so her husband thought, how much of that shy, hopeful child must live on in the self-

possessed women thirty-two years old. In the meantime, what betrayals. Poor little girl . . .

In his faultlessly modulated voice, the auctioneer
was taking bids for one of the day's last and most
coveted lots. Everyone knew this was the sort of
item in which Mrs Adams specialized. The best of
the paintiangs had been bagged by Mallory Lydiard
from the Tate. They had included the Arthur Devis
portrait of the house's first master and his family,
all stiff silks gleaming against bare floors and panelling. Sylvestre and Gell of Old Bond Street had purchased the day's most splendid lot, a Tabriz carpet
with jagged spandrels hooked in ivory, indigo and
rose madder. Maria herself had topped offers phoned
in from the Smithsonian, who were after the Ocea-
nic art collected by one of the house's Victorian
owner. In particular, there'd been a Maori amulet
in greenstone and a ceremonial model outrigger,
sturdy but delicate, amde to hang in a chieftain's
house in the Ralik islands, the 'sunset' isles of Micronesia.

There was enough interest to round off the day
rather well as Maria repeatedly raised the little
white bidding paddle with her number on it at ten
thousand pounds a gesture. The auctioneer
managed to keep his voice excitement-free, in spite
of determined opposition from two youngish Japanese prepared to pay cash. the Japanese couple certainly looked loaded. Their clothes, in the exquisitely
tactful colours described as natural, were good
enough to have grown on them spontaneously.

At length Maria triumphed, and she had what she'd come for. It was a jade Buddha, attributable, like part of her own ancestry, to eighteenth-century Hawaii. There was a polite stir throughout the great room, as if the very sum she'd bid were admirable.

Preparing to leave, Maria Adams thought it was no wonder her purchase price had surprised people. But so what? Nothing could cost too much, when it was for her only daughter.

A few days before Maria gave the auctioneer her quarter-million-pound nod, her father-in-law had been leaning forward to speak into a dubbing-booth microphone.

'The family, then, is a subversive organization. The very loyalties that bind parent with child breed an independence of outlook for which tyranny of any kind has little use.'

Digory Adams' reading voice was perfect for material like this. The executive director, a cautious man, was openly impressed by his delivery. Even in private, Digory's urbanity suggested a character as substantial as Mount Rushmore. The series editor admired the edge of authority, like a killer current beneath calm waters, that saved Professor Adams's prose from blandness. And the microphone adored his strong, Bostonian-tinged baritone. Whether or not his best years as a scholar were behind him, his media career was still expanding. He was at that point of success where each public exposure brought a demand for more.

'The dictatorships of big business, the impiety of fundamentalist religions, the chaos of totalitarian government – these have small attraction for anyone whose childhood has bestowed the values of self-certainty and tolerance . . .'

Both as originator and presenter je was the man for the job. Everyone at Flamingo Productions Ltd knew they were lucky to have him. As he read into the mike, several of the production team were waiting out of sight for him to finish. The hospitality room, where they sat, was lush but scuffed, like prime pasture after a marathon rock concert. Its ashtrays were full and the coffee rings on its glass tables were wet. Padded swivel chairs faced each other in disorderly groups as though a number of urgent ghosts were in conversation.

Jenny Wheatcroft, the editor, was flicking through Digory's script. It was a twelve-part documentary on the history of the United States as a colonial power, entitled *America and her Empires*.

'Next Sunday. This lunch party scene, with people's children and what have you.' A crew was going down to Digory's country house in Gloucestershire to shoot the film that would go with today's voiceover. She glanced at Owen Ellis, the director at the British end of things. 'Will this voice work cover the whole sequence?'

Owen stubbed out a cigarette. 'I thought we'd fade up Digory's voice against a background of conversation. We can't use library stock —'

'Why not? asked Ralph Frenkel, tugging at his

10

moustache and frowning. He was their executive director, imposed on the project by the All-America Broadcasting Service as a condition of air-time. He had to query his British colleagues' every move, just to give himself a job.

'Ask Candida.' Owen smiled, a shade self-consciously, at his thoroughly nubile research assistant. 'Library material wouldn't match up.'

'Especially,' Candida said, 'if we want the sound to synchronize with close-ups. For example, Digory's daughter-in-law has said she'll be there to be filmed.'

'I should damn well hope so,' Ralph said. 'I thought the whole point about this family structures bit was to tip a nod at the Adams household's own – uh —'

'Biographies?'

'Calamity?'

'Scandal?'

Jenny asked, 'But will the camera do justace to the fearfully wonderful Mrs Adams? It can take against the most unlikely people.'

Owen yelped with laughter. 'Oh, come on! I mean, whaddya think?'

'Seriously,' Jenny said, 'a lot depends on what the viewers already think of her. All that state-of-the-art couture and commercial success.'

'Well, good God, at least the woman's putting the best face on what must have been every parent's nightmare. She may look as though she's re-made herself. But no one, since, has been allowed to touch the kid's bedroom. Take it from me, it's a fucking shrine.'

'But I still don't see why all this stuff on families.' Jenny, a veteran of Eritrea and Beirut, knew how to wash in a teacup of water and treat half a dozen kinds of snake bite. She found Owen's aproach to documentary-making too arty by half.

'But this has never been at issue,' Ralph insisted. 'The good professor's family are one hell of a selling point, no matter what. People remember seeing them as a package in the news media. So that's how they've gotta have them from here on in, amen.'

'So,' Jenny asked, 'do we get to film Digory's son and heir?'

Everyone looked at Candida, who gave a heartless smile. 'Sorry. The wonderful Maria, yes. But not the equally wonderful Edmund.'

'Why not, for Chrissake?' said Ralph. 'He's around, isn't he? What in hell's name went wrong?'

'Nothing's gone wrong.' Owen said. 'Adams junior refuses to edge into shot, so what? His old man has worded this sequence so that we just cut in a few frames of *The Storm Drains*; there's no one here who won't love it.'

In the dubbing booth Digory read on.

'Say what you will of popular American culture, it is shared alike by shanty-dwellers and by people rich enough to buy themselves the Presidency of the United States. Moreover, it is democratic enough to be found on movie screens throughout the world.

'Yet within the States themselves, there is another empire. America has many internal colonies. Some integrated one with another; others waging bloody but undeclared war. Every township throughout the Union is home to several unofficial nations. Down the years their inhabitants have spoken a Babel of languages, from the Greek-Texan fisherman on the Gulf of Mexico to the Russian-American logger whose ancestors settled in Alaska when that part of North America was governed by the Tsars.

'How, then, can we explain the insularity of America – a country in which fewer people hold real passports than have bought a ticket to the fantasy lands of Disneyworld? For if America is an empire, her attitudes are those of an island – a small island at that – set just over the horizon from the doings of the world at large . . .'

'If we must cut in part of an Edmund Adams's movie,' Ralph said, 'I hope you know which part. No way is anyone in this company going to ask Digory to do today's voice work a second time. I'm sorry, but I mean that.'

'All will be well, no sweat. Right after Digory's piece about America and chauvinism, then we have our sequence from *The Storm Drains*. The one where they're in the Oceanworld theme park – where the alien joins the manatee and the otters behind the glass wall.'

Jenny brightened. 'Where he forgets to pretend he can't breathe under water?'

'The same.'

'And the grown-ups don't notice because they're busy probing their kids to see if he's an immigrant from the trailer park.'

'That's the one. Honestly, I think with the winsome Maria on camera we should have all we need of America's most newsworthy couple.'

'Not supposed to be much of a couple these days.' murmured Candida.

'Yes, but that's how the public still sees them.'

Ralph persisted. 'I'm sure you've given this a lot of thought. But, seriously, Mr Zlotnick himself has said how he'd like this done.'

Owen turned pale and bridled. Hastily Ralph said, 'I know, I know. The production values are supposed to be yours alone – '

'Supposed to be! You know damn well they are!'

'Owen, I'm merely repeating what Mr Zlotnick said. He simply let it be known it would please him if Edmund Adams, as his one-time college buddy, would sit up at table and be filmed with everyone else.'

Jenny said, 'I reckon the guy's on an ego trip to nowhere, if that's what he wants. Did you see the bad-mouthing he got in *Private Eye* last week?'

'I'm sure they exaggerated,' said Ralph squeamishly.

'No, but honestly,' Owen put in, 'have you heard what Zlotnick did to the air hostess, the time they hit an air pocket and she split boeuf Bourguignonne on his shoes?'

The phone bleeped. It was Ralph's assistant, buzzing through from the sound engineer's booth to say they'd finished recording.

A few seconds later Digory's heron-like figure emerged. Even for a young man he would have been tall.

'I hope that will please your masters,' he said, as Ralph strode up to him, followed by the others.

As ever the professor was at pains to be agreeable. The courtesy of princes, thought Owen.

Ralph was saying, 'I'm just sorry Edmund won't be at the Rectory next Sunday. That splended evening Catherine and I shared with him at La Gavroche will have to serve for all.'

'Oh no, he'll be there, even if he does stay out of shot. I suspect Edmund feels you'll have enough, how shall I say, over-exposed faces. Since I gather your own overlord will be breaking bread at my table.'

Everyone tried to hide their surprise. 'Zlotnick – Mr Zlotnick? asked Candida.

Digory gave the phantom of a smile. 'So my secretary tells me. In the meantime, should any of you hear from young Zlotnick, give him my sentiments.'

The studio car was announced, and Ralph and Owen went outside to see the professor off. Such attention was the least thing due to the world's most publicized living anthropologist and the Grand Old Man of American liberalism.

15

Sentiments indeed, Owen thought. At least in announcing Zlotnick's arrival, like that of a pantomime devil through a trap door, the old boy hadn't expected anyone else to look pleased. You had to give him that.

Lunching over Greenland, Jimmie Zlotnick was without doubt the most sociable man on board. In a setting like this, it was something he did supremely well.

All his life he'd been different things to different men. And women. He was neither strikingly ugly nor very good-looking: light brown hair, light grey eyes, average height, weight, everything. When it suited him his physical ordinariness could make him invisable. At other times his charm hit like a strobe.

He was dealing out goodfellowship now to the leader of one of the British parliamentary opposition parties. the politician had paused in the aisle to greet Zlotnick, hands clasped behind his back like royalty on walkabout. Most Concorde passengers greeted each other with this kind of casualness, like commuters on a suburban train. Probably a lot of them could be found here more often than almost anywhere.

If servant class had existed, however, that was how some of Zlotnick's fellow passengers would have been flying. A few rows back three employees of Allied Consortia each wore an invisible sign saying, 'May Be Wanted on the Flight'. There was

Lalage Dalling, the English ex-diplomat who was Zlotnick's principal assistant; Crispin Wayne, Lalage's secretary, and Harry Baum from one of the firms of Lawyers Zlotnick kept on retainer. Zlotnick was hot for being seen to waste the time of people who cost him a bomb. No way would Harry's services really be required in the couple of hundred minutes it took to scorch across from Kennedy to Heathrow, but Zlotnick wore a lawyer in his entourage the way a fourteen-year-old car thief had to sport a knife. His official career – the one everyone knew about – gave him excuses enough. Along with All-American Broadcasting, Allied Consortia's interests included weapons manufacture, real estate. oil, mass travel and catering.

The debris of lunch removed, Crispin was transcribing some of the instructions Lalage had been given in the limo out to Kennedy. Most of them he found predictable. There was a call to be arranged from a gossip columnist who wanted something extra on Mick Jaggar's life as country squire. Also an appointment was to be made for tea at the House of Commons; an MP from a marginal constituency in the shires wanted the local press rooting for him instead of his opponent. Zlotnick's informal career, as a fixer, had no equal to everyone who counted he was at least a close acquaintance.

It hadn't always been so. A trainee researcher at ABS had once confided to a friend at the *Village Voice* something she'd heard about Zlotnick's early life as a farm labourer in Gloucestershire. Two days later she'd gone to work to find a security guard on the door of her office, and not so much as her spare packet of Tampax returned by way of a kiss-off.

Crispin was nursing one or two future indiscretions of his own. Meanwhile, some of his instructions had him foxed.

'What's this? he murmured to Lalage. 'He hates the opera. And why are these other guys scheduled to creep about upstairs at the Savoy, like old-time house guests out to score on the side?'

'They're the lawyers for a British radio station. Just *entre nous*, he's selling its owners some of the newspapers. To raise a few readies.' As a maker of powerful connections, Zlotnick had haphazardly picked up various private assets. they included a debt collection agency, some housing developments, a couple of ocean-going yachts and a group of newspapers in the West of England.

'What's he going to buy?'

'Nothing. He's going to give it to the poor.'

'I just love it when you play me around, you know that?'

'It's true. Up to a point.'

'So he is going to buy something else?'

'In a manner of speaking.'

Lalage knew better than to glance over her shoulder. During her years with the Foreign Office she'd risen to British Consul at one of the hottest spots the Persian Gulf could offer.

'He wants to make donations to some charities. Speaking of which, there's something else. Not now, though; on the way from the airport.'

18

Crispin guyed his own surprise. 'And I thought you and I had no secrets from each other.'

. An hour later, on the motorway into the West End, she confided what was the most important thing about their trip.

'First, I think it's time you called up a favour from your chum at *Private Eye.*' Though officially resident only in New York, Crispin laid claim to a social life on several continents. 'One on which the sun never rises though I say so myself.'

'The *Eye?* I'm not ready for enforced retirement yet.'

'You *can* tattle, Crispin darling, can't you? On demand, that is?'

Crispin put his hand on his heart and opened his eyes wide. 'Me? Well, only under contract, of *course.*'

'Freddy Debbs,' said Lalage, naming the British manufacturer of weaponry and other hardware whose Anglo-American career most resembled Zlotnick's. 'I'd say it was time your friend passed on the news that Freddy's on for a gong this Honours List. Mr Zlotnick says, tell them a Knight Grand Cross rather than any old knight. Order of the Bath, natch.'

'But he loathes Freddy. And who are my sources?'

'Of course he does. And I can be your source. I met Freddy last month down at somebody's place near Savernake. Besides, Freddy will be so thrilled when he reads about it. He's a dear man, always has been. But he'd just love to get his K – almost more than, uh —' motioning ahead to where Zlotnick's hired Daimler was just visible in the outside lane.

19

Understanding spread over Crispin's face in the form of a shit-eating grin. 'God help us, then, if our own fearless leader doesn't get one. Sir Jim Zlotnick, Sir Jimmie. No, what am I saying – Sir James! But they ration these things, don't they? Why's he fixing a puff for the other guy?'

'Because it'll look like self-publicity. If you do it right. Also Freddy doesn't want any old knighthood. If he expects to be a Knight Grand Cross – you're getting all this, aren't you – and he's offered something only nine-tenths as good he's almost bound to refuse.'

'Leaving the field further open. Neat – as far as it goes. But I hope no one's planning to dance on *my* grave if our master wakes up on the Queen of England's birthday and finds he's still Mister.'

'It's the New Year list, not the birthday one. And this is just as idea that came to him in the lift this morning. You wouldn't believe some of the other things he has in mind.'

'What about his age? Is fortysomething okay?'

'He's well enough in with this government. Actually it might get trickier for him later – if the other lot win the next election. And besides' lowering her voice, 'ten years from now, say, he mightn't be clean enough.'

On the approach to the Chiswick flyover, all three lanes of traffic dawdled to a stop. They were in a landscape of golf courses and distant pre-war semis. A pick-up in front held half a dozen men in overalls, two of them wearing turbans. Four impossibly handsome Turkish guys dressed like first-division footballers were stuck in the fast lane in a BMW. One of them was leaning out of the window to comb his hair in the wing mirror.

In the Daimler Zlotnick was taking a pre-arranged call from Ralph Frenkel. At the sound of Ralph's voice, without identifying himself or his subject, he demanded, 'Will the local press be there?'

'Yes, Mr Zlotnick. The features editor of the *Oxford Daily Press* will be at the Old Rectory on Sunday. Also the *Gloucester Enquirer*. *The Sunday Times* Colour Supplement will be sending someone too.'

'I didn't ask you about The *Sunday Times*. How many of the local papers have agreed to send a photograph?'

'I can't believe they won't send one, Mr Zlotnick.'

'I don't have to ask you twice. *Will the photographers be there?*'

'I'll see that they are. Right away, Mr Zlotnick,' said Ralph, an instant after hearing himself cut off.

Zlotnick hitched the receiver into its rest as carefully as if it were made of confectionery. As a businessman he might be aggressive and slipshod; to make up for it physically he was a precision itself. In his days of partying with Roy Cohn, for conformity's sake he'd spoken schlocktalk like everyone else at Studio 54. But even then, nobody had really heard him split an infinitive.

Right now, on his third change of accent in twenty years, he was becoming more English by the mile as he headed for a series of strategic encounters around Mayfair and down at people's houses out of town.

Never before had he wanted something so much that the thought of failure filled him with sick dread. If a change of government lasted long enough would his chance be lost for good, while his most powerful allies retired or died? Would he not be rewarded after all for his work in setting up the British Industrialists' Protection Society? Zlotnick had put so much into the Society's political fundraising, from ots ex-directory office in two rooms off Lord North Street. He could hardly believe it might be for nothing.

Sir James. With an English title he'd consider himself made for ever. In his lifelong quest for self-regard, maybe he'd even die for such a distinction. Certainly he'd kill for it.

The limo, heavy as a traction engine, swooped up to the raised part of the motorway. Above the crumbling Victorian rooftops of West London it blew in towards town with the ease of a witch's brooms-tick. It crossed the crowded, litter-strewn gulch of the Earl's Court Road running so quietly that every-thing outside was unreal. On Constitution Hill the grand leafless trees of Green Park might have been a movie projected inside the car's windows.

Sir James. On the pretext of several weeks' busi-ness, Zlotnick was headed for an epic of favour-chas-ing and quiet confidence in dignified rooms. What-ever the terms of cinching his knighthood, he was psyched up to meet them. Only one thing could be allowed to interrupt his mission: the chance to be there with the camera crew at Sunday's shoot, in the village where he grew up.

22

CHAPTER TWO

It was the professionalism of the job that was to keep the Serious Crimes Division so interested. That, and the beauty of the boat before the incident took place.

The yacht *Dominique* wasn't the flashiest vessel ever to enter St Katherine's Dock. A floating gin palace she was not. But she was certainly one of the most classically crafted. Out on the Thames, she'd stood out from the lighters and floating restaurants like a thoroughbred among seaside donkeys.

No one had taken much notice of her arrival, however. It had been raining and half dark when she had puttered into the deep tidal alleyway linking the river with the dock. Her masthead lights had been invisable against a glare of rush-hour traffic high above on Tower Bridge. And once inside the *Dominique* was merely part of the scenery.

St Katherine's Dock had always been rich. When Britain had boasted an empire, raw material from half the world had poured into the vast East India Docks further downstream. Here under the shadow of the Tower the anchorage had been too shallow for any but the most valuable cargo. In those days the dock had been pungent with the smell of imported spices. Now it stank of money.

The harbour's head of security often pondered this as he made his rounds at midnight. Sometimes he would amuse himself by totting up in his head the value of the boats moored there – but usually lost track well before the Inner Lock at around fifteen million quid. Most of his life had been spent in the merchant marine, and he found it hard not to be rude to the City sailors, arriving by taxi from the glass towers of the financial district. For three years' worth of his income, they were prepared to buy a Navsat system that told them to within a dozen metres where they always were – moored alongside a converted Victorian warehouse selling electronic toys and Breton fishermen's pullovers. He was just thinking that such a garment should never be worn unless you happened to be both Breton and a fisherman when something coughed loudly and kicked him headlong on to the cobbles.

The explosion in the seventy-five-foot, Finnish-built Swan was nothing like the movies. No orange flame blossomed in the night sky. The nylon rigging didn't get a chance to drip liquid fire. The boat died in the first fraction of a second.

About three ounces of Semtex had been enough. As one anti-terrorist copper was to observe, Gaddafi had given away fifty tons of the stuff to almost any fruitcake so long as the mischief was loosed on the West. It was untraceable. Placed under the port Maytag diesel, probably in the sump, the explosive burned at five thousand feet a second. For a brief moment the weight of all that German engineering directed the blast downwards, cutting a neat, round, five-foot hole through the hull. Then the engine smashed up through the rear cabin and into the deck. For another millisecond the overpressure in the engine room was contained; then the bulkhead bowed outwards and burst. a hail of brass, steel and fibreglass tore through the guts of the boat like shrapnel. On the starboard side the second diesel was blown out below the waterline. The sudden difference in stress loading, from the stern to the prow, snapped the boat's spine like a twig.

The only casualties were the security head's personal dignity and a nearby Riva which sustained twenty thousand pounds' worth of damage when the rear mast of the Swan toppled on to its flying bridge.

The *Dominique* had been slaughtered as efficiently as a racehorse despatched with a bolt-gun.

The Daimler struggled through the London traffic like an ant labouring over loose sand. At last it whooshed up on to Westway, a sound-proofed room on overdrive. The day had begun.

Zlotnick sat in the back with a newspaper open at arm's length, in a posture identical to his chauffeur's. It force of will could have powered his motor, he would have been airborne.

The raised motorway swept over a series of townscapes, all irrelevant as shadow-play. It crossed a skateboard park in the lee of a line of tower blocks like striding giants. A hill of old car bodies was shiny with gashes from the claws of the junkyard crane. One could see into twenty attic windows a minute. The traffic jams beneath, glinting in the low morning sunlight, flashed under the throughway one after another. On a muddy strip of ground between a railway and another motorway, a settlement of caravans was packed tight inside corrugated-iron palings. The Daimler overtook a large Bangladeshi family in a Triumph Dolomite. On the Triumph's back seat, small children overflowed three glum women in nylon saris.

Zlotnick was filled with a queasy mixture of elation and hope. In pursuit of his knighthood he was on his way to use the Adams family one more time. It could be their punishment, he told himself. For having once had so much more of everything than he'd had. And then for patronizing him, by offering to share it.

On the motorway to Oxford, then on minor roads into Gloucestershire, he brooded. He was as certain as he could be that there was nothing about him to displease the Cabinet Ceremonial Office. If his knighthood demanded the usual local connection, no problem. At least, not if he involved the Adams household. And as President of ABS he knew there wasn't a thing Digory Adams could do to keep him out of their home. Eighty miles out of town he was still savouring the fact, while being driven down into the Cotswold valley where Stinscombe Old Rectory stood.

Stinscombe was really tow places. The village proper, and a caravan site a mile away on a disused railway siding where Stinscombe Halt used to be.

The village was a place where everyone knew his neighbour's business. Not because the villagers regularly drank together at the Golden Fleece across the lane from the churchyard with its famous yew walk. Nor because they stopped to gossip on the stone bridge across the shallow River Eyne. When local news was swapped, it wasn't against the background of wild country dancing in the medieval tithe barn, as the peasantry celebrated Harvest Home and their kinship with the good earth. What people had in common here was that they were forever meeting in the same airport lounges, viewing theatres, mid-town restaurants and drying-out farms. Everyone knew that Digory had a visiting professorship at Oxford, and that he lived part of every year at the Old Rectory. It went without saying that most of the village knew he was expecting a film crew and why.

The Daimler crested a horizon of ploughlands and crumbling dry-stone walls. Below a coppice of beeches the roofs of the village came into view.

Stinscombe's main street elbowed its way down the hill between cottages with stone tiles like sliced blond gingerbread and made blind corners round barns solid as an abbey church. A cross-fringed brook was overlooked by a Georgian gazebo. The street forded the brook by a village green whose grass was as cherished as the lawn of the brook by a village green whose grass was as cherished as the lawn of the Great Court in Digory's college. Smoke drifted from cottage chimneys against a steep background of trees. In Stinscombe at this time of year most people warmed themselves at an open fire. Only one's live-in staff made do with central heating.

The Daimler crossed the packhorse bridge spanning the Eyne. A grey-haired woman in a sheepskin coat waited in one of the parapet's niches while they passed. Under each arm she held a dachshund. A couple of fishermen in green waders stood in the gravelly river, casting for trout and fretting at the brightness of the day.

Across a flat meadow stood the Rectory, at the foot of a wooded hillside. It was a square, elegant house, built of old-gold limestone three hundred years before, in the reign of Willaim and Mary. Other homes might be grander, but not as beautiful: in his guide to the county Nikolaus Pevsner had rated it one of England's twenty finest buildings.

Zlotnick certainly saw it as the standard against which he measured everywhere else. Recently, offended at being beaten to a mansion once owned by Gloria Swanson, he'd had a copy of the Rectory built on a boulevard in what passed in LA for down-town. Next door stood a Weald of Kent farmhouse with built-in garaging for five cars. On the other side was a Swiss goatherder's chalet with twenty rooms floored throughout in marble the colour of dried blood. Zlotnick's house, shadowed by palms the size of oil derricks, had been built behind elec-trically operated gates mounted with remote-con-trolled television cameras. By contrast, Digory's Gloucestershire home was half a mile from any other building. In spring, its beechwoods bloomed with wild garlic and dogs mercury, or quaint rare plants like lady's mantle and butterfly orchid. The banks of the lane that led to it were scuffed with the trails of foxes and badgers.

The Daimler turned in through the Rectory gates. Among the other vehicles drawn up on the drive was a patrol car. Zlotnick gave an inward scowl. Even though it could be nothing to do with him, his day was too tightly geared for any interruption. Only Lalage had his number. And today not even she was to call him.

They pulled up and the chauffeur got out to open the door for him.

Beside Zlotnick the phone rang.

The two police officers had asked to speak to Digory first. While Zlotnick was still awaited, the other guests loitered, curious, in the dining room, where they were being organized for filming. There were

29

the Northrops, who lived nearby in a converted watermill above Nether Shipcote bridge; Charlie Northrop was a former actor who produced TV advertisements, and Agnes was a journalist. The Kempes were there too, from Stinscombe Manor, behind the churchyard. Harry Kempe farmed three thousand acres of breezy wold around his private airstrip. His wife, Victoria, in a Barbour and pearls, was the essence of fresh-faced county womanhood.

Each couple had brought their young children; Digory's voiceover would be to do with changes in family life. It had to be said that, as a setting, the Rectory's dining room was a shade privileged. The panelling dated from 1692, and Digory's tall, scroll-backed chair had been made for a Doge of Venice and looted by Napoleon. Still, they could always come in tight on homely features like the handpainted candlesticks and the Staffordshire jug of spindleberries. And a lot could be done by focusing on hands and profiles; especially the children's.

Maria, dressed down in a loose skirt and open-necked white shirt, was liaising between the TV crew and the caterers, based in the big stone-floored kitchen. A reserve set of table linen was needed, so she went upstairs to the walk-in airing cupboard.

In the bathroom next door her name was being mentioned. Agnes and Victoria must have been adjusting their makeup in the big Rococo looking glass.

'I always feel I let this mirror down. It is *so* scrumptious.' Agnes's voice echoed slightly. The room looked underfurnished, even with twin baths on either side of a four-seater rattan sofa.

'Who put in those mahogany baths, do you suppose?'

'Edmund and Maria did that . . . when they were newly married.' At the twilit sadness in Agnes's tone, Maria nearly left, to get the damned linens some other time.

'Why *did* they become, er, estranged, do you know?'

'I gather there was a row, four or five years back. Maria flew to LA meaning to stay, and came straight back east on the red-eye.'

Maria stood among the dim closet shelves with her head bowed. Mindlessly she smoothed a tablecloth against her arm, over and over.

'At least she hasn't fallen out with the family as a whole. I must say, one does admire Digory for giving her the chance to grow up here. And her, too, I suppose, for adjusting so well and being so grateful.'

Maria fled. Turning a corner she nearly bumped into Edmund.

It was hard to remember when they'd last met alone. Even harder not to compare the present with the dizzy days and tender nights of courtship. Halfway back to being strangers, nowadays they treated each other with careful courtesy.

'I wanted to ask you something.' Edmund thrust his hands into his jeans pockets and looked at her guardedly. He was a tall man with Black Irish features, dressed in the seedy clothes of a backroom billionaire. There was still no grey in his shaggy hair; like Maria, he was a long time in reaching the finished version of his looks.

'Ask me about what?'

'I'll need to be in New York this month.'

'That's okay. I shan't want the apartment for a few weeks yet.' They were joint owners of a duplex on Fifth Avenue, overlooking Central Park.

'I could stay in a hotel, if you'd prefer.'

Neither fully understood the wreck of their marriage. Meanwhile it was partly out of consideration that Edmund kept his distance.

'Thanks, but no. I promised Digory I'd be in this country until after the New Year.'

'Speaking of him —'

'Yes?' she said faintly.

'It may be none of my business —'

'No.'

'But don't you think he demands too much from you? Or are you maybe offering him more than he has a right to?'

Nowadays, Maria's readiness to please Digory did seem endless. Earlier that year the television people had stayed several days at Digory's other country home, an experimental shingled mansion built a hundred years ago on a Vermont hillside. Maria should have been in Milan, at the opening of one of her galleries. For Digory's sake she had stayed behind, swapping an Oldfield suit for deck shoes and linen Bermudas, and showing the calm in-

32

itiative of the perfect chatelaine. A month later, Digory had made another polite but masterful request and Maria, giving up an important party at the Guggenheim, had flown with him to a former nuclear testing site in the Pacific, to be filmed looking out towards the radioactive site of her dead family's home.

'You never owed him that much,' Edmund urged, 'whatever people may say.'

The conversation Maria had just overheard hadn't been the least bit unusual – more like the background noise to her whole life.

She avoided looking at him. The sight of her husband made her think of a quotation from Shakespeare: *My heart is turned to stone; I strike it and it hurts my hand.*

'Don't.' She was standing with her back to the room that had always been the nursery. As a small boy, Edmund had crawled around its floor crooning stories to himself and playing with a vast set of toy soldiers from the Coronation procession of 1953.

From downstairs the clatter of crockery was audible, as the second-best dinner service was laid. It had been the best, until its tureen had been smashed. Maria had hurled it at Digory, flinging home-grown-artichoke soup in an arc across a ceiling and two walls.

Edmund said, 'I hope you don't think you have to make some kind of expiation, either.' Five years ago he'd been appalled at the things Maria had said to Digory.

'Of course not,' she said brusquely. 'Don't you try to keep busy simply for the sake of it?'

'Perhaps.' Edmund was anxious to back off. Both knew a silence must pass before they could pull back from the abyss and each go about their business. He added, 'I suppose Digory would like me to show up for a moment in the dining room?'

'I think so. I didn't know how soon we might start filming. Digory said the police were still waiting.'

She meant, for Zlotnick. Neither of them mentioned him if they could help it. But she knew Edmund would want to meet him, if only so he shouldn't seem to be hiding.

At the head of the stairs he stood aside for her, like a dutiful relative making the best of a forced meeting. The first time they had met after the crisis of their estrangement their contained behaviour towards each other had been more than Maria could bear. Afterwards, she had run out to her car, driven ten miles to a remote place, laid her head on the steering wheel and wept until she was parched.

When Zlotnick arrived, the police were still with Digory. Scarcely the wiser after a call from Lalage, Zlotnick was shown into the green drawing room, so-called, and asked to wait.

Like most of the house, this room served as a haphazard extension of Digory's study. It wasn't green in fact, but a shade of umber. Three generations back one of Digory's in-laws had had its walls covered with figured silk the colour of moss, and the description had stuck. The furnishings were mostly what his art-historian wife had described as country-house tat – not that the late Mrs Adams had used the term disapprovingly. A couple of Bokhara carpets in need of restoration may have been valuable. The furniture was plain but certifiably antique, in oak, walnut or satinwood. A couple of thousand books were stcked anyhow, regardless of whether they were first editions. One glass-fronted bookcase, five yards across, had been made for the wife of George III. It looked splendid enough to be the tradesmen's entrance to heaven. Most of the books had been written by Digory; over thirty titles, each in several translations. They included such set reading as *Myth Versus Legend*, comparing the Old Testament with stories from other cultures worldwide, *Lost Tribes; The Prehistory of Pacific Migration*, and of course the work that had made his reputation, *Anthropology Anew*, based on the months he'd spent in his twenties as a member of a formerly unknown Stone Age tribe in the highlands of Papua. Even the rare pieces of furniture looked used. None of the Rectory's owners had fancied themselves as collectors. It was just that two lifetimes had gone by since anyone had thought to fix the place up.

The two plain-clothes men came into the room. the older one, down from London, introduced himself as Detective Inspector Coleman. With him was a fit-looking young guy named Shepherd, a local man who'd come along for form's sake. Coleman was a bald-headed man with a gut; but for his manner, he might have matched the popular idea of a pub landlord. His first words took Zlotnick utterly by surprise.

'Are you prepared to confirm that you're the owner of a yacht registered under the name *Dominique?*'

'No. Why?'

'Are you sure?'

'Should I be?'

'It would help my colloeague and me if you were, sir.'

Zlotnick made a placatory gesture, wanting to gain time. His ignorance was genuine: he'd never heard of the damned boat.

Or had he? Once he'd been meticulous in playing small assets for all they were worth, but he had since reached the point of worldly success where he was no longer sure what he owned. He could easily have been given an expensive toy like this as part of some kickback, and forgotten about it.

'The vessel we're concerned with, sir, is formally registered under your signature. As it has been for the past four years.'

Zlotnick's digestive tract gave a blip of unease. 'I'm sorry. I just wish I could help you people.'

'Then I take it you have no serious regrets. Seeing that no insurance policy would offer cover in such a case.'

'Whatever's happened, I'm sure that's fine by me.'

Coleman noticed how Zlotnick's eyes were glassy with false certainty. 'The yacht *Dominique* was set on fire and sunk last night at her mooring in St Katherine's Dock. By means of an explosive device. Ownership *is* registered in your name, sir, but it will be hard for me to commiserate with you, much less make useful inquiries here, if you're not prepared to acknowledge the official facts of the case.'

There was a moment's silence, during which doors could be heard opening, and footsteps passing across the hall's chequerboard marble floor. Probably some of the local press had arrived to record Zlotnick's triumphant return to the scenes of his youth.

His mind was working with the quivering energy of a rat sniffing a trap from the inside. One thought stood out: how could he avoid compromising his knighthood? At least the damned boat hadn't been lost off the Florida Keys, so it was that much less likely to have been loaded to the gunwales with the makings of a tonne of crack.

The two men eyed him with dead-weight neutrality, waiting for him to speak. In order not to appear at a loss, he said, 'Look, it's not impossible that you've got the wrong owner.'

'Isn't it?'

Shepherd spoke up. He was standing, hands in his blouson pockets, against a blur of cool autumn sunshine from the lawns outside. His haircut made him look like a successful villain.

'Are you here this morning on business?'

37

His drift was obvious. Both men were bound to have examined the old file that featured Zlotnick's name so much. A fighter for fighting's sake, Zlotnick returned Shepherd's look without a tremor.

'Since you knew how to find me, I can't belive you don't know what I'm doing here. This house did use to be my home.' All the evidence of five years ago was on his side. These clowns knew they were blowing their cool to no purpose.

'My colleague and I appreciate that,' Coleman interrupted.

'Then no doubt you both appreciate that I'm here by Professor Adams's personal invitation. As I've often been in the past.'

Yes, you poncing crud, thought Coleman. But not in recent years you haven't.

In the drive, shoulders hunched against a rising breeze, later the two policemen compared impressions. From habit they kept their eyes up and their voices down, even though Coleman's driver was the only person who could have overheard.

Shepherd declared that Zlotnick was a tight-arsed prick who deserved to find himself in deeper shit than he ever would.

Coleman took a more cheerful view. 'I don't give a damn what he hasn't done. We needn't kiss him goodbye yet.'

Zlotnick joined everyone else in the dining room, opening and closing the door as precisely as if it were part of an assembly kit.

'My dear fellow!' Striding up to Edmund, he held out his hand. Anyone would have thought Zlotnick was the host, being gracious to a guest. 'How delighted I am that you could join us today. And how well you look!' This, between ex-buddies once close enough to address each other mostly as 'asshole'.

Edmund was visibly embarrassed. He grunted out a few politenesses – Zlotnick's journey – had he met the crew? – his own regret at having to leave them, to make some calls to another time zone. Even the weather, for God's sake. As soon as decency allowed he turned to Ralph, on the pretext of asking something about the day's filming.

The crew from Flamingo Productions were busting a gut in their effort not to stare at Edmund. Here, in frayed sneakers and a sweatshirt with the elbows gone, was Movie Success incarnate. Not only that, but Hollywood's One Just Man, if you didn't count that business with his wife. Since his virtual separation from Maria, Edmund had spent much of his energies in setting up an organization for parents of missing children. In groups around the world its members supported one another. It spread awareness of how to reduce risks to children in public places, and it staffed centres in areas of danger, from Soho in London to King's Cross down in Sydney. There'd been a time when Edmund had felt victimized by his own fame. Subsequently he'd learned to use celebrity for all it was worth, raising funds or blackmailing the networks into giving free publicity for his cause. Even the Salvation Army rated what he'd achieved.

As Owen ordered people to their places ready for filming to start, the room was thick with respect. Edmund excused himself and left with the wading motion of a man too tall for ordinary rooms or furniture.

The script called at first for background conversation. Everyone sat down and started talking about the least controversial thing they could think of.

'Try some of this, old son,' Charlie Northrop suggested to his elder child. 'It'll do great things for your number twos.'

'I find it helps if you pre-chill the ramikins,' said Victoria, who didn't actually know any other way to talk.

Her husband was declaring, 'No, no question about it; another grain silo. But I'm borrowing yen this time, not marks.'

Standing out of shot, Owen and Digory began to relax at how well everyone was performing. Zlotnick gave his roguish laugh at even the most banal remarks, and Maria made a touching sight with Agnes's nine-month-old daughter on her lap. The baby was just old enough to help herself from a feeding bottle upended in both hands. Between gulps she looked around, her glance jerking at random this way and that. Every time she caught sight of her mother she crowed excitedly, gaping with delight.

The opening shot was supposed to give a general view of the meal. It meant that really everyone was sitting bunched together like the Mad Hatter's tea party. Only when the close-ups were being filmed could they spread out.

'Half-time thanks, everyone,' Owen said at length. 'This is your one chance to have a nicotine fix, scratch where it itches or go to the john.'

As if on cue the baby on Maria's lap turned red, then began to cry. Maria laughingly smoothed her skirt with one hand where the child had peed on it. 'Nice timing,' she told Agnes. 'She could easily have done it on camera.'

Across the room Zlotnick gave a smile as wide as an elephant trap. 'As well as on you, dear lady!'

Everyone laughed, thinking him as good-humoured as he looked. Maria hurried from the room. As she finished sponging down her skirt, she could hear someone rattling the bathroom door from the outside with deliberate irritation.

Opening it, she found Zlotnick.

He said, 'You have finished, I take it. One would hate to think of those lissom, oh-so-slightly-tinted thighs still being smeared with shit.'

In the old days Zlotnick had often talked like this – though only to Maria, a shy, unhappy schoolgirl. Everyone else had been too useful to him.

She ignored him. Seeing Agnes pass with the baby newly changed, she remarked to her, 'Now I know why they say one should never perform in public with animals or children.'

Zlotnick waited until they were alone again. 'No doubt if you'd supplied the child yourself it would have shat ice cream. On the other hand, you and

41

Adams haven't been too effectual in reproducing yourselves, have you? One looks in vain for evidence that the line is due to be continued.'

Maria paled. 'How like your real self to say so,' she managed to blurt.

For the rest of the meal no one could understand why she had fallen silent.

After everyone had packed up and left, Maria got into her car. For half an hour she drove with her foot down hard, doing seventy on country lanes and blaring the horn at every bend. In a side street in Oxford she slewed to a stop and got out without bothering to lock up. Stiff with unpurged fury, she stalked tearlessly through the by-ways leading to the wide space of St Giles Street.

Among the bare boughs of plane trees, drizzle made a halo around every street light. Maria sat down at the foot of the memorial to the Protestant bishops who four centuries back had been chained up on that spot and ceremoniously seared to death. The steps beneath her were soaking, but she was indifferent to glances from the few passers-by. All she could think of was what this place meant to her, and what she intended to do about it.

It was here, five years ago, that Zlotnick had been allowed to bring Maria's daughter to the fair, against her will. And it was in this place, with Maria elsewhere, crying out from the pangs of still-birth, that little Sarah Elizabeth Adams had last been seen, dead or alive.

CHAPTER
THREE

The decisive moment for Maria's life came six years before she was born. From twenty miles up-wind, among a shoal of brilliant Pacific islands, a hydrogen bomb was detonated in her grandparent's coconut grove.

After four seconds the bark and fronds of trees three miles away where dissolving in smoke. Half a dozen heartbeats later, the site of Maria's family village was several million degrees Fahrenheit. At twelve seconds from detonation the scorched stumps of palm trees were lashing in a five-hundred-miles-an-hour wind, almost flat to the ground. By now a mushroom cloud had risen several miles into the sky. Radioactive particles billowed out from it in a spectacle of extraordinary beauty.

As it rose above the ocean the pillar of fire from the explosion carried all sorts of remains. Fragments of cement floors and outdoor latrines. Toy boats from the bottom of the lagoon made of coconut husks with potato-chip packets for sails. A presidential photograph of Harry Truman from the back room used as an office by Maria's late uncle the magistrate. The vaporized remains of termites, stormy petrels, tuna fish, dolphins, and a bewildered abandoned dog. Decorations from the village burying ground – coloured shells, tinsel streamers and the broken bottles used nose down to make picket fences round the graves.

And, with the other tainted dust streaming twelve miles up, the bones of most of Maria's recent ancestors.

Plenty of islands were left from the archipelago where the US military had tested their bomb. Maria was born on one, six hundred miles to the south. In advance of the test, her mother had been put on to an American naval destroyer along with several hundred other islanders. Their exile was supposed to have been temporary; as a government spokesman put it, 'There will be just a little bit of poison and then you can settle down again.'

The new island was one of a chain of coral specks around a wide lagoon; a piece of bright heaven fallen into the foam of a perfect sea. It was untouched; almost no one had even visited there.

In a part of the world where land was a scarce resource, there was a reason for this. The pigs and goats brought along in the destroyer's hold were soon gone, as people found they hadn't a hope of supporting themselves on a patch of ground no bigger than a golf course. Water from the new settlement's four taps was rationed to an hour's supply per day. Official visitors to the island were dismayed to find it had become encrusted with shanties, many of them built on stilts over the water's edge to save space. Low tide stank.

From the military base over the horizon some welfare did get paid out, even though in return the islanders could offer nothing. Thinking they were merely loaning their land, they'd obediently made America a present of all they had.

Or almost all.

'These people,' said the area's military governor, 'are tending to depend too much on American aid, and are losing their self-reliance.' But a hundred or so, through with being all washed up beside their bacteria-soup lagoon, accepted the offer of another move. Their settlement would be on another uninhabited island, but there were fish over the reef and they could harvest coconuts, pandanus and arrowroot. also it was within a day's sail of their original home.

Not long passed before the new settlers began to respond to the quantities of caesium, strontium, americium and plutonium that made up so much of their island. After a few years more, their pleas for medical help brought at least some response. Researchers from the Department of Energy commented on the scientific usefulness of the exiles' birth defects and missing hair and fingernails. Their

45

report was written with suppressed excitement, as if an archaelogical party had found a lost Aegean site full of statues with broken noses and no arms. 'These individuals provide possibly unique information about the effects of radioactive fall-out on human beings from detonation of nuclear devices.'

Of the babies born at the islanders' first place of exile, little Maria was one of the strongest. This might have been unlucky if she'd fallen ill, for she would have taken that much longer to die. When she was four, she found herself orphaned. Her mother had been ill for some time before a bout of pneumonia finally killed her; so Maria didn't realize right away how much of her childhood had been plundered. She mainly remembered the night her mother died because there'd been a tornado. The wind had ripped off a nearby corrugated-iron roof and turned it into an airborne saw that felled an electricity pole. For a week there'd been no heat or light.

The little girl was fostered somehow, here and there. Everyone around her was interrelated; her own father, insofar as she'd had one, had been some sort of cousin to her mother. He'd bred and sailed away, to be last heard of working in a tuna cannery in American Samoa. Such things happened a lot. Meanwhile enough people saw to it that Maria was at least fed. There was usually somewhere she'd be allowed to sleep at night, and most of the other children let her play with them. She even got a few weeks' schooling in the tin tabernacle church hall, through the intervention of a Presbyterian neighbour who spent her life pestering God and the minister with displays of piety.

At eight years old, Maria had a home of her own again. She was taken in by an aunt who'd returned newly widowed from the exiles' other island to join the local aristocracy of labour. Aunt Fahi became one of the people, mostly Koreans and Okinawans, with a pass to work as a maid on the island where the Americans had built part of their military base. It was a place of irrigated lawns, with a big shopping mall. The elegant white dishes of its missile tracking station dominated a low skyline of palm trees.

Meanwhile Maria hadn't become a foster child so much as a surrogate wife. She had to shop, cook, clean the two-room hut she shared with her aunt, and queue for water. Shortly after her aunt's arrival it was Maria who had to dispose of the blood-soaked cloth containing a newborn creature like a turtle with its shell hacked off. Luckily the thing hadn't cried out, and it had only gone on pulsing for twenty minutes. When her aunt later fell sick from heart disease and migraines, then from thyroid dysfunction, it was also Maria who did what nursing was any use.

At twelve, big for her age, she managed to get on to the 'Americans' island'. Using her aunt's pass she became a breadwinner, along with the other cleaners and gardeners. She was ready to learn everything she could. Her employer, a meteorologist's wife, became all too anxious to ignore any irregularity in the girl's documents. 'Maria is a treasure. I just couldn't get on with my life without her.'

Digory knew none of this, the second time he met Maria. But he could guess it, down to the search by military police that had finally taken away her job.

She was bound to have been investigated some time, if only because she was getting too pretty to be ignored. Came the day, in the queue for the evening ferry, when two young Marines from Louisiana, one white, one black, singled her out. The island's daily immigrants weren't allowed to leave with goods from the Americans' shops, so the two lads were happy to know they were only doing their duty in asking her to turn out her pockets and show her pass. No harm was meant; they just wanted an excuse to talk to her – to have their uniforms admired and maybe have her say something in reply. 'Hello' would have been just fine.

But even a pretend scrutiny of Maria's ID showed her up. Not as Mrs Fahi Darlene Balos, aged thirty-nine, but as an underage imposter. Maria's future looks were indistinct, like a classical statue seen under water. The photo on her pass showed a woman with a neck like a bull's and a face heavy with stoicism.

The two teenage Marines were overcome with embarrassment; but they dared not turn a blind eye. Maria could hardly bear to look her bad luck in the face.

Digory's first meeting with Maria had happened a few days before this. He was in the Trust Territory as an independent observer, invited by legal counsel for some of the dispossessed islanders. Lacking a hotel, he'd been put up privately. His host was Maria's employer. Like Digory, the meteorologist, a civilian on short-term contract, was due to give evidence on patterns of fall-out.

As Digory was being driven back to the airfield in his hosts' family sedan, Maria was in the back.

'I'm so delighted,' his hostess said, 'to have the chance to do Maria this small extra favour, and drop her off.'

They made small talk, with Maria as a silent onlooker. She was a shy figure with a smile like a clear moonrise. From habit, Digory noted her probable future. Narrow prospects, possibly cruel. As to the girl's history, there was decidedly a touch of Slav about those dark eyes. Sealers; maybe whalers. Or perhaps the military early in the last century. In the 1820s, before the Russians had decided their empire was over-extended, the Tsarist flag had even been flown on Hawaii. Interesting how on some mixed-race islanders – Pitcairn was the most useful example – racial characteristics depended on people's sex. The men there could look like English squires. The women, on the other hand, often looked entirely Polynesian – as if Magellan himself had yet to sail his rat-infested cockleshell into the Pacific.

At the landing stage Maria got out. Digory acknowledged her departure with scrupulous politeness. So often the rest of the world found such people invisible.

'Not one of the others has been as deserving as Maria,' his hostess said. 'The one before got terribly sick, too. So I was really grateful that Maria was there to step in at short notice.'

By the time they'd crossed the causeway to the civilain airstrip, Digory knew a lot about Maria, even including her aunt's recent journey to Cleveland. Mrs Balos had been flown to the States by the navy. She was one of several islanders whose liver, kidneys, thyroid, blood or other organs were at last being properly investigated.

'I think it's wonderful,' he was told, 'what they're doing now for the poor Micronesians.'

Digory's own quest on the islanders' behalf was interrupted. There was a book to be finished, up at his home in Vermont where he and his wife spent much of their time. A conference in Heidelberg couldn't be missed. It was a month before he was back.

This time Maria was the first thing he saw. She was squatting pateintly by the road, outside the airfield's torn perimeter fence. Like a leper seeking alms, he thought, at the gate of a medieval city. Beside her an assortment of junk was displayed on a mat. Half-perished fruit had been carefully piled next to a sheet of postage stamps curled under itself from the damp. There were some polystyrene ornaments that anyone from the air-conditioned part of the atoll would have paid to keep out of their home.

She was so obviously begging that Digory, on principle, wouldn't have dreamed of cutting her. Telling his driver to stop, he leaned out of the cab window to ask the price of one of her wares. At random he pointed to a pink spider with wobbly legs made from squared-off foam rubber.

Close to, he realized how young she must be. She looked bewildered at finding herself there. Her desperation belonged to a child, not a young adult. She was wearing a T-shirt patterned in vile fluorescent colours, too-big jeans and broken plastic sandals. It depressed Digory beyond measure to think that she couldn't be more than twelve. Hurriedly he overpaid her, anxious to be gone. Not wanting to cause a jam, his driver gunned the engine.

If the cab had moved off three seconds earlier, they'd have been out of the feeder road and away. As it was, on the main road the first jeep of a passing convoy had come up just too close. Components for a new tracking station started trundling past, carried on eight giant transporters. With its escort of outriders, the convoy took several minutes to go by.

Trapped for the time being, Digory lowered his window again. Maria was about to sit back down beside her display of pathetically overpriced tat.

'You're unlikely to remember me,' he said.

It was the small things about this encounter that would stay with them. Maria was at a time of life when everything new is vivid. An age of such psychic energy, Digory was thinking, that some said having an adolescent girl in the house could make the very furniture shuffle about. For her, this instant would always be brought back by, of all things, the smell of the Americans' island. It was a compound of car exhaust and decayed crabmeat. The crabs liked to sun themselves on the hot tarmac. Unfortunately they were no good at avoiding traffic, and the blacktop was dotted with pats of mashed seafood.

What Digory noticed in this part of the world was the wind. What must it be like to have lived nowhere but here? A place where the salty sky was rushing at you night and day?

He too felt he was rounding a corner in his life. At forty-six he was doubtless nearing the height of his powers. Meanwhile his existence had become predictable even in its success. His eventual Grand Old Manhood seemed assured. The family fortune, it went without saying, was unassailable. It had been built on an alp of money old enough for his grandparents to have looked down the Vanderbilts as parvenus.

Why, then, was he so angry and frustrated? He observed Maria, noting her shock at having tumbled through the trap door that led from frugality down into destitution. Digory knew that look well. He'd seen it in places from Macao to Penn Central; but he'd never got used to it. In Victorian London she'd have been selling matches, or diseased sex.

With all he had he still couldn't save the whole world, only his own life — that was what grieved him. Neither he nor the Congress of Micronesia could get the results he wanted here. No humanitarian agency on earth could be made to get what he was after. He couldn't even save a few hundred God-fearing peasants trying to live harmlessly three thousand miles from the nearest freeway intersection.

'Yes,' Maria said. 'I remember you.'

She was telling herself it was rude to stare. The tall American, with his aura of power quietly worn, was like no one she'd ever seen. 'I'm sorry that I've forgotten what your name is. You are the visitor in the front seat of my old boss's car, who knows the people who took away my aunt.'

Trying to sound kind, Digory asked, 'Have you had news of your aunt?'

The child shook her head. Loneliness and terror were written all over her.

He watched the sea breeze snatch at her clothes and stream through her hair. Nowhere more than on the windy atolls of the Pacific was Digory aware of inhabiting a whirling lump of rock in some insignificant part of space. And after the rock had orbited the sun a few more times he would be an old man. He had to strike out in a new direction.

What if the child were uprooted from these islands? How would she cope? The idea didn't enter his mind gradually; it jumped him fully formed.

'If you like you could give me your aunt's name and I could ask after her.'

Maria nodded, near to tears.

It was then, quite on impulse, that Digory decided what he wanted to do. He hadn't realized how frustrated he'd felt here. Questioning those ailing poor bastards from further north, dumped where the earth, water and air virtually crackled with radiation. Fighting in vain, afterwards, to spread what he knew. Worst of all, sitting still for all that fluent ungrammatical horseshit from the Pentagon, who weren't admitting a damn thing.

He presumed the child's luckless aunt must still be alive and in her hospital room overlooking the icy horizon of Lake Erie. He would certainly do what he'd promised Maria. And more than that, for God's sake. the least he could be allowed was to change the world for someone – for just one child out of the multitudes of the lost. He was damned if he would go on being completely helpless.

Digory was confused in his motives, much as the two young Marines had been when they too had intervened in Maria's life. But there was no doubt about *what* he wanted to do. It seemed he couldn't personally save any part of the Pacific; so he would salve his ego by saving Maria instead. He wopuld adopt her as his own.

Maria's last contact with home was in a hushed, pristine room wrapped around by an Ohio snowstorm.

'What worries me about how I am is Gary and Jean. Do you think they'll ever be back together?' Maria's aunt, now forty pounds lighter than her niece, was lying back among her pillows surrounded by remote-control devices. Her face was the colour of spoiled milk. A twenty-seven-inch RCA 1200 stood in the corner, cooling from an episode of her favourite soap opera, *South-West General*.

The room's picture window was curtained in crisp chintz, more like furnishing for a resort cottage than a suite twenty floors up. In the bathroom next door the lavatory bowl had been sealed with a paper strip, as through waiting for royalty to sanction every dump with a ceremonial pair of scissors.

Forty-seven other people from the same island at the north of the archipelago were now living or dying somewhere like this, courtesy of the Department of Energy. 'Surely we have paid our tab on this one,' a spokesman had said, reviewing the cost of a mass shipment of islanders to America for medical investigation.

'You see, they've been taking so long to understand each other. When they do, I might not be here.' The aunt, like her young neice, spoke the careful English of someone using it as a second language. As she talked, she looked from Digory to Maria, too far gone to move more than her eyes. In better health her words might have been accompanied by an ironical guffaw. As it was, she couldn't speak without sounding pitiable and urgent.

Digory could only guess what she was talking about. Maria knew right away. Back home the 'Americans' island' had been the perfect place to learn about mainland culture. Whether in the

base's supermarket or on its airwaves, nothing had
been spared to hold off disorienting foreign influ-
ences and remind our boys of the homeland they
were guarding. Maria's idea of current affairs was
vague: Vietnam, for example, was a vast embattled
empire off the coast of President Nixon's home state
of California. But she could name every character
who'd appeared more than once in *The Flintstones*
or *The Beverly Hillbillies*.

She'd been ushered into the room amid lowered
voices. the new winter clothes bought on a stopover in
LA felt heavy, like wearing a roll of bedding. Maria's
manner had confused the store assistant, who'd also
been unable to fathom the relationship between
father and adopted daughter. Playing it safe, she'd
dressed the girl as an adult, fashionable but restrained.
Maria was wearing knee boots under a calf-length
coat and matching hood trimmed in artic fox fur. She
didn't look like someone transplanted from the equator; more a Blackfoot or a Nez Perce wearing white
women's clothing for the first time. Her face, Digory
thought, was a kaleidoscope of human types.

Seeing her aunt like this had jolted Maria; for the
moment she wasn't even aware of grieving. In the
hospital lobby Digory had bought her a dozen tight
red roses to give Mrs Balos. Ever after, the smell of
roses would be inseparable in Maria's memory from
the whiff of corruption mingled with floor polish
and disinfectant. Digory had hinted that any of
these visits might turn out to be a final farewell. He
was watching the child for some reaction – any-

56

thing. Thank God what they could see of the poor bloody woman didn't have any bits missing.

When it was time to go Digory stood up to shake hands with immaculate formality. He would wait outside, he said, and Maria should take as long as she liked. Digory may have prided himself on his tact, but he was also capable of genuine kindness. Outwardly he gave the impression that nothing in their lives couldn't be fixed. Still clasping Mrs Balos's hand he said, 'You must tell Maria the details of the television programme you mentioned. I know some of the people involved, so if you like I can get you an advance copy of next season's scripts. They won't have started filming yet, but you'll still be able to find out what happens to the characters.'

Whether from gratitude or physical weakness, Maria's aunt shed tears.

Sometimes, Digory could lord it over death itself.

In time Maria too found the fates of *South-West General*'s star-crossed Gary and Jean, watching in a deserted eight-room *pied-à-terre* on Fifth Avenue.

Other business had left Digory too hard pressed to stay with Maria in Cleveland while her aunt was dying. When could he hope for another mission, however unofficial, to Hanoi? In his place an agency had provided a temporary governess-companion. She was a flustered French-Canadian girl of twenty-two, embarrassed half to death by Maria's grief the night they were summoned to watch Mrs Balos finish fading away.

The week, after a month spent mostly in airports, Digory flew back to Cleveland from Stockholm, having cut short his role in that year's Conference on the Human Environment. there was no one else, after all, to see that the funeral was decently financed. He and Maria were the only mourners. At the graveside, every time the child sobbed aloud Digory patted her shoulder as though dusting down her coat. His own face was stonily dignified; it was impossible to know if he was at ease with the situation or not. The weather was so cold that the topsoil had to be broken into with a pneumatic drill. After the ceremony, the gravediggers shovelled mixed earth and ice on to the coffin, like a grit sorbet.

In New York there was no twenty-seven-inch screen in the room Digory's secretary had furnished by phone for Maria. Fitted shelving covered a whole wall, carpentered to match the apartment's massive cornices and skirting boards. It held a record player with stereophonic speakers, a short-wave radio, several hundred newly purchased books and a built-in desk whose top could be angled to make a proper draftsman's drawing board. The little portable television, like a fishbowl with a window, seemed an afterthought.

In town and out, Digory had some urgent appointments before they could complete their journey together, from Micronesia to the Cotswolds.

'You must see the next few days as a stopover,' he instructed her.

58

'There's no need to think of an inhospitable place like this as home.' He gestured past a wall hung with a twelfth-century icon and a seventeenth-century silk kelim. The colours in the kelim were echoed by a Sisley showing a meadow in high summer. Outside, Central Park lay beneath sunlight snow.

Maria nodded, in good faith. She was too ignorant to see Digory as richer or better informed than any other American. Everything about her new country was a jumbled, brilliant circus parade of prime-time plenty, enjoyed by people of undaunted frivolity or solemn joy. To her every American, in life as in the TV commercials, had perfect teeth and whole limbs and the chance to be anything he or she wanted.

Meanwhile, still with no one around to call her own, she waited for her new life to begin properly. Between whiles she would wander into the service part of the apartment and marvel at how much water Elvira, the live-in housekeeper, used in cooking a meal. Once, she ventured out into the gnawing cold and the crowds striding indifferently by, only to find that for her the street signs might as well have been in Gujerati. The rest of the time she watched television.

It was the only sure link between past and present. Each week the same people were guaranteed to appear at the same time and be predictable. They were Maria's substitute family, among whom certain conventions could always be counted on. People on television never went to the bathroom, no matter how much coffee they'd drunk while helping each other get in touch with their feelings. No one got diseases that lingered; they died from a rare fever or in a car crash. Above all, they were apt to lose their memories so that they no longer knew who they were or where they'd come from.

The same programmes taught Maria that poverty, in some unimaginable place called 'the other side of town,' made people nasty in later life, if only for a while. In the newer series, for a woman to be acceptable she had to be everything at once but never show strain. Unlike the wife of Maria's employer back on the atoll, television mothers roused their children for school wearing a suit rather than stained pyjamas. The woman on the show never hurried in with a briefcase in one hand and a dirty disposable in the other. And at the end of the day, her offspring in bed, she wouldn't dream of recharging with a slug of vodka tipped into the baby's mug of leftover orange juice.

Maria noticed, too, that blameless people could be framed, and that a love triangle could keep conflict alive for years.

The only puzzling thing, in all those shows located around a family settee, was the role of Dad. He was always a soft old guy in elbow patches, whose pretty permed wife and wisecracking moppets forever shrugged and sighed at him behind his back. Digory was nothing like that.

'You must choose only what you yourself want,' he ordered, on an expedition to buy clothes at Bloomingdale's.

The thought made Maria uneasy. She knew that in her newfound world what one wore could easily give the wrong signal. On the soaps, a whole episode might turn on somebody wearing something mistaken, while Pop, Mom, Ricky, Bud and little Sis did a double-take and rolled their eyes.

But she dared not argue. With an eye that had known only the fierce light and smiting colours of the equator, she chose to leave the store wearing a long-sleeved minidress in scarlet angora and cream kid-leather thigh boots. Their colours made her glossy hair look as dark as the stamens of a poppy. Whatever Digory had really had in mind for her, it had to be said that she was striking.

'You're past it, man,' muttered a young jerk in the crowd as they stepped on to the down escalator. Digory, next to a wall of mirrors, didn't even deign to glance in the youth's direction.

They went on to his club. Feeling that Maria could no longer be left alone in the apartment like an unexercised dog, he'd promised to take her for lunch with his publisher.

Even in the sanctuary of that muffled, much-upholstered place, people had their doubts about Maria. Was she an underage tart or someone's gutwringingly pretty niece from the boonies? But not by the twitch of an eyelash did anyone show what they were thinking, from the former ambassador to India down to the invisibly polite man who took their coats. Not for nothing was Digory one of the club's fourth-generation members.

His publisher was waiting in the bar. Bob Freed was an affable fellow with hair a little too long for his age, and a red bow tie. Knowing about Maria, he was full of friendly attention. Partly for her own sake, but mainly out of respect for her father.

Entering the dining room, Maria was overwhelmed with deference. Bob treated her too small talk about the blizzard outside while Digory guided her by the elbow and the maitre d' showed the way. A waiter brought up the rear, ready to make Maria jump by whisking her chair beneath her and snapping her napkin open. Forty pairs of eyes, all old or over-seasoned, pretended not to look at her as their group went in.

Somewhere else new. It was unnerving and exhilarating, like so much about Maria's changed life. Each time she entered a different room it was as if she'd stepped on to an undiscovered planet. Bloomingdale's had been full of people strutting their stuff in tight flares they must have washed while wearing them. Everyone in this room was perfumed, powdered, artificially tanned, massaged, tucked, rhinoplasticized, dyed, bleached, permed, or worked with the aid of surgical implants. The combined impact of their discreet will power was as obvious as having half a ton of sunshot Pacific surf fall on your head.

Maria stirred with pleasure as well as curiosity. She had no idea who all these ancient people were, let alone what compromises pocked their histories, but suddenly she realized that being young could feel good. Young, strong, blameless and full of unknown opportunity. For the first time since coming to America she felt cheerful.

There was business to be done, but not before the coffee. Bob went on putting Maria at her ease, by asking if she liked New York.

'Yes. I do, thank you.' The girl didn't know she was expected to answer at length, like a talk-show guest given a sound bite.

'Is there anything you enjoy in particular?'

'I like looking at families in their homes. On television.'

'Maria doesn't have much experience of family life,' Digory pointed out.

'I see,' said Bob, accepting a menu the size of a small billboard and greeting the waiter by his first name. 'And how do you imagine life will be, now that you've got a family of your own?'

'I think families all talk at once, and they often have a big dog. But I cannot understand how they keep warm in cold weather —'

'Mam'selle,' said the waiter, thrusting a menu at the bewildered Maria. Quickly Digory signalled for him to take it away.

'Why is that?' Bob asked.

'They own so many things. But their front door always opens right into their sitting room.'

'Who told you that?'

'No one. I see it on the television.'

'Ah,' Bob said to Digory. 'The ever-present eye. Those of us who live by the printed word are lucky to be alive, let alone sitting here.'

63

'Maria has also been watching *Sesame Street*.' Digory could see she found it hard to understand everything Bob said.

'Excellent,' turning to Maria. 'And do you find *Sesame Street* useful?'

Her confusion grew. Reading and writing weren't useful, just daunting.

'Maria's progress is good. Over in England she'll be starting school next month.'

'So Elizabeth is still based over there? I trust things go well at . . . the Tate, isn't it?'

Digory nodded, scanning the menu. 'We're in Gloucestershire this Christmas. I've told Maria' – glancing up to show she was included in the conversation – 'how happy her new mother will be to meet her.'

'And vice versa, no doubt. You must be looking forward to your new home,' Bob told Maria. 'What do you think you'll like about it most?'

Maria smiled shyly. 'Everything.' She laughed, a sound as unselfconscious as birdsong. Digory was startled to realize he'd never heard her laugh before.

'I look forward to having a father like Professor Adams —'

'Digory,' he corrected her.

'Digory' – laughing again, at the strangeness of having a father and of calling him by his first name – 'because I have often been told how he has tried to do many helpful things for the people at home – at the place where I used to live. He has tried to be like Moses leading the Israelis to a safe place. And I am happy to think he will do the same for me.'

64

CHAPTER
FOUR

Unlike families on television, Maria's new parents showed their affection calmly.

'How are you, dear?' said Digory, giving his wife a kiss and holding tightly on to her hand for a moment afterwards. They were in the VIP lounge at Heathrow. The family didn't normally bother with meeting each other at airports. They travelled enough to meet by accident at JFK or Frankfurt, slipping round the world as freely as daytime in pursuit of night. This reunion was held here on Maria's account.

'I'm well, thank you, Hello, Maria.'

Digory's wife was an aristocratic-looking Englishwoman three years his senior. Among her colleagues in the art world she was well regarded, and her energies were spread thin over endless committees. A life among objects of beauty had put her off making herself into a work of art. Her fair hair was nonedescript and she wore a grubby sheepskin. Even at meetings of the Trustees of the National Gallery she looked as if she'd just been inspecting the home farm.

'Hello, Elizabeth,' said Maria, bravely informal. Thinking it was expected, she put out her hand.

Elizabeth took her hand but kissed her on the cheek as well. If she was fazed at what her husband had done she didn't show it. She was a well-meaning woman, secretly panicked at displays of emotion.

With Elizabeth at the whel, a nearly-vintage Jensen carried them out of the flat West London suburbs and through the motionless woods of the Chiltern Hills. Maria thought it must be dusk until she worked out that they'd been driving for nearly two hours. As they swooped into the vale where Oxford lay, there was a band of colourless clear sky along the horizon. By the time they reached Stinscombe, one shire further on, the clouds were gone. Out of a brilliant sky the last of a shower of snow twinkled down.

Maria's new home was quieter than anywhere she'd imagined. People there spoke as though nothing could excite them. If the sky above Stinscombe Wold had been scrolled away by a giant hand, Digory would have remarked, 'I see the world's come to an end. Or should I say, the universe, inasmuch as we *can* be cognisant of its spatio-temporal extent.' And Elizabeth would have replied, 'Oh dear, I see you're right.'

66

They dined by candlelight, at a table that had been polished shiny as water some lifetimes ago. There was macaroni cheese grilled brown on top and home-grown brussel sprouts followed by bread-and-butter pudding with double cream. the room smelt of pot-pourri and burning logs. Chimes from the grandfather clock in the hall could be heard right the way up to the attics.

. Maria was almost too tired to speak. Her new parents talked mostly to each other, about their work. They seemed to inhabit a world of organizations referred to by their initials and run by people who only had first names. By nine o'clock her eyes were watering with fatigue. Only the good manners learned from her aunt kept her sitting upright. At last it was time to go to bed. Beneath the spindly canopy of her four-poster, exhausted by anticipation and anxiety to please, she wept until she thought her bones would break.

'Elizabeth,' called the housekeeper next morning, 'there's a trespasser in the bottom field.'

It turned out to be Edmund, taking a short cut up the snowy meadow below the ha-ha. In a landscape of pure, unbroken shapes he was the only untidy thing: a loping figure with a rucksack.

'*You're* early, aren't you?' exclaimed Elizabeth. She was pink with delight at her son's unexpected arrival.

'I know – hello, Digory – I hitched.'

'From Heathrow?' Like his wife, Digory was trying not to look as pleased as he felt.

'No, from Klosters.' Edmund had been skiing with a party of friends, most of them from his year at Winchester. 'One of the guys I was with got me a lift in his father's plane. His old man and his step-mother were on their way over here for Christmas, so they dropped me off.'

He'd walked three miles through snow-covered lanes from his last lift, on a milk tanker. Flushed and out of breath, he radiated pleasure in every-thing: being home, being healthy, being eighteen.

'It goes without saying,' Digory remarked, 'that your mother and I are glad to see you. But I hope your hosts didn't mind that you whiff rather abom-inably.'

'Edmund, if you smelt much worse, you'd have a fuzzy outline,' Elizabeth said.

'Ah, this garment. No problem. I plan to burn it forthwith.' Edmund was wearing a thin denim jacket, shiny with dirt. The sleeves were too short to do up, which made him even lankier.

'It is a bit small,' Elizabeth guardedly remarked.

'Fear not. I can explain everything.' He pulled it open at her in a gesture of spoof menace.

'No, Edmund, seriously,' she exclaimed, flapping her hand in front of her face and laughing.

'I swapped it with a guy I met near London. He was hitching to South Wales to see his children for Christmas. Only he wasn't getting too many lifts.'

'Oh, Edmund, I hope you didn't give him any-thing you were fond of,' said Elizabeth before she could stop herself. 'I mean – too fond . . .' She and

68

Digory were squeamish about him applying their liberalism to his own life.

'Well, what the hell?' muttered Edmund, uncomfortable at being found out. His own jacket had been an Artic-issue Swedish infantryman's coat, good as new, with sleeves like bolsters. It hadn't cost much and he had several wardrobes of clothes anyway, one at each of his family's addresses. But it had been dear to his heart; offering it had been a wrench. To change the subject he said, 'So where's – um —?'

Maria was loitering in the doorway of her bedroom. Would she be intruding? Or was it rude to hang back? Digory introduced them to each other. Awkwardly they shook hands: the privileged youth in denim tatters and the orphan correctly dressed in a short cashmere sweater and a midi-skirt.

There was a silence. Though Edmund was fearless in debate with any of his parents' distinguished friends, his new sister was too young and strange for him to be at ease.

'I am very pleased to know you.' Involuntarily Maria glanced at Digory to see if she was saying the right thing. 'You are the first man of my family.'

Edmund looked anxious. He'd never met someone from such a genuinely oppressed minority. Nobody could have been more concerned to say the ideologically okay thing. On the other hand he hadn't realized there might be a language barrier.

A furnace-breath of embarrassment scorched Maria, too. 'I mean, you and Digory.'

'I think Maria means she's never lived with male next of kin,' Digory explained. 'Where she's come from, most of the men become migrant workers.'

'Oh,' said Edmond, relieved at having someone to interpret. 'You mean like you, Digory?'

His joke went awry, however. Maria's face was stamped with dismay.

'You will each go away?' She realized her new family were often on the move. 'I want to ask, who lives here all the time?'

'I'm sure you needn't worry about anything like that,' Digory said. He paused, visualizing his work schedule. 'We'll all be down here for – oh, part of the Christmas vacation at least.'

'Christmas,' Edmund later informed Maria, 'is when the suicide rate is highest in this culture. Most of the population can't beat all that enforced jollity. And the rest feel lonely. I shall ignore the festivities and stay indoors until they're safely over.'

For every day of the holiday there was at least one invitation. Some parties were in spacious Victorian mansions in north Oxford, others in Cotswold manor houses or in former barns or weavers' cottages, extravagantly converted. Maria, introduced around by her new parents, spent most of them watching television alone in a playroom somewhere.

Edmund virtually disappeared. the phone rang so insistently that his 'indoors' became a choice of non-stop house parties, in Oxford, London and places beyond. A couple of times he showed up in his new MG, followed into the drive by two carloads of his friends. Wrung out by partying, next day they'd rise at noon. His parents half killed themselves pretending not to wonder how often he was getting laid, and by whom.

Maria was treated with self-conscious curiosity in her role as the Professor's very own third-world orphan. Most of Edmund's friends were as scruffy as castaways, and worked hard at hiding the accents they'd got at Westminster or Rugby. Overawed by their loud bonhomie towards each other, Maria watched and listened, a scout in no-man's land.

Every conversation turned a searchlight on her ignorance, whether she knew it or not. One day she and her new parents were lunching with the Warded of Digory's college, at a grand Baroque house in the secluded heart of Oxford. Even during term this part of the city was quiet. The narrow lane outside echoed to footsteps, voices and the occasional bicycle bell. Every few minutes in some nearby tower an ancient mass of clock machinery clanked into action to strike away another quarter, followed all around by competing chimes or solemn deep strokes.

Lunch was a family affair, arranged for the Warden's niece. She was a feature writer from *Nova* magazine who was doing an article on adopted children of famous people. Unluckily it was the Warden's mother-in-law, old Mrs Lunt, who dominated.

71

'Isn't she sweet? . . . You Polynesians are so lucky in your looks, you know.' Mrs Lunt took a forkful of turbot in mangetout sauce and patted the corners of her lipstick with her napkin.

'Micronesians,' her eminent son-in-law corrected her. He pictured the flesh spilling over her too-tight shoes and wondered what new excuse she'd find tomorrow for not going home.

'I suppose you can be ever so helpful to Professor Adams in his researches. Can you show him how that barkcloth stuff is made?' In search of the wilder shores of tourism, Mrs Lunt had once joined a party spending a fortnight in the Honolulu Hilton. 'You must be glad to be so useful to him, in return for everything.'

Looking up, heavy knife and fork in hand, Maria sought a new way to say, I do not understand. She was getting used to making such excuses: How do you mean? I'm sorry? I beg your pardon? What was that, please?

Digory said, 'Maria's culture has been too thoroughly demolished for that. She's nothing if not a *déracinée*.' Concious of speaking for the record, he was grimly urbane.

'What a shame. But Helena' – turning to the journalist niece – 'surely you should have photographed Maria to make her look like a South Sea islander. What you ought to do is to have her standing barefoot under a palm tree in the Bontanical Garden.'

The niece continued to eat. 'Our photographer

has been and gone.' She was dressed with knowing informality, in a cowl-necked belted sweater and a calf-length suede skirt. Her hair was twisted smoothly up on top of her head.

'Did you take your picture out of doors? It would have been a pity not to, in a lovely place like this.'

'I saw no point in asking anyone to take off their shoes. But we did go out into the cloister.'

In fact it had been a job to make the professor and his adopted daughter look okay. The girl had photographed well enough on her own, coming over as wary but sweet-natured. When she'd stood next to Digory, though, they'd both been subtuly transformed. He'd looked like a corrupt colonial official; she, like an underage bar girl decoyed from some innocent paddy field on to the streets of Saigon. In the end the photographer had pretended he'd finished, then sneaked another shot. It was the light of relief in Maria's face that had made this last attempt perfect.

The Warden's wife, anxious to elbow Mother out of the conversation, asked Digory about one of his recent journeys. As part of an unofficial delegation, he'd been to Hanoi. Everyone listened as he described daily life in cellars and fortified bunkers beneath the scorched ruins of the North Vietnamese capital. In every way it was the flip side of the planet, compared to the room where they sat overlooking the garden of the Warden's Lodging. Outside, amid melting snow, redwings hopped on a half-acre lawn bounded by a medieval city wall. An

73

ancient mulberry tree was supported by wooden crutches. As Digory talked, a maid came in and silently cleared plates and glasses.

Several times he'd seen streets of people fleeing an air raid, like wheat bending in the wind. He thought it would be tactless, though, to describe what it was like being bombed. Instead, he dwelt on the certainty that the North Vietnamese would overcome all.

'Naught for our comfort, then,' said the Warden's wife.

For once Maria thought she could follow what was being said. 'But the president does not say that.' She looked puzzled and hurt, like someone knocking themselves out in a game whose rules have suddenly been changed. 'I have seen him myself, many times. He has always told us that South.Vietnam will help us win the war. I never heard anyone from America say anything different, when I watched television in my boss's house, before here. President Nixon and other men from the government have told the television interviewers that the South Vietnamese know what to do. Because now they have America to help them with their lives. They will bomb the liberal Democrats into nothing, and any other foreigners that threaten America from outside.' Maria looked pleased and anxious, as though reciting a difficult lesson correctly. 'Is that not the truth, Digory?'

Getting ready for bed that evening, Digory said to

Elizabeth, 'I've been reconsidering Maria's schooling.'

'Have you?' The mirror on Elizabeth's dressing table reflected her surprise. 'I thought we were going to try for Ipchester.' The high school at Ipchester, a former market town near Oxford, selected its pupils by one of the stiffest exams in the country, based on intelligence rather than knowledge. Several of their friends had children there.

'I thought we should give Aynesford Hall a try instead.'

'Oh.'

'What do you mean, 'oh'?'

'It doesn't have much of an academic record. Of course, those pony-worshipping little girls do tend to look quite cheerful . . .'

'How do you know she would be? Just because being seen with her isn't perfectly easy yet —'

'That's nothing to do with it. Do you seriously want her early mistakes made in front of people she might know all her life?'

'At Aynesford Hall she'd certainly be lost from view. But it's so snobby there. Do we really want the poor kid to graduate *cum laude* in nothing but sneering? Or being sneered at, more probably.'

Elizabeth knew she couldn't win. Digory's liberalism tended to stop short of his own household. It could only be counted on outside, among the serious matters of the real world.

'Look, it's not as if I'm unwilling to spend on the girl without limit.' In adopting Maria, Digory

75

reckoned he'd made his grand gesture once and for all. Good God, were people now going to cast doubts on his generosity?

Out of a glum sense of duty, Elizabeth persisted. 'Why not sent her to the nearest state school? At least there'd be a decent social mix.'

'Would you really want me thought parsimonious?' Digory was rigid with impatience.

'Well, for that matter, do you really want to be seen supporting undeserved privilege? Especially by putting her among rich dimwits who won't be fit for anything better than finishing school.'

'Do you seriously imagine that I care what people think?' Digory's face was dark with the effort of believing his own words. 'Look, if you've got any criticisms, can't you just come out with them? Exactly what is it you're trying to say?'

Elizabeth gave an inward sigh. 'Nothing, Digory. Consider me persuaded.'

'You can't come past here; this is Alpha territory.'

The six girls who'd voted themselves the most popular in the third year turned to look at Maria. They were lounging on a pile of matting in the converted coach house that served as a gym. Next door was the former tack room, where art classes were held. Unlike Eton and the local secondary modern, Aynesford Hall School was not purpose-built. It had been fudged together from an early Victorian mansion and its outbuildings. the main house was all stucco battlements; its garden was shaded by wellingtonias. Holm oaks screened the former stable block. From the headmistress's study the view of elm-shaded fields was as English as a country dance tune. As she told every parent, 'We do like to offer a good atmosphere.'

'This isn't private,' Maria said. 'You just want it for yourselves.'

The six Most Popular Girls brightened without moving. They, their copies of *True Love*, *Tatler*, *Roxy*, *Pony* and *Vogue*, together with Anabel Cliffe's transistor, were nestled in behind the gym horse, barring Maria's way to the art room. It was Saturday, when boarders were expected to make their own entertainments.

The art room was Maria's sanctuary. Alone at last, she could be ignored. She could also be doing something at which she already excelled. In her first week there the class had been set to make a charcoal drawing of a pair of gardening boots. Finding how swiftly Maria absorbed what she was told, and how surely she used it, the art mistress had blossomed. Maria felt almost ashamed at causing such enthusiasm so easily.

'I like to get by, please.'

A shiver of expectation ran through the members of Alpha. With someone's Etonian cousin from Pop in mind, or maybe Enid Blyton's Secret Seven, they'd formed a clique and given it a name. They shared a particular way of turning up their shirt collars, and som, slang expressions which were now *their* words. There was only one way of carrying a school bag – slung backwards over one shoulder, *never* under the arm. Most exclusive of all was the secret membership sign, which consisted of cutting off the spike in the middle of their school berets. The only thing they lacked, to confirm how super they were, was a guaranteed outsider.

'How do you know you like,' said Anabel Cliffe, 'if we haven't let you yet?'

The others squirmed helplessly, mewing with delight. As Joanna Wickham later confided to her best friend Gulietta Pettergill, she'd lauged so much she'd actually dribbled some you-know-what.

'If you haven't let me do what?' Maria was learning to protect herself by answering a question with a question. What she couldn't do was avoid turning pale with fury.

They conferred in whispers.

'Shall we let her?'

'No, look . . .

'Make her answer . . . I know what we can ask her . . .'

'Oh, yes – *yes*!'

'Would you like us to let you through?' Anabel challenged. 'We could, you know.'

Maria ignored them and laboriously picked her way past. Thwarted, they fell back on examining the treasure trove of her past mistakes.

'Tell us about Karl Marks and Spencer's Maria.'

'Maria, who told you to put your slip on under your bra?'

'Maria – Maria —'

'Oh yes, ask her *that* one!'

'Maria, do tell us. Where's the island of Yoko Ono?'

Digory unfolded the school's termly report. Maria said nothing as he looked it over. On the wicker garden table her Lapsang Souchong cooled in a wide, semi-transparent cup.

She and her parents were having tea on the Rectory lawn on the first mild day of the year. A wash of green was deepening beneath the naked trees framing the bottom field. Violets flowered among drifts of dead leaves in the hedge bottoms. Edmund was there, too, stopping off on his way to join some friends on a yacht in the Dodecanese.

With a frown of concentration, Digory read, then re-read. Maria tried not to look at him as she waited, perched on a big basket chair with Liberty print cushions. After the noise and bareness of school the faded comfort of the Rectory's garden furniture felt like unsurpassable luxury. In three months she had grown even longer-legged; already her school uniform was too small. She wore an unfashionable pony tail, reaching nearly to her waist. It was a regulation style, as was her navy and yellow uniform with its braided emblem on the blazer pocket. Badges, Latin mottoes, house sashes: Aynesford Hall was hot for that sort of thing. It meant parents could see what they were getting in return for the arms and legs they'd invested in school fees.

'Maria's progress in art speaks for itself,' the headmistress had written. The art teacher couldn't have been more enthusiastic if she'd written a sonnet.

'Her aptitude for science subjects is also remarkable.'

Maria had felt a shock of pure joy on realizing that the languages of algebra and chemistry were almost as new to the other girls. Like a centre forward butting his way to the touch line, she'd seized her chance. I hate you all, was her thought the first time she'd got an A.

'In the latter part of term, Maria has shown herself committed to the cause of learning,' her headmistress summed up. 'So much so, however, that she appears willing to put the pursuit of excellence before making herself popular with her classmates.'

'What exactly does this criticism mean, Elizabeth?' asked Digory.

'You've had so much to do with the woman as I,' his wife replied, with strained patience. The sharp April light made her face and hair colourless. She really should tell her family about the trips she'd been making to the man in Harley Street. Wa it only weeks ago that she hadn't known what a histology was?

'They probably don't know what to make of Maria,' Edmund said. 'Most of the girls there are too moronic to mix with an IQ in treble figures.'

'Don't belittle Maria's achievements,' said Digory. He really meant that he didn't want his choice of school criticized.

Maria asked, 'Are end-of-term reports very important?' Some of the girls had gone home in tears of apprehension. Phoebe Weatherby's face had been swollen and leaking for a whole day.'

'It depends who reads them,' Edmund said, wavering between aggression and the desire to reassure Maria. He still treated her with careful awkwardness.

Aloud, Digory read: '"Perhaps Maria should now try harder to take advantage of the social opportunities that Aynesford Hall School offers its pupils."'

'I thought you'd found a friend,' said Elizabeth.

Maria blushed. 'I spend a lot of time with Phoebe Weatherby. But she's not really my friend.' It was to make up for her shyness and imperfect English that Maria had struck out for the top of the class. Once she'd got there, though, she hadn't been admired by the other girls; just resented. Only one pupil was as lonely, if not as clever. Indeed, clever was the one thing poor Phoebe could be counted on not to be. Phoebe, who wheezed and hung around her teachers and was cut by everyone because she was so very dim. Awesonely, denser-than-a-black-hole dim. It had been suggested in the staff room that Phoebe's lack of intelligence deserved a monument, to be inscribed Tomb of the Unknown Teacher. As the two loners in their year, she and Maria were destined for each other.

'You hate it there, don't you?'

'Edmund,' said his mother, 'don't make Maria feel she's giving evidence before a committee.'

81

'It's important.' Edmund was at the age when the world owed him and everyone else a truthful answer, and damn the consequences.

'Ought I to be happy?' asked Maria warily. 'Our headmistress says the school's great virtue is that it makes you or breaks you.'

Edmund scowled at his father. 'You've sent Maria to a craphole. They're too pathetic to stop her being bullied, and they pretend it's a selling point.'

'*Are* you being bullied, Maria?' Elizabeth's brow wore a crease of concern. She hadn't asked to be presented with a half-grown daughter, but now that it had happened she wanted to do her duty.

Maria blushed and squirmed. 'They leave me alone now. Since my English has got better.'

'I hope the other girls haven't made an outcast of you.'

'Oh, yes they have,' said Edmund.

That afternoon he'd been the one to pick her up from school. Even in the time it took to fetch her luggage, he'd noticed. The crowded entrance hall had resounded with tearful farewells and exclamations of undying togetherness. Maria had wlaked straight out, looking neither to right not left.

She'd even ignored the squeaks and murmurs set off by Edmund himself. At the sight of the dishiest man in the country – with Maria Adams of all people – the entire school building had nearly elevated a foot off the ground. Maria had shown nothing but indifference as Edmund's MG had surged away with her in the passenger seat, her

82

beret knocked slightly askew by the doorframe. Meanwhile it took only a few shared gawps of disbelief for her status to become – oh wow – I mean this honestly – I mean, really, really different! By the end of the school drive she was a full member of the human race even as defined at the Stinscombe Pony Club.

After a couple of miles in near silence, she fetched a huge involuntary sigh and yawned with relief.

Edmund had been saying, 'I hope that place isn't too bad.' At his words, Maria suddenly looked defeated.

'It's okay,' she muttered. 'I can manage.' They'd been almost home before she'd come clean.

After she'd gone indoors to unpack, Edmund confrunted his parents. 'Maria's not happy. Something should be done.'

His confident voice carried to Maria's bedroom, where she was dutifully putting away her winter things in perfect order. Being tidy was something she couldn't help; it was a spell, to ward off bad luck.

On the lawn Digory sipped his tea with the dignity of a man whose household affairs were supposed to be taken care of by others.

'What exactly do you think we should do? asked Elizabeth. 'Unhappy how?' She glanced towards Digory, but he just crooked a sarcastic eyebrow at the middle distance.

'She's been sent to Coventry. Almost from the start of term.'

Digory said, 'I think you'll find your sister is exaggerating, if only to herself. You're taking altogether too much on trust.'

'What your father means is that Maria may have had false expectations. For one thing she mightn't have known her English would be a problem.'

'The other girls barge into her in the corridor. They knock things off her desk accidentally-on-purpose.'

Digory went on looking angry and closed. Elizabeth said, 'Are you sure she's not exaggerating? To herself, of course.'

Edmund made a noise of exasperation and shifted in his chair. 'It only came out when we were driving up from the village. She'd been nerving herself all the way here.'

With a pang, Elizabeth saw that he was bewildered at them both. Now she envied her son's readiness to run headlong at the world's ills. She wanted him to stay young and fearless for ever.

Behind the half-open bedroom window Maria hurried to finish upacking and flee to where she wouldn't overhear any more. She didn't think she could bear to hear her defeats at school described again. Wanting to stay out of sight, she wandered down into the black lobby and opened a cupboard where some of the garden things were stored. Croquet balls and mallet in hand, she went out to practise her aim alone on the north side of the house, where a little-used area of lawn was set with hoops.

84

Digory meanwhile persisted in being stonely impatient.

'You can't hold your mother and me responsible for the behaviour of adolescents the world over. Maria will have to give it longer.'

Edmund stared back at him. He didn't understand that the more Digory wanted to see himself as supremely generous, the less willing he was to be challenged in this way.

'But you've always said that when the strong oppress the weak, excuses count for nothing. Nothing counts – you said – except the viewpoint of the weak!'

He himself had always had whatever he asked for. It still hadn't ocurred to him that Digory might see Maria as the family's second-class member.

Elizabeth could no longer bear the ache in her own conscience. 'With due respect, Digory, if there is a case for sending Maria somewhere else, like Ipchester High, I think you should hear Edmund out.'

'That's what you want, is it?'

'Yes,' in a brittle voice. 'I'de like you to listen.'

'Don't be vague, Elizabeth. There's something more than that, isn't there?'

'That's right. That's what I've already said.'

'Yes, but what is it? What do you want?'

Elizabeth's patience broke. 'I don't enjoy trying to mediate between you, you know. Playing the fond whimpering matron – not even on Edmund's behalf. But if Edmund chooses to be more generous than you are towards that luckless girl, I'm damned if I'll let you ignore him. this one time, be man enough to show respect for your son's better nature.'

In defeat, Digory still insisted on having face, usually by being decisive. Maria must be summoned immediatley, he declared, as of his wife or son might somehow take it into their heads to hinder him.

Elizabeth hurried off in search of her. Seeing Maria on the croquet lawn, bending anxiously over her mallet, she felt a rush of guilt and sadness. The girl looked so lonely, tinkering away like that at a game made for conviviality. and what in God's name could croquet mean to someone transplanted from a shanty town like hers, a speck of urban squalor lost in a salt-water nowhere?

Too shy to come straight to the point, she said, 'You mustn't think you've got to master this game, you know.'

'But Anabel Cliffe said she couldn't imagine life without it.'

Elizabeth tutted, more crossly than she'd intended.

'Even the things they teach you formally at school aren't that important.' From the first Elizabeth had sensed Maria's feeling that she had to excel in every way or something terrible would happen. 'Besides, this game is awfully dull for just one person.'

'I don't mind,' Maria murmured. Elizabeth noticed nonetheless that she politely made as if about to put the mallet and balls away.

Trying not to find the girl's awkwardness catching, Elizabeth said, 'I was looking for you —' She faltered seeing Maria's look of alarm. 'It's all right,' she added. 'It's nothing to do with your school report. It – your report – is excellent, anyway . . . You do realize that, don't you?'

Maria looked down and said something inaudible. Moved by the sight of her stoicism, Elizabeth braced herself to speak on, as kindly as she could. 'You mustn't take your headmistress too seriously. Or anyone, for that matter, who tries to discourage you. She doesn't always know what she's talking about, not in my view. And we are – all of us – very proud of you indeed. Do understand that, Maria, won't you – please?'

Such pleading reassurance from one of her adoptive parents was more than Maria's shaky self-control could stand. Suddenly she found there was nothing she could do to stop the snobs wrenching their way out of her. Elizabeth was appalled at what a few well-meant words could do. As she and Maria embraced at last, she was also relieved at the realization that the way to the poor child's affections was wide open.

It was some time before Maria, her eyes splashed with cold water, was ready to rejoin the others. Edmund looked surprised and embarrassed at her swollen face; Digory, too, was shocked, and made an effort to speak gently. He came straight to the point nonetheless.

'Are you happy at your school, Maria?'

She had no idea what to say. As someone who

always told the truth, she found it hard to pretend she hadn't overheard some of what they'd been saying. Besides, her aunt had told her how with her new family she would always have to appear grateful.

Elizabeth understood. 'What Digory means is that you're evidently not perfectly happy there. You aren't, are you?' Her own voice still quivered from the effort of comforting the girl.

Maria gave a cautious shake of the head.

It was all that was needed. In less time than she had taken to walk back out of doors, the whole thing was resolved.

'Don't thank me,' Digory told her. 'This is Edmund's doing.'

I thought so, Maria nearly replied. Instead, she managed to say nothing more than, 'Oh.' It was as close as she could get to declaring that Elizabeth and Edmund were both henceforward her heroes.

CHAPTER
FIVE

As Maria was riding her new bicycle up the cool, deep lane from the village, four men slowed alongside her in a van.

It was early summer and she was dressed for hot weather, in cutoffs and a tank top. Her heavy hair fell smoothly down her back. They would have wanted a better look, even without an excuse to speak to her.

'Which way to the Old Rectory, sweetheart?'

The foreman leaned out of the window, his mates' interest like a wall of heat at his back. None of them really needed directions.

Trying instinctively not to look interesting, Maria pointed up the hill.

'What d'you reckon?' she overheard one ask as the van accelerated away.

'Yeah, all right, I suppose,' said the twenty-year-old of the gang, Jimmie Zlotnick.

As they turned into the rectory drive Edmund, home for half term, was unloading some movie equipment from the boot of his car.

'Show us where it is then, mate.' They had come to cut down some trees dying of Dutch elm disease.

'Oh – sure,' said Edmund, carefully putting down a carton of something heavy and striding towards them. He was anxious not to shame himself by looking too much the young master of the big house.

As he was pointing out the way, Maria free-wheeled into the drive. She propped her shiny four-speed Raleigh by the wrought-iron bootscraper, gave them a cautious glance of acknowledgement and went indoors.

Since the day was warm the front door was propped open with a giant fossilized ammonite dug up in the garden. Inside, the house looked cool. The floors were freshly polished and on one of the hall tables an antique Japanese vase held branches of flowering cherry. A passage wide enough to hold an oak settle led to the sunlit dining room.

Maria ran upstairs, calling out a greeting to the housekeeper. Jimmie Zlotnick and the other men watched her disappear.

'Is that your sister?' The foreman's question was by way of a warning to the others to watch it. It was the obvious thing to think. The two fine-looking young people both had long legs and dark colouring.

'She looks like you,' Jimmie Zlotnick quickly

90

affirmed. He was gazing past Edmund, into the house with its doors and windows open to let in the air.

When Maria later carried out four mugs of tea, she was treated with poker-faced caution. Only Jimmie Zlotnick was ready to put himself forward as she balanced her tray among a litter of branches and fresh sawdust. He hurried to relieve her, adroit as a waiter in a crowded restaurant. The noise of two chain saws made speech impossible. He flashed her an impish grin instead and gave a double thumbs-up sign.

Maria couldn't help responding to his determined show of charm. Being tallish for his weight, he looked younger than he was. He had thick, light brown hair and an Eastern European face very broad across the cheekbones. Zlotnick wasn't as pretty as the young Truman Capote, but he would always look more upright and freshly pressed than Andy Warhol.

When the break came for lunch he made a point of taking the tray back indoors.

'Jailbait, Jimmie, it has to be,' murmured one of the others from out of earshot.

It wasn't Maria he was stalking. The fact was, Zlotnick hadn't made up his mind who he wanted to meet.

One thing he had recently discovered. Someone, somehow, had to give him a leg up in life. Pretty damn quick, now his twenty-second year was bearing down on him. With the short perspective of youth, he'd started feeling as cheated as someone twice that age.

He hadn't always figured life as something you tried to direct. At sixteen he'd left Ipchester Secondary Modern without a single exam pass. The curriculum had mostly consisted of football anyway, played on a bleak campus fringed with cramped new executive homes. The one thing pupils had in common there was that they'd failed to make it into the grammar school. Faced with that, there wasn't too much the staff could do to fire up anyone's ambition. Most boys took it for granted that if you kept your nose clean you could simply get through life with no particular trouble. The same as Mum and Dad, right?

Zlotnick's own parents had split during his infancy. His mother was a mild, weak-minded woman whose children were all by different fathers, long gone. Only Zlotnick senior, an Air Force mechanic from the big American base down the road, had stayed long enough to leave his signature on a marriage certificate. After comparing his own disordered home with those of other boys, young Jimmie came to several conclusions, starting with the fact that having no man in the house meant having the power cut off a lot. From the beginning, he grew up despising women and children for their helplessness. The summit of his ambition had been no commitments and a steadyish wage.

He'd been a supermarket assistant, then a trainee clerk with the Rural District Council. Twice he'd applied for work as a salesman, impressing his interviewers with his power of self-projection. But both times, his contempt for the public had him busted back to the Labour Exchange within days. If they didn't fall for his patter he was vindictive. If they did, he sneered. Thereafter he'd been a tractor driver, a logger for the Forestry Commission, a brickie and now this job.

It was his meeting with Joyson, the class buffoon, that finally shook him alert to his future. Joyson had been the fat kid in Class 5CZ. Not the one who suffers endless humiliation, but the guy whose size makes him associated with extroversion and good humour. As a career slob, he'd taken no pains with anything – but in such an agreeable way that even his teachers liked him for it. He'd lived in a leafy road near Ipchester golf course. Usually, on that side of the town, if you failed the eleven plus your mother wept in her bedroom for a day then went out and got work, as a doctor's receptionist maybe, to pay your fees at the nearest private school.

Nothing about Joyson had cut much ice with Zlotnick. Instead, he'd tried to make up for being the poorest kid in the class by running with a gang who went as close to the edge of the law as most of them dared. Then a couple of things happened. Through school and after, Zlotnick had been the sidekick of one Forrest, the only gang member with the battle honour of a Borstal record. Last Saturday night Forrest had lost both legs in the wreck of a stolen car during a chase with police on the Oxford bypass. The following Monday Zlotnick had gone for an interview as an apprentice shopfitter, to find himself sitting across a desk from Joyson – *Joyson!* No matter that Joyson's father turned out to own the business. Shit! thought Zlotnick, comparing their careers with the shakiness of a man just missed by a fall of masonry.

It was time to change sides. Already he'd fixed an interview for a job with prospects, on a local newspaper . . .

Inside the Rectory, Zlotnick looked through doorways to right and left, treading carefully in the quiet house.

He heard the sound of typing. Edmund was working in a small study off the back lobby. Zlotnick peered through the half-open door. He could see the back of Edmund's shaggy head and part of a T-shirt bearing the Grateful Dead logo. At the clink of empty mugs on the tray, Edmund noticed him and jumped to his feet.

'Oh, can I help you?'/'I hope I'm not interrupting,' said the two scruffy young men, each on his best behaviour.

Zlotnick could usually slip in and out of the local accent without thinking. This time, trying too hard to sound like Edmund, he defeated himself. 'Iyoop Ayim nu' interrupting,' was how his words came out.

Not a bit, Edmund said, leading the way to the kitchen: he'd been needing a break. 'They say if you're writing something that's supposed to be or-

94

iginal, you can only keep going about as long as a football team lasts on the pitch.'

'Oh. You're studying for the university, are you? That must be interesting.'

'Yes, it is.' Edmund took a sideways look at Zlotnick. He had no idea how the other four-fifths lived, apart from what he'd learned via textbooks and the movies. 'But this isn't for an exam. I'm writing an article. About current films.'

'You're a reviewer! Aren't you, like, young for this job?' Zlotnick assumed Edmund must be contributing to a school magazine or some such, but he saw no reason not to use flattery.

'Dunno, – maybe. For all I know' – modestly slandering himself – 'the *Oxford Gazette* only commissioned a couple of articles from me for the sake of family connections.'

Zlotnick laughed aloud. Without making it clear, however, if such thing seemed impossible or wickedly likely. As it happened, it was the *Gazette* that had offered him an interview. How's that for a – he was about to say, when the wall phone rang on the far side of the kitchen.

The call was evidently for Edmund. After watching him for some moments, saying yes and uhuh with a look of concentration, Zlotnick left, knowing he'd lost his chance.

He wasn't to be thwarted for long. Driving through Stinscombe next evening in his nearly new Cortina he saw what he was looking for. Edmund's two-seater had been left outside the Golden Fleece, among the Land Rovers and Lotuses beneath the churchyard wall.

Hastily Zlotnick double-parked, and ducked in under the low doorway of the Fleece's saloon bar. The room was full of loud men in old tweeds or corduroy accompanied by women in sensible shoes. It was hard to know who were big-time farmers and who were merchant bankers down for the weekend.

Edmund wasn't there, of course. his crowd was too self-consciously democratic. They were crammed around a table window in the public bar, the girls only just longer-haired than the boys.

It was even more cheek-by-jowl in here. Among a group of middle – aged men by the bar was Zlotnick's foreman, dressed up for the weekend. Zlotnick ignored him, even though he had to slide by close enough for them to exchange body heat. Though he didn't smoke, Zlotnick bought a packet of Weights at the bar with his lager. Easing his way past people's elbows near Edmund's table, he made a show of pausing.

'You got a light, please, mate?' he said to one of the other lads there.

No way was he going to ask Edmund, even for something as small as this. If the guy wanted to patronize him by doing any kind of favour then fine. But let him do it, and compromise himself, on his own initiative, okay?

'Hi!' said Edmund, recognizing Zlotnick right behind him.

'You can get a light at the bar, sunshine,' muttered Zlotnick's foreman on the other side of the room.

'Hey!' exclaimed Zlotnick with fake surprise. 'Hi there! How's it going with that article?'

The other lad, Bob Danvers, had to stand up to get his Zippo out of his pocket. His jeans, loose enough in the leg, were punishingly tight round the crotch. While Bob was fishing for his lighter, Edmund said, 'Jockey yourself a pew if you like. We can fit you in.'

Zlotnick gave his disarming grin and the thumbs-up, and everyone was introduced.

'Hey, you know what's amazing?' he said, easing himself in next to Edmund. 'I never saw you before yesterday. Haven't you been in that house very long?'

Edmund said something to hide the fact that his family owned four homes. Did that mean, he added, that Zlotnick was from Stinscombe too?

'Yes. No! – God, what am I saying?' with a mime of smiting his own head. 'No. We live down by Stinscombe Halt. I mean, my mother and my brothers and sister and me.'

'What is it at Stinscombe Halt?' asked Bob, who was reading PPE at Christchurch. He was a stooping young guy whose beard would never curl thickly enough. 'Is it another village, or a railway station, or what?'

'It's a caravan site. But it's okay, it really is.'

Everyone took in the suggestion that Zlotnick's

family actually lived down a crack in the roof of hell. He said to Edmund, 'Look, this is an incredible coincidence. What I mean is,' adjusting the facts, 'I found out this morning I've got a job interview with that paper you said you were writing for.'

'Doing what?' asked Iona Helford. She was their group's odd girl out. Her ambition, narrow as the flight path of a bullet, was a good marriage to someone who could keep up a decent house in the country. She placed a lot of importance on having been at school with Princess Anne.

'It's only in the post room,' Zlotnick said, trying to address nobody but Edmund. With the eye of one user for another, he and Iona had each other figured at a glance. 'I haven't decided,' he lied, 'whether I want another job like that. You know what I mean?' He was confident (a) that Edmund wouldn't, but that (b) he'd feel he should. 'It's okay for a couple of weeks. Then you realize you might never do any of the things you want.'

'What *do* you want to do?' asked Iona, with a stony hint of challenge.

'All sorts of things!' In fact Zlotnick had never had an interest for its own sake. He just wanted to avoid taking orders from Joyson or anyone else he'd thought of as an equal. Mindful of Edmund's contacts, he added, 'What I'd really like to be is a journalist, but what's the post room got to do with that?'

'Depends' – 'More than you think,' said one or two people.

Zlotnick knew the job was better than he made it sound. Nonetheless he said, 'You reckon? I thought I'd give it a miss.'

'Hell, no.'

'Give it a try, at least.'

Edmund said, 'As far as the *Gazette*'s concerned you could've come along at exactly the right time. Old Everard Higgs is in his late forties and he's been running it since the war ended, for God's sake. Maybe after VE Day there were people who never wanted anything to happen to them again. The way Higgsy runs things, he must figure his readers'll actually pay to be reassured how boring their lives are.

'But now – seven or eight years after everyone else – his owners have stumbled on something new. Us – their lost generation. Lost by them, I mean. With more readies to whack out than most people's poor bloody parents ever had. And now that they've found their mistake, they're scrabbling after people our age, no bribes barred. We've got so much collective spending power they think we're touched with inner vision. If you're ancient enough to have voted in a General Election, the best thing you can do is to lie about your age.'

Zlotnick was watching Edmund steadfastly. 'Did it help you at the newspaper office, being, you know, young? You said something else as well – I mean, I know you were being funny – about your family. Family connections, you said. Is your father sort of a journalist too?'

Edmund said, yes, he bet being young and ignorant had helped; and no, an anthropologist. He also
advised Zlotnick that no way should he show up for
interview with straight gear or a haircut.

Zlotnick solemnly concealed the fact that he
hadn't a clue what an anthropologist was. 'So what
should the *Gazette* do that's, you know, a change?'

Edmund gestured with his pint, caught in mid-
swallow. 'First they need to change their format.
They're still catering to a readership who've never
seen a television. Who'll buy any crap you like so
long as your printer's raw materials haven't been
pulped by a Nazi high explosive. Then they need to
redesign and do something about their typefaces.
Those headlines set in Baskerville make it look like
an instruction manual. They need more features,
too. Stuff about what's on for people who'd rather
commit harakiri than stay in on Saturday night.
About politics as well, the sort whose movers have
never owned a tie . . .'

Zlotnick listened, then excused himself to go to
the lavatory. Locked in a cubicle he felt through his
pockets till he found an old parking ticket. On it he
wrote the words he needed to look up. 'Format';
'tipeface'; 'Hara Keary' . . .

'I'll tell you what,' said Edmund when Zlotnick
returned. 'Whenever we're both in here again, let
us know what happened. I bet you the price of
every round that Higgsy gives you the job.'

CHAPTER
SIX

Maria looked at the view with glazed eyes. Twenty
miles of olive groves and chestnut forests were piled
up towards the Apennine hills. The vista from their
hosts' medieval fortress was wonderful. It was also
hateful, now that everything was tainted by what
she'd found out.

She could hear Elizabeth up on the terrace with
the others. It was unbearable that her new
mother's voice might soon be stopped for ever. No
one could have substituted for Aunt Fahi, who'd
always been ready to josh Maria when she looked
serious or share her confidences. But however
reserved Elizabeth was, she'd been an ally. If
Maria felt anxious that Digory mightn't love her
like a father, Elizabeth could be counted on. Until
now.

On the terrace they were talking about her. Maria
and her parents were guests of the Professore Gio-

vanni Arrigoni, one of Elizabeth's former colleagues, and his wife Francesca.

'How Maria's English has come on,' their hostess was saying, 'since we saw you last.' Francesca, mostly known still as Fanny Hinkemeyer to her circle, was American – just. Her family had been established in its own palazzo in Rome since the middle of the last century.

It was the first afternoon of the Adams's visit, during the week of Maria's half term. Conversation was circling nervously round the one thing that would have to be mentioned. Elizabeth was on a brightly upholstered recliner with a glass of champagne she didn't fancy. She looked as if the sunlight could pass right through her. Out of sight in an enclosed garden, Digory was being athletic in the pool.

'She's not bad, is she? By Easter she was down right idiomatic. And now – well, you could never guess how violently the poor kid's been uprooted.'

'For that matter,' ventured Giovanni, offering more champagne and being quickly refused, 'I notice she's started learning Italian. I heard her on the telephone earlier, asking about admission times at the Boboli Gardens.' Giovanni himself, a large, ugly, attractive man, spoke English quite as well as his guests.

Elizabeth gave a feeble smile. 'Yes. I'm glad to see she's got used to the phone, never mind in which language.'

'Perhaps,' said Fanny Arrigoni, 'she doesn't rea-

102

lize how little is expected of Americans abroad.'
Fanny herself looked thoroughly native. She wore a
white bandana and white tunic and pants strongly
printed with turquoise and azure. This far south,
London or New York fashions, with their discreet
earth tones, looked wretched in the bold light.

'Ah, there you can tell she's an immigrant. She
thinks she's expected to do everything superbly.
She imagines everyone east of Hawaii has a doctor-
ate of some sort. I overheard her the other day
talking to our new cleaner about Pieter Breughel's
genre paintings, as though everyone in Stinscombe
knew that kind of thing.'

'What did your cleaner say?'

'She said, Pieter Breughel the Elder or the
Younger? We get our floors shined by an Australian
girl at Ruskin, who's trying to stretch her grant.
Not that Maria was to know.'

Fanny laughed, then fell silent. Below a parterre
of box hedges and lemon trees Maria was leaning
aimlessly against a balustrade, pulling tufts of moss
off its stonework. Wanting time to run backwards,
perhaps; or at least to stall awhile. How dare Elizabeth have kept her in ignorance for so many
months? How dare she get so sick at all?

Digory was in limbo, too, however resolutely he
might be splashing through his twenty lengths. Outwardly he hadn't changed since the result of Elizabeth's last tests. Every page of his appointments
diary had been struck through, however. From now
on he was going to be with her all the time.

Sombrely, Fanny asked, 'How is Edmund?'

'You mean, does he know about me? ... I'm afraid I haven't been altogether honest with him yet; he's got exams coming up. We told Maria on the way over. We couldn't have brought her here and still kept quiet. So, Edmund's fine. I'll tell you what —'

'What? What can we do?'

'Nothing much, thanks all the same.' Elizabeth struggled to find whatever it was she'd wanted to say. She suddenly found her eyes had filled with tears.

Below them Maria was imagining how it would be when Elizabeth had whispered her last word ever. The sound waves from it would vibrate out into space, getting thinner and more distant in every direction. Leaving a centre with nothing in it.

'I want so badly to bore you by saying what I really feel. Just this once, why don't I brag and tell you just how well my son has turned out?'

'... Okay, then,' said Zlotnick. 'To sum up. More features, right? Items about what's on, for people who'd rather commit harakiri than stay in on Saturday night. About politics, too – the sort of politics whose movers have never owned a tie. You don't want all of us too young to have voted to be, you know, another lost generation. Lost by the guys who own your newspaper, I mean.'

Everard Higgs went on doodling. He had the squared-off, battered good looks one might expect to find under a senior commando's beret. His hairline was receding, with each hair on top of his head visible in silhouette. The cramped view from his office at the *Gazette* showed courtyards and fire escapes. Next to the service area of a supermarket stood an uneven row of medieval houses. Their rendering had been heavily restored, then painted in shades of umber, bottle green and dusky pink.

'What you say is interesting. But that's what I'd expect, since you say you're a good friend of Edmund Adams. But let me give you some advice. If you're the sort of man I think you are, it should benefit you for the rest of your life. Whenever you find yourself on the coat-tails of an articulate comer like him, by all means announce his insights as your own. But do try to avoid his rather characteristic turns of phrase. Except when selling yourself to people who haven't met him, obviously.'

Zlotnick's face was emotionless. He was thinking he couldn't wait to hear the jerk damn himself even more. As soon as he'd heard Baldy out he'd shake hands to show that he, at least, knew how to behave. Then he'd leave, okay? Without stopping to say another thing.

'I shan't offer you work in the post room.' Higgs had been looking Zlotnick steadily in the eye. Now he started doodling again, as if working out his thoughts as he spoke. 'There's a particular problem with hiring people as young as you – and I do count your youth a disadvantage. It is that neither you nor we can be sure of what you're fit for. But my guess is that as a reporter you would do at least as well as most. The fact that you can give such an account of yourself, if only on the basis of mixing with young Adams, shows that you've an excellent memory and a good ear for a telling phrase. You also seem to have the ability to choose an opinion, if not to form one of your own. Correct me if I'm wrong.'

Zlotnick grimaced, trying to look judicious. He was rigid with concentration. So Baldy mightn't be useless. By God, though, Thingy back at Stinscombe Rectory owed him for putting him through this.

'I'm surprised your CV doesn't mention employment as some form of salesmen,' Higgs added. Zlotnick said nothing. He'd kept quiet about any job lasting less than a month. 'That, after all, is where your talents seem to be concentrated. As one of our reporters, if that's what you'd like to be one day, such talents would be indispensable. In interviewing strangers you would be delivering a sales pitch. The only difference is that you'd be selling yourself, as a good listener. Also I think you'd have persistence whenever you wanted someone to do something for you. To talk, for example.'

Zlotnick's features had changed. He was no longer an expressionless foe but a solemn ally. A spark of triumph kindled within him. Edmund Adams might have dropped him in a pit of shit, but it would be the perfect revenge if Zlotnick could show he'd got a job out of Baldy anyway.

'There may be disadvantages to what I'm going

to suggest. For you as well as for us.' Higgs capped his pen and twiddled it absent-mindedly. 'You have, I suspect, two shortcomings. One is an inability to see people on their own terms. To sympathize, in other words. The other, as I've suggested, is a lack of any opinion of your own. However, this may not be a problem; we're not the Manchester *Guardian*. There's no demand here for finer feelings, nicely put. Not compared to the kind of wham-bam reporting I think you can be trained to deliver.'

Higgs looked up at Zlotnick, who responded with a rueful twitch of conspiracy. Bugger me! Zlotnick was thinking. Not just a job, but a job like Edmund Adams's. A new idea had begun to occur to him: work was not just what you did to get by; it was how you told other sons of bitches what you thought of them. He held Higg's eye, careful to seem attentive but not over-eager.

'Let me tell you what I've got in mind. In the short term, a job for you selling advertising space. I'm confident you're better suited to it than anyone else I'm likely to see. Think about it. Or indeed, don't give the idea another moment, if you feel it won't do.'

Zlotnick mimed indecision, but not for an instant longer than he had to. A quarter of an hour later all details had been explained and agreed to. He was his most delightful self as he stood up to shake hands.

Seeing him to the lift Higgs said, 'Give my regards to Adams senior as well, won't you?'

107

'Right; right. Will do!'

'Since you know his son so well, I must say I'm a little surprised that you haven't named Professor Adams as a referee. He's bound to be a useful contact for anyone as closely acquainted with him as you are.'

'Well, you must know how it is with old Edmund's father.' He watched Higgs press the button to bring up the lift. 'The Professor's schedule . . . need I say more?'

The lift showed no sign of arriving. Higgs noted Zlotnick's technique of saying as little as possible when, presumably, he wanted the other person to talk. A useful instinct in a journalist.

'To be honest, one reason why I've offered this job – assuming in due course you do want to be one of our reporters – is because of your association with Professor Adams. Not for reasons of snobbery – don't get me wrong. Though knowing him does put you in touch with a network most trainee journalists would covet.'

'Too right!' said Zlotnick, looking serious and nodding. No way was he going to risk anything by asking the guy to explain. Not now the job was in the bag.

'The thing is that you're in a position to compare Digory Adams and his circle with a very different scene. I mean, with your own family experience, as an underage breadwinner living in sub-standard accommodation. Not all our trainees have had such a breadth of social experience. Ah, here we are.'

Seen from the departing lift, Higg's feet swooped upwards as though he were a stage angel on a flying wire. Well, I'm damned, thought Zlotnick, frowning with surprise at the other man's parting words. Maybe he'd have to deal differently with Adams. At first he'd decided to take the job, but show his independence by having nothing more to do with him. The guy needn't think he could treat him, Zlotnick, like some kind of sidekick. He probably thought he'd done him a favour.

Well, Zlotnick had turned the tables on him, hoisted him with his own whatever the bloody word was. And why? Because the job Zlotnick had gone out and got was damn well better than the guy had meant it to be. What's more, Zlotnick had done it in spite of him – on his own merits, right?

Go back to that house? He hadn't been meaning to, really he hadn't. But look at it this way: he owed it to himself to go. He wasn't letting anyone think he was in their debt, not without making them pay. If there was any more to be had from those people at the Old Rectory, maybe by getting it he'd serve them right.

Maria pulled open the heavy front door. The summer afternoon was friendly as a contented cat. Swallows chased farmyard insects, and a cuckoo was calling from the far side of the valley. Bumblebees flew through the sunlight like translucent blobs of pollen.

It was Zlotnick, standing in shadow on the doorstep, who'd pushed the big old brass buzzer.

'I'll tell you why I'm calling,' he said, before Maria could speak.

He looked apologetic but self-mocking. Immediately she felt like some kind of fellow conspirator. 'I've got some news Edmund wants to hear. Look, I know this is daft, but I couldn't wait to tell him personally. Face to face.'

Maria's liking for him grew. Not just on account of his charm, but because he'd taken the trouble to drive over. Anyone who thought that well of Edmund was bound to be all right.

But – she was sorry, but – her brother was in London. He and Digory were staying there for the time being . . . yes, it was at short notice.

'I'm getting a lift to the station this afternoon, to go up to town as well,' she told Zlotnick, her look of pleasure in his company fading away. 'Normally I'd be at school tomorrow, but Digory's asked me to go and stay in London, too.'

Maria wasn't always so confiding towards strangers; like many orphaned children she'd grown careful that way. Zlotnick was so eagerly responsive, though; she found it hard not to keep talking. She added, 'Would you like to come in? If you want to use our phone, you might be able to get Edmund —'

Zlotnick's refusal was all earnestness. 'No, no; no way. Thanks but no thanks, really.'

'He'll be at the hospital a lot of the time, seeing Elizabeth – visiting my mother. But you might catch him at home.'

110

At the mention of hospital he froze and looked solemn.

'... Yes,' said Maria, who seemed to shrivel as she spoke, 'it is, I'm afraid.'

But Zlotnick was hastily backing out of earshot. 'Are you sure you don't want —?' she called after him.

Looking stricken, he gestured his refusal and hurried away to his car, parked at a respectful distance outside the gates.

'What it is is, I don't want to intrude on private grief,' he afterwards told a colleague over several lunchtime pints in the Brasenose Arms.

'Then you're in the wrong business, aren't you, mate?' said Trevor, the other young guy from the advertisements department. They each spent the day on the phone, selling space by the line to local curry houses, and people with an outgrown baby buggy on their hands. Both wore their connection with journalism with a swagger, Trevor more openly so since he wasn't the new boy in the office.

'Seriously, if you want to be sure the woman's safely underground, check the deaths column. It sounds as if she'll be in *The Times* as well as the *Gazette*. That way you won't risk pitching up among the sackcloth and ashes, when no one'll want to know.'

So, daily without fail, Zlotnick studied obituaries in every one of the likely papers, local and national. Maria, her father and her brother took turns by

Elizabeth's bed, in the bright, hushed terminal wing of a hospital with a view down into one of London's Royal Parks.

Elizabeth was doped throughout, and in any case nearly gone from this world. Of the things that wanted easing, in her last days, the worst was Maria's grief. There were moments when the child seemed to be drowning at the bottom of a well of tears.

'I feel rather guilty about all this,' she told her husband. To the end, Elizabeth was apologetic about dying, even if she was too restrainedly English to mention death by name. 'This must be the third time the poor kid's been orphaned. The least I can do, if no one else minds too much, is to leave her reasonably well funded.'

The time came when Zlotnick got his reward for watching and waiting: a column or so each in *The Times*, the *Telegraph* and the *Guardian*. Behind the respectful prose and the flattering photographs, meanwhile, there was a lot of private tutting. When Elizabeth's will came to be read several wealthy households, in Gloucestershire and London, were scandalized at how much had been left to that child the Adamses had adopted from the Third World. No one from that sort of background would be used to that much money, let alone know what to do with all the real estate. Even though it was held in trust, in the long term the child would only be made restless by being given so much. She probably didn't even know how to use a knife and fork.

A month later there was a memorial service in the chapel of Digory's college. The *Gazette's* reporter listed every mourner who'd appeared regularly on television but neglected just about everyone else. The presenters of prestigious cultural series such as *Art Now*, *Forum* and *Viewfinder* got a mention, as did Harold Macmillan and John Betjeman. The Minister for the Arts and the Director of the National Portrait Gallery were ignored. A photograph showed Edmund and Maria looking sombre as they climbed the chapel steps half a pace behind Digory and Sir Kenneth Clarke. Edmund was almost unrecognizable in a well-cut suit. The unfamiliarity of formal dress made his part-Irish looks more striking than ever. Maria was leggy and wan in a soft linen minidress and flat-heeled shoes. Lifted by a breeze, her hair belled out about her elbows. No one in the picture looked dressed up; merely right for the occasion.

Zlotnick studied the photograph. He had no idea who most of these people might be, but he stared at them with a mixture of adulation and bile. Six months back he wouldn't have given any of them a thought. Since then, however, his indifference had been undermined, subtly but for ever. It had happened suddenly, in the moment when Edmund looked up from among his friends in the public bar of the Golden Fleece and said, in so many words, be one of us.

Though Zlotnick now cared, he still didn't know what he wanted. But he knew exactly what it was he feared.

Exclusion. Edmund's friendliness hadn't filled him with hope. Instead it had become a source of dread. Sure, he'd put one over on Higgs, no problem; and anyway wasn't that how you stayed alive? But what if he couldn't do it again? What if this Adams guy was a shitter, who'd only act like some kind of mate in the short term then dump you?

Zlotnick knew about perfidy. At sixteen he'd been meticulous in organizing the persecution of one of his classmates. The kid, by name Cruikshank, was a shy lad who'd been the runt of the gang and had suffered all sorts of unpredictable treatment. Zlotnick had arranged that no one ever spoke to him unless Cruikshank spoke first. There'd been the occasion when the boy's mother had been seen at the shops without her false teeth. For a month, the gang had cut him, more or less triumphantly; Zlotnick himself had been as righteous as a government minister nearly caught lying.

Possessed by formless dread of all the put-down artists in the world, Zlotnick left it several weeks before driving past the Rectory. For three evenings running he cruised past the gates. On the fourth day Edmund's MG was there in the drive. Zlotnick pulled over and went to ring the bell.

It was Maria again who opened the door. 'Oh, hello —!' she started to say.

He cut her short with a speech of sympathy. For days he'd rehearsed what he'd say, adapting a routine he'd learned as an apprentice salesman. Like

114

most foot-in-the-door patter, it couldn't be interrupted, or he'd lose the thread.

'What counts is this,' he concluded. 'It's not just a loss. It's your loss.'

Maria was caught unawares. Through all the condolences on Elizabeth's death, the handshaking, the wreaths and the eloquent letters, she'd been ignored, as though none of it concerned her. Now, shaken with gratitude, the poor child shed tears.

Edmund, coming into the hall, noticed this.

'I was just telling Maria – well, what can one say about your loss?' Zlotnick said. He went on to give another modified speech from his sales course. His face was wry with the effort of showing concern.

Edmund was grateful too. 'Yes, there isn't too much one can say, but it's good of you to think of Maria as well.'

Zlotnick didn't stop to wonder what Edmund meant. It still hadn't occurred to him that Edmund and Maria mightn't be blood relations.

'Look,' Edmund said, 'I'm glad you're here. I've been wondering how you got on with old Higgs.' Not thinking to see Zlotnick again, he was flattered at being remembered.

The three young people loped upstairs to the thirty-foot-long attic where Edmund slept. His bedroom was cluttered but functional; he'd pursued his teenage enthusiasms with single-minded method. There were maps of the night sky and an astronomical telescope the size of a rocket launcher. At each end of the room stood a wall of well-used books. Plastic toy boxes were stacked with back issues of *Zap* and *Mr Natural*. A structure like the skeleton of an outsize albatross was slung from the ceiling: a home-made flying machine. Edmund, aged twelve, had figured out its construction from the drawings of Leonardo da Vinci. Originally he'd planned to get it on to the coach house roof, climb into it and launch it, all in secret from his anxious parents. But, though careless of his own safety, he hadn't brought himself to risk damage to his lovingly carpentered craft with its brass fittings and oilcloth wings.

In the middle of the room stood part of a project Edmund was just reviving, after the weeks following Elizabeth's funeral. An easel supported a big cork-backed notice board covered with a grid of paper rectangles. Each rectangle bore a pencil sketch above a lengthy handwritten caption. Scene by scene, Edmund had been storyboarding his first movie.

Carefully hitching his trousers at the knees, Zlotnick sat down on the edge of a battered horsehair sofa. He launched into a jokey but doctored version of his interview at the *Gazette*.

'So it worked?' Edmund said. 'Higgsy really did go for what you suggested?'

'Loved it! Of course,' looking roguish, 'I thought it best to pretend it was all just me.'

'Terrific!' Edmund was cheerfully incredulous, enjoying Zlotnick's aura of conspiracy. 'So you managed to keep quiet about knowing someone else from the *Gazette*?'

'You bet. Maybe by now old Higgsy knows I know you. I suppose I should feel bad about it, really. But yes, when he gave me the job – hell, he hadn't a clue!'

Edmund laughed out loud. They both did.

The movie might have been Edmund's first, but it too was being handled seriously. The crew were mostly friends from school. Taking their cue from him, they were keyed up if necessary to work sixteen hours a day. The cast itself was made up of professionals, mostly just out of RADA and hungry as hell beneath the horsing around that had gone on in rehearsals.

The equipment wasn't amateurish, either. No cheapo stock from the local chemist, and a minimum of hand-held camerawork. Edmund hadn't hesitated to invest in sixteen-millimetre film to be used on a big Bolex that had been expensive by the standards of any private citizen.

In mastering his craft, he was realistic about saving money as well as spending it. First he'd written a budget – and only then a script. Sure, the action was set in deep space, but it was a part of space that did its damndest to imitate life on earth. The main character was a sentient asteroid that kept changing its form into a series of houses. Which house, at any time, depended on the histories of the people who landed on it. The Rectory was scripted to feature; so was the ugly new house of one of Maria's friends from Ipchester High, all picture windows and acrylic-brocade upholstery.

117

One twist was that the asteroid worked inconsistently. Sometimes it was a house in the distant past and the actors had had fun practising 'authentic' sixteenth-century English, to be matched with subtitles. Other events might belong to the future. There was also an alien, friendly but misunderstood.

Maria was one of the helpers, taking phone messages and making coffee and sandwiches. She sketched alterations to the storyboard, sometimes over and over, until Edmund was sure whether he wanted a tracking shot or a succession of fades. 'Hey, Maria, you've cracked it!' he'd exclaim, careless of taking credit for himself.

Praise from Edmund filled her with joy. She was proud, too, to be part of his crowd, seemingly so old from the perspective of thirteen. But what really counted was belonging to him as one of his family. Digory, by turns encouraging and distant, had done little to make her sure of her world. Elizabeth, who might have become her best friend, was now scorched to dust, her remains scattered nearby in Highcombe Wood. Maria was sensitive as ever to any sign that her adoption might be regretted. Only Edmund could be counted on to make her feel she belonged.

At the Rectory and elsewhere Zlotnick worked to make himself welcome. When Trevor left the *Gazette* to become a junior reporter on another local paper, Zlotnick, seeing his promotion as a personal challenge, responded on the spot. He started chasing Trevor's boss, a hard-working, overweight, articulate girl with an unpleasingly thin-lipped mouth in a rubicund face. Poor Carol had never known such ardour. Two evenings at the cinema at Oxford, three expensive meals in half—timbered alleyways off the High and the Cornmarket, a round of late-night avowals over a bottle of Calvados at her place and she was his. Undone, with a plain woman's lifetime of brisk stoicism blown to pieces. Zlotnick pursued her with passion, inspired by the fear of being professionally outdone by a dumbfuck like Trevor. 'You've saved me,' he whispered as they lay between her only-just-afforded Laura Ashley bedlinen. 'You've changed my life.'

Of course he wasn't going to be seen in public with such a dog. Where the rest of his world was concerned she would have to be kept at arm's length. He invented an estranged wife, still living in the same house with him, whose feelings mustn't be hurt.

· What could she do for him? she wanted to know. In no time, Zlotnick had got himself a crash course in basic journalism. Bargain-basement sociology, too; no point in selling yourself as rough trade if you hadn't a clue what was going through the other guy's mind.

As a journalist he was going to need a speciality, according to Carol's advice. The most obvious thing, given his connection with the Rectory, was the cinema. No matter that Zlotnick knew as little about movies as he did about anything else. He let Carol point him in the direction of the nearest picture house showing art movies, then joined a film society.

'Quite simply, it's what I've always wanted to write about,' he confided to Edmund, half apologetic at his own earnestness. 'Only, when I was a kid, well, you know, we didn't always have enough money for a television licence. And, let's face it, down at the dear old caravan site, Bunuel wasn't exactly mainstream viewing.'

He also let Edmund talk him into meeting some people from the film industry, at a party on the river near Oxford. Their host was the father of one of Edmund's school friends from Winchester, an independent director much in demand with the BBC.

'Yeah, great. But they'll have to have me on one condition: I've only got tat to wear.' When in doubt about black tie or white, flaunt one's shortcomings. Zlotnick was learning fast.

Hell, only the girls dress up. If they want to.'

The party was on a former college barge, all broad decks and white wooden balustrades. Others followed. One was in a former artisan dwelling full of furniture from Heal's in the once mean streets between Oxford railway station and the canal. Another was in London, in a house in Holland Park with stuccoed pilasters and balconies in frilly Regency ironwork. It belonged to someone's parents, who'd gone to Umbria for part of the summer. Someone else, still up for the summer vac, gave a breakfast party in his rooms in New College.

120

'You won't believe this,' Zlotnick remarked afterwards to Edmund. 'Really you won't. But until recently I hadn't realized the University was colleges in the middle of the town round quadrangles with lawns and stuff. I thought it was a big house out in the country.' Sometimes even the truth had its uses.

At these bashes, Zlotnick proved good at saying no more than enough. His best pitch was inviting people to talk about themselves; in his company, all sorts could be made to feel interesting. Towards the end of summer a group of Edmund's friends and their girls persuaded him to come along on holiday. By day there was windsurfing off a private beach in the Aeolian Isles. Afterwards there was much talking on the terrace till dawn; the kind you expect among people about to go to university, to whom time and opportunity seem infinite. They were at an age when anyone is greedy for new people and high on hope. Most people there would have been confident enough to hold out a hand of friendship to the whole world.

CHAPTER
SEVEN

It was a perfect green and gold afternoon in late September. Maria was being driven home from school in a twin of Edmund's MG. Zlotnick had bought it that week, on his promotion to trainee feature writer. The road swooped over wolds of stubbled fields. Along the skylines it ran in and out of the shadows cast by long coppices of beech trees. Maria sat with her legs aslant to make room for a bulging school bag. She held her long pony tail twisted round one hand; if she let it go, it streamed forward and whipped her across the eyes.

'Thank you for giving me a lift,' she said. 'I hope you didn't have to make a big detour.'

Zlotnick laughed as if at a witticism. 'I am running her in, you know' – patting the steering wheel. 'Not bad, is she?'

'It's very nice,' said Maria diffidently. She hadn't ridden in an automobile until she was twelve years old.

122

'You were on my way in any case.' He gave her an ironic grin, to show that this wasn't meant ungraciously.

'Oh.' Remembering that conversation was supposed to consist of rallies, she added, 'Were you?'

'Been down to London, haven't I?'

'Oh. To get the lens for Edmund's new Bolex?' Zlotnick had been tireless in running errands for Edmund's improvised film crew – or anyone in the Adams household. Sometimes he more or less invented them. Recently Digory had mentioned that the 1892 Purdey he'd inherited from his grandfather needed an overhaul and Zlotnick had insisted on making a special journey to London to deliver the gun to the Purdey workshop in South Audley Street.

'Yup. Just been to Wardour Street.'

Edmund had told him, 'You won't half look out of place. The guys picking up stuff in there are usually middle-aged musclemen dressed twenty years too young. You'll probably spot your first long-haired baldy.'

'Didn't they mind handing you something so expensive? Edmund said most of us look too young to be buying equipment like that.'

'Nah, no problem. I didn't fit in, mind. You know the type you see in there. No kidding, today I saw my very first long-haired baldy.'

They turned on to an empty stretch of Roman road, switchbacking across the breezy countryside.

123

A distant curtain of smoke leaned into the sky above a line of small fires; it was the season of stubble-burning. A baling machine two miles away moved along lines of harvested straw, transforming it into rectangular bales like giant caterpillar droppings.

Zlotnick changed down for the turning to Stinscombe. 'So how's school?'

'It's not bad, actually. The only problem is that next year Sally and I will have to start making choices.' Sally was the friend whose house was featured in Edmund's movie. 'Sally can't decide if she wants to make Latin and Greek her main subjects later on. Her parents are really fed up about that – they want her to stick with the natural sciences. I don't know whether I'd prefer doing art right through to the sixth form, or going for physics, with pure maths plus pure and applied maths. The thing is, Elizabeth used to say the art world was too political even for good artists to have a chance. It was pointless, she said, if all you'd got going for you was talent, skill and hard work.'

Zlotnick didn't realize that by 'political' Maria meant clique-ridden. He preferred to keep quiet, though, rather than ask what the hell Parliament had to do with it. Being contemptuous of ignorance in others, he was very careful how and when he owned up to it himself.

'Of course, Elizabeth did say lots of bad artists do okay, if only in the short term. But that doesn't stop lots of good ones being overlooked. Especially in mid-career. Early on, you might get taken up as a prodigy, being dead is a help – you can't devalue yourself by suddenly overproducing. Of course, you can make a good living by portraiture, but you need contacts for that, too. That's what she told me, anyway. And she said most people who commission portraits want a particular style. They even want the right kind of conversation while they're sitting. Either way, it wouldn't count as being paid to do what I wanted, would it?'

'God, no!' said Zlotnick, without much idea of what she meant. This was the first time they'd had a conversation alone. He added, 'But no one could say contacts were what you were short of! As well,' flashing her a grin, 'as talent.'

'Do you think so? About having contacts, I mean?' Maria had taken it for granted that Zlotnick knew she was adopted. And not only that, but chronically insecure.

He answered with a chuckle of disbelief. Privately he told himself to find out what it was she meant. 'And if you decided not to become a world-famous artist, know what I mean, a nudge is as good as a wink to a blind man, then . . .?'

'I'd do a D.Phil. Then research, naturally.'

'Naturally.'

'The problem is, pure mathematicians usually burn out early.'

'Yes, indeed.'

'And in some ways it's just as risky as being an artist, even if I did turn out good enough.'

'Well, yes.'

'You could work away in a particular direction for a couple of years, my maths teacher says, only to find that some other researcher, in Australia, say, or California, had published the same findings a fortnight earlier.'

'I'll say.'

'Not that she doesn't want me to stay in her class.' Maria looked thoughtful. 'But then so does the art teacher.' Virtual civil war had broken out in the staff room in the contest to recruit her. Anyone less modest, or less single-minded in doing what interested them, would have been amused to find themselves the centre of such rivalry. Embarrassed at talking so much about herself, she said, 'What about you? What are you going to do next?'

Zlotnick laughed, as if flattered at such extraordinary interest. In fact, it was a difficult question. He had no ambition, apart from seeing that other shitters didn't do him down by doing better in life than he had.

'Whatever I do so – say no more, irons in the fire and all that – I'm sure it'll be very different. From your plans, I mean. Even if I had your talent, and I mean that very seriously, well, at my school, we weren't taught too much of those sorts of things.'

Maria had never known what to make of Zlotnick's stories of poverty. In particular she didn't understand why mention of the caravan site was supposed to cause a tremor of sympathy. Back on the atoll, watching her employers' television over her shoulder as she vacuumed and polished, Maria had been shown many versions of Anglo-American home life. Locations in Bel Air or Newport had left her unimpressed; living in a mansion had been too different from her own reality. The fantasy that pleased her most had been the one in which she went home to find her aunt's shanty magically transformed into the luxury of James Garner's trailer from *The Rockford Files*.

The road crested the hill above Stinscombe village. Immediately the Cotswolds stopped being a place of wide skies where no one lived within five miles of anyone else. The meadows of the Eyne valley were threaded, one every ten minutes' walk, by ancient stone hamlets with manicured gardens. To cover Maria's silence, Zlotnick said, 'Sally must be a bit bright, to be in your class so young.' Maria's best friend was short and dainty, with a round face framed by curly hair that she was trying to grow straight. She looked like Shirley Temple impersonating the young Queen Victoria.

'Everyone thinks Sally's two years younger than me instead of just one; it makes her terribly cross. It's probably because I'm so much taller.'

'This can't be a rude question at your age – know what I mean –? But how old are you?'

'I'm thirteen.'

'You're kidding!'

'No, honestly.'

'Really?'

'Really.'

'That's amazing,' said Zlotnick, quite truthfully. 'I always thought you must be at least sixteen.'

Maria blushed with pleasure at such seeming interest. To be accepted by Edmund's friends was the next best thing to being treated like a real sister by Edmund himself.

Zlotnick added, 'To be honest with you – no messing, really – it's not only how you look and sound. I would've thought you were older just from the way everyone else talks to you.'

'Oh, most of Edmund's friends are really okay that way. But with a lot of people I've met – mostly to do with Digory – it's different. Some of them only give me the time of day because of him. It wasn't until recently that I realized how a lot of people see Digory as an important man.'

Partly to show his own respect for Maria's father, Zlotnick threw back his head and laughed disbelievingly.

'Seriously. Last winter in New York Digory took me along to lunch with his publisher. To be fair, I think Bob was okay. But if I'd had nothing to do with Digory I'm sure he wouldn't have tried quite so hard to be nice to me. Since I've been here – God, Jimmie, you'd be amazed at how many people have been like that.'

'Really?' Zlotnick was all concern. Even by his standards he couldn't have been more attentive. Since I've been here? What the fuck was that supposed to mean?

This was not a moment to parade his ignorance, however. No way was he going to lower himself by asking Adams's sister right out what it was she meant. Especially given the suspicions he now had. Too damn right she wasn't to be trusted. Come to think of it, there were other things he remembered her saying.

Nonetheless, to be on the safe side, he went on trying as hard as ever – almost – to be agreeable. Few people could have noticed any change in him.

Certainly Maria didn't. Not yet.

Meanwhile in the Rectory's drawing room, three time travellers had arrived. They were looking on at an encounter between a sheep-stealer and a bailiff, plus a foxhunting clergyman pickled in port wines of about the 1820 vintage.

The cameraman was Edmund, perched on a crude trolley improvised to allow for tracking shots. Bob Danvers was hunched over the recording apparatus, a pair of headphones pressed on to his candyfloss hair. The sound boom was operated by Neville Underhill. Neville was a tall bony guy with a look of premature middle age. Like Edmund, he was about to start his last term at Winchester. He was currently smarting at having been dumped by Iona Helford. She'd taken up with a titled cousin of his whom she'd met at a party in London, off the Boltons. With both arms raised to support the boom, he looked as if he'd been asked to prop up the whole world.

'I know you want me to ask pardon,' said the young actor playing the sheep-stealer. The scene needed him to look haggard; conscientiously, he'd

129

prepared himself by going a night without sleep. 'And I would, but that you, sir, pride yourself on being vengeful. On being pitiless, bloody and base.' He was doing rather well at portraying not only cold anger but an edge of embarrassment; his character was due to hang publicly before a curious audience of thousands.

The time travellers were in a position to save him, but at a price. On returning to the present, they risked finding they'd annihilated his widow's descendants by another husband.

One problem during filming had been noise from outside. A system of speakers had been rigged so that shooting shouldn't be disrupted by someone using the lawn mower or the kitchen radio.

'I could indeed let you live.' As Maria and Zlotnick got out of the car, the amplified voice of the actor playing the clergyman boomed around the garden. 'But see it as a man must, in my position. What if you did become an object of forgiveness – of an act of moral virtue on my part? It would be you who conferred a favour on me. How can I give a man in your station even that much advantage over one of his betters? It would be to call into question the very foundations of society.'

Maria and Zlotnick waited, listening, for the take to finish, then slipped round the drawing room door to join the others. Zlotnick was carrying the new lens in its tight polystyrene package. He handed it to Edmund with a neat flourish and a look of anticipation, as if it were a surprise he'd thought of on his own.

'That's bloody good of you, mate; that really is.' Edmund was bright with pleasure at his new toy and at the trouble Zlotnick had taken.

The others had been talking about the script's next sequence. Several people held that most of the locations were too samey and well furnished.

'Another setting would be fine,' said Ronald Fairbairn, who played the clergyman. 'But not if you had to distort the story to fit it in. Personally I think Edmund's done a good job of turning every difficulty so far into an advantage.' Ronald, the cast's only member over forty, was also its only amateur. He was an English don at Digory's college and a long-time friend of the family.

Bob said, 'I still reckon an extra location at this stage would do us no harm. Don't you think?' appealing to Edmund.

'I'm anybody's man. I've revised this script so often I'd have to put it away in a drawer for two months before I could even make sense of it.'

'If something different is needed,' ventured Ronald, 'we do have the footage shot in that box room in Oxford with a view of the railway.' He looked doubtful, though, and no one hurried to respond.

Maria spoke up. 'Jimmie, maybe you could help. Do you think we could set scene twenty-one in your mobile home?'

'Hey,' said Bob. 'How about that? Maria may have hit on it.' Everyone looked at Zlotnick.

He laughed apologetically. 'I only wish I could help.'

'What's the problem, Jimmie?' Bob asked. 'It's a great idea. If it's okay by you.'

'It's a terrific idea. And as far as I'm concerned it would be fine. I just wish it was possible. Sorry about that, folks.'

'Your mother wouldn't mind, would she?' Edmund asked. Despite the number of times Zlotnick had slept over at the Rectory, no one had ever been invited back to his place. They had a clear enough idea of his home life, even so. His mother was a mild, friendly woman, ever ready to see things from her children's point of view. By contrast, his sister Dominique was the very stuff of spirited proletarian earthiness.

'Naw, she wouldn't mind. She'd knock herself to pieces for us. That's the problem. My mum wouldn't stop at cleaning the windows; she'd feel she ought to be .getting in new furniture. And, well, you know,' addressing a roomful of respectful faces, 'I don't really want that.'

Though the subject was dropped, later it gave Edmund an idea.

'Doesn't your sister feel left out? I mean, with you being up here with us so much of the time?' There were also two brothers, but according to Zlotnick they were too young to be interested in anything he did.

They were manhandling the camera trolley back into the coach house for the night. It was a clumsy-looking thing, fudged together from planking and bits of old floor joist. The wheels had been can-

132

nibalized from a second-hand baby buggy; the seat came from an ancient haymaking machine found in a patch of nettles behind a barn.

'Dominique?' Zlotnick looked concerned. 'I'm not too sure about that. No reflection on anyone else, but she might be a bit overawed. You know what I mean?'

'Er . . . I'm not sure I do.' Edmund peered to see if the front wheels were going to clear the sill of the coach house door. The trolley handled well, but only on a level surface. 'I know we're all much older —'

'Well, there you are. Not that the kid's a wimp, God knows.'

'Maria's the same age, isn't she? Younger, even?'

'Yes, but Maria . . .' Zlotnick's tone implied that any sister of Edmund was bred from the playpen up to put people at their ease rather than the other way about. 'For one thing she's travelled more than most kids – most girls, I mean – her age.'

'Aw, come on. Not till last year, anyway. Oh, bugger.' The trolley, making heavy weather of the ripply brick floor, was stuck. Its front wheels had wedged themselves into the shallow channel built to drain a row of stalls. 'Hang on, I'll fix it. You pull while I lift.'

'No shit? I mean, hasn't she? She talks about this place – this house, I mean – as if she's hardly ever had time to be here.'

'Well, that's not surprising.' Edmund was stooping to grasp the front of the trolley platform. 'Considering her history.' He glanced up to see if Zlotnick was ready to brace himself against the handle. Instead, Zlotnick was staring at him.

'Isn't it?' he said.

Briefly Edmund mentioned where Maria was from, and how she had come to live at the Rectory. 'Okay,' he said, holding the edge of the trolley, 'pull now!'

The wheels jumped free. 'That's incredible,' Zlotnick said, struggling to keep his voice calm. 'I'd never have guessed that. What an amazing story. Bugger me.'

Edmund tried not to look self-consciously pleased. Sure, he'd taken Maria's part against Digory once or twice, but he was proud of his father for all that. Not many rich liberals you could name had paused to snatch even one Third World child out of the path of the US war machine.

'We're just relieved that she's so little fazed by being here. It's only a year since Digory first met her.'

'That's really great. Really it is. That's terrific. That's the most amazing thing I ever heard.'

'I reckon so. Considering what might have happened to Maria if she'd stayed where she was.'

'Too right. I mean, you know better than I do, but . . .'

Taking his cue, Edmund gave a few details of Maria's former life. 'So even Washington can't deny that the island's got the highest population density on the entire goddamn planet,' he concluded.

134

'Well, I'm buggered,' said Zlotnick, looking serious – though to him any density figures were meaningless. They'd have stayed meaningless, he reflected, even if he had given a flying fuck for any of those tinted folk located up the arsehole of the world.

He was furious. Not with himself, obviously, but with the coon bint. There'd been signs she'd been phoney. The clincher – Jesus, he deserved every bit of credit for this – the clincher was that he'd noticed her fingernails. Not many people would have been wise to that one. He recalled how one night in the pub he and Neville Underhill were the only ones to hear Iona Helford slagging off a former classmate from Kampala, part-English, part-Indian. 'When your closet nignog has tidied up everything else about themselves, you can still count on their hands to give them away. There's nothing so reliable as a pale crescent at the base of their fingernails. It shows up even the tiniest lick of the tar brush.' He'd noticed Underhill's embarrassment, but had thought it was the sort of thing you'd expect in a chinless git like that, all sandals and adam's apple.

No – if he, Zlotnick, had been jerked around, at least he needn't blame himself. But by God, he told himself later in one of the Rectory's downstairs johns, it was someone's fault.

'Fuck the fucking fuckers.' He was sitting on the lavatory and straining, with his pants round his ankles. 'Fuck the lot of them,' he repeated, without knowing who he really meant.

That very afternoon the bint had let him chat her up. Without anyone else there to see how well he did it, right? But his main grievance was far more bitter. He'd done bloody well at overcoming his drawbacks as an outsider. Running their errands. Giving the bint lifts. Playing up those same drawbacks for all they were worth. And at every turn, without even trying, she'd upstaged him. She'd known that, compared to her, in the deprivation stakes he was a non-starter.

And she'd let him do it, he told himself. She'd tried to lead him into it. It would have taken a pocket calculator to follow the pluses and minuses of racial status in Zlotnick's mind as he analysed the DNA cocktail of Maria's ancestry. The way he now saw it, she rated only a few points ahead of Carol. And that was after subtracting extra from Carol (a) for letting him shag her and (b) for giving away perfectly useful professional information to him for nothing. Gritting his teeth, he strained over the lavatory one more time, crimped with frustration and rage.

In the hall Edmund hailed him.

'Jimmie! We're nearly ready.' The house resounded with people scampering to get changed, and shouted conversations through bathroom doors. They were going out to eat by lamplight in the garden room of the Woolsack, a coaching inn on an upland crossroads near Chipping Campden.

'Could Maria have a lift in your car?'

'But of course!'

Outside, the autumn dusk became lit by four sets of headlights. Zlotnick stalked over to his car, stiff as if he'd been goosed, and got in. He was willing Maria to notice that he hadn't opened her door for her.

Putting his hand on the car roof, Edmund leaned down to speak through Zlotnick's open window. 'Hey do you know your way to this place?'

'Not so far I don't.'

'Okay, follow me. And if you get left behind, Maria's been there before.'

'Terrific.' Grinning, Zlotnick gave the thumbs up.

After half a mile Maria wondered at his silence. Of all Edmund's friends, no one kept the conversation perking more freely than Jimmie. Was it her fault? Maria may have changed in recent months, but she was still the polite child whom her aunt had taught never to leave their island's corrugated-iron chapel on Sunday without saying thank you nicely to the minister. She guessed it couldn't always be Jimmie's turn to put himself out.

She asked, 'Did Edmund find that book he wanted to lend you?'

Recently Zlotnick had regretted aloud that he hadn't read more. Edmund had responded by lending him a yard of books, happily reliving his own discovery of some favourite authors. Zlotnick had already wondered if he should get Carol to tell him which names to drop, but Carol was self-educated and couldn't have been counted on to give the correct ones.

As they slowed for Stinscombe bridge the traffic light turned green. Zlotnick changed back up with the abruptness of someone being harassed. He replied, 'To answer that, I'd have to know what book you meant.'

Maria flushed with surprise. For nearly a mile, neither of them said anything. At length, since her good manners were ingrained, she tried again. 'When Edmund shows us his finished print, will Dominique and your mother be able to come?' There was to be a party at the Rectory on the completion of filming.

'No.'

She looked at him. Every muscle in his face was set hard. His manner announced that he shouldn't have to put up with being probed like this. Where the road ran through Withycombe Woods they lost sight of the others' lights. Following Edmund's lead, everyone else must have taken a different route. Maria said, 'Would you like me to tell you the way, from here on?'

'There wouldn't be much point in giving directions from further back, would there?' For the rest of the way Zlotnick's silence announced that 'bear left' and 'turn right' were the most foolish things anyone could have said.

In the Woolsack's restaurant, all quarry-tile flooring and glass-domed lamps, one long table had been booked for their party. There was a subdued cheer for Zlotnick and Maria as latecomers. It was Friday night; work on the movie had gone well and, miraculously, there even seemed to be universal good will among the cast and crew.

Edmund was passing a carafe along. He twisted round to look up at them. 'We thought you might be lost.'

Zlotnick laughed his delightful laugh at the mere idea. 'Maria was terrific. She must know every inch between your place and here. Let's face it, Adams, you old bastard, your sister's too good for you.'

'If you think something's wrong,' Edmund suggested next day, 'maybe you should ask what it is. But you've heard yourself how well Jimmie thinks of you.'

Maria recalled the cold zest of Zlotnick's hostility. She decided she'd pass.

Over the following week, filming was finished. The celebration party extended through every room in the house. On the lawn a marquee had gone up, part of an end-of-shooting present from Digory. Throughout the first part of the night the world, his girl and his cousins roared up the lane and disembarked by the carload, credit-card hippies every one. The noise of greetings was tremendous; out of hundreds of people nobody, it seemed, was a stranger to anyone else. In the garden soared the music from a jazz quartet of guys still up at Oxford, whom Edmund knew as mates. They were good; their Finals Year was already going to be seriously holed by professional bookings in London.

Towards midnight it was obvious something

139

special was about to happen. A free-fire zone was cleared in front of a pair of speakers half the size of Stonehenge. Behind it apparatus to match was hustled into place by men who'd done the job before. At the stroke of twelve searchlights went on and The Who were choppered in. They arrived to tremendous applause from a flushed, rumpled audience crowded five deep along the rim of the ha-ha to cheer them as they touched down in the bottom field.

At sunrise four dozen people were still there, sleeping fully dressed on improvised beds as though taking refuge from a natural disaster. There was a lingering brunch, at which the party's survivors browsed among smoked salmon, eggs Florentine, Cumberland sausages or scrambled eggs with cream and herbs. The last guests finally revved off into the bright autumn countryside, full of the pleasant feeling of unreality that goes with wearing ostrich feathers or a rumpled caftan when the driver in front is going to work on a tractor.

Helping to clear up, Maria found a missing book Edmund had wanted to lend to Zlotnick. As the party had broken up into boppers, smoochers, people-collectors and the serious-talk faction in the kitchen, Edmund's attic had been where most of the dope had been smoked. Tipped off to look out for half-smoked roaches, Maria was peering under the bed when she found his lost copy of *Fear and Loathing in Las Vegas*. It had been keeping company with six dirty glasses, a couple of hastily half-cleaned ashtrays, three empty bottles of Taittinger, five empty pint bottles of Guinness, a pair of woman's throwaway paper pants, somebody's contact lens and an issue of *Black Dwarf*.

Last night had also marked the end of Edmund's school vacation, so he was no longer around. Maria wasn't in any haste to meet Zlotnick; but she could always deliver the book to his home when he was out at work. Going round to the coach house she got her bike and rode out of the drive, happy and impatient at the thought of doing a favour for her brother. It was only when whizzing down the shade-splattered lane to the village that she remembered: no one at the Rectory had ever had Zlotnick's precise address. But once she got to the caravan site she could ask around; someone would know.

It was a still day, bright as a painting in a medieval manuscript. In Stinscombe village smoke from autumn bonfires rose up unwavering. Rooks wheeled noisily in and out of the trees massed above Manor Farm. By the village green, the river's tiny tributary could just be heard, flowing invisibly through a tunnel of watercress. The lane along to Stinscombe Halt ran between water meadows and the course of the old branch line. Where the farmers hadn't reclaimed the track, a row of broken fence posts hewn from sleepers was overwhelmed by scrub: young ash trees and seedling birches, dogwood, hawthorn, field maple and rose hips. Old man's beard was seeding fluffily, festooning everything like a Hallowe'en cobweb.

141

On a good-tempered day like this, the caravan site looked homely rather than mean. The little Gothic railway station was used these days by a dealer in cattle feed. It stood some way back from the lane, behind a tussocky piece of ground that had once been gravelled over as the station car park. Down the middle of the railway track itself a narrow trail had been churned to mud, then baked hard; at this point it was a bridle path.

Half a dozen caravans were ranged close to each other, like elephants at a watering hole. Several cars, from a Wolsey to a beat-up Ford Capri, were waiting to be cannibalized, or just mouldering amid the brambles and rose hips of a neglected hedge. A tall ancient fridge painted with dark green gloss was leaning at an angle on the uneven ground. The caravans, with a few improvised sheds, were clotted together beneath an angular skyline of television aerials, lines strung with limp washing and power cables suspended from poles. The scene looked like a picture vandalized by a toddler with a felt-tipped pen.

Three chained-up yappy mongrels guarded the site. Back in Micronesia, settlements like this had also included chickens and pigs scratching about and rooting for edible rubbish. Unconsciously Maria registered how little queueing must go on here to get water at the standpipe. It was a weekday, so there were few children about. Except for the absence of human voices and the mildness of the sun, she could have believed herself on an improved version of the island where she'd been born.

142

She picked her way through rank grass, and dock leaves booby-trapped with dog turds. This place might be halfway familiar; but to anyone peering out at Maria she obviously didn't belong in any part of rural Gloucestershire. She wouldn't have looked foreign in Liverpool or the East End of London, among Cypriots and Pakistanis, but her honey-coloured skin and luminous black hair were out of place on this dusty site inhabited by the families of farm workers with names like Pauncefoot and Priddle.

Her clothes were incongruous too. Maria was dressed correctly to the point of dowdiness, in a Viyella shirt, a divided midi skirt, knee socks and lace-up shoes. Without knowing it, she was in mourning. She had started to dress for pleasure while Elizabeth was still alive, but she'd gone back to choosing her clothes for invisibility's sake, just as when she'd first arrived in England. 'A white man's good nigger,' was how one sixth-former at Aynesford Hall had described Maria's out-of-uniform wardrobe.

She looked around, hoping to ask the way from a woman rather than men or boys. Her time before England, as a street beggar, had made her careful when dealing with strangers. Outside one caravan she noticed a row of terry-towel nappies. They were turning crispy-dry on a line strung between the television aerial and a crab apple tree in the boundary hedge. She reached up to rap on the door.

Before she could knock it was opened anyway,

by a young woman with a baby on her hip. 'I hope you don't mind me asking, but are you lost? Only I saw you from the window.'

The woman – girl, really – wore a recently fashionable pinafore dress gone bald at the hem and well-polished shoes whose uppers had started splitting away. Her hair was strained back into a rubber band. She wore no make-up and no tights.

She added, 'I would have opened the door sooner, seeing you coming, but I was finishing changing the baby's nappy.'

The child was a pretty creature of fourteen months or so. At the sight of Maria she'd fallen silent with curiosity. Her feet were bare; otherwise she was elaborately dressed. Over her nappy a nearly outgrown pair of pants bristled with carefully ironed broderie anglaise frills. Her frock was two sizes too small, but expensive and scarcely worn: a rich child's hand-me-down. The woman, in her out-of-date good clothes, reminded Maria of a classmate back at Aynesford Hall whose father had refused to pay any maintenance other than school fees.

'I'm looking for someone who lives here —'

'What, here?' asked the woman, glancing behind her as if Maria could produce a stranger from inside the caravan. 'Oh, I see. You mean you're looking for a friend or whatever. When I saw you holding that book I thought maybe you were doing a school project. I couldn't think what else it could be.'

'No, this book's for a friend – for someone I know, I mean – who lives here.'

144

'Oh right. I used to do a lot of reading myself, before. You must have thought I was stupid or something; it's just that we don't get a lot of new faces round here. Who are you looking for, if you don't mind me asking?'

Maria unwittingly clocked another similarity to life on the atoll. This was a place for women and children whose men were gone for good. 'I wanted to leave it with Mrs Zlotnick. Could you show me where she lives, please?'

A surprising thing happened. At the mention of Zlotnick's mother the woman's manner changed. It was as sudden as a total eclipse of the midday sun. She looked as if Maria had inflicted some kind of personal shame on her.

'Well – yes, er – I mean, I could, of course.' To cover her unease she leaned round the door and pointed. The baby, unconcerned, tipped backwards on its mother's hip like a rodeo rider. 'It's, er, that way, you see.' She made a show of peering towards the road, as if to guarantee that what she said was true.

Maria was mystified. Why had she been made to feel as if she'd just played a shabby trick?

'Look,' said the woman, noticing her bewilderment, 'I can show you the way, really I can. Only – are you sure you've got the right name?'

'Have Mrs Zlotnick and her family moved, then? I thought they lived here.'

The woman looked at her with wary concern. 'They've always lived in the same place, up the

145

road.' She hesitated. 'I don't want to sound rude, but if you haven't got the right address anyway, does that mean you don't know them very well?'

If this was meant as a warning, Maria didn't notice. It was surprising, though, that they didn't live at the caravan site. Trying not to sound disbelieving, she thanked the woman and cycled back to the road, standing up on the pedals as her bike rode over the bumps in the track.

She'd been directed to a late Victorian villa originally built to house the halt's station master. Its garden, all burdock and brambles, had a jagged wall of Cotswold stone as solid as a tank trap. Fretwork bargeboards in poor condition still decorated the slate roof. As Maria went up the path a large part-Alsatian strained against his lead, barking at her as if he'd only been put on this earth to do her harm. Still thinking she must be at the wrong address, Maria knocked on the open door. Inside a corniced ceiling was crusted with dulled brownish gloss. The dirty floor was tiled in concentric diamond shapes of black, blue, white and terracotta.

At the other end of the hall a girl stuck her head round a door. Her face was blank of everything except curiosity. She edged her way towards Maria, past a dusty bicycle with a missing wheel and a child's buggy doing long-term service as a coat stand. Maria tried to fit her into the picture of his family that Zlotnick had drawn: the salt of the earth, with a robust sense of humour and a hold on reality that was denied to people from softer, more privileged backgrounds.

146

'Yes?'

The girl might have been fifteen. Or, since she was forty pounds overweight, she could just as well have been ten years older. Her miniskirt was either a mistake or an act of bravado. Looking at her knees, Maria remembered Edmund saying that most pantyhose advertisements didn't feature women at all, but male models with shaven legs. Her hair was slick, with a dull purple tinge from being dyed; there was no guessing its real colour. It lay in two lappets over her ears, as if she was growing out part of her fringe.

'Is Mrs Zlotnick in, please?'

'Mum!' shouted the girl, holding the door open in front of Maria.

'What is it?' The other woman sounded older than Maria had expected. 'My mum's a worrier,' she recalled Zlotnick saying. 'It's the way, you know, that she's had to live.'

'Someone to see you,' yelled Dominique.

'Oh.' Mrs Zlotnick's voice wavered somewhere between apprehension and wanting to make a good impression. 'Who is it?'

'It's a girl,' Dominique called, fearlessly eyeing Maria.

Mrs Zlotnick put her head round a door in a timid version of her daughter's curiosity. 'Well, don't you think you can ask her in?' Physically she was an older version of Dominique, with every surface and hue buffed away and faded. It was hard to tell how she might have looked when young.

147

Without saying anything, Dominique held the door further open to show that Maria should come in. She led the way through the hall, where a trail the width of a goat track had been trampled clear of dust. It opened into a back room with a cooking area at one end. On the floor vinyl tiles curled at the edges like a week-old sandwich. The cooker stood on bare boards, with yellowing newspapers spread out to catch spillages. It was an old four-legged gas model that Maria recognized as having no bottom beneath its racks. Once, on the atoll, the woman in the breezeblock hut next door had used one like this to bake a big tuna head, only to find a mouse had climbed up into the dish and been cooked as well.

The room was dominated by a huge TV. It stood on a glass-fronted sideboard topped with imitation marble formica. Inside the sideboard, which held unmatched crockery and old newspapers, a broken fluorescent tube had been designed to illuminate a mirrored back. Three chairs with rusty metal legs had backs and seats in blue plastic. Along one wall stood a black button-back sofa, also upholstered in plastic, which someone had tried to mend using insulation tape. It had spindly brass legs and seat cushions in crimson and black acrylic. Next to it a cardboard grocery box had served too long in place of a vegetable rack.

On the island where she'd been born, Maria had rarely seen so much furniture in such a small room. Nor had she seen so much dirt. The walls were a faded orange gloss speckled with ancient deposits of grease. Looking about her with the eye of an ex-housemaid, she noticed that even the light bulb in the centre of the ceiling had a grubby sheen. Its frilled nylon shade had gone brown at the edges like an elderly smoker's moustache.

The two women stared at her, with the expression of cows gazing at a stranger over a hedge.

'I'm Maria,' she said, the confidence draining from her voice. Neither of them said anything, so she added, 'Edmund's sister.'

'Oh, yes?' Dominique said, meaning, who's he?

'You know,' responded Maria, senselessly. 'Edmund Adams. We live at the Old Rectory.'

Urgency as well as confusion dawned on Mrs Zlotnick's face. 'Oh, right.' She clearly had no idea what Maria was talking about, but she figured that if Maria was the daughter of one of the local clergy she was bound to be important somehow. 'Well, as I say, won't you sit down?'

Maria perched herself on the edge of the sofa. Mrs Zlotnick sat down by a formica-topped kitchen table with splayed metal legs. Faced with an outsider, she looked anxious, as if this were no longer her own home.

'I've brought something for Jimmie. From my brother.'

'Oh, yes?' Dominique sounded interested, if not polite. 'What is it, then?'

'Edmund wanted to lend him this book, so I thought I'd bring it down here.'

149

'Oh.' Dominique's voice fell like a lead balloon.

'What's that, then?' Mrs Zlotnick asked, craning for a better view of the cover. She read the title aloud, clearly making nothing of it.

'I was thinking maybe I could give it to Jimmie, if he's going to be home soon.' Maria sensed that she didn't trust Edmund's property with either of these women.

'So why've you brought it round here?' Maybe from an instinct for advantage, Dominique had stayed on her feet.

'What?' Maria looked up at her, not understanding.

Mrs Zlotnick tried to explain. 'Jimmie's a very busy boy these days. He isn't here, most of the time.'

'I'm sorry?' Sometimes Maria's English still let her down. 'Does that mean he is here some of the time?'

Dominique scowled. 'Look, are *you* trying to tell us?'

Maria wondered what to say to stay out of trouble. Did they see her as a spoiled brat down from the big house for a spot of slumming?

'I thought this was where Jimmie lived. Have I come to the wrong place?' She looked at the other girl's heavy features, adorned with white pendant earrings and purple eyeliner. Dominique bore no likeness at all to Zlotnick. In him, the well-defined bones of his Eastern European forebears were combined with the light colouring got from generations of Gloucestershire labourers. His sister was a pair of sharp black eyes in a pudding face.

'He doesn't live *here* any more,' Dominique said, as if Maria were the one who owed an explanation. 'He hasn't lived here since he left school.'

'But he would if he could,' insisted his mother. 'Only it's like I say; he's ever so busy these days. You stay there,' she added – though Maria hadn't shown any sign of getting up. With the haste of someone not used to moving quickly, she scuttled over to the glass-fronted sideboard.

'Do you know, I never realized how important my son's job was. Until I was in the shop – oh, it was earlier this year – and I saw this. Now. You look at these.' Mrs Zlotnick put half a dozen copies of the *Oxford Gazette* on the table. She was probably animated for the first time in years.

Maria politely reached out. First though, Mrs Zlotnick wanted to read something aloud.

'"Battling bog. The cricket scene, by J. Zlotnick. Bledington village team were staring defeat in the face during Sunday's away match with Kingston Bagpuize, but fine batting from Bob Evans (39) who was ably supported by Pete Easton (41) managed to save the day . . ."' She read laboriously, giving each word the same emphasis, like a primitive voice synthesizer.

'. . . So you see, that was the first time I even guessed what my son had managed to make of himself. If you can't imagine how astonished I was, just ask Dominique.'

But Dominique, bored, had left the room.

Mrs Zlotnick held out the pile to Maria. 'Go on, help yourself. Take a look.'

Maria reached for the top issue. The paper already felt sandy with age. 'No – no; here you are,' Mrs Zlotnick insisted. Maria took all of them on to her lap, self-consciously, like the audience member asked to choose the conjuror's playing card. Slowly, so as not to hurt the woman's feelings, she turned over the pages one by one.

Everything must have been there that had so far had Zlotnick's byline. 'Teenage Teresa sprains ankle in unguarded hole.' 'Bank holiday fair fun.' 'Show-jumping Simon beats the clock.' Eventually Maria asked, 'Is Jimmie pleased that you've kept a copy of all his, er, work?' Even as she spoke, she blushed at the hypocrisy of such a question.

'Oh, I'm sure he understands – you know, that I'd keep anything that's got his name on it in print. Even though he doesn't know I've found out about his new job. You know, like deep down he must understand.'

'So – if he's not here very often, maybe I'd better keep the book till later,' Maria said.

'Oh, no! I'm sure there must be some way we can give it him.' Mrs Zlotnick looked urgent. Presumably she hoped this would be a way of making contact with her son.

Outside the dog began to bark. He stopped, then started again in the hall. The front door crashed open, its glass panes rattling. Two boys aged between ten and thirteen stormed into the room, shouting with glee as they teased the dog. He was trying to seize his lead from them, leaping and twisting in the air. A foot away from Maria's face he snapped his teeth with a sound as sharp as a broken bone.

Neither boy took any notice of Maria. From what Zlotnick had said, these were his brothers, Terry and Keith. The former looked vaguely Italian, with heavy brows and brown eyes. Keith, the younger, bore a ghostly racial resemblance to Maria; perhaps the local US air base had had a Filipino among its personnel.

Seeing their mother the boys stopped tumbling about for a moment. The dog lashed his tail hopefully, waiting for the fight to begin again.

'Mum —!'

'— We need five quid to go out.'

'Six, dickhead.'

'We need six quid.'

'Make her give us six, that's what we need.'

'I've told you there isn't any more this week,' pleaded their mother.

Both lads stared at her. Keith scratched his inside thigh. 'Yes, there is,' replied Terry, for lack of anything else to say.

'Hey, I know where she keeps it,' Keith told him.

'Fuckin' hell!' Terry glanced at his mother, triumphant.

'Oh, you boys are awful. You know I don't like you touching my things.'

153

Tittering, the boys rushed from the room.

'I don't know what you must think of us,' Mrs Zlotnick said. From the moment her offspring had disappeared, she was all placid unconcern. 'But what I say is, where's the real harm? You only have one chance in this world to watch your kids grow up and let yourself spoil them.'

Dominique reappeared in a white PVC mac that covered her miniskirt while leaving her legs almost entirely exposed. She looked as people do in the dream where they discover in public that they haven't put on their trousers.

'Are you going to give us that book, then?'

Maria found herself clutching Edmund's paperback as though it were something far more precious. 'It's all right, thank you. My brother can post it.'

'As I say,' remarked Mrs Zlotnick, 'I'm sure we can find some way to give it to him.'

'Thank you,' said Maria, floundering, 'but I expect my brother will want to enclose a letter.'

Dominique said, 'So why've you come down here if you're going to change your mind?'

'I thought your brother lived here,' said Maria. 'If,' turning from daughter to mother, 'you don't mind, I'll get it to him some other way.'

'But it's no trouble,' insisted Mrs Zlotnick. 'I was talking to one of Jimmie's friends from school's mother only the other day. Maybe she can tell me where he lives. I know she said he'd got a flat in Oxford. I mean, that's something to start from, isn't it?'

'I'll bear that in mind.' Maria got up. 'Thank you
—'

'Don't you trust us, then?' Dominique broke in.

Facing down the other girl's scowl, Maria realized that Zlotnick did have something in common with his sister. In Dominique, as in her dapper older brother, the spirit of competition had found its ultimate embodiment. Win or lose, neither of them could resist a scrap.

'So why don't you want to leave it with us?'

'I'd rather my brother sent it, thank you.' Maria edged to the door.

'You mean you aren't Jimmie's girlfriend?' Dominique said. 'Isn't that why you came here?'

'No!'

'Oh, that's a pity,' Mrs Zlotnick interrupted. 'It's like me. I was thinking the same thing.'

'How old are you, then?' Dominique demanded.

'Thirteen.'

'You what?' The other girl's face was total cynicism.

'Thank you for your help,' said Maria. She turned to go. Terry, Keith and the dog could be heard thumping their way downstairs in a series of concussions that shook the house.

'Like I say,' Mrs Zlotnick called after her, 'it's a shame if you are only that old. Next time you see my won, you tell him from me I think you're a really nice girl.'

CHAPTER
EIGHT

Edmund wasn't the leader in everything he did. At the end of the autumn term he left Winchester with eight months to fill in before Harvard. The following week he took off for Africa, the only teenager in a six-strong party organized by a young cousin of the Queen. They planned to drive across the Sahara to the mud-pie city of Kano, through the Congolese forests to the Mountains of the Moon, and on via someone's uncle's ranch in the Rhodesian uplands to the South African border near Kruger National Park. The send-off party virtually took over Annabel's. It ended at sunrise on the river terrace of a Georgian mansion at Chiswick, with a breakfast of spit-roasted sheep given by Carlos Fitzmarney, the expedition's Anglo-Argentinian. Late that afternoon, in an unseasonal flurry of snow, their three Land Rovers set off for Portsmouth and the ferry to northern Spain.

Christmas at Stinscombe was lonely. Digory wasn't there much, and Maria spent a lot of time waiting in the echoing house for lifts to her friends' homes. It was a relief to be back at school.

From mid-January, the place wasn't lonely enough. Going to the bathroom one morning, Maria saw that someone must be using the main guest room with its view over the big yew hedge into the orchard. The wardrobe had been filled; shirts, jackets and pullovers were hung up or stacked with aggressive neatness, as if in a window display. On one of the early Victorian slipper chairs a set of clothes had been arranged ready to be put on, all right angles or parallels. An emperor's corpse couldn't have been laid out more carefully.

No one was there; but Maria's bathroom, which she shared with Edmund when he was around, was locked. Someone was showering, while listening to *What the Papers Say*.

At breakfast, Maria went downstairs to find Zlotnick at the table. He was neglecting his kipper while talking eagerly about Digory's forthcoming address to the British Humanist Association. Maria, in her uniform ready for school, sat down on one of the high-backed dining chairs and tried not to look surprised.

The phone rang in Digory's study. Zlotnick went to answer it, in a whirlwind of discreet haste. Maria had meanwhile guessed what he might be doing here; she hoped she was wrong. Reaching for the silver salt cellar, with its coke-sized spoon, she asked, 'Has the agency replaced Janice yet?' One of Digory's PA's, a former personnel director, had given up work at the Rectory to go overseas with her husband.

Before Digory could answer Zlotnick came back. 'Wouldn't you just know it! A wrong number.' He sat down by Digory again, alert to anything the older man might say or need.

Digory told Maria, 'Your brother has done us a favour. On his initiative, Janice has been metamorphosed into Jimmie.'

To hide her dismay, Maria asked, 'Have you heard from Edmund, then?'

No, Digory said, but a telegram had gone ahead of him to Algiers. Before crossing into Africa, Edmund's party had lingered in southern Spain, spending Christmas at a borrowed villa overlooking the Alhambra. 'I know he'll be pleased that Jimmie feels he can take the job.' As Digory looked up at them from his plate, a ghost of Edmund's goodwill gleamed in his face.

'It has to be said,' he told Maria, 'that Edmund did suggest Jimmie partly on your account. He thought it would please you to have one of his friends squatting here, since there's not much else going on at this house.' Out of tact Digory's eye avoided Zlotnick, who was modestly staring at his plate.

Maria struggled to hide behind a look of gratitude. 'Oh. Right. Right on, I mean.'

All too soon she was dismayed at how swiftly

he'd changed – and went on changing. 'That young man *has* come on,' remarked the Fabian mother of one of Edmund's friends from a grand house further up the valley. It was the better part of a year since Zlotnick had first padded hesitantly into the nearly deserted Rectory in his workman's overalls. During that time he'd worked at transforming himself, with quiet, furious zeal. At the *Gazette*, for what his subject-matter was worth, he'd proved Everard Higgs's damning praise right. As Zlotnick dutifully toured the county, reporting weddings or motorbike accidents, he was honing the skills that were to serve him for the rest of his life. His memory for detail was formidable; near-strangers, re-meeting him at parties, would exclaim, 'Hey, you re-membered that!' as he told them something they'd mentioned about themselves months before. On anyone's terms he was good at holding up a mirror to people. One of his most disarming traits when interviewing as a reporter was to repeat what the other person had just said in the most flattering terms possible.

The one thing that hadn't improved was his spell-ing, but from now on he would have people to deal with that sort of thing for him. At the Rectory his correspondence was dictated to an enthusiastic girl out of the sixth form at Aynesford Hall, whose parents had told her that working for Professor Adams would be more stimulating than finishing school. To her, as to almost everyone, Zlotnick was careful to turn his best face, full of engaging mock-

159

disrespect. Only in his dealings with Maria was he obstinately unaltered.

She learned not to be alone with him. He was meticulous in making her feel she had no right to be there. If he found her watching television he would stalk up to the set, stiff as if he'd had his bum pinched, and change channels without a word. His taste in programmes had been correct; suddenly he was ready to watch hours of quiz shows, if he thought it would thwart her. Once or twice, washing a sweater or cleaning her teeth, she forgot to lock the bathroom door. He'd reach past her to the tap, then watch her start back as a scalding or freezing explosion of water burst over the floor and wall.

'Ten points if I get its underdeveloped tits,' he told Trevor in the Brasenose Arms. 'Twenty if it stands there asking to be squirted in the eye.' The supply of woundable females to bad-mouth was down now that Carol was off the scene. Since Zlotnick stopped taking her calls, she'd been staying at her mother's house with indefinite leave of absence and a renewable prescription for Valium. It wasn't on to mention anyone who was that much of a loser.

One weekend there was a lunch at the Rectory for a former colleague of Digory's from Princeton over with his wife and teenage daughter. The meal was a success. Maria's looks and perfect English were admired and Zlotnick was suitably solemn or amused at everything that was said.

160

'Almost a surrogate son,' the Princeton faculty wife murmured on her way out of the dining room. 'At least while that good-looking boy of Digory's is on his Grand Tour.' Over coffee she remarked to Maria, 'It must be good to have another young person in the house while Edmund is away.'

Maria was still smarting from her latest humiliation. Zlotnick had waited to let a door slam in her face while she was carrying the coffee things from the kitchen. If he'd dared, he'd have made her smash them. Kneeling to fill their cups, she looked up. 'As far as Jimmie's concerned, this is just somewhere he dosses. His main address is in Oxford. At least, that's what his mother told me when I met her at her house. Right, Jimmie?'

Zlotnick sipped his coffee carefully. After a silence meant to embarrass her, he said, 'I would have thought it was impossible for anyone to take Professor Adams's – sorry, Digory's – hospitality as lightly as that. Especially,' looking straight at Maria, 'when it's shared with someone like you.'

Maria had to wait to find out her real punishment for catching him out in a lie. A few days later she was cycling back from the village. On the levels by the river she had to ride through a wide puddle to avoid an oncoming tractor. As she wobbled along she failed to see Zlotnick's MG. He accelerated and overtook. The sheet of water from his wheels smacked her from head to foot with the force of a solid object. Inside the tractor cab, the driver and his buddy were creased with glee at the sight of Maria with mud in her eyelashes and ears.

161

When she got home there was a peevish call
from Sally. 'What's going on? This is the fourth
time I've tried to call you since Friday.'

Standing in the hall with an inch of icy water in
her wellingtons, Maria asked, 'Who took your
calls?'

'A young guy.'

'Er . . .?'

'Can't you talk right now?'

'No.'

Later she rang Sally from the call box in the
village. After Maria had talked for some time, Sally
asked, 'Why do you put up with it? I mean, any of
it? Three evenings last week he made you wait at
least an hour at school.'

'Who would believe me?'

'I believe you. So do my parents.'

'You're not someone he wants to impress.'

'I still think you should complain to Digory. If
he's really serious about being your father.' At thirteen, Sally could be deliberately tactless or, as she
preferred to put it, bullshit-free.

So one evening Maria went to appeal privately to
Digory. Embarrassed but dogged, she stumbled
through what she had to say. Digory prided himself on
being seen to listen. As his adopted daughter struggled
to confide in him, he was all friendly attention. At first.

'Now let's get this straight. What you're objecting
to – among other things – is that over the space of
a few days Jimmie Zlotnick was several times seen
to light a cigarette. Am I right?'

'Well, yes. But only when I had chemicals on my hair.' There'd been an outbreak of head lice at school. Maria had had to soak her hair in something serious and wear it pinned up under a scarf amid a haze of flammable vapour.

'He briefly took up smoking, and you didn't like that. Is that what you're saying?'

'I know it doesn't sound much, but —'

'I'll say it doesn't sound much.' He looked at her with contained impatience. 'Do you seriously expect me to concern myself with the sort of details you've described? Even assuming you're not deluding yourself about some of them?'

Maria blushed, but pride made her persist. 'He took up smoking the day I had to put the stuff on my hair, and he gave it up the same day the treatment finished. I did have to avoid him for safety's sake – several times.' Seeing Digory look at her without speaking, she added, 'I know some of the things I've mentioned must seem trivial, truly I do. But it's because they're trivial that they can happen so often. Maybe several times a day.'

'Have you been keeping count of these alleged incidents then?'

'Well, it's obvious, isn't it? If he shifted my things out of the bathroom cabinet twice a day for a month —'

'This is monstrous. Can you really be in the grip of such an obsession? I feel as if I've brought someone into my home, to be raised as my own – alongside my own son – whom I don't know after all. And why, in God's name, instead of tattling to me, can't you talk sensibly to Jimmie about whatever it is that seems to offend you?'

'He wouldn't listen!'

'How can you say that? Have you tried?'

'I know he wouldn't. I've told you how he won't speak without being spoken to whenever he drives me back from school. Or at any other time, come to think of it.'

'"Come to think of it"? You mean you're making up these accusations on the spot?'

'No! For months now, he's treated me as if I've no right to be here.'

This did shock Digory.

'Maria,' he said quietly, 'do you realize what you're saying?'

'Ye-es.' Her voice wavered, full of uncertainty at what he meant.

'I hope you don't. Can you really believe I would employ someone, here under my own roof – or anywhere else – who would be guilty of racism?'

Seeing his face, she didn't dare argue. 'Well, no.'

'I should hope not.' He studied her in silence, then spoke as if weighing his words. 'Jimmie Zlotnick doesn't just keep an appointments diary for me, you know, the way a head typist would in an office. He is the person to whom I've given responsibility for arranging who comes to this house. To my own home, where they're as likely as not to meet Edmund and you.' He emphasized the last three words, looking her hard in the eye. 'And when he picks you up from school, he does so on his own initiative. Not – and it's important that you understand this, for the sake of future relations between you and me – not as a personal servant. Yours or anyone's.'

Maria paled. 'Why do you think he mightn't like me?' she ventured.

'I can't see how he can possibly bear you a grudge. He may be frank, even outspoken, but, good God, how else do you expect honesty to show itself? And if he seems flippant – believe me, once you're grown up you won't expect to find yourself among many people as good-humoured as he is.'

Digory was rocklike in his sincerity. Maybe in family matters he was impatient, like any self-respecting man when faced with nonsense from the women or children. But nothing could stop him showing loyalty to his employees. True, at some half-conscious level much of what Maria said did niggle him. It took only a guilty fraction of a second, however, to stuff such an insight further towards the back of his mind. Jimmie Zlotnick had made himself too well adapted to Digory's needs and routines and the inconvenience of listening to tattle against him wasn't to be countenanced. 'Now I've heard you out I'm glad for your sake that Jimmie doesn't know any of this, because what you say disturbs me. If you can accuse someone like him of jealousy – a man you ought to know well by now – all I can think is that you're suffering a classic case of projection. It's you who see him as a usurper, not the other way about.'

'How could I?' she blurted. 'He's one of Edmund's friends.'

'I'm glad you appreciate that.'

Maria was silenced. At length she murmured, 'But will you think about the favour I asked you? If I don't mention any of this again? May I become a boarder next term? Please?'

'You want your school life rearranged for you yet again.'

'I'm sorry.'

'You realize that if I thought you were trying to avoid one of my staff I should have to say no?'

Maria sensed victory. She held back tears of relief. 'I could spend more time with my friends. And no one would have to give me lifts.'

'We'll have to see. But I'd like to think your life here won't always dissatisfy you.'

In early summer Edmund came home, almost unrecognizable. He was bearded and deeply tanned. Harsh vertical sunlight had bleached his hair to a coppery colour so that it was almost lighter than his skin. He brought presents: for Maria a Moroccan necklace of amber and coral with links of beaten gold, for Zlotnick a smuggled flag of the underground African National Congress.

'We all ended up looking like this. Not on the road, during our time at sea.' His party had come back by liner from Capetown. 'Apart from stuffing our faces or boozing, there was nothing to do on board except read, use the gym and cultivate melanomas. It was like being a five-star gangster in a low-security nick.'

In fact, after the privations of the journey south nothing could have been a better contrast. On the thready highway linking the Mediterranean with the Sahel they hadn't washed properly for nearly a month. Most of them had been prostrated by the trots somewhere in Zaire – 'probably from squeamishness, after we found we'd been fed baby monkey'. Fording a river near the Masai Steppe, one of their Land Rovers had been caught in a flash flood and damaged beyond repair. Edmund had done the last two thousand miles by motor bike, on a second-hand Norton.

'After the South Pole, Amundsen said adventures were what happened when you'd bungled. I can't wait to do something like that again, but we did cock up, several times.' Edmund never did tell Digory how nearly he and another man had been drowned.

At the end of the week he was off again, to LA. He was due to fill in the rest of his time before Harvard with a gophering job at MGM, where Digory knew some corporate heavies.

'I'm supposed to be an office messenger,' Edmund wrote to Maria. 'But because of how I got the job, guys all the way up to corporate vice president scamper to hold the door open for me. Even if I were the token black around here, people couldn't laugh louder at my jokes.'

Digory didn't have that many contacts on the Coast. To Edmund, though, even with only an undistributed home movie to his name, it seemed that

167

the whole town wanted to show him its tribal rites, whether a barbecue for a couple of hundred famous neighbours in Laurel Canyon or flying to Palm Springs for tennis. The evening he arrived in Hollywood, disoriented by a thirteen-hour flight over the Arctic, he found himself at a party where half the guests were made up professionally as monsters.

'But not Orson Welles. Someone asked him how he could expect to look horrific without green latex carbuncles. He said, no problem; he'd come as a studio finance director.'

Edmund sensed that fate and his own talent would one day drop-kick into this town for real. 'Living in southern California isn't my ideal. But if you want to make movies, it's one of the dues you have to pay. After Africa, being here is like finding yourself locked up in a sense-deprivation chamber. No fast-friends, no heartfelt enmities, no downtown, no out of town. And a climate but no weather – every day's the same. Also, a world turned upside down. The two ultimate status symbols belong to the money men. First they can make it without all the hassle of being famous afterwards. Second, they're allowed to be old and ugly . . .'

Even on air mail paper, Edmund's letter was almost too fat to fold. If Maria have received it she would have treasured it, like everything she'd had from her brother. But instead for months it kicked around unread in a bedroom drawer at the Rectory before being lost or thrown away. It had come enclosed with something else: another letter, about

– hell, everything – full of frankness and enthusiasm, in an envelope addressed to Zlotnick.

'It's free to be given its letter,' he told Trevor. 'Any time it wants. All it has to do is find enough brain power to ask if Adams has sent it anything.'

One cobwebbed morning towards the new school year, Maria got up to find another sudden change. Zlotnick had vanished. In the bathroom his badger-hair shaving brush was gone, together with the rest of his shaving kit on its silver stand and his leather-and-canvas toiletries bag. In the drive his MG was gone. After several months of his company, Maria was so relieved she could almost see a hole in the air at the spot where he used to park his car.

He hadn't just disappeared; he'd left the country. 'Did you really not know that?' said Digory, who happened to be down at Stinscombe that week. He looked at her, disbelieving. It had taken some doing, but Zlotnick had managed to leave without a word to Maria.

'Suits me,' she told Sally afterwards. 'You know that scene in Act Three of *Fidelio* – the one where the freed prisoners come up into the light? Well, that's what it's like now at home.'

It had been Edmund's idea that Zlotnick should join him Stateside. In the event, Digory had needed persuading before he'd agreed to let Zlotnick go. Not fire him, but let him go onward and up. From all over Oxford he'd arranged for Zlotnick to have private tutoring. The result had been splendid refer-

ences plus a neatly bagged brace of SATs. All Zlotnick had lacked was a quick spot of research on
how best to exploit his Englishness once he'd arrived
in Harvard Yard.

Digory had good reason to hesitate before putting
him through college. Not that the idea didn't appeal;
other rich men paid out far more for a racehorse or a
football team. The trouble was, Zlotnick had become
so damnably useful. No one could match his memory
for names and faces – let alone personal histories,
whether found out from *Who's Who* or from common-
room gossip. He was adaptable, too. No one could
have taken more pains to cultivate the more tiresome
guests – usually rather old or a bit young – who
sometimes had to be invited to the house.

In the end, it was Digory's view of himself that made
up his mind. Hadn't his theories always declared that
nearly anyone could be made upwardly mobile? In
some cases from the dole queue to *Debrett's* in half a
generation? It was something he'd insisted on in all his
works, from *License or Liberty? A Plan for Post-War
Europe*, through to his latest, controversial book, *The
Pursuit of Unhappiness: politics versus the people in
modern America*. How could he pass up this chance to
prove himself right?

He acted with characteristic energy. In the same
term that Edmund started his effortless pursuit of a
master's degree in social anthropology, Zlotnick
went with him to study business finance.

For a long time to come, Maria really believed
she was home free.

PART II

CHAPTER
NINE

Once this room had been a sweatshop. Rows of women with ankle-length aprons and scrappily pinned hair had clattered away at their Singers in an atmosphere as soupy as a poisoned holding tank.

The people here today weren't sitting in rows. They were standing in leisurely groups or drifting round the walls like browsing angel fish. Their surroundings were as dignified as a cathedral cloister, all recessed spotlights and sandblasted brick. The pristine carpet positively slurped at one's feet.

Everyone was here from the usual magazines: *Connoisseur, Art in America, Harper's*. Their declared reason for attending was to write up the rising artist whose vernissage this was. In fact several were at least as keen to interview the new young owner of this, one of SoHo's best-rated galleries.

Bruce Christian, the artist, was a Californian by

birth; by descent he was a Pitcairn Islander. His early work had been uncompromisingly abstract: quirky three- and four-dimensional sculptures about nothing but themselves, in wire, fibreglass, spectra gel and plaster. Then a grant to travel had taken him away for several months. He'd gone to the South Island of New Zealand, where on a lonely crossroads his grandparents had owned and run a general store. Thence he'd gone to Pitcairn, to see the smallholding in a grove of breadfruit trees where his great-great-grandmother had raised fifteen children. His journey had ended by taking him to Tahiti, and the Frenchified, crime-ridden port of Papeete. As he'd journeyed back through his family's history, Bruce's schedule had grown lazy, then chaotic. His work, on the other hand, had prospered. Instead of being cramped by fashionable theory, it had grown confident as he'd learned to borrow what he wanted from real life.

Maria had certainly thought so, taking her gallery manager's advice to put on this show. She'd just been back to the Pacific herself, for the first time since childhood. As an early twenty-first birthday present Digory had chartered a yacht in the Society Islands for Maria and five of her friends from Radcliffe. Looking at Bruce's latest work, she found she could recognize new forms from their common heritage – not just taken from carvings in museums, but from living seascapes.

The gallery was also a coming-of-age present in a way. It had been part of Elizabeth's bequest kept in trust for Maria, whose birthday was tomorrow.

174

'How do you see your role here,' The manager, Costas Joannou, was being asked, 'now that you have a new owner?' His questioner was Judy Kravitz from the radical magazine, *ArtWorkers*. She was short and fierce-looking, with a mass of reddish hair that seemed as if each tendril might twitch of its own accord.

'I see my role with great pleasure. Maria is more than a beautiful object to be viewed as part of our display.' Costas was an Athenian who had moved to New York to avoid the regime of the colonels. He had crisply curled black hair and a profile that astonished anyone who didn't know that classical Greek statuary had been done from the life. His reception desk tended to be staffed by luscious boys.

'Will you be working with Maria Adams, or for her?' Judy persisted, eyeing him as levelly as she could from eighteen inches below.

'Oh, the former, decidedly. I know what you must think of Maria but I do assure you you're terribly wrong.'

'What do you think I think?'

'Why, that these premises are the plaything of a whimsy heiress. What you mustn't forget is that six years before she started college, Maria was already a trader in her own right.'

Judy ignored this gallant attempt to dress up Maria's period of beggary. Having done her homework, she'd already decided to head her article 'Poor Little Rich Girl' and angle it accordingly.

'If you're working together as equals, does she

175

accept guidance from you? We're talking about someone who hasn't yet finished college.

'No – and yes. She takes advice from me on general business practises. I yield to her judgement as a buyer.'

'So really she's settled for what many rich, college-educated girls would see as the glamorous end of your business?'

Costas laughed in the melodious way he did when utterly disagreeing. 'I think you overestimate Maria's readiness to be an honorary Wasp. Her career as a slum child has had far more of an influence. When we discuss business, she's as serious as my grandmother.'

Judy refused to smile back. She always figured most of the job was deciding what it was you wanted to discover, then rooting out that and nothing else.

Seeing Maria arrive, Judy was convinced her angle had been the right one to go for. Maria looked as carelessly cheerful as any Daddy's girl. Other people there might wear their social faces and work the room; she came in with a rush of bonhomie and a readiness to talk longest to the people she liked the most. Life at college, with its freedom to make and unmake friendships without limit, was suiting Maria.

One or two press photographers also knew in advance what they were after. Much was made of Maria's waist-length mass of blue-black hair as she and Bruce posed, pretending to examine one of his sculptures. The idea being, of course, to point up his own connection with Oceania. In fact there was no resemblance: Bruce was slightly shorter than Maria, with grey eyes and spiky auburn hair. For the sake of his party she was formally dressed, out of jeans for the first time in months. She wore a gathered cream skirt in raw silk, with a matching jacket for protection against the gallery's fierce midsummer air-conditioning. Bruce was obstinately scruffy. He was nervous as a cat, for all that. With no powerful friends in the art world, and no private capital, it had cost him to get this far.

After the photocall Maria in a group of several people was introduced to a new arrival. Loretta was a heavily groomed ash blonde. Her eyes were a handsome shade of amber. Looking at her with the judgement of a professional colourist, Maria noticed that every accessory had been chosen to match them, down to the cloisonné buttons on her sharply cut suit.

'Do you paint, too?' In the melee of introductions Loretta had only caught Maria's first name. It discomforted her not to know if she was talking to someone important.

'Not as much as I'd like to. So far I've only exhibited in England.'

Loretta, who worked in a nearby art agency, took a narrow view of the world beyond Manhattan. Mishearing 'England' for the name of a New York gallery, she asked, 'Where?'

'At the Mulberry Tree, first time off.' This had

been in a converted livery stable up a cobbled byway off Burford High Street. 'It's in a small town in the Cotswolds.' After that, Maria had graduated to London, and premises of Campden Passage in Islington.

'After Islington I got lucky: Mayfair, and Swyndell and Devine, in Cork Street.'

Loretta seemed unfazed at the mention of places so far out of town. She was thin, with the skin around her elbows unusually slack for a woman under thirty. Evidently she's been dieting with fearsome determination. She asked, 'Do you sell well over there?'

The noise in the room was rising as more guests arrived. 'Do what?' said Maria, leaning closer.

'Sell?'

'Overall, or compared to other people?'

'Compared to other people was what I meant.' Loretta looked prim at this implied slur on the competitive impulse. Envy was good; it sharpened you up. Everyone knew that.

'Haven't a clue,' Maria said, heretically cheerful. 'I've never had time to check on everybody else.'

'But what does your agent tell you?'

'I haven't got an agent. Maybe I ought to look for one, if I could stop work for long enough.'

'Well, you're bound to be losing on sales otherwise.' Loretta's manner suggested, And don't you think you should feel sorry? Maria was put in mind of an impatient mother telling her daughter to smarten herself up and make more of a play for the men.

Loretta squared her padded shoulders, wondering who she should talk to next. 'You mean,' she said, in a voice with a dying fall, 'you only paint for pleasure?'

'For pleasure?' Maria was thoughtful. 'I wouldn't say that. It's only just something I do.'

Scanning the room, Loretta's eyes skidded across the gallery's front window. Outside in the steamy afternoon sunlight backed-up traffic went at walking pace. A strawberry blonde was roller-skating through it in a satin singlet and purple and scarlet running shorts. She had a Walkman pressed to her head. Swooping up the centre of the street, she was twirling about to face alternately forward and back.

The only thing Loretta noticed was Edmund, coming through the double set of glass doors with an overnight bag.

She seemed to know him – and to care. 'Well, hi there!' Giving what was supposed to be a social kiss, she gambled on throwing her arms around his neck. His smile was tighter than ever.

Edmund looked much as he had when he'd left England for Harvard, eight years before. Marginally, he was tidier; his hair had been trimmed to collar length and his clothes were no longer ragged, merely indifferent. He looked like an athlete who couldn't afford decent training gear.

With a nod and a word or so, he and Maria said hello. But Loretta noticed more to them than that. Edmund looked untypically hesitant, as if he'd found himself in the wrong place. Maria's eyes had grown darker and her mouth more vividly flower-like.

179

It surprised Maria to realize that for years now every encounter with him had been like this – in a crowd, or on the way to an airport. Their trails had crossed but never run parallel. After Harvard, Edmund had gone on to film school at Berkeley. Afterwards, whether or not he was due to knock the socks off the movie-going world, he'd still had to start short of the top. He'd moved back East to help on adverts for TV before making an increasingly successful series of rock videos. On the basis of brilliant work done as a student as well as in the Apple, he'd since been in and out of New York on location as second unit director on his first feature film.

The same thoughts were running through his own head. 'An extraordinary thing just occurred to me.'

'What? What is it?' Loretta leaned towards him like a heliotrope in a heatwave.

'I can't believe how little Maria and I have seen each other recently. Do you know,' addressing Maria, 'in the last five years the number of words we've swopped probably only comes to a few hundred?'

Loretta froze. One should have been able to hear her fingernails grow. 'People without much to say,' glowering anxiously at Maria, 'do best not to talk, don't they?'

Edmund didn't hear her. He was listening to Maria, who was saying something about her birthday celebrations. They were both due to join Digory at the house in Vermont for a party to be held the following night.

A few moments later the demands of other guests split their group. For the dozenth time in two months Loretta was thwarted in her attempt to consolidate things with Edmund, or die trying. Her claim on him so far amounted to dinner, a pass by her and a night of moderately okay copulation. She hadn't stopped to wonder if he'd agreed to fuck for politeness's sake.

The party started breaking up. From behind his elbow, as he finished some goodbyes, she made her best play. 'Don't forget what we agreed. You're welcome to share my cab.' So they could travel together to the airport, she'd scheduled a flight of her own. Her neglected parents, back in Toledo, had been surprised as well as pleased to have her suddenly invite herself for a weekend.

When only half a dozen people were left Maria came back out of the gallery's office with an airline bag. On the hot sidewalk the three of them paused.

Searching for a cab Edmund said to Loretta, 'Thanks for offering to share.'

'Oh, not at all!' She gave a jagged smile. If an intruder was going to ride with them her whole trip was pointless.

Maria said, 'I hope we're not putting you out.'

'Oh, I wouldn't let that happen,' Loretta told her, doggedly watching Edmund's every look. 'But I hope you realize that Edmund and I are both on our way to the airport. I'd just hate to take you out of your way.'

181

'We can all go together, can't we?' said Edmund.

Loretta's smile widened painfully. 'Why ever not?' She was suffering the torment of someone who lived by inflexible rules, but has suddenly found herself in unknown terrain. Every self-improvement book she'd ever read said that nailing your man was just a question of going for it. Only now did she realize that not one had offered sample scripts to show how you trampled the opposition. 'Though if you do want to come with us,' she told Maria, 'we wouldn't care to make you early, so you had to hang about at the airport. I mean, on your own. Would we, Edmund?'

He'd been paying only just enough attention. 'There's no question of that. Maria is coming home too. We're joining our father for her birthday.'

For once Loretta was shocked enough to be spontaneous. 'Oh, I *see*! She's your – I mean' – turning to Maria in a tizzy of making amends – 'Edmund's your *brother*!' Relief cascaded through her, visibly.

Edmund laughed excitedly without taking his eyes of Maria. She wore a huge smile too. Encouraged, Loretta set about making an ally of her. She knew from instinct, as well as from lifestyle manuals, that it was the guy's sister you should go for rather than the guy himself. The sister was your Trojan horse, to carry you triumphant into his home, his pants and his affections. By the time they reached the airport, Edmund had never been so ignored in his life.

'Well!' breathed Loretta at the foot of the escalator

to the departure lounge. 'Enjoy your weekend with your disreputable brother. I'm sure' – putting a hand on Maria's arm – 'he's not as bad as you suggest. Not *really*.'

Her smile of farewell was beamed up at both of them, all the way to the top of the escalator. It could have been held to the front of her head with elastic.

On board, neither of them had much to say until the plane was taxiing. 'Let's order champagne,' proposed Edmund in an undertone, as if everyone in the cabin was eavesdropping.

At last they were rushed along their runway and snatched into the sky. The plane banked over a blindingly bright sea and levelled out in clearer air.

Under its hot dun haze the city was gone. Its eight million people, enmeshed in one another's doings had ceased to exist.

The champagne came quickly; it was mid-afternoon and a Thursday, so the plane was half empty. They felt as if truanting from school.

Edmund raised his glass. 'To – uh . . .'

Maria flunked as well. Too many wishes, too many hopes. For some reason she wanted to giggle.

'Hell, we'll fix on something' Edmund said. He too looked like someone trying not to guffaw out loud in church. Maria found she'd caught the eye of another passenger progressing gingerly down the aisle. An old lady dressed, as if she didn't fly very often, in what must have been her best suit.

'I hope you don't mind me saying this,' she told

183

them both. 'But my sister and I couldn't help noticing you two young people, back when we were on the ground.' She was holding on to the seat in front of Edmund. Though there was no turbulence she seemed to think she'd hit the fuselage ceiling at any instant. 'May I ask you both a very personal question?'

They nodded, pink with the effort of looking serious.

'It's none of my business, of course, but anyone as good-looking as you two are must have gotten used to being noticed together. And, my Lord, where's the point, at my time of life, if you still care what others think? Are you both on your honeymoon?'

They shook their heads in idiotic unison. A pair of guilty three-year-olds couldn't have been more solemn.

'No, I'm afraid.' Edmund could feel laughter surging inside him like a whale about to surface. 'We're not.' To speak at all was an achievement.

'I'm afraid we must have misled you,' added Maria, her voice stretched as thin as it would go.

'Oh, I am sorry,' said the woman. 'Only, my sister and I would have had a bet on it, if we hadn't both of us been so certain.'

As she moved on down the aisle, Edmund tried to speak again. 'She's my sister!' he whispered, teary with the effort of keeping his face straight.

Luckily the woman was out of earshot. Such apparent sarcasm would have been taken very unkindly indeed. As it was, they both had to duck behind their headrests in order not to shame themselves. Suddenly they could bear it no longer. Crouching out of sight, they choked on silent laughter until their eyes and noses ran.

'Oh, God!' Edmund gasped at length, heaving himself upright. 'Oh, God – excuse me! I've just realized how badly I need a pee!' And sprinted towards the front of the fuselage as if a fire drill had been announced.

They touched down late, into an evening so still the only thing moving was the shadow of their aircraft. Not wanting to keep Digory waiting at the house, Edmund drove their rented car from the airport as fast as he dared, with a frown of concentration and much changing of gears as the roads got smaller and more hilly.

Digory wasn't there; he'd phoned from Chicago saying dinner should be delayed for an hour. Edmund went down to the stone-built cellar for some Taittinger and they went to kill time on the terrace, where the dinner table stood ready like part of a deserted stage set. At each place stood three antique wine glasses and an array of heavy silver cutlery. A butterfly paused to probe a cut rose swathed in baby's breath. The damask tablecloth and the fat cushions on the wrought-iron chairs were becoming invisibly speckled by gnat droppings.

Below, the lawn and driveway rolled down a long valley into the shadow cast by woods of hemlock and white pine. One forested skyline stood beyond another, all the way westward to the green summits of upstate New York. In a setting of such dreamy solitude, the shingle-clad house looked improbably large and comfortable. It had been built in 1878 and was much visited by students of architecture.

Narrowing their eyes into a sunset the temperature of body heat, they opened the champagne.

'What an absurd thing,' Edmund said, 'to rediscover someone you've known for years.' Perhaps it was the prospect of getting squiffy, but he sounded drunk already.

'I can't have changed that much. And if I had, everything that had gone before would have been a sham. Wouldn't it?'

'You're exactly the same. Only more so – and in ways I'd never have guessed. You're different, too. In ways that make sense only now.'

His open-hearted nonsense was irrestistable. Hurriedly Maria said, 'I'd like to be like you —'

'How?'

'You know the way it is with some people. You find yourself saying, he was cute back then. Or, some day he'll be good-looking —'

'Is *that* what you've thought of me?'

'Never! You've always been exactly right for whatever age you were.'

'You can't say that. How can you know what I was like before eighteen?'

'Everyone says you were. An eighteen itself is

usually so disappointing in males. Have you ever seen a photo of James Dean at that age?'

'You know what seems extraordinary? Growing up with neither of us knowing the other existed.'

Inwardly Maria smiled; it wasn't like Edmund to talk in chlichés, even ones based on a bedrock of truth.

Indoors the phone rang. It was Digory, still waiting for his connecting flight. It was unfortunate, but the evening's reunion would have to be limited to a drink together.

Suddenly they were hungry. Mrs Wisniewski, the elderly emigrée who with her husband supervised the house and grounds, brought out their meal before saying goodnight. There were oysters, fennel sorbet, then a cassoulet, followed by goat's cheese and a fresh strawberry tart. At every moment the luminous sky looked as if its colours would die. Instead, it turned from lemon yellow to green, then to a warm silver that left a night-time gleam down the sunset-facing sides of tree trunks and walls. For a long time only half the sky got dark enough for starlight. The air was as hot as new bread.

Inevitably they spent a long time at table, putting the world to rights. When the candles had burned down under their glass globes, they went on talking in near-darkness.

'I'm sorry to gabble,' Edmund said at length.

'Come off it. When you die and go to heaven, there'll be one thing wrong with you. There won't *be* any potential improvements I can hear you talk about.'

Neither of them said anything for a while. Then Edmund remarked, 'Speaking of the wider world, it must be some time since we've both been together with Digory. He's missed the last two Christmasses. Thanksgiving too.' Digory had recently served as US ambassador to one of the larger South American republics. He'd resigned when his second wife had left him for a rancher from the Andean foothills whose life was spent on the international polo circuit.

'It wasn't Digory's fault that Joanna lost patience with diplomatic life.' Edmund's gaze rested on the furthest silhouette of the Adirondacks. Their outline was much clearer now, against a deepening twilight, that in the humid brilliance of noon. 'He hadn't realized she was better suited among rock stars and titled hoorays.' His voice held a twinge of cynicism. All his life, Edmund had been out of his father's company for long periods. Nonetheless their bond of pride and affection was formidable.

'I haven't seen him since then.'

'For a while I think he avoided anyone who'd known Joanna. Someone less proud might have started screwing teenagers. We ran into each other only a month ago, in fact. In Paris. My outfit's clients had wanted a video with their lead singer looking stormy against a mountain of industrial derbis in rust belt. Then there was a purge at their head office and they came back wanting the same, only pretty. So instead of New Jersey I took everyone off to France. We ended up doing our stuff in front of those colour-coded ducts wrapped around the Pompidou Centre.'

'How was your – how was Digory?'

Edmund noticed her slip of the tongue, but pretended not to. It jolted him. The pretty, obliging child may have become a woman of feeling intelligence and smitting beauty, but she still saw herself as an arm's length adoptee, his family's second-best.

'His hair's completely grey now. I think Joanna's defection gave him his first taste of death. I mean, as something that advances on you one crisis at a time. But to anyone who doesn't know him, he must look as indestructible as ever.'

Mari stretched her arms above her head. 'All this talk of love and death . . . What do you think we should do if he doesn't get here soon?'

By way of reply, soon afterwards the phone rang. Edmund got up to answer it. He was slightly drunk and stepped carefully in the gloom. On the terrace the darkness had been lit only by stars, bright enough to tremble. Now moonrise was casting a great silvery bonfire of light through the treetops above the house. The terrace began to sink into deeper shadow. Edmund reappeared in the doorway. He was a code of dim shapes, barely readable as a man.

'Do you think I've talked enough at you for one night?' He sounded foolishly earnest.

Maria got to her feet. She too was just a collection of outlines; not a real woman, but the glimmering notion of one.

'Enough about death, anyway.' she ventured. 'And the other big questions.' In the luminescent gloom he could hear that she was smiling.

'That was Digory. It seems we ought to go to bed.' There was a blip of glee in his voice. And, to be fair, a hint of dread.

When he slid inside her, it was with the groan of a murdered man. The sound of him was wrenched up from so deep he couldn't believe he hadn't come already. But release was unbearably far off.

How could he endure it? He was nothing and everything; he'd had no idea raw sense could be so blank. Nor that emptiness could be so vivid. A cathedral of sensation was building, made of singing stones with him as one of them. Someone had said something was a ribbon of dream. Had they meant this eternity – or this one, following on? Sure, if you like – sure. Maria strove beneath him, yelping as sweet and beastly as a mermaid. The cathedral crumbled upwards. His senses pooled. Patches of music made colour; sanctified bones blossomed as pinnacles.

How could this nothing lead on to what smote you back to life?

Wasn't this the end?

Wasn't it?

He had held in perfect suspension, pleading not to be released. Then he was free, blasted away and ripped clear.

Edmund giggled weakly. Maria's invisible mass of

190

hair was warm under his face and tickled his nostrils. A cool breath moved across his back from a
night breeze that had strayed through the open
window. The curtains stirred, as though the planet
was a ship that had wandered into a contrary
wind.

'Well, I'll be fucked!'

'Oh!' Me too.'

Not being able to see her made him uncertain
again. 'You're not laughing at me?'

'How could I do that,' she said, with the deliber-
ateness of someone trying not to drowse, 'when
I've just been rogered to death?'

He could have died himself, from smugness.

Two hours later they slept in a mess of sticky
sheets and limbs too heavy to disentangle. 'Surely I
can't do it again,' he finally said. And had fallen
asleep, moments before the headlights of Digory's
car enterd the valley.

CHAPTER
TEN

Until they put on their scarlet robes, the six men and women had looked as ordinary as any bus queue. When they began to sing they became superhuman.

'*Surge propera, amica mea, columba mea . . .*' Arise and make haste, my beloved, my dove, my fair one, from that far land of sorrow, and come to this land which I will show to you.

Maria and Digory were walking into a wall of sound. The music was Tudor, the work of William Mundy; the choir was Schola Sanctae.

'They're up there with the Tallis Scholars,' Edmund had said happily. 'And the Hilliard Ensemble. Maybe early Eric Clapton, too.'

He and Maria, high on the discovery of each other's heart and body, had lost no time in declaring themselves to the world and arranging to get married shortly after Maria graduated from Radcliffe. It had been Edmund's idea that their marriage should be solemnized in Oxford cathedral, inside the college walls of Christchurch.

'But you're not a churchgoer,' she'd teased. 'Just a connoisseur of rituals. An amateur anthropologist.' He'd once told her that out of curiosity he'd attended the ceremonies of maybe thirty denominations. In San Francisco he'd looked in on the House of Love and Prayer. As a boy, taken along on a field trip by Digory to a mountainous region of Ethiopia, he'd heard the last fragments of church music to have survived from the Roman Empire.

'I don't care. If God does exist, I want Him there when we get spliced. Besides, you can't have big-time ceremony without religion; it looks daft. Think of those Soviet weddings with the bride and groom swapping pasteboard crowns at the feet of Lenin.'

When Maria had suggested a small wedding, he'd added, 'I want everyone there, rooting for us the best they can. Neither of us is getting married as a dress rehearsal for something better a few years up the road.'

He'd had another reason for wanting her to marry him wearing bridal slipper satin by Bellville-Sassoon before a capacity congregation. Edmund hadn't forgotten how she'd nearly described Digory as 'your father', as if nothing could make her quite accepted into the family. He wanted everyone there who could be. 'And even if this were 1968, I'd like them dressed for the occasion. Or wearing shoes and a watch at least.'

193

If Digory had planned anything different for his son, he didn't say so. It was as well, one or two members of the congregation whispered, that he was the one to give away the bride. It did so help to make him look as if the whole thing had been his idea. Certainly no one could have carried off the occasion with such easy dignity, like a friendly magus – not even the learned reverend Archdeacon waiting for them at the end of a forest ride of Early English pillars. Digory was perfect in today's role: not an ageing character actor, more a presiding genius at the height of his powers.

Most other people were in tune with the occasion too. The cathedral nave was packed with well-wishers in a state of suppressed light-heartedness; barely an invite had been given out of duty. At first Maria had been doubtful about a ceremony with a congregatoin divided into 'his' and 'hers'. How could she claim anyone as her own?

'Aw, come on,' Edmund had said. 'Lots of people will be friends of us both. What do you bet that anyone who's worked at the NFT knows at least half the staff of the Slade?'

'*Veni ad me,*' sang the choir, '*dilectissimum amatorem tuum, prae omnibus adamata . . .*' Come to me, your most dear lover, for I have loved you above all others, and I will bestow upon you my kingdom.

Walking up the aisle in flowing, tight-waisted draperies that could have graced a sea nymph, Maria wore a blush of seriousness. It deepened when Edmund turned round to watch her. He'd

194

meant to give her a reassuring grin. Instead he found himself looking idiotic with delight.

Zlotnick was also awaiting her arrival at the altar steps. He too fitted the scene, as best man; a less vivid presence than the bridegroom, but utterly presentable. His morning suit looked as if its style had been invented for him alone. The closer Maria got to him, the harder she tried to look only at Edmund. She and Digory reached the steps.

'*Te omnes caeli cives summo desiderio exoptant videre* ...' All the host of heaven with great desire are longing to look upon you. '*Veni veni, veni caelesti gloria coronaberis. Amen.*'

In a vast new silence, broken only by the smallest noises, the Archdeacon began to speak.

No one processes through the streets of Oxford with much pomp, whatever the occasion. Most of its thoroughfares are too narrow, or lead up some cobbled gulch to a high wall with a barred gateway. It is a city turned inside out, with its grandest façades looking into hidden courtyards or secret gardens. There was no procession from the church on the day Digory rose to the demands of his famous social conscience and gave away Maria in marriage to his own son. The couple and their guests walked unceremoniously up the street to Digory's college, chatting under a great noise of bells.

It would have been impossible to find the reception for anyone who didn't know their way around. The college was closed to the public, so the guests

195

had to go through the huge gates one by one via a postern not much bigger than a cat flap. Maria needed help to manoeuvre her wedding dress undamaged over the high wooden sill. At the far corner of the main quad, with its eccentric Jacobean sundial and its lawm as smooth as a moleskin, shallow steps led up to the chapel. Inside one alabaster monument showed an Elizabethan fellow of the college twice over. Once splendidly laid out in his gown and ruff; and again in a niche below, as he'd expected to look after he'd been in his coffin for a year. Vanishing behind his tomb, the guests went through a small side door, as hard to spot as Alice in Wonderland's rabbit hole. They came out, squinting in strong sunlight, in the cloisters opposite the Fellows' Library and Garden. The Library was a Georgian building, well made as a fine sonata, with a spiral staircase built broad enough for two sedan chairs to pass one another. Part of the reception was being held here, the rest out of doors.

Most of the guests were gathered beneath the giant planes and horse chestnuts beyond the Library. The Fellows' Garden was a sunlit space at the axis of the city, lost to the rest of the world. Sir Christopher Wren's Tom Tower peeped over its walls, and the pinnacled spire of St Mary's on the High. Treetops were visible in a meadow of rough grazing that gave on to the distant Thames and open country.

People were there from every continent on the planet. Some, from New York, had been at last week's pre-nuptial party in the loft Edmund had kept on in SoHo. Ruaidhri O'Dowd, who claimed to be the only half-Laotian Irishman in Australian TV, was looking seriously jet-lagged, having telescoped his schedule to be there. Maria had been filmed by him for an issue of the weekly programme *Expression*, about rising artists from Oceania.

Hugh Oxenham, in cowl and sandals, was also the worse for travel; he'd arrived only that morning on Concorde from Rio. He and Edmund had been at a school for children of the international community when Digory had spent a couple of years teaching in Tokyo. Few people had seen him since he'd become a holy Jesuitical father and disappeared into the underside of Brazilian politics. Across the lawn, laughing at something with Zlotnick, were his diplomat father and his small, ageless French mother. Hugo's father, straight-shouldered and heavy-set, looked pure Foreign Office beyond the powers of any sitcom actor to imitate. He'd been a friend of the Adamses since Digory was a youth, up at Oxford as a Rhodes scholar.

As well as Whitehall, Fleet Street was there. Maria's schoolfriend Anne Hattenden had recently landed a byline in the financial pages of one of the posh Sundays. She'd turned up as an item with Adrian Fetchett, the editor of *Strobe*, a new radicalism-and-entertainments magazine that looked set to score more libel writs than *Private Eye*.

Congress House was represented too, by Eileen Westcot, whose mother had been a charlady at the

Rectory. Eileen, deputy secretary on the Union of Amalgamated Clerical and General Workers, was the ultimate in middle-aged chic. She led a punishing working life supported, at her Edwardian terraced house in South London, by a field unit of nannies and home helps.

Of several lawyers present, the youngest was Mark Wearing. Where other people were jet-lagged he was merely short of sleep. At half past two that morning he'd had to get up and go to Islington police station to help sort out a case of arson as a legal aid solicitor. Mark was another second-generation friend of the Adams family. His mother, head of a Cambridge college, had served with Elizabeth on various parliamentary committees to do with the arts.

Networks, cadres, alliances. But not everyone was there. The local press hadn't bothered to show up, hearing there'd be no movie stars. What use were pix of underground actors? Or the ancient French director Jean-Marie Ventre, who after the war had been the supreme *auteur* of Existentialist movies? The glossies sent no one, either. This wasn't a society wedding as they understood it, with beefy young Oxfordshire nobs sharing a barf amid broken glasses.

In New York too, people had found themselves making sour-grapes noises. Calvin Pfeiffer, the hyperwired demon princeling of the modern art scene, was astonished not to have been asked. Pfeiffer's small, eccentrically dressed person embodied the very fulcrum of fashionable life. He'd made his name simply by knowing the whole of New York. His fortune had been made after he – or someone around him – hit on the idea of making original artworks in the form of giant helium balloons. Each balloon was a life-size replica, meticulously detailed, of its owner's house. It was made to be moored, at legendary cost and inconvenience, about the house itself. The secret of Pfeiffer's commercial success lay in putting as much obstruction as possible between the customer and a completed deal.

'Okay,' he'd said, 'so everyone is telling everybody else how this is going to be the wedding of the season. So, okay, I can get what I need, because Jimmie will see to an invite. I mean, it's like Jimmie Zlotnick has been my dearest friend for ever.'

Zlotnick wouldn't have dreamed of it. Pfeiffer was a sleazeball, never mind how much time they'd spent together.

Besides, he couldn't let the different compartments of his life break down too freely. Not now he was beginning to establish himself as a fixer. What point would there be in devaluing his currency?

In America, Zlotnick had adapted socially every inch of the way. 'Radical chic was invented for a fast-talking sonofabitch like you,' one of his more sceptical tutors had said. Nonetheless, once Edmund had moved on to New York to make TV adverts, the easiest patronage Zlotnick could pick up had been back home. In Oxford, Digory had helped him to a job in the firm of his own accountant. Even in this role Zlotnick had been overstretched, lacking the chance to advance purely on blarney. Just in time, good news had come. Not only had Edmund got work on the first of several feature films, he could also see Zlotnick all right in LA, as an assitant financial supervisor.

Zlotnick was beginning to prosper in California, with gophers to do his job for him while he honed his act. As a young British guy new in town he was learning to pose as a puckish brat with a regional accent and areadiness to chat up anyone. Already he was looking forward to smuggling his name on to some of the hottest credits going.

Recently too, he'd embarked on a new, informal career – one whose possibilites expanded at every turn. In America not every mover belonged to a world as interbred as that of the guests mingling on the lawns of Digory's college. Zlotnick, with his appetite for being close to men of power, was finding himself in business as a maker of introductions between important people who had a use for each other.

Each discreet encounter gave him a bigger buzz. He was a broker, not in wheat or uranium but in big-timers themselves. To date, his unholiest thrill had come from a three-cornered deal between a studio casting director, a promising actress whose mother had once been The Blonde in numberless westerns, and Edmund. The director had wanted the actress to boost the saleability of an indifferent caper movie; the niece, sold on the notion of *auteur* movie-makers, had wanted to do one of Edmund's scripts; and Edmund, as a hot but newish indie-prod, had need the studios help with distribution.

No matter that the kickbacks had been negligible. What counted was that he, Jimmie Zlotnick, had reached the point of acting as patron to one of them, the Adams family. Afterwards, exulting, he'd looked more tightly wound up than ever. He never smiled when alone, anyway. As he drove back to his apartment that night, no one could have looked more contained.

Like others, Sally had noticed Zlotnicks's aura of prosperity. 'Thanks for not making me a brides-maid,' she told Maria. 'I couldn't bear having to pal up with a best man like him.'

Sally was dressed with absent-minded chic in a full skirt and a short-sleeved jacket. She still looked a little like Shirley Temple, only with a narrow body beneath her deceptively round face. 'He would have frozen me to death. Especially since I'm no professional use to anyone outside the stargazing biz.' She was an astronomer on the staff of the Royal Observatory.

'We couldn't figure what bridesmaids were for, anyway. Since you mention work, do you ever come out over your drawbridge these days?' Sally was based down in Sussex at Herstmonceux Castle, with a view across the moat to a skyline of high-tech domes.

'We aren't cut off from the rest of the world, if

that's what you mean. I was at Palo Alto only last month. And just try jumping the queue for decent international facilities – there's so much sex and politics, it's like wanting to be a royal mistress. Speaking of toadies, do you mind if I hide in the lavatory when your best man gets up to speak?'

'You won't need to. Edmund's going to make a speech saying there won't be any speeches.'

'Seriously,' Sally added, 'I hope the man won't be too much in your pocket once you're living in LA.' She rolled her eyes sideways to indicate where Zlotnick was laughing voilently at something the Vice Chancellor had said.

'Too right.' Suddenly, pleased and surprised, Maria exclaimed, 'Good heavens – Ephraim Turpin's here after all!' She hastened across the lawn to greet a frail eldery man, her floor-length veil on its Juliet-cap eddying out behind her. The man was looking around inquisitively as he shuffled into the garden, helped by two women: his retired secretary and his sixty-eight-year-old daughter. Lord Turpin of Paddington was probably the last surviving Labour politician to have been gaoled during World War I for refusing to fight. Nowadays he looked and moved like an old tortoise; almost none of him worked properly apart from his mind. At public functions it was his role to sit with a blanket over his knees while people took it in turns to file past and say respectful things.

'It's rather like lying in state, only without the palaver of dying,' was his comment as Edmund and

Digory settled him on a bench under a large magnolia tree. 'You're looking extraordinary beautiful,' he added, looking up at Maria with the candid gallantry of a man thirty years too old to be on the make. 'It's enough to make me think of marrying again.' To Zlotnick he said, 'You're a very useful young man. I remember you from before.' With a flourish, from somewhere Zlotnick had produced glasses and a newly opened bottle of champagne. 'You used to work for Professor Adams, didn't you? Are you sure he hasn't adopted you, too? From the way you seem to be everywhere at once, I could've sworn you had a debt of gratitude to work off.'

Zlotnick laughed, pretending to ignore the slyness behind Lord Turpin's geniality. 'On the contrary,' he said, deftly folding a napkin round the bottle. 'I have become a patron, as the lovely Mrs Adams can tell you.'

Seeing Maria look puzzled, Edmund interrupted. 'Jimmie means a patron of the arts. He's just bought one of Maria's paintings. I don't know what the deal shows up best: Maria's reputation or Jimmie's good taste.'

Maria did her best to be gracious. Zlotnick had only shown up as a buyer because *Artforum* had said she was a sure thing. 'It was probably a rip-off. The sum on the cheque was very handsome.; I only hope the painting is, too.'

Ephraim obligingly gave a look that said, Indeed? Digory explained. 'It depicts a landscape in Gloucestershire. Maria doesn't paint in a very realist style

203

– it's more a vision of hills and valleys resembling the human body, if you like. Wish Stinscombe Wold as a large pair of female haunches. Of course, I'm not qualified to compare it with earlier schools.' At fourteen Turpin may have been employed as an ostler, but Digory hadn't forgotten that he'd also become Minster for the Arts.

'I'm sure,' said his lordship, smiling, 'that women's bodies were shown even meatier in my day.'

'What a group they make,' remarked the Archdeacon's wife. 'Look at the bride and groom, standing one on each side like that. I hate it when people get sentimental at weddings – really I do – but doesn't it look exactly as though one of the Wise Men had wandered out of his period for drinks in the Garden of Eden?'

Zlotnick finished dispensing champagne and waited till he could catch Ephraim Turpin's eye. Raising his voice, he announced, 'As best man, I can't let this moment pass without doing my duty. And none of us can let Edmund and his delightful consort fly back to the Coast without us drinking their health. Your lordship, ladies and gentlement, I give you America's favourite couple!'

CHAPTER
ELEVEN

Maria seized the bucket of white pigment with both hands and threw its contents on the floor. It fell in a neat three-foot arc. She was sloshing a quart of sticky new-made ground on to a fresh canvas. It was messy work, as well as laborious; she wore a bandana around hair bound as tightly as a ballet dancer's and paint-encrusted dungarees that ballooned tightly over her belly. For the second time since her marriage, Maria was pregnant.

It was getting hard to imagine spending her working life any other way – alone, under a north-facing skylight in her garden studio. She and Edmund had lived here in Coldwater Canyon for several months while he finished setting up his new movie.

But had she relished her time here? It was impossible to say whether she enjoyed what she did, or dreaded it, entering her studio each morning like an actor with stage fright. She only knew she hated the thought of giving it up. It was bad enough that the obstetrician had ordered two months' complete rest with every tool of her trade locked away.

In the studio, a clutter of apparatus signalled efficient disorder: shelving, workbench, racks of brushes suspended bristles down, a rack of knives, glass jars of lumpy resin and dry pigments pretty enough to eat, funnels, saucepans, heating rings, blocks of pumice, a stack of sandpaper, a stone slab and its cylindrical stone muller, a tray of nails divided into a dozen heaped compartments, and a no-nonsense metal toolbox. Maria was hurrying to complete one last commission before her pregnancy began to occupy her full-time. Already it was getting hard to reach things; to smooth the white ground on to the canvas she was having to use a broad brush fixed to a handle instead of bending down.

Other pictures, not for sale, hung indoors. The main house was a rambling, anonymous series of white rectangular shapes half hidden by jacaranda trees. Inside, its rooms were wide, cool and sparsely furnished, mostly with artworks.

That morning, they'd stayed in bed for breakfast, despite Maria grumbling at the waste of time.

'Good practice,' Edmund had said, 'since you've got to watch it for a couple of months anyway. Doing nothing is far more demanding than being a work junky.'

Their bedroom opened on to the pool, which was shut off from the rest of the grounds by a high white wall. 'That settles it,' Maria had said, when they'd been looking for a place to rent. 'If Sarah won't be able to toddle in here and drown herself, this is the place for us.' The light from the pool made wavering patterns across the bedroom walls and ceiling. On the far side of the garden wall a single palm tree stood against an empty blue sky. They'd bought a house on a mountaintop in Colorado only to discover that here was where work was to be found.

Over breakfast on a shared tray, they'd played the popular local game of When the Big One Comes. What would they pick up and run with, if the San Andreas Fault finally came right apart?

'Sarah's outside anyway,' Edmund said. 'I can hear her.' Their little daughter was playing in the garden with her nanny. 'Sweep up, sweep up,' she was chanting. She was sixteen months old, and only a practised ear could make sense of anything she said. Her parents, listening, knew what she was doing. The gardener had been made to give up his broom, and Sarah was staggering about with it, trying to sweep the sun deck. Every so often she would sit down with a bump on a puffball of a nappy barely covered by her sundress.

Maria levered herself into a more upright position. She was too big to lie face up without feeling crushed by the weight of her other, unborn, child. 'Sure – everyone else is out of doors when the first tremor goes off. Then what?'

'I'd take whatever script I was working on, plus

207

your first sketch of Sarah.' Maria's drawing in pencil with watercolour wash showed the baby asleep on her back, one arm flung wide. Delicate spikes of dark hair lay flat against her head, which was turned to one side. Her other arm was slowly uncurling where her thumb had been in her mouth.

'What about you?' he asked.

'I'd take the ancestor figure Digory gave me when Sarah was born.' On the birth of his first grandchild, Digory had been full of restrained but genuine concern. Maria treasured his present both as a sign of affection, and for its own sake. In a previous century it had probably supported a housepost, part of some Polynesian chief's thatched communal home. Even with no proof to hold up, it looked like a figure of ultimate strength. The face was rugged but elegant, the legs bowed and foreshortened. Its shoulders wore muscle like a set of plate armour. Every millimetre was incised with whorls or zigzags, as if the blood vessels and nerves had risen to the surface.

It stood in Maria's studio. 'To keep standards up. And to remind me of the dear old atoll.' What she didn't mention was that the statue made her nostalgic for the dreadful polystyrene imitations she'd sold from the roadside in Micronesia. 'Hoem', as she still found herself thinking of it, though she'd long ago cured herself of calling it that in public. 'If there was time, what else would you take?'

'That one.' Edmund indicated a big canvas over the door. In pale acrylic colours that seemed to shimmer, Maria had shown semi-abstract scenes from the life of a famous eighteenth-century beach-comber. 'The seriousness of being among us,' the title read in irregular white lettering curving across one side of the picture. The beachcomber had been ceremonially drowned and eaten. Afterwards his bones had been made into sail-making needles.

'Why that one?' Maria asked. 'I only painted that depressing story to find out what I really thought of it.'

'It gave me an idea for the script of *Van Dieman's Land.*' Edmund was about to start a thoughtful, voilent and seductively photographed movied to do with an Australian convict settlement. While the opening sequences were being filmed in Britian, among the blunt-topped green mountains of Kintyre, Maria and Sarah were to stay in Stinscombe.

'Let's suppose,' Edmund said, 'we had three clear minutes after the first tremor. That should give you time for one more thing.'

'Easy. I'd take the Hockney. Not because we're in it, but because it's the view from this bed.' She paused, the said, 'Actually, I've rather liked living here.'

Edmund noted with private pleasure the echo of his mother's oh-so-English voice. Maria's accent had been lately described by a columnist from the London *Times* as mid-Atlantic. Whenever they returned to London, though, or to the damp breezy countryside of the Cotswolds, she unwittingly became more British.

'Yes, I'd belt indoors for that one, too.' David Hockney had painted them standing on each side of the sliding glass doors that gave on to the pool. Maria looked straight out of the frame; Edmund was staring across it. 'Both superbratty as hell,' was the comment of one friend. Most of the picture was a rectangle of sky, punctuated in one corner by a chunky green astrisk of palm leaves.

'I've had a use for that bit of sky,' Edmund added, pointing out through the open doors at the original of Hockney's view. 'Whenever I've got to work on a sequence that won't come right it's where I project imagimary rushes.'

'You stay of that sky; it's mine. How do you think my preliminary sketches get figured out?'

Moving laboriously about in the studio, Maria smiled to recall that conversation. Truly the last five years, lived mostly hereabouts, had been busy and productive. It was near here that Sarah had been born. Before that Maria had frequently worked fifteen hours a day, often not even going indoors to eat. The housekeeper had carried out a tray to the studio every four hours, bringing the sort of food one could consume without stopping to sit down.

'Hag-ridden by the muse,' was Edmund's comment. 'Just as well the fickle bitch delivers for you.' Certainly demand for Maria's work had gone on growing. It was admired by private buyers and public galleries alike. In particular, for its combination of precise technique and primitive style.

Maria stretched to ease her back and looked at

her watch; time to start clearing up. As she was scrubbing her fingernails at the sink there were voices outside: the soft-spoken burr of the Scottish nanny who lived in the guest bungalow across the lawn, and the squeaks and burbles of Sarah. A tap on the door and they came in. Moira, the nanny, was a pretty young woman thirty pounds overweight from eating up leftover baby food. She had to stoop sideways to reach Sarah's hand, held straight up above the child's head.

Every evening it was the same. Sarah seemed to think her mother the most wonderful thing in the world, but also the most surprising. Seeing Maria, she was too delighted for noises of glee. Instead of toddling forward she put her hands to the ground and her bottom up, then straightened again, two or three times over. Her face gaped with joy.

Relish it, Maria reminded herself, as she enfolded the little girl with murmurs of greeting. Nobody of any other age could love one so.

Such was her life as she and Edmund prepared to leave for England and the birth of their second child. Everything to hope for. And nothing to fear.

CHAPTER
TWELVE

Zlotnick nearly fumbled, he was that anxious to open the door and be the first to greet Digory's principal guests. It had taken some finely judged negotiations, but the people from Allied Consortia had finally agreed to adjust their schedule and show up at the Rectory. Zlotnick, who'd set everything up, didn't want a false move from anyone. If he'd known how to he'd probably have cooked the lunch himself.

'Hello, stranger!'

His internal organs tried to do a back flip without waiting for the rest of him. At the sight of her unsmiling face, his hands and feet tingled with shock.

'Surprise!' his sister declared. 'I bet you didn't expect to see me!'

If he was appalled, she didn't seem particularly glad either. Dominque's look of suppressed energy was one he recognized from way back – she was quivering with readiness to be insulted. She must have walked here; pushing a baby buggy up the lane had left her out of breath. A small infant lay in the buggy, maybe five or six months old. Most of the child was obscured by a towel used as a blanket, the rest by a too-large bobble hat.

Under the impact of astonishment, Zlotnick's face had turned to stone. 'Hello there.' If his manner was freezing it was also polite. His horrible sister was the last person he could tolerate finding him in the wrong.

'Aren't you going to ask me in? I know how well in you are with whoever it is lives here.'

'And what makes you think that?'

'Mum heard it, down at the shop.' Dominique was staring at him with disbelief. Not at his manner, which had hardly changed, but at his fifty-dollar haircut and the understated suntan he'd got while playing tennis with some people at Aspen.

They hadn't met since Zlotnick's teens. In other circumstances he'd have been glad to see how she'd realized his worst expectations. The truculent brat had become a garish hundred-and-ninety pounder with chipped nail varnish in dayglo colours and a pus-embedded nose ring. Some women her size, blooming with superabundance, might be called voluptuous. Dominque was merely heavy and ageless, her skin and hair dulled by nicotine and cheap

213

cosmetics. From the look of her, there was no doubt that life and her own recklessness had dealt her some blows.

Behind him, Zlotnick heard the drawing room door open on the voices of the guests already arrived.

'Can I be of help, Jimmie?' asked Digory from across the hall.

'Everything's fine, thanks.' Zlotnick gave a grin, putting his head with utmost casualness back round the door. As Digory retreated he willed him out of earshot with every molecule of his body. The image on which Zlotnick had laboured was shot through with street-cred, notwithstanding his flash linen suit and solid gold Rolex. But publicly acknowledging his sister would be something else.

What in hell's name was he going to do with her? At any moment he expetected the arrival of the two head honchos from Allied Consortia. It had been damn ticklish getting Digory to front an epis-ode of their series *The Birth of Civilization*; it had been even more touch and go to get a particular group of West German investors to cop for most of the backing. Thank God there were still schmucks around who thought culture was sexy.

He wanted this one so badly that just brooding on it left a taste in his mouth. He wanted to pull Digory from his pocket like a rabbit from a hat, to be made to perform before several million viewers at a time. In a roundabout way the deal would also put Zlotnick so much in pocket he could hardly bear to think about it. Not while negotiations were at this delicate stage.

'Are you getting ready to have a party?' Dominique was peering past him into the house. 'You can always ask *me*, you know.'

'My host is getting ready for a business meeting.' Zlotnick restrained himself from looking at his watch. He knew that any sign of anxiety would make her seize on the chance of tormenting him. In the low voice that could get him through two secretaries a month he demanded, 'Does something seem to be the matter?'

'You what?'

'I said, what is it you want?' He spoke with biting eveness, thinking how his tone, if not his words, might be overhead indoors.

'I've come to see you, haven't I?' Dominique's expression was as righteous as his. Having let her words fall into an expectant silence, she went on staring at him.

'I see. You're paying me a social call.'

'Well, I haven't walked all this way just so's I can wave through the bleeding window, have I? And the car's laid up.'

The baby stirred. Beneath its wrappings, it was just visible as a pair of pale curious eyes and a dainty nose. It looked as if it might start to cry.

'Look,' said Zlotnick, 'this isn't an ideal moment.'

'For you, or what?' she challenged.

'For both of us, I'm afraid.' Resisting the temptation to look over his shoulder, he closed the big door behind him as quietly as he could. 'Perhaps we can talk later.' He took her by the elbow and half led, half pushed her over to his scrupulously restored thirty-year-old Jaguar. His face was dark with self-control. 'I'll give you a lift back.'

He reached to unlock the car, but was blocked by Dominique. 'Is that all?' She gave him a significant look.

Relief trickled into him. She did have a saving feature – she'd come to cadge. And to judge from the look of her, no one could be bought off much more cheaply.

Keeping his back to the drawing room windows, he got out his wallet. 'You can't expect me to be carrying that much sterling,' he lied, taking out a couple of twenties. 'I'm leaving the country tonight. Most of what I've got is in dollars.'

'Is this for me, or have I got to share it with Mum?'

'Get in the car and I'll see what else I can spare.' He didn't dare look at his watch, but surely to God by now the Allied Consortia people were late.

'Why can't you give it to me now? Do you think I won't go away? Is that it?'

'I'm perfectly delighted to see you. Now – get in the car.' He seized the child, not knowing it was strapped down. The buggy left the ground and thwacked against the side of the car. Only the risk of being seen from the house stopped him from throwing it violently back on the ground, infant included.

'You watch what you're doing with my kid!' Dominique sounded resentful rather than anxious. It was only from envy of her brother's rumoured prosperity that she'd come up here. She'd had an ill-thought-out impulse to feed her own jealousy by seeing for herself. Of course, if he wanted to be patronizing and offer her charity, that was his problem.

As ever Mrs Zlotnick headed a household without men. Terry and Keith were long gone: one last heard of as a minicab driver in London; another on a construction site in Abu Dhabi.

Zlotnick was breathing heavily as he spoke. 'You can have the same again, in dollars. I'll give it to you in the car, and you can change it into pounds sterling at any bank. But you'll have to accept that this is all there is. I'm due at Heathrow later today.'

'All right, all right.' She put the child on one shoulder and kicked the buggy shut, glowering at him with the look of a woman whose displeasure was to be feared by anyone, if they knew what was good for them. The baby's head lolled like a newborn's; Dominique had smoked throughout her pregnancy, evern after finding out how far gone she must be.

Zlotnick drove through the village at a careful thirty. He was damned if he'd let her see he was in a hurry. She sat without speaking to him, not bothering to use the safety belt. On her lap the baby grizzled.

They drew up in the lane leading to that only

too-well-remembered house. 'Oh, for Chrissake shut your noise,' she sighed at the child for the fourth time. Noticing where they were, she said, 'Why've you gone on, then?'

'I beg your pardon?' In fact Zlotnick had stopped short of the house by a couple of hundred yards.

'I said, why've you gone on? We don't live here any more, in case you're interested. In case you find us so facinating you're bleeding dying to know.'

'Oh, yes?'

'I mean, you've gone past our turning, haven't you?' As if her meaning were obvious, Dominique pointed back at the entrance to the caravan site. 'The landlord went and died, didn't he? Some people would've made it their business to know something like that.'

Zlotnick backed up, braked hard, and got out. Strolling round to the rear nearside door, he yanked out the buggy with the force of someone pulling a tooth and handed it over in silence together with the money.

'Is this it, then?'

'What?' Not bothering to speak aloud, he mimed the word with a grimace.

'I said, don't you want to know how we are?'

'How are you?'

'Okay, since you ask.'

Small thanks to you, her face said in his rear view mirror as he drove off.

Roaring back through the village, he jumped the

218

light as he crossed the river. Okay, so some schmuck in a Range Rover was nearly on the bridge at the other end but Zlotnick had known – almost for certain – that the guy would bottle out if he ran straight at him. By the time he was back at the house, he must have done a couple of miles in just over a hundred seconds, blind corners and all. And no questions asked when he got there.

From the distant past back to a seriously feasible future. In two minutes. No shit.

A few days after Zlotnick's sister had appeared, like an exasperated jack-in-the-box, Maria too was wishing him ill.

On the surface the scene in the Rectory garden was everything it should be. The September weather was placid and warm after days of weather in the harsh greys of winter. On the far hillside pasture and stubble were the same tarnished shade; only the dull green of Combend Wood gave a contrast. Maria was sitting in a basket chair among the fallen leaves of the big tulip tree that grew against the back of the house. She made a picture of calm fecundity, with baby Sarah playing at her feet on a rug scattered with toys.

They were alone in the sunshine. Edmund was in Scotland with his crew, filming with one eye on each day's costs and another on the weather. The empty, strong-featured coast of Kintyre didn't have the kindest climate, but it did let them pretend it was 1825 without having to film every location in fog, or with the horizon as close as a hand in your face. At home, Digory was shut away indoors, consulting with Zlotnick on the script for *The Birth of Civilization*; the deal had gone through. For his own convenience, Digory had pressed Zlotnick to stay a while longer as a house guest.

On the lawn Sarah was talking earnestly into a plastic telephone with wheels and a face. 'Oowuh!' she said, in self-possessed greeting. 'Showallalergh ... Erg?... Uh ... Uhuh ...' It was a grown-up conversation, perfectly imitated in scribble.

Normally Maria would have smiled to hear her own voice mimicked; instead her face was shaded by a frown. She was picturing the Rectory as a giant museum piece doll's house with its façade lifted away. From here, how many rooms would you see where in the past few days her little girl had been deliberately put at risk?

The landing. From the start Zlotnick had obstinately left the safety gate open, seeing it as an infringement of his rights and liberties. One morning Sarah had waddled towards the top of the stairs two paces ahead of Maria, who was too bulky and tired to move fast. Holding on to a baluster, the child had stepped laboriously down towards the first tread. Each step was half as high as she was. She heard Zlotnick coming upstairs and looked up, curious.

'Sarah – darling – go down backwards!' Maria hadn't cared to sound harried in Zlotnick's hearing. But she knew her daughter's concentration couldn't last.

The little girl had tripped, lost her balance, and tumbled. Too surprised to make a sound, she'd fallen with a distinct thump each time, over the edge of fourteen uncarpeted oak treads. She might have pitched down only five. But Zlotnick, seeing her fall towards him, had stepped aside, with chilly nonchalance.

Maria had squeaked with fear and hurtled downstairs, her big belly wobbling. Kneeling, she'd tried to shush the shrieks of her terrified child. Zlotnick had glanced at them, rigid with disdain for everyone who couldn't handle themselves.

The back lobby. One afternoon while Maria had been putting away the folding paddling pool, Sarah had wandered to the open kitchen door. She'd been fascinated by the sound of someone grinding stewing steak in the blender. Out of the corner of her eye, Maria had seen that the child was standing with her soft unformed fingers in the hinge of the lobby door. At that moment Zlotnick had come by. Without shortening his stride, he'd looked pointedly at Sarah's endangered hand and seized the door. He'd shut it behind him so hard that a spatter of plaster had fallen down from the dodgy bit of ceiling by the boiler.

Maria had been quick enough to snatch Sarah backwards by her hair. It had taken some while to calm her screams of bewilderment. The bathroom —

'Dadda! Dadda!' Indoors the phone was shrilling. Hearing it, Sarah was tugging at her mother, wild

221

with excitement. Once a day Edmund rang, and she'd come to think every call must be from her father.

This time it was. Maria could see the housekeeper gesturing at the kitchen window and mouthing Edmund's name.

But she'd forgotten to bring out the damned cordless phone, hadn't she? On her way out it had been on the hall table as usual, but her attention had been taken up by something else. The front door had been propped open in spite of Maria's pleas to keep it closed, and Sarah had duly done a runner. Maria had caught her investigating the chassis of someone's car from underneath.

For the twentieth time Maria regretted Moria's absence on a long-arranged holiday in the Sierra Nevada with three other ski-bum nannies. Her replacement was taking a week off. Officially she was visiting a sick relative; in fact she was almost certainly having an abortion. That left Sybille, the ageny au pair, who spent most of her time out or on the phone. Clutching Sarah in her arms, she clambered hastily upstairs to take the call in her own room. She felt dizzy with effort as she sat down on the bed. Her unborn child went on moving steadily about, like a sleeper beneath a tight coverlet.

Talking to Edmund she was careful not to sound harassed. She'd been on location with him herself, and knew how many crises an ordinary day could present. There'd been stunts that wouldn't work, an outbreak of food poisoning via the mobile canteen, an actress breaking her nose in a road accident, and, throughout everything else, demands from the backers for a shorter schedule. At least Edmund had kept control of the script this time, despite a studio's worth of executives each needing to sound off his or her half-penn'orth of nonsense. He'd even adjusted it to take account of bad weather – only to have the endless Highland drizzle displaced by a heatwave. His empty nineteenth-century sky had been criss-crossed with vapour trails, and the hillsides were crowded with trail bikes and hang gliders.

'So I'm going to be a single parent a while longer?' Maria couldn't help smiling at the sound of Edmund's voice. He was always on a high during filming, despite everything. Years of hassle were behind him for good, and only weeks were left to go.

'I wish you weren't. Is that Sarah I can hear?' They talked for half an hour before ringing off.

As Maria put down the receiver she realized how desperately she needed a pee. No doubt the new baby was doing a headstand on top of her bladder. The bathroom wasn't safe, though. She was sharing with Zlotnick, who was pointedly defending his territory by leaving his razor and any other hazard he could within Sarah's reach. In the downstairs lavatory, then, next to Digory's study, Maria tried to pee while Sarah pulled at her and started to cry. There was a sharp sweet whiff of baby shit; the little girl was going to go on crying until she was taken upstairs and changed. She was upset at being put down, too, and getting tired.

Back in the hall, she was accosted by Digory.

'Is something the matter?' It was his polite way of complaining about the noise of crying. From inside the study door, Zlotnick looked up at her, sitting at Digory's big desk.

'Not really, thank you. Sarah didn't like being shut up with me in the downstairs loo.'

'If the child is going to be distresed, you can always get someone else to keep an eye on her, you know.'

'That's all right, thanks.'

'I mean, good heavens, if no one else is about at such a moment, why don't you ask Jimmie or me to help you?'

In a lowered voice, Maria said, 'If you don't mind, Digory, I'd rather not ask Jimmie Zlotnick's permission every time I use the lavatory.'

Digory looked displeased but said nothing. Later, he knocked on the door of Maria's room. Sarah had been lulled to sleep for the night next door in the nursery, and Maria was lying on the bed watching television.

After a few remarks about his granddaughter's welfare, Digroy said, 'I've been noticing your behaviour since you've been back here.'

His tone was benevolent but the goodwill in his voice sounded conditional, as if an ungrateful word from her would make him change at once. 'Is there some problem you ought to have mentioned?'

'Nothing I can't cope with, thanks.' Now that she was an adult, Maria knew better than to criticize Digory for not keeping his house in good order. Zlotnick's hostility would have to be endured in silence.

He looked at her for a moment, as if offering her one more chance to be more helpful. 'I know you need to sleep a lot, but don't you feel you're being unsocial, staying up here quite so much?'

Maria levered herself to her feet. She didn't want to face this line of questioning while lying down. 'It's the most convenient place, at a time like this.' In fact it was lonely as hell, taking refuge in her room. She'd forgotten how isolated she'd often been, living here as a child.

'Another thing I've noticed is that you haven't gone out of your way to be agreeable to Jimmie.'

'I'm every bit as agreeable to him as he is to me.'

Digory frowned. 'As a favour to you, I'll ignore such a meaningless remark. Are you seriously cherishing the same resentments towards him that you expressed as a child?'

There was no doubting his earnestness; the deal he'd made through Zlotnick had seen to that. He'd agreed to risk himself before the cameras for a whole hour of prime time. No man of his reputation would do anything so public for someone he didn't respect.

'Now as then, Digory, I mean every syllable.' Maria tried not to think how unappealing she must look. She'd been too tired even to keep herself tidy. Just standing up left her breathless and palpitating.

'I don't understand how you can say such a thing. As I recall, your complaints against Jimmie Zlotnick were nothing if not frivolous. Indeed – and my memory does *not* fail me – you soon withdrew everything you'd said.'

'Yes, under duress! I remember what was said, too. And how I was made to stand in awe of you.'

He looked at her, astonished. For a moment he said nothing; the idea that he could have abused his own power was too incredible. With a show of self-restraint he asked, 'Are you sure you're not feeing unwell? I mean, in the sense of being over-wrought?'

'I'm of perfectly sound mind, thank you, Digory. Even if I do need to go to the lavatory every half hour. And don't worry; I won't embarrass you by picking a fight with Jimmie Zlotnick. Any more than I'd give him the satisfaction of driving me out of here and into a hotel.'

Digory stared in shocked disbelief. 'Good God, I should hope not! Have you any idea how such a thing would affect Edmund? I can't believe you've even considered it. To have him leave everything and fly down from Scotland? Merely to deal with the upshot of a pre-natal whim?'

Maria was too frustrated to speak. Throughout a long silence she struggled to keep back the tears of rage.

In a quieter voice Digory eventually said, 'Listen, Maria, because people have been generous to you in the past, you shouldn't think of anyone here as

226

weak. Not me, nor anybody else. There's one thing you must understand. By refusing to humour you now, I'm actually showing respect for your basic judgement. I know – and I trust you will, soon enough – that any delusions you may have about Jimmie Zlotnick treating you as a usurper are, as I say, a passing whim. They're the effect of a mind temporarily unbalanced by a difficult pregnancy; nothing more.'

Maria didn't trust herself to go on looking at him. She turned away to a window. The warm evening landscape lay balanced at the very turn of day into night. A tractor's headlights spilled twin beams as it moved across a distant hillside; behind its plough, stubble was turning to fresh earth.

'I'm not going to quarrel with you,' she said. 'For Edmund's sake, and because of the children.' Unconsciously she stroked her belly. 'And in return, you can damn well let me look after *my* daughter in whatever way seems best to *me*.'

Brave words, no doubt. For what they were worth in the end.

Some days the house felt as remote as a space station. When the police later arrived at the Rectory to take statements, most of the household would still be out. Sybille had been shopping in Oxford with a fellow au pair from home. Mrs Rosenberg, the housekeeper, had gone off on a fifteen-mile drive to the nearest decent supermarket, having left a cold lunch for Digory and Zlotnick outside the study.

227

Digory's assistant was at his rooms in college, giving dictation in her dogged monthly bid for the bottom of his in-tray. Deborah, the middle-aged divorcee who came in to clean, was also in Oxford, doing some background reading for her Prelims. Today she was making no headway at all at her desk in the library of the Theology Faculty. The trees outside had sprouted a hideous crop of loadspeakers and were simultaneously blasting out Bill Halcy, Bod Marley, and the massed trumpets of a big band from the 1940s. On this Monday each September medieval custom dictated that St Giles Street be closed to traffic, to become a public fairground.

Maria was alone with her daughter in their quiet upstairs room at the Rectory. Sarah had been waddling up and down, pulling a segmented plastic caterpillar on wheels. Inevitably the string had caught around an axle. She was looking up at her mother, jerking her arms up and down in rising frustration.

To divert her, Maria picked up the television's remote control. This was the newest, favourite game. She pointed the gadget at the child with a smile of complicity. 'Zap! I'll shush you! I'll shush you!' she exclaimed, with a mime of pressing the volume control.

The little girl laughed helplessley, until she couldn't stand up. Sitting down with a bump made her chortle even more. Maria thought she'd never seen such bliss.

Even as she was laughing too, the realization flashed upon her that something was wrong. Between her legs there was a hot gush.

It was what she'd feared all along – even so, she was rigid with disbelief. 'Oh, no – God – no,' she found herself mouthing over and over. Gingerly she got up from the sofa where she'd been sitting. The bloodstain she left steamed briefly. All the way down to Digory's study Sarah's laughter followed her. 'More! More!' she heard her exclaim as she tapped on his door.

Digory took charge irresistibly. 'Sit here and don't move. Jimmie will get anything you need.' He looked around; but Zlotnick had already sprinted upstairs, his face inscrutably solemn.

'I'll get the car round.' As Digory hurried outside, Zlotnick came back with Maria's handbag. He was carrying it masculine fashion, at arm's length with the strap trailing. Rather than hand it to her, he put it on a nearby table without speaking or looking in her direction.

Upstairs she could hear Sarah calling for her. Risking further loss of blood, she got up. When Digory returned, he exclaimed at her in surprise. 'God Almighty! What are you doing?'

Watched without comment by Zlotnick, Maria had laboured upstairs and back. She now sat with Sarah on her lap; beside her lay the beach bag in which her daughter's change of nappy and spare clothes were kept.

'I'm taking Sarah with me.' She heaved herself off the chair and made her way outside. Balanced on her hip, the little girl blinked in the sunshine. The inside of one of Maria's sandals was squelchy and warm.

Digory followed. 'But – good God! This is an emergency! We can't take a child with us at a time like this. Can't Sybille take charge?'

'Most other people cope, Digory. And Sybille's out; she's not due back for an hour. No one's asking you to achieve anything out of the ordinary. All you have to do is sit in the waiting room and play horsey-horsey and pat-a-cake, like the other grandparents there.'

'Far be it from me to accuse you of being willfully impracticable, but can you really not think that Jimmie won't be willing to help you out?'

Maria opened her mouth without a sound and slowly doubled up. Dropping the beach bag, she let Sarah slither to the ground. Across her abdomen and upper thighs a dismal stir of discomfort grew stronger. It swelled to a drum-roll of pain, as the first contraction hinted at its approach. This is nothing, it said. You wait.

At last Maria's breathing eased and she straightened. Digory said, 'Quick, get in the car. Don't think about anything else.'

'I'm not leaving her here.' Maria spoke in an urgent undertone. At their feet Sarah stood gazing up at each of them in turn. She wore a vacant expression of concentration, unsure whether to be excited or scared.

'Just do as you're told and get in the damn car!'

'Damn *you*, Digory! I'm not leaving her behind! *Here*? Without the care of a fit person?'

He could hardly believe that his authority was

being challenged like this, here, in his own home. 'You choose to say that to my face? *You* do? All the generosity Digory personified in public was gone. 'You think you can make me do what you want by insulting my choice of colleague?' Conscious of Zlotnick standing in the doorway, he too was speaking in a near-whisper. 'I used to think you were a sensible woman, at the very least. Do you not have the smallest idea what would have become of you if I'd left you where you were?'

'Patronize me if you must, Digory. Congratulate yourself, even. But don't leave someone as helpless as this – who never harmed you or anyone – in the care of a man I don't trust.'

Maria had sworn she wouldn't weep in front of them. She slammed both hands against the car roof, enraged at the tears and snot oozing out of her face for anyone to see. For privacy's sake, she knelt down and put her arms round Sarah, to hide her face in the child's clothes. Sarah whimpered anxiously.

'She won't be any trouble, I promise she won't!' she exclaimed, looking up at Digory. In the crisis of the moment she'd stopped being the sophisticated creature Digory liked to boast of as his own work. Instead she was just a pleading, dishevelled woman; a rather embarrassing sight, frankly.

The pain stirred again, like the noise of a mighty rumour out of sight. This time it was no rehearsal. The child inside her didn't feel like another creature. In was a fifth limb, to be torn from its root with a

231

creak and snap of bloody sinews. Maria let go of Sarah and crouched face forward on the ground, enduring it. She couldn't even hold on to the thought of Sarah, left behind to wander the house in bewilderment, cynically half ignored by Zlotnick. A tree of pain climbed and shimmered inside her. Only one thing was left in her mind: don't let them hear you cry out.

Through a barrier of anguish she heard footsteps; Zlotnick was hurriedly picking up the baby and her things. 'I can take the child into Oxford,' he muttered to Digory over Maria's bowed head. He bristled with quiet-spoken tact.

'That's good of you,' Digory exclaimed after him in an undertone, as if it meant Maria wouldn't hear. By removing the infant, Jimmie had found a quick way of bringing the whole ridiculous scene to an end.

Unbelievably, Maria felt the pain grow less, then vanish. Her face bore a ghostly glitter of sweat, like gold-dust. Zlotnich got the little girl, then himself, into his Jaguar, strapped her in and gunned the engine. By the time Maria stopped gasping and climbed up off her hands and knees, he'd left nothing behind but a cloud of exhaust. His machine could go from nought to sixty in eight seconds.

Without a word, Digory held open his front passenger door. Maria half sat, half fell on to the seat, weeping convulsively. In silence, they drove off. She might have displeased him past all forgiveness, but it would still have offended his pride not to get her to hospital as fast as he could. He was a good driver, unflappable and bold. Before slowing for the bridge, they overtook Zlotnick. Sarah recognized Digory's vintage Jensen; excitedly she started chanting something – probably 'Grandpa' over and over. Zlotnick didn't look round. He was hauling on his seat belt will still down in first, changing from one hand to another on the wheel. On the far side of the bridge he roared past and disappeared for good.

Maria was carried past without a word. There was nothing else she could do; at that moment another contraction had taken hold of her. Groaning through clenched teeth, she found herself being crushed to nothing in a vice of pain. She never even saw them disappear.

'Proud Old Time Horses Rode By All With Joy'. Curly gold letters a foot tall spelled out the words around the pie-crust top of the big merry-go-round. The fairground filled the wide leafy street of St Giles from end to end. Above the stalls of vendors selling hot dogs and cheap toys the Voyager-Starship Biowheel rose forty feet in the air. There were ghost trains, helter-skelters, a gleaming nineteenth-century traction engine, and a Ferris wheel with a view into the upstairs galleries of the Ashmolean Museum.

Once a year, amid the smell of generators and the din of public address music, the University and the townspeople of Oxford mingled with each other. Several people were there from the Senior Common

Room of Digory's college. One, a high-caste young Hindu with a chair in astro-physics, was trying to win a pink teddy in a shooting gallery for his small brother. With his four elder sisters the boy stood a few respectful paces behind. He was holding the hand of his sari-clad mother, who giggled a lot in company but rarely spoke. Ageing punks loitered under the gateway of St John's College with elaborately shredded black jeans and the accents of rural Oxfordshire.

Questioned afterwards by the police, Zlotnick would come to know by heart how he'd killed time that afternoon. Hoisting the child on to his shoulders, at first he'd kept her quiet with a bag of cashews bought at a hamburger stand getting the scare of all time when she'd nearly choked on a nut. She'd had to be hurriedly lifted down and held by one arm while he smacked her hard between the shoulder blades. The blow had started her screaming, so another bribe had had to be offered. He'd bought an ice cream and plonked her down to eat it inside St Giles's Church, away from the crowds.

A couple of Australian tourists, later coming forward, could confirm that they'd seen the child there. She'd been running up and down the nave with squeaks of pleasure at being on the loose, while melted chocolate ice cream ran down her wrist.

Inside the church, Zlotnick sat in a pew, consulting his watch every minute or so. On the walls above him stone-garlanded memorials named eighteenth-century squires who'd been affectionate to their children and kindly condescending to the poor. Outside, a fairground speaker in a yew tree was belting out 'Sympathy for the Devil'.

Screams of dismay inevitably echoed through the nave as soon as the ice cream had melted enough to fall off its cone. Zlotnick carried the child outside, washed her in bottled mineral water bought for the purpose and silenced her again, this time with a silver helium balloon depicting Thomas the Tank Engine.

Dominique saw him before he saw her. She was staring at him from the far side of a crowd of people queueing to buy candyfloss. He knew he'd have to acknowledge her.

'I thought you'd had to go away somewhere abroad.'

'I got called back again at short notice,' he fibbed, 'It happens a lot.'

'So you're staying at that big house again?'

'No.' It would be true any day now; thank God, he wouldn't have to risk meeting her again.

Savouring her envy of him, she asked, 'And did you drive here in that car of yours?' It wasn't social chat, offered with a smile of politeness. To Zlotnick's sister, smiling was alien – something chimpanzees did perhaps when they'd had a fright. Not that anything could frighten Dominique.

'I drove here in my own car, yes,' Zlotnick replied, coolly patient.

'And is this your little girl?' Like a trespasser

stretching to peer over a fence, she stared up at Sarah, who was perched on Zlotnick's shoulders. 'It is a girl, isn't it?'

'It is.' Privately he was wondering how he could escape. What would it take to shake her loose without a scene? 'The child belongs to the people at Stinscombe Old Rectory.'

'Oh, those people.' Dominique sounded grandly disdainful. The Adams family, her manner suggested, had been born wealthy out of personal spite. 'She belongs to those rich friends of yours, then?'

'That's right,' replied Zlotnick, whose patience was growing murderous.

'Are you here with them, or what?'

'No. I'm not here with them.'

'You're like baby-sitting, then. I mean, kind of on your own?'

If there was a drift to her questioning, Zlotnick didn't notice. 'Uhuh,' he said, on automatic.

Suddenly he caught sight of someone he wanted to buttonhole. Moving away through the crowd was the figure of Sir Leslie Rumbold, the moral philosopher and media figure recently appointed at Digory's college as the new Warden. With an effort not to be disagreeable, he added. 'I'm doing the family a favour.' If Dominique took offence, there was nothing like being in a public place to make her throw a big number.

Sourly she said, 'I thought people like that had someone to do all that for them.'

'One would, wouldn't one?' Furtively anxious, Zlotnick watched Sir Leslie's departing back.

It didn't occur to him to ask after Dominique's infant. She wasn't looking the least like a parent today. No child, no buggy with shopping in the rack; not even the flat shoes and sensible clothes of early motherhood. She wore a quilted nylon-satin bomber jacked in electric green over a baggy thigh-length T-shirt. Her thin black trousers looked like tights, lopped off at the calf.

Without warning the air filled with screams. Zlotnick found he had a possessed creature wrapped round his head. The string attaching the helium balloon to the the child's wrist had come undone. Flashing silver in the sunlight it was drifting away, up past the street's big plane trees and over college roofs with Cotswold stone dormers. The child's anguish was deafening: a first taste of loss.

Zlotnick did a hasty mime at Dominique, pointing out some more balloons for sale. They were floating in a tree-sized bunch above the crowd. With the child still screaming, he did a runner.

'Don't you want no change nor nothing?' the balloon seller called out, holding Zlotnick's fiver.

He didn't stop to answer. With the child silenced, he hurried away down the deserted alleyway that had been made by pitching a line of booths with their backs close against the housefronts. Quite apart from fleeing his sister, a social word in Sir Leslie's ear was bound to be a good investment, long-term. And then he could get the hell out of here and go back to Stinscombe.

The child shrilled with delight, being piggybacked around the hazards of guy ropes and stone doorsteps. The air throbbed from the power of several dozen generators. 'Pink elephants rule the world, pink elephants fool the world,' sang the amplified voices of a sixties group whose drummer had fatally OD'd on acid. Zlotnick scurried past the homely seventeenth-century front of the Friends' Meeting House. 'Pricks and kicks and pricks and a fix,' chanted a punk band called Anal Kanal from a speaker outside the Eagle and Child pub. Past Pusey House chapel and the Oxford bookshop he was pursued by the sound of a long-gone group of blondes with beehive hair singing 'He was seventeen; he was heaven, see; he was mine.'

From the far end of the street, by the Martyrs' Memorial, Sir Leslie wasn't yet in sight.

'Horsey!' cried the child, holding out both arms.

The merry-go-round was one of the finest. Pennants fluttered from its top. Victorian engraved mirrors gleamed on its central pillar; princial-boy figurines beat time with the music. The wooden horses, in paintbox colours, had gaping eyes and trumpeting nostrils. As they circled, they rode up and down to a medley of the oldest and best of fairground tunes. There were painted cupids, lions, tigers, panthers, elephants and Union Jacks. A series of minor nineteenth-century royalty had knobbly coronets and eyes as bulgy as the horses'.

'Horseys!' cried out Sarah, triumphantly naming the most wonderful thing she'd ever seen. She grew urgent. 'Horsey! Horsey!'

The music and the riders slowed to a stop. About thirty people got off. They were as assorted as the rest of the crowd. Two cheery teenage girls with bushy pink hair who'd shared a horse; a thin, donnish woman with grey hair riding behind a five-year-old boy; a middle-aged couple in silly fairground hats who'd been waving noisily to a group of friends.

The child was about to wail with frustration. She strained towards the merry-go-round. At that moment Sir Leslie came into sight again, moving purposefully through the fairground en route for tea with his publisher at the Randolph Hotel. He strode along as if he were the only solid thing there, and the rest of the crowd was a vast holograph.

Quickly Zlotnick stopped a boy of ten or so who was scambling to take his place on one of the wooden horses. 'Do us a favour,' he coaxed.

The boy stared at him, curious. He had short spiked hair and one gold earring. Zlotnick glimpsed himself as he must look to any kid who was halfway streetwise: too clumsy with the baby, and too sharply dressed, to be a father. He said, 'I'm looking after the kid for her mother, okay? Can she sit in front with you? I need a word with someone.' He started reaching for his wallet.

The boy ignored Zlotnick's readiness to bribe him. 'Yeah, okay,' he said, indifferently easy.

'Cheers.' The child was bundled away in the strange lad's arms and put on a horse, looking ecstatic. Zlotnick turned to raise a casual hand in greeting to Sir Leslie.

'Surely not the issue of your own loins?' Sir Leslie asked, indicating Sarah. The music started up.

Zlotnick gave a self-deprecating laugh. 'I fear not. Seriously, though . . .' Looking solemn, he explained the crisis at Stinscombe that had brough him here.

At length, to show they could stop sounding melancholy on Maria's behalf, Sir Leslie said, 'How glad I am, as a mere male, to leave the mysteries of gestation unfingered. Let the ladies, God bless 'em, take the credit for that particular achievement.' He was a large brick-coloured man with smooth hair turning grey.

Zlotnick chuckled. 'Speaking of achievement, I believe I saw you being interviewed the other night.'

'Ah. On Channel Four.'

'The very same! And what a remarkable debate it was, dare I venture to say.' In fact he'd thought it crackpot, being to do with life after death.

Sir Leslie sensed this. 'Your reservations do you credit. If it weren't for so-called balance of opinion, they wouldn't have invited even one rationalist sceptic to challange their line-up of cranks. Did you note the woman who held forth about experiences outside her own body? The one with the long grey hair and the blouse that looked as if she'd hired it?'

'Oh, good God, yes!'

Suddenly Zlotnick's merriment became strained. Behind Sir Leslie, on the other side of the merry-go-round, he could see Dominique.

She was waiting. But not for him, even though

he was in full view. What drew her attention, above the crowd, was Sarah Adams, whirled along laughing on her painted horse. Dominique's eyes were bright and hard. She looked as if she were holding her breath in expectation.

'. . . Of course, I was only the producer's first sub. They'd really wanted Freddy Ayer, but he was on the Coast.'

Round and round flew baby Sarah – as the tabloids would be calling her by lunchtime tomorrow. Round and round, puzzled and delighted at how bright and fast-moving the world looked from so high up. All about her, circling to the music, other pleasure-seekers were smiling or larking about. Behind, on a blue horse with a carved green mane, rode a pretty boy of her own age. He sat wedged between two grandparents in beige cardigans and neatly pressed trousers, both of them smiling at what idiots they must look. Another little girl might have been Sarah in two years' time. Very proud of sitting in front, she was clasped protectively against her daddy's T-shirt. On his back, her little sister peeped out of a baby carrier. The horse next to them carried two older children. The girl was about five years older than Sarah. Her big brother was sitting back to front, guying around for the benefit of his family: mother, father, grandmother and a slightly younger aunt and uncle carying a new baby between them in a Moses basket.

Meanwhile, rapt among the onlookers, there lurked the one woman in the world who could dismay Zlotnick. His half-sister; fifty per cent flesh of his own flesh, he thought with a shudder.

Later, he'd realize he should have asked what had become of her child. The youngest Zlotnick hadn't gone on looking out at the world with such bland, intense curiosity for long. Three days after Dominique's appearance at the Rectory, the baby girl had died of pneumonia in her grandmother's arms during a long, dreary row about electricity arrears.

'. . . Of course the studio fee can barely be said to cover one's expenses. Nonetheless I felt one had a duty to puncture the illusions of the credulous . . .'

Zlotnick was beginning to feel dizzy with the effort of smiling at Sir Leslie while watching Dominique. It was almost as if the merry-go-round was a blurry UFO about to detach itself from his view and swoop away. For some reason it gave him a strange sensation to see Dominque, a lumpish ghost from his despised past, looking up like that at Edmund Adam's firstborn.

'Surely, Sir Leslie,' he rallied, 'one could say you were simply being generous to the viewing public.'

Even before the child had been conceived its prospects had been splendid. Without knowing it, Zlotnick was savouring much the same resentments as his dour, hot-eyed sister, watching and waiting over there. It should have been mine, he was thinking.

'Interesting, that.' Sir Leslie was having to speak up, over the noise of the merry-go-round's organ. 'I mean, your use of the word "could". "One *could*

say one was being generous." A foursquare example, in that not, of the way in which systems of
pure linguistics should yield to considerations of
context?' Though they were nearly shouting, no
one looked round at them. Such talk was com-
monplace beneath the walls of Balliol College.

With every moment Zlotnick was feeling more
odd – like two separate people. Physically he was
fine; braced, like an athlete just warmed up. But
with each turn of the whirligig he could feel his
rancour towards the Adams child hardening and
taking shape.

'What I appreciated most,' he heard himself saying,
'was your put-down of the mystic in the long frock.'

Around Dominique the crowd was beginning to
move again. As the merry-go-round slowed, people
got ready to help their children down. Others, queueing, moved forward to take their turn.

'Ah, the Bishop. Dear old Huddersfield is a great
pal of mine – has been for decades. He knows these
occasions are more of a ritual joust than a serious
letting of arterial gore.'

Watching out of the corner of his eye, Zlotnick
couldn't believe what might be about to happen.
'Tell me,' he said, not daring to look directly in
Dominique's direction. 'since you're his friend,
you'd know this: but isn't it true that people are
unkind enough to call his diocese the Dead See?'

And it was going to be his own doing. All he had
to do was – nothing. Killing someone, the first time,
must bring on a high as queasy as this.

Dominique thrust her way through the crowd and disappeared behind the central pillar. The horses had almost slowed to a stop; on the nearer side the lad holding Sarah was getting ready to slide off with her. Catching his eye, Zlotnick acknowledged him with the thumbs-up.

'Poor old Huddersfield!' Sir Leslie, seeing Zlotnick's gesture, turned to catch sight of the boy and the little girl as they were carried behind the pillar at one mile an hour. 'But no, that's a different dioecse altogether – Is something up?'

Zlotnick was watching the merry-go-round. A troop of emotions crossed his face. Each looked less welcome than the one before. He was making damn sure of that. Intense concentration. Then concern. All the horses in sight were now empty.

The rest of were revolving into view, one every few seconds. He adjusted his face to show dismay – then desperation. 'Jesus Christ. Look! Look at that!'

Every horse was empty.

Dominique was hurrying away into the crowd, not checking to see if he'd noticed her. On one hip she held Sarah. The child looked about in bewilderment, impulsively turning this way and that.

For one moment more, Zlotnick could have done something. Then they were gone.

Of course they hadn't really vanished, he told himself. All that had happened was that his sister had been dumber than ever. What it God's name did she think she could achieve? Did she imagine she could scare him? *Him?* The mere idea gave him an adrenalin high. He felt as if he were floating two feet off the ground.

What she didn't realize was the opportunity she'd given him. He could blackmail her out of his life for ever now. The first chance he got, he'd drive over to their mother's and sort her out. Hell, he was overdue for a visit.

Meanwhile the Adamses would have the advantage of learning a lesson. They should have made proper childcare provision.

They could have their brat returned by tonight, sure.

Well. Maybe tomorrow.

CHAPTER
THIRTEEN

The police car moved uncertainly over the tussocky ground. Down on the shore the actors were the first to notice it. Four of them were impersonating fishermen beaching a rowing boat. Five more were on horseback, in the top-hatted uniform of the nineteenth-century British police force. The car turned on to the hard sand below the tide line, and Edmund shouted to the cameras to stop. Since the movie policemen were supposed to be making an arrest, there was a spatter of laughter at the sight of real coppers.

On the water's edge the group of actors were out of earshot. They watched as both men got out of the car and Edmund stepped forward to meet them. The ones cast as fishermen were particularly fed up at the interruption. They were wet through and anxious as hell to get back to the warmth of their trailer, up behind the beach where a village of Portakabins had been set up for the duration of filming here, complete with canteen, hairdressing salon and medical staff. Everyone's curiosity increased as Edmund, seeming anxious and confused, walked back with the policemen to their car. Without exception, the thought in everyone's mind was that such an interruption could start costing at the rate of several hundred a minute.

'We've nothing definite to tell you,' was the first thing one of them told him. 'But it does concern your child.'

Emdund's thoughts, involuntarily, were running on that day's filming. 'But we can still go ahead,' he nearly said aloud. 'We can use the other one.' The script had called for a baby. To cover themselves against illnesses they were using identical twins, turn and turn about.

He wrested his thoughts away from make-believe. Growing inside him was a dull reluctance to hear anything that could possibly follow. 'What?' he managed to say. Had something fearful happened to Maria or the new baby? 'But she was all right – my wife was fine – only a few hours ago. I spoke to her.'

Both of them looked at him. Something about their faces made him feel as if he were suddenly losing body heat, for the inside out.

'Your wife's come to no harm, sir. She's in hospital. You father's waiting there to see you as well.' As they reached the car the man opened a rear door, indicating that Edmund should get in.

His astonishment was visible all the way up the beach where a tight crowd of nearly fifty people were staring at him: the cameraman had his assistants, the lighting engineers, focus — puller, sound engineers, script editor, continuity girls, make-up artists, properties manager and his crew, the wardrobe people, plus the usual proportion of lovers, spouses and other camp followers. The whole scene was dominated by a semicircle of fierce lights raised aloft like so many one-legged giants; even at noon they could make every blade of marram grass cast an extra shadow.

'But – look —' Edmund was saying, as they both waited for him to get in. 'Can't you tell me? What's happened to the child? The doctors must have told your people something.'

He was too agitated to notice the two young men's response, or he would have seen them exchange an unprofessional look of surprise and dismay.

'It doesn't concern any medical —'

'What do you mean? You said my wife was in hospital. Has she lost the baby? She didn't miscarry at home, did she?'

'Your wife did miscarry, I'm afraid.' The man was serious enough as he said this. He also sounded as if it were by the way. 'But we're not here because of that.'

Watching from beneath a blinding bank of Panaflexes and Krieg lighting, the crew could hear nothing of what was being said. At length one of the officers took Edmund by the arm and said something in a lowered voice. For a moment Edmund didn't move or speak; then even the group of actors standing way out in the waves heard him howl, 'What? *What?*' Without another word he and the policemen hurried into the car and drove back up the track. The crew found themselves staring in silence at their departure, amid the rustle of the wind and the piping of oystercatchers. Only when they were out of sight did the cameraman, as Edmund's deputy, say, 'I guess that must have wrapped it for today.' One by one the monstrous lights went out.

'I'm very sorry. Really I am.'

It was the obstetrician, back at Maria's bedside already. He gave her hand a squeeze, to show reassurance, she supposed, as well as sympathy. Maria shifted her knees sideways, oppressed by the weight of the child inside her. She was trying to avoid the doctor's eye, as if it would stop her understanding what he was about to say.

'I'm afraid the baby couldn't have survived. I can't tell you how sorry we are.'

Maria wasn't sure she wanted words of comfort. They made it harder to hold her features together in a mask of indifference. After the humiliating scene outside the house, her determination not to weep in public had become even stronger.

'We're going to see everything happens as quickly and easily as possible. The midwife will be here immediately.'

'What for?' As soon as the words had popped out, she realized how pointless they were. Even the littlest corpse had to have been born some time. She would be giving birth after all.

The police arrived soon afterwards. Both of them, a local plain clothes man and a uniformed woman constable, were taken to where Digory was waiting on a bench in a corridor cluttered with stacked chairs and trolleys of soiled linen. In the delivery room Maria was concentrating on lying still. The anaethestist was trying to stick an epidural catheter into her spinal column without risking damage, which meant that even the smallest hiccup of grief couldn't be allowed. 'There's a good girl. That's a very good girl indeed,' said the anaesthetist, a young woman who looked about eighteen.

It was at that moment, outside the door, that it was decided to wait for Edmund's arrival to let him give her the worst news of all.

Maria screamed. Her head was thrown back her eyes were rolled into her skull. In her lap her hands hung limp. Nothing counted except emptying herself of sound.

Edmund clung to her as tightly as if she might turn to vapour in his arms. His face was washed blank; nothing showed in it except shock at her response. She screamed again, every vein standing out. He could hardly believe she had the strength to make such a sound, over and over. When he'd been shown into her hospital room, filled with terror of his own news, she'd been lying back exhausted, as if she'd never sit up again. Her face had been the colour of old ivory; her eyes had sunk from dreary, passive weeping. Past any hope or fear, one would have thought.

She heaved another breath into herself and howled again. Edmund held her head against his own. To think that outside this room the world carried on as before. People were walking out of the reception area feeling better. They were watching television at home; they were flying overhead on the airline that had taken him north only last week. To the place where, without knowing it, surely he'd had the last contented moment of his life.

Grief and fury had used Maria up at last. She twitched in Edmund's arms, parched and dizzy. Her head flopped convulsively; her tongue lolled.

When the doctor and a nurse hurried in, they found her thrashing feebly on the bed. Edmund was holding her hands in one of his, reaching again to ring for help with angry desperation. For their own sakes, everyone was only too relieved once the poor bloody woman had been held still, shot up and straightened out, ready for a long, deep sleep.

Edmund got up feeling hollowed away to nothing. He couldn't think what had to be done next. Some mountain of a task, no doubt, far beyond his strength.

As he opened the door a man in a doctor's white coat forcibly jammed it wide with his foot. Another, who might have been dressed to pass as an orderly, aimed a camera at him.

They nearly got what they wanted: a photograph for their paper of Edmund Adams looking straight out of the frame in unguarded shock. On instinct, though, he feinted with his left arm at the guy holding the door, then grabbed the photographer by his jacket. During the time it took for the corridor to fill up with people exclaiming and hauling them apart, they circled, staggering in a grotesque dance. The photographer was hanging on to Edmund's coat in self-defence; Edmund was trying to shake him loose. First he wanted to smash the camera, then fracture every bone in the hungry fucker's face.

The ratpack had covered every exit from the hospital.

'Mr Adams, what did your wife say?'

'Edmund – hey, Edmund – look over here!'

'Where do you think your daughter could be at this moment?'

An unmarked car took him and Digory away. Later that night the inspector in charge of the case told Edmund, 'One more thing, I'm afraid. I know you'll dislike doing it.'

There followed a drive forty miles across country through a night that seemed to have become permanent. In the centre of Gloucester the streets were empty of everyone but the odd drunk. They entered an anonymous building where windowless corridors led to a large neon-lit basement with tiled walls and floor. Edmund had been wanted to identify a corpse.

On the far side of the room one surface bore what looked like a pile of something under a covering. It seemed too small to be human. Wanting to be reassuring, the officer sent to accompany him said, 'It's just that in a case like yours we do cover ever possibility.' A rubber-gloved assistant reached to show them the body. Edmund Adams, future founder and president of Friends of Children in Peril, nerved himself to look at his first dead baby.

They'd brought him here for nothing. This pale, dirty stranger wasn't a bit like his own daughter. Even soaked through, her hair was too light and wispy-straight. It was still fastened in a top-knot, by an elastic band ornamented with plastic teddy bears. There was no way she could have been mistaken for someone asleep.

Edmund studied the child for a long time. He knew she was going to stay near the forefront of his thoughts for the rest of his life.

'Do you know how she died?'

'Exposure,' the officer hazarded, glancing at the mortuary assistant behind Edmund's back. The assistant nodded in confirmation.

'A lot of misadventures like this don't get much attention,' the officer added. 'You wouldn't know about them if you didn't read the local press.'

Inevitably Edmund's thoughts were with the parents. 'But it's now —' He looked at his watch; it was nearly daybreak.

'Let me put it like this. Assuming this one isn't already on our missing person's file, I'd be surprised if the next of kin don't contact us soon.' He had three young children of his own, and knew it would be tactless to speak of some parents' indifference. It was only a few days since there'd been a case of a cot-death baby found in the family dustbin.

Edmund went on looking at the corpse. With its muddy ankle socks and missing nappy. He hoped with all his strength that the child had been loved by someone throughout her short life.

How many more times would he be fated to find himself in a place like this? It occured to him that if the search dragged out they could be showing him the remains of babies who'd been dead for some time. But at least, he thought with a grim quiver of irony, a bundle of bones couldn't hint at any personality. He was profoundly grateful that his first body hadn't been shown signs of torture.

As they left the room the officer held the door open for him and asked, 'How will we contact you?'

Edmund momentarity failed to understand. He was in that state of fatigue where sleep itself seems impossible. Surely the whole night had been an evil hallucination.

'What?'

'Are there friends you can stay with? Or will you be at a hotel? While public curiosity is running high, that is.'

'Of course; forgive me. I see what you mean. I can't go home now, can I?'

Zlotnick was awestruck at what he'd achieved. He was a little boy playing with matches who couldn't believe how easy it was to produce dozens of grown-ups with real fire engines.

The risk, the suddenness and the ease of what he'd achieved had left him beside himself. Questioned by one official after another, his show of remorse, adrenalin-fired, had turned out brilliant. What higher cause was there than self-defence, anyway? Especially when the whole circus was the fault of that silly bitch Dominique.

Too charged up to sleep much, inwardly he went on slagging her off throughout an inconvenient night spent at a hotel. His instincts had urged him to go straight to Stinscombe Halt. Reason warned him otherwise, as he realized how cramped his choice of action was. With Sir Leslie as his witness, it mightn't fit his story too well if anyone saw him chasing up his sister in the small hours.

So here he was first thing, driving west along the breezy hilltop road that led towards Stinscombe. In a few minutes everything could be sorted out, one way or another. Eager to be doing, he ran his mind over the other business of the day and keyed in the Rectory's number on his car phone.

He was answered by Deborah. Damn. The wrinkly cleaning woman with aspirations to self-improvement.

'Deborah, this is Jimmie Zlotnick. I won't say good morning, on a day like this.'

'No, indeed.' Deborah's voice was guarded. Apart from her ex-husband she had less time for Zlotnick than for anyone.

Briefly he had the irrational feeling that she suspected something. Then he remebered that she usually sounded this way. 'I shan't inflict any regrets on you,' he said. 'I'm sure you've heard enough as it is. Now, I'd like you to do something for me . . . Can you hear me?'

'I can hear you.'

'I take it the Street of Shame have got the place well staked out?' He ventured to sound grimly good-natured. God damn the old bag, he thought; there was no getting her to do anything without putting oneself out.

'That's right.'

'It's good of you to be there.'

'Think nothing of it,' said Deborah with toneless dignity. Her shrivelled, resolute manner occasionally got her mistaken for a reformed alcoholic by people who didn't know about her messy divorce.

'Yes, well, as I said, I want you to do something for me.' As curtly as he dared, he described the possessions he'd left behind at the Rectory. ' ... Could you see to that? I'll be outside the Golden Fleece in half an hour.'

'I can assemble them for you, if that's what you want; but you'll have to come here to get them.'

'Look, uh, I'd honestly prefer not. Can you really not drive half a mile down the road?'

'Mrs Rosenberg and I can't leave the house empty.'

She had a point. He pictured the group of cars in the lane, the waiting men and women, bored but tense. They'd be standing around with their recording equipment, sharing routine noises of cameraderie with rivals from other newspapers and broadcasting companies. Everyone would know everyone else via any number of assignments like this. And no doubt they prided themselves on stiffing each other even more than on getting any story. If the place were empty, at the very least they'd have turned the dustbins over and scabbled through the household rubbish.

'Okay, fine. So you'll be there for some time, right?'

'No doubt.'

'Well, this is what I'd like you to do. I'll send a girl, later today. Perhaps you could give her the things I've described.'

'If she doesn't mind walking the last bit.'

'I beg your pardon?'

'I said, she won't be able to drive up here.'

'Look, I know we're both deeply upset by what's happened, but could you explain that, please?'

'By all means. The lane is blocked. With people, mostly. I had to leave my car on the road to Aynesford.'

Zlotnick felt a pang of surprise. Rather than show it, he remarked, 'I'm sure she can cope,' and rang off. He drove the next two miles looking preoccupied.

Probably she was dramatizing. The chances were this was the only noteworthy thing that had happened to the woman since her old man had handed out her marching orders.

On the other hand the road was unusually busy. In the one direction, too. At the turning for Stinscombe Zlotnick got another surprise. Every vehicle was hanging a left and dipping down into the village.

Here was something. Zlotnick's own experience as a journalist had involved covering flower shows and interviewing women who'd just had twins. It fell a long way short of this. Even outside the village, cars were parked at the roadside; the first sightseers had arrived. There were families with parents pushing baby buggies or leading children by the hand. A group of teenagers had arrived on scooters. On the village green two ice cream vans were doing good business and a whiff of holiday was in the air. The lane by the Golden Fleece was double-parked; outside the pub a group of Japanese and a couple of leather-jacketed Frenchmen were hung about with serious photographic gear. They were waiting for opening time and the chance to do some interviews in the bar.

Zlotnick drove on, inwardly fizzing with excitement. What a way to end this era in his life! He'd first entered the Rectory as a day labourer. Now that the Adam's family's role in his career seemed fulfilled, who could gave guessed that he'd be moving on with a flourish like this? It was dizzying, watching his own handiwork. If one thing was certain in the eyes of the law it was his innocence; he couldn't even be suspected of complicity with the lad on the merry-go-round. They'd probably never find the boy, and if they did Sir Leslie had spotted him momentarity, empty-handed in the distance. They'd tried to give chase, but in vain. Zlotnick himself was Mr Clean; conspicuous but untouchable. He almost wanted to celebrate by giving a few interviews of his own.

There'd be plenty of publicity, though, once his sister had been made to hand back the brat. Already he could picture the headlines describing his remorse at the child's unaccountable disappearance and his stricken decision to re-establish ties with his old mother. Over the wheel of his car he cawed with inward laughter and another thought. Adams's wife would have to be publicty grateful for the infant's accidental discovery. It was almost too good to be true.

In his quest for self-advancement, Zlotnick might

well have become the most calculating man on earth. For him, though, ambition itself was over-ruled by his competitive obsession with the Adams family, as his first patrons. In his desire to influence their lives, he was prepared to outdo even the mind-less Dominique as a risk-taker.

Parking by the muddy entrance to the site, he knocked in vain on the door of the nearest caravan.

Irritated, Zlotnick rattled the door handle and rapped on the windows. It was the same at four other caravans on the site, even though most showed some sign of occupation: a nearby line of washing or a parked car. He wondered what to do next.

'Hey, you want to know something?'

Two boys of about eight and ten years old were tittering and staring at him from behind one of the cars. They'd obviously been told to stay away from journalists, and had only come up to him because they'd dared each other.

'Depends, doesn't it?'

'Are you from the papers like up in the village?'

'Uhuh.'

'What do you want to know, then?' asked the elder one. The other boy demanded, 'Are you look-ing for old Ma Zlotnick?'

'Will you pay us?' his brother said.

Zlotnick gave them a cool look. 'Which is their caravan?' They reminded him disagreeably of his brothers at the same age. He didn't have to be here, he told himself. It was strictly as a favour that he was doing this.

'Depends what you mean by "theirs",' the elder one told him. Both fell about with sniggers of delight at such subtlety.

'Where are Mrs Zlotnick and her daughter?'

'Dunno.'

'No, dickhead,' whispered the other boy. 'Make him pay first.'

'Is that their caravan?' demanded Zlotnick, indicating the second one he'd tried.

'Yes,' the younger boy said, eyeing him. 'How much will you give us?'

'Depends what you know. Is anyone in there?'

'A hundred pounds, then,' said the boy, naming the biggest sum he could think of. 'Go on, give us a hundred pounds.' He giggled helplessly at his own wit.

A woman appeared, a neat fierce looking creature. She wore a flowered apron over Crimplene trousers, unfashionably flared.

'Will you get inside!' she exclaimed. 'What did I tell you? Go on – what did I say?' Without waiting for an answer she rushed at the two children. 'Didn't I tell you not to talk to anyone?' The scampered out of her way, half shamed, half laughing. She turned to Zlotnick. 'Don't you dare come in here, interfering and corrupting young kids!'

He'd been about to take out his wallet, but now he put it away with a look of contempt at such slander. 'I'm not a journalist. I'm from the rent agency.'

The woman laughed with what she thought was

crushing scorn. 'My God, you'll have to think of something better than that! I'll tell you just one thing, and I'm not going to tell you twice.' She pointed to one of the caravans. 'They've gone. Now, have you got that?'

'Mrs Zlotnick and her daughter? When did they go? Where to?'

'I don't know and it's no good thinking I do. Like I told you, that's all I'm saying. So now you can damn well go away and I won't ask you to pardon my French because I don't care if you do quote me.'

'They've definitely disappeared.'

'Look for yourself. Of course they have.'

CHAPTER
FOURTEEN

'Keep him away from he, won't you?' murmured
Maria.

. They were going home.

Edmund changed down for the road into Stinscombe. He stole a look at her, not needing to be
told what she meant.

'Damnit, Maria – darling – look . . .' His voice
trailed off.

He was close to feeling lost. Everyone had
assumed that he, if anyone, was a man who could
take it. The police, the doctors, the hospital chaplain, his colleagues – they'd all shown the utmost
sympathy, but they'd behaved nonetheless as if
Edmund alone knew how he and Maria would carry
on their lives.

'Darling . . . I can't make a promise like that. Not
where my own father's concerned.'

'I know,' she said, in the dull tone of a woman

determined to give no more trouble. 'Don't let him make demands on me, that'a all.'

'What sort of demands?'

'Oh, Edmund, for God's sake! No – I'm sorry; I'm sorry. Just don't ask me to be false, and smile, and say hello nice to see you again. And what bad luck, being responsible for something like that for the rest of your life.'

Edmund was shaken at how steady her voice was. This was no passing whim. He swerved to the side of the road and pulled up. 'We don't have to come back here,' he said, with a tremor of effort. It felt as if he were being pulled in every direction at once. 'If you'd prefer somewhere else, it's okay by me.' As a reasonable man and an affectionate son, he thought Digory was to be pitied rather than blamed for what had happened. Even so he sensed there was little point in arguing with Maria.

'No,' Maria said, trying to speak lightly. 'I'm sorry. And I'm sorry I keep apologizing, too. It must be unbearable.'

He wanted to take her hand, but he dreaded her lack of response. In the last few weeks talking to Maria had been as frustrating as confiding in a voice synthesizer.

She added, 'It's that I can't decide on anything. What to say. What to think. What to put on in the morning.' Fall back on habit, the hospital psychiatrist had advised her. Stick to what's automatic and familiar. For better or worse the Rectory was what she thought of as her childhood home; returning there counted as touching base. 'We might as well go on.'

At Maria's invitation, Sally was a guest at the Rectory, taking leave from Caltech. From an upstairs window she caught sight of the car turning into the drive. Nothing, she thought, could be more melancholy that this home-coming, on a damp autumn evening with the distances closed off by drizzle. The lane outside was deserted at last by reporters and sightseers. Since September, police, press and talk-show hosts throughout the country had been harried by any number of alleged sightings of a child resembling Sarah. Hundreds had made silly accusation towards some neighbour; a few had made an impossible 'confession'. But no one had been worth holding for serious questioning. Zlotnick himself had gone back to the States. Now, no one loitered outside the house in the sheepskins or waxed cotton of people accustomed to hang about for long periods in the cold. The media's absence declared the case closed as far as they were concerned, even though the police had hundreds of people working on it, from switch-board operators on an open line to a team of frogmen.

Sally watched Edmund get out and open the passenger door. Maria emerged stiffly, like an ageing woman pretending to be young and vigorous. Outwardly she was fine, really. She was brightly dressed, in a new coat of yellow cashmere. Her make-up had been carefully put on and her gleaming hair was elegantly piled. But Sally, like most people there, knew better. Maria's surgical scars were

265

almost healed, where they'd had to scissor a wider passage for her stillborn child. She was coming back as an invalid nonetheless, her life organized for her by anxious onlookers.

Digory waited at the open front door. Wordlessly, he gave Maria a peck on the cheeck, he tried to hide his relief when she mumbled 'Hello' without resisting. Mrs Rosenberg, her own knowledge of bereavement got young and hard in wartime Czechoslovakia, embraced Maria and disappeared again. Digory introduced Evelyn, the ex-policewoman, hired to live in as a secretary. Her job included fielding any remaining calls from madmen or journalists. No one raised their voice.

After supper Maria invited Sally upstairs, where a log fire had been lit in the bedroom. They sat in front of it with a bottle of Armagnac.

'I feel bad about one thing,' Maria said. 'Guilty, I mean.'

Sally looked surprised, but said nothing. She knew her job was to listen.

'Edmund needs an easier time of it. He could do without propping up a distraught woman.'

'He doesn't see it like that.'

'I make things harder for him by blaming his father. But what else can I do? Digory was to blame, almost as much as thingy.' This was as close as Maria could get to mentioning Zlotnick's name. 'It was Digory's responsibility to stand up for us – to ensure the safety, God damn it —' She gulped, tears in her eyes. 'Of me and mine.'

Sally put out her hand, but Maria said, 'it's all right, this isn't the start of another big weeping session. Thank God.' She blew her nose. 'So you see, there's a barrier between Edmund and me. I know that in his teens he was ready enough to speak out against his father, but even then they were close. Honestly, I do try not to make Edmund take sides; his wife, or his parent.'

'Why did you come back?'

'To show I could do it, I suppose. Maybe to hasten the day when I can stop feeling like this. Unstable, I mean. Unpredictable. It frightens me, not knowing what I'm going to say or do next. The worst thing is that everyone seems to have a fixed idea of how long I should take to . . . "adjust" is the word most of them use. Not that I mind being told what to do. Today you get up for the first time. Tomorrow you phone a friend, all on your own. But supposing I can't meet their schedule? I feel as if I've got an exam coming up and I've lost my notes.'

It seemed Digory was wary of her, at least; but Maria found that he too had ideas about her best route to normality.

'There's something I'd like to ask you,' he told her one evening when they were along. 'Have you considered how soon you might try for another pregnancy? The people at hospital suggest you do, no doubt?'

'Of course some of them did. They sounded as if I'd fallen off a horse, and all I had to do to get back

267

my confidence was to climb straight back on. And from the way they talked, anyone would think the police – and I – had given up hope.' Maria was on the phone to the police every day, pleading or cajoling them for news of something – anything – however insubstantial. 'Forget it, Digory. Never again.'

He gave a pained look and her unhelpfulness.

'It's like this,' she explained. 'Any new pregnancy would be an unbearable piece of nostalgia. And having responsibility for another young child would fill me with more terror that I could describe.'

Later Edmund said, 'Darling, he only wanted to help.'

'He can do that by saying as little as possible. I didn't lose just the idea of a child, something stamped out in a mould. I – we – lost an individual. Oh God, and now I'm weeping again. Is there no end to it?'

The subject of replacement babies were dropped. A few days later, however, Mrs Rosenberg came to see Maria. She appeared uneasy. 'I'm a bit confused about one of Digory's instructions, so would you mind telling me what to do, instead? What I mean is, what would you like done with the things from the nursery?'

'What?' said Maria, as if someone had cannoned into her in a crowd. She hadn't pictured the favourite stuffed toys and the pop-up books being piled away in darkness or carried off somewhere in bin liners.

'I don't know what you think – but Digory mentioned it to me earlier – he said the nursery should become an extra guest room.'

'I'd no idea he was in such a hurry to rid his house of reminders. Maria was surprised to find herself palpitating from anger and dismay.

'I did say I thought you mightn't like it,' said Mrs Rosenberg, embarrassed at finding herself put in such an unwelcome position.

'No doubt that's why he didn't suggest it himself.'

She tried phoning his number in Oxford, so hastily that she had to redial three times. He was unavailable, of course.

Over supper that evening she told him, 'I'd rather the nursery stays as it is. I haven't asked you for much else.' They were alone. Sally's leave was up, and Edmund was in London. Rather than throw away years of preliminary deal-making he'd hired someone else to finish directing his movie. Now it was being edited.

'My dear girl, the change was proposed with your interests at heart. If you're determined to avoid any further pregnancy – and the choice is yours; don't think I don't appreciate that – then it surely can't be good to live with a locked room in the house. Any more that if you'd shut up a part of your own mind.'

'If you think it's such a great idea, why didn't you ask me yourself? And why don't you let me decide what happens to all those things?'

He put down his soup spoon, the better to meet

her eyes. It occured to her that he'd never once said he was sorry. He'd offered his regrets, of course, like everyone else who'd shown up at her bedside while she lay doped into semi-stupor. But his fault? An apology?'

'It was you who said you wanted to look forward instead of lingering among distressing memories.' He started to eat again, glancing up as if to make sure of her silence.

'They're my memories, Digory, far more than yours. And I'm the one to say when I can bear to junk them.'

'No one's asking you to junk anything, for God's sake.'

His quiet impatience stung her. 'Then why am I being chivvied? Told in so many words to act like a grown-up and snap out of it?'

Digory frowned with surprise at hearing his own thoughts so bluntly spoken. 'No one's asking you to snap out of anything. I just think you could make life easier for yourself.'

Maria slammed down her spoon, so hard that the other cutlery jingled. 'How? Go on, tell me. How do I do that?'

'I would have thought that was obvious; by not labouring under a burden of resentment and blame.'

Maria didn't trust herself. She got to her feet, turned towards the door, then turned again, at a loss.

'What are you doing?' His voice was casual but guarded.

'I can't believe what I hear. Resentment? Aren't you going to take that back? Resentment? She gaped at him, terrified of her own anger. It felt like a distant rushing wind about to break every window in that quiet house before tossing away the roof.

Digory didn't flinch. If any sense of guilt was burrowing in him, it only served to make him more obstinate. 'Do sit down, Maria, for God's sake. A woman of your intelligence ought to know you're only proving my case, with every word you say. It's high time you came to terms with your own feelings. If you ask me, the best way you could lighten your emotional load would be to get in touch with Jimmie Zlotnick.' He looked at her coldly, waiting in vain for her expression of shock to clear. 'I realize you mightn't agree with such an idea. But regard it from his point of view. Believe me, if you want to do yourself a favour, as well as him, you couldn't do better than to contact him personally. To reassure him that you bear no ill will.'

All through the house Maria's howl of pain could be heard, together with the crash of something heavy and fragile. Evelyn and Mrs Rosenberg ran in to find her screaming and clawing Digory, resisting any restraint. A quart of cold soup dripped from the silk wallcovering. Maria's language was something no one could have imagined. Digory was visibly relieved once she'd screeched herself hoarse and started weeping instead, staggering about with exhausted sobs.

The doctor was sent for, and Maria sedated.

271

Before she passed out she said to Digory, 'Live a very long time, won't you? It could improve your change of dying as slowly as Sarah might have done.'

At first Edmund thought he'd opened a suicide note. It was the evening after Maria's row with Digory.

'How can I write to you like this?' her letter said. 'Yet how can I bear to stay? The harder I try to recover, the more I pull myself down. Worse, I'm a great weight about your neck, too. I've always known I could cling on to you, but what help have I given you in return . . .'

He burst into Digory's bathroom, where his father had just finished showering.

'What did Maria say to you? Do *you* know where she's gone? When did she leave, for God's sake?'

Digory was towelling his hair, a bath towel wrapped around his waist. In the irrelevant way one does at time of crisis, Edmund registered that his father was still a well-made man; it figured that he was stalked by an extraordinary variety of women.

'What's happened?' Digory paused, noticing Edmund's bewilderment reflected in the mirror. 'Wasn't she in town with you, earlier?'

'She says she's gone!' Edmund brandished the four pages of Maria's letter. 'No' – seeing the expression on his fathers face – 'not for good. But where? And for how long?' He thrust the letter at Digory, then just as impulsively snatched it back. A

272

man didn't get something like this from his wife merely to show it around.

Digory wasn't as worried as he pretended. The girl's accusations last night had been so insulting it was as well Edmund hadn't been there to be embarrassed by them. The most charitable thing one could say was that she must have been hormonally disturbed.

'She says she isn't telling anyone where she's gone.'

Digory avoided looked Edmund in the eye. Though he'd raised the girl himself, it still went without saying that no one would have been good enough for his son. 'Really?' he said, in a sceptical tone.

'Maria wouldn't lie to me,' Edmund said. He was standing in the middle of the room, irresolute.

At the sight of Hollywood's finest at a loss, Digory felt a surge of wounded affection. He also suffered a moment's disloyalty to his own theories. Had he done his son wrong, those years back, by introducing a stranger from the Third World into his home? Surely some other wife could have pulled herself together with less noise and mess than Maria?

'Of course she wouldn't lie,' he said automaticaly. 'But she could be deceiving herself. Consider the facts. She's a woman of extraordinary beauty, among her other assets, for whom things were normally bound to go well. I mean, once she'd become one of our family. How much easier, then,

273

for this particular tragedy to knock her askew. Maria can't know what she's saying. To you or anyone. Any day now, she's bound to be back.'

Digory's impatience with Maria was clear enough. If he was also sexually jealous of his own son, Edmund didn't notice. He was too surprised and irked at hearing his wife criticized.

'You mean you only took Maria in as a show-piece? Is that it? I've disappointed you in marrying her?'

At the sight of his son's angry distress, Digory backed off.

'No – good heavens, no. I was only trying to put myself in her place.'

'I see. Forget I said anything.' Edmund was disillusioned all the same. Right into manhood he'd idolized his father. It disconcerted him that Digory could be unjust in such an ordinary way, like any other parent who thought their darling boy had married beneath him. He left the room, resolved never again to confide in his father about Maria. Even though that did leave no one else on earth. It would be better – safer – if he and Digory could avoid each other for a while. Twenty minutes later Edmund was on the road to London.

Maria's letter went into Edmund's wallet, to be endlessly taken out and re-read, as if by staring at it he could get a clue to where she was, and in what state of mind.

'At least let me be alone,' she had written, 'until I know I shan't shame you or humiliate myself.'

There was no apology for any of the things she'd said to Digory. Edmund guessed that one reason for disappearing was her anger. Maria was possessed by such rage that all she could do was to hide herself away.

Alone in London, he lived for a while like a squatter in a corner of the Chelsea house overlooking the Thames. Now that the movie was edited, he made no effort to do anything but eat, sleep and log on to every address file he had in search of some friend or acquaintance who could help him find Maria. If he'd been an ugly old woman, meanwhile, people might have thought it natural for him to be on his own. But since he was a beautiful young man they felt they had a duty to be supportive. He was invited to dinner in garden rooms in St John's Wood or Hampstead, and parties in converted warehouses overlooking the Pool of London.

Everyone meant him well, but so much talk and laughter was hard to take. Worse, it seemed everywhere he looked his friends were starting a family. Frustrated in his search for Maria, he found himself wanting to flee.

But where should he go, now that he wasn't working? And with no responsibility to anyone, what should he do with himself? Edmund had always dreaded being at a loss, the victim of his own wealth and freedom. He wondered whether to fly to Venice for a few days. On second thougths, such a thing would be unbearable; that was where Maria and he had spent their honeymoon. And since nowhere else attracted him, what was there? In the end he took himself off to their mountain top house in Colorado, with it's view across twenty miles without another building in sight. If other people's company grated, maybe silence and vast space would prove painless.

Once there, Edmund gave up trying. He found himself not shaving; then not washing. Each day he slept later and started drinking earlier, until breakfast came out of the drinks cabinet. One noontide he woke up fully clothed, so thirsty he couldn't believe he'd ever pee again. A fragment of daylight, escaping the drapes, made him feel he was being trepanned.

Was Maria living like this somewhere? He'd half expected to find her here, too.

At first he watched his own downhill progress with curiosity. So this is how such people feel. The ones you try not to stare at on the street. Then, one evening, he noticed something new. He'd been looking for a dropped lighter on the living room floor among the day's litter of empty cans, strewn newspapers, bottles, dirty plates and bits of silver paper with traces of nose candy. His housekeeper was stepping out on the sun deck to sweep it clear of snow. Out of the corner of his eye he saw her share a conspiratorial look with the strong, diminutive old Cheyenne who worked there as gardener and maintenance man. He saw the same thing in both their faces: disdain.

Edmund had been talking to himself. He realized he hadn't the slightest idea what he'd said.

It was one thing to explore the lower depths as a tourist; another to lose your return ticket and get banged up there for life. Where to now?

A few days earlier he'd had an invite to fly to the Coast as a guest of Vince Schwaab, an agent he knew from some way back. Schwaab was a man Edmund might normally have avoided. When introduced at parties he gave everyone ten words in which to prove they were useful before cutting them. His wife, the much-photographed Morgana, lived to postpone their inevitable mega-buck divorce. She planned each year around a bout of cosmetic surgery, sneaked in during a socially dead period when no one was seen much anywhere. But whatever Edmund might have done once, he now seized on their offer as if it were the last airlift from a lost battle zone. Alone on his hilltop he'd understood why people deliberately killed themselves when they didn't really want to die. If you couldn't snuff yourself temporarily, permanent extinction had to do. No matter how, he had to be dragged back to the world of work and effort.

So, as the Schwaabs' Lear jet took off and Pikes Peak became as flat as a dropped snowball, he felt a dogged sense of hope. The little plane nosed about, seeking its trail to the golden West through a sky crowded with people piloting themselves in for the skiing. Edmund wondered where he would have gone, if not LA. Maybe once he was there some project might crop up to interest him. If not, he didn't know what he would do.

'Doesn't he look sincere with a beard?'

At a poolisde barbecue lit with flaming torches, Morgana Schwaab was greeting two hundred of her best friends. Her gown, white, gold and malachite green, made her look like a figure on a carnival float rather than someone for viewing close up. She sported a cleavage fit to make Dolly Parton look like a starveling boy.

No one, but not a soul, was allowed to overlook the fact that she'd got Edmund Adams for a house guest. Seeing her beckon he came over, drink in hand, to be introduced yet again. 'Hi there,' he said dutifully, this time to Lizette Sorenson. She was a once-lovely brunette, immortalized in post-war French films as a nymphette, via serveral movies of the Nouvelle Vague. Recently she'd made a comeback in a TV soap as an indomitable, all-wise matriarch.

'This is Eleanora,' Lizette said. 'My astrologer. Every day she gives me the knowledge I need so that I can relate to the rest of the world.' Eleanora had teased blonde hair. She wore several yards of pink silk chiffon, draped like an opera designer's idea of Boadicea. Edmund reckoned she must be under orders from her cosmetic surgeon never to smile in case the back of her head fell open. 'And this is Robert.' Lizette indicated a tall young man with a too-eager smile. 'He's going into the movies as a lawyer.'

'I really am pleased to meet you sir – I mean, Edmund. Wow, I really am pleased.'

The three of them made an unlikely-looking item, even though it was obvious that they were chauffeured everywhere together.

'Edmund's gotten more good-looking than ever, hasn't he? said Eleanora, as if she knew him personally. 'You know what I think about you?' turning to him. 'Now you're so hot as a director, I'm sure you could get into acting. You could, you know. Micheal Douglas has.'

Emdund smiled politely. 'I'd rather be invisible.'

They laughed as though he'd meant something really funny. Eleanora persisted. 'I'm serious, you know. You should let me read your signs. I'm sure things would turn out good for you that way. You know whose signs I read last year who's a friend of yours? Jimmie Zlotnick. He's here tonight, isn't he?'

'I believe so. We've not seen much of each other in recent years.'

Edmund had deliberately been getting drunk so he could face meeting him. He could still walk and talk; but any minute now, surely he would cease to feel.

Eleonora ignored him. 'Last year at Lizette's house one time, I said to him, Jimmie, I said, you've no need to worry. Your studio *will* make another hit like the last. And do you know what happened?' She looked at Edmund, who obligingly shook his head.

'*Prom Queens IV!*'

Once, he'd found this town hilarious in its awfulness. In the days when he'd been a promising outsider, he'd laughed at it feeling like the only person at a party who hadn't come overdressed. But everyone was clawing at him for something, now that his last movie but one had made him hot. It was true what they said about belonging. It was only a big deal if it hadn't happened to you. And now that everyone did want him on their credits, wher was his zest for movie-making itself? Seeing Zlotnick in the distance, he made an excuse and loped in the opposite direction.

A halfway sympathetic face. It belonged to Jeannie Meredith, a showbiz journalist trying to transform herself into a scripwriter. Life in Hollywood was either boom or bust so most people tried to cover themselves by having two trades.

'It's like riding a pair of circus ponies with a foot on each one,' she told him when he asked after her. 'At least I'm not starting cold, like you did in the mail room of whichever agency it was. Or have you made a point of forgetting that time?'

'Hell, no. It was bad, but it was a laugh. I had to score for the boss, as well as drive his receptionist's piranha to the vet. And what did I know then about dealers?'

'None of that gophering for me, thank God. The other side of the coin is my age is against me.' Jeannie was a daintly middle-aged woman like a small egret, with pretty fair hair. Her nose was the same shape as everyone else's there whose face had been surgically remade. 'I could lie about how old I am, but I've piled up so damn many bylines. Credits, too. The studios hate it if you're not inexperienced enough to boss around.' She adjusted a long silk scarf over one shoulder of her smoking jacket and mimed delighted hellos at three people in succession. 'Now you're one of the elect, tell me it will've been worth the effort.'

Van Dieman's Land, once it was released, looked set at least to consolidate Edmund's reputation. His biggest hit so far had been *Hanging Loose*, a feature about an American Princess running with the Weathermen. Over by the pool in a group that included Zlotnick its praises were being sung at that same moment by Lizette's toy boy, Robert.

'But don't you see? The guy was a groundbreaker with that movie. I know just about everyone's been to see it, sure. I know it's commercial. But the beauty of it is he cut a new path between the genres.'

Until recently Robert had merely been Lizette's hired bodyguard, paying his way through law school. Having accepted her advances, it had gone to his head to find himself among what he thought of as the grown-ups.

'It's not a gangster movie. It's not hippy nostalgia crap. And it's only incidentally a road movie – that's what's so great about it. All those schmoozers who put it into turnaround – they all said he'd fall between genres and hurt himself. And I mean, badly. But then, don't you see' – appealing directly to Zlotnick – 'your buddy and mentor had them fooled.'

281

Zlotnick was looking sleek enough to have worn his suntan at birth, and despite the promotions that had come his way it pleased him less than ever to have a pipsqueak see him as Edmund Adam's side-kick.

'Fair enough,' he said, in a voice that meant no such thing. 'But what you should know is that the studio only let him make it because they wanted old Henry's esteemed niece.' The latest and brightest Fonda, Kathleen, had been the star of *Hanging Loose*. 'Let's face it, what that lady plays in goes.' What Zlotnick didn't mention was that before Kathleen Fonda had shown an interest he too had tried to give Edmund's script the thumbs down.

Meanwhile Edmund was seeking alternative entertainment. Six martinis had left him in need of something different, to fend off sodden depression. The Schwaab's half-acre mansion was the sort of place its inhabitants rarely left, even for deal-making. That meant any best-grade Columbian was probably being tooted upstairs, not in a bathroom or bedroom, but in Vince's vast office.

On the way indoors he was stopped by Harry Verbeeten, a producer who'd turned down one of his earliest submissions ten years before. The idea behind Edmund's script had been the story of Marie Celeste, rewritten as a black comedy on board a nuclear sub.

Harry shook Edmund's hand with both of his, and started in on a speech. It was one that Edmund used to hear almost every day. In each case it could be summerized as, Ride with me, baby, and you'll take me to the top. Not that Harry's version was bad. He'd come a long way by looking and sounding the way Ronald Reagan used to.

'. . . Didn't I always tell you you were great?' he finished by saying.

'Sure,' Edmund replied, by now too fuddled to be cautious with anyone. 'I remember sending you one of my very first outlines.'

'Me too,' lied Harry. 'How could I forget?'

'You don't think,' asked Edmund, inventing wildly, 'it was too risky, setting the entire movie in a Japanese monastery?'

'No, no. It made the whole thing just great.'

'Not even when they said grace over a real panda? Spit-roasted, with the ears left on?'

'Believe me, Edmund, I said to myself at the time, nothing puts posteriors on cinema seats like something new to do with pandas.'

'It wasn't a problem, having every character under a vow of silence?'

'Baby, no one writes purist, dialogue-free material like you can.'

'On the other hand, I wasn't too sure about the parachuting sequence.'

Harry Verbeeten was less of a fool than he acted. This was a conversation he'd had many times. He always ended it with the same line. 'The dream sequence, right? That's the stuff you do better than anyone. Hey – Vince!' Seeing their host, he nobbled him as deftly as a rodeo star cutting out a calf from the herd. 'Great party! Uh – look . . .' And fell to talking some other business, work being the only topic at a bash like this. He was after a script Vince's agency had on offer.

Vince, however, was playing hard to get. 'Of course we're wild for this one; who wouldn't be? But I can't show it to just anyone and his guru.'

Edmund meandered upstairs, morosely intent on stupefying himself. When he came back Vince was still stalling. Suddenly, no doubt as a prearranged signal, he put out his cigar in his realy full glass of Bollinger. At that moment a very beautiful girl nearby, with a cloud of dark hair and superfine features, began to groan. No one within earshot took any notice; Except young Robert.

'Is this an epileptic fit?' he asked Edmund, as the girl's moaning grew louder.

'Nope.' Edmund was finding it hard to take in very much. His face felt as if it had been frozen off. The garden and everyone in it seemed to be tilting, over and over, as if seen from a whirligig. (No, don't think about merry-go-rounds, not even when blasted.) He could barely register how few people were even looking curious at the sight of a woman standing there faking an orgasm. Edmund had heard this ploy of Vince's, but he'd never seen it used before.

'Ain't she something?' Vince was saying to Harry, who was still trying to make him negotiate. 'No – no – this is something you ought to watch.'

'Is she trying to get a part?' asked Robert, in an awed voice.

'Nope.' With a drunk's frown of concentration, Edmund added, 'She's helping Vince do business.'

'No shit!'

'It's his way of saying, I'm made, so why argue? The other thing he does, in his office, is have the cops chuck you out for trespassing.'

'Is she an actress from his agency?'

'Naw, he uses hookers. She'll disappear when she's done this.'

Robert said nothing. He looked like someone awoken by a strange noise; maybe he'd only just noticed the likeness between his role and the girl's. She reached a crescendo, legs apart, toes turned in. Every part of her was raw sinew. The instant she finished she walked away, once more as demure as a beauty queen whose only interest was working with children. There was a spatter of cynical applause.

Before long Edmund wanted to split too if he could only find his suite. The whole party seemed less real every moment, as if in a bubble rising out of his head.

He was delayed by Harry Verbeeten, trying to nail him with yet another deal.

'This outline, I swear, is only for you ... Sure, it's by a first-timer, but so much the fresher – Jeannie Meredith. You know her? Yeah, well, I took one look at it – the outline, I mean, not the broad, sure – and I went, like, this is fantastic. I mean, who can we get to rewrite it? And you know who came into my mind?'

Edmund shook his head, ignoring that Harry didn't want an answer. It made him less dizzy than nodding.

'Believe me, if you took this one on, dealing with my boss isn't half as bad as they say. But then Jimmie Zlotnick's a pal of yours, isn't he? He's a sweet guy. Okay, if you rewrote and directed, there'd be one or two special requirements. Like, you know, I figure he'd think it a real nice gesture from me if I got next year's Silver Shadow written in, so's the studio can let him buy it back as used. But that's only what I guess, you know? That's what I like about the guy; he;'s not pushy in that way, you know what I mean? If there's something he wants, he lets you work it out on your own initiative. I like that . . .'

Quitting the party, Edmund wondered how he'd feel in the morning. Like a mangled polyp, that's what. No harm in that. If you want to forget badly enough, nothing worked like a nice predictable dose of physical pain.

In the hall the hooker was waiting for her cab, perched on a hideous post-modernist chair up-holstered in scarlet and blue leather. Her fee earned, it was bad form for her to stay in view. She didn't sit as if exquisitely made, but like an ordinary woman at the end of a day's work. Edmund found she'd caught his eye.

'If you're lookng for the john —' she began.

'Uh?'

'— he's outside.'

It must have been the oldest wisecrack in her trade. Still she hadn't had to acknowledge him.

'You're being kept waiting,' he slurred. 'Call that justice? I don't. Do you?'

She shook her head, suddenly alert and winsome again. Momentarily, if occured to Edmund that she must have recognized him. 'Fear not,' he said. 'I have all you need.' He fumbled for his car keys, then realized they must be upstairs. 'Correction: I shall have everything you need. Don't move from there. All will be well.' Too drunk even to care that he'd nearly collided with Zlotnick, he set off up the stairs. On the landing he fell, bringing down a horrible free-standing brass lamp like a semi-abstract snake.

Zlotnick had clocked both of them. Summoning the hooker, he turned to Edmund. 'Not hurt, Adams, are we?' he said. 'Not injured, I trust? No mangled metatarsal? No fragmented femur?'

Edmund tried to get up. 'I'm taking this lady home.' He heard himself sounding naff, but could do nothing about it.

'Your gallantry buggers description, mate. However, this time around it is we who are taking you home.'

The inevitable meeting between them had happened. Edmund felt relieved. He let them help him up, his arms across their shoulders. His feet stumbled and dragged.

'Up the marble hill to Bedfordshire,' Zlotnick said, in a voice of cheerful purpose.

They reached Edmund's bedroom. On Zlotnick's instructions the woman undressed Edmund, then herself. Helplessly spreadeagled, Edmund though about what they were going to do. It would have been better if he'd been the type to commit a proper suicide. That way, no problem. As it was he could always kill off bits of himself and see how it felt. Look, no heart. No gall, either. No hard feelings; no spleen. Everyone knew the kidnap wasn't Zlotnick's fault. Besides, think how he must feel.

And since desire was supposed to be the source of all wretchedness, let's kill of a yearning or two.

The death of desire; the death of hope. The death of regret. With luck.

CHAPTER
FIFTEEN

Digory's heart sank. Why here?

He was also relieved. If Maria had been missing much longer, his unease would have turned to desperate worry. He finished saying goodbye to his lunch guest, a fellow-member of the Social Science Research Council, and went into the foyer.

What state would she be in? After an absence of some months, what excruciating surprise was she about to spring on him? Here, of all places.

'Digory! I do hope I haven't inconvenienced you. I asked Michaelis not to give you my message until you were free.'

Maria brushed her cheek against his, giving off a cool perfume. She wore a charcoal suit by Chanel and a coral silk shirt whose stock was fastened with a diamond pin. In the past she'd disdained piercing her ears' but now her earrings were diamonds, too. Her hair, which she'd usually worn loose or in a plaid to her waist, was bound in a flawless chignon. Her shoes and purse looked as if they'd cost most people a second mortgage. Or get them accused of endangering a species.

As she sat down with Digory he was filled with relief at seeing her safely back again – but also with surprise at the change in her appearance. He hadn't known she could look so different. Say what you would, diamonds did suit her.

'We worried about you,' he said, once they'd asked after each other. 'How could we not?' At the warmth in his voice, one or two people looked up. 'Even though you asked us not to track you down.'

'It was an unavoidable interlude,' she said lightly. Then, with the slightest contralto tremor in her voice, 'How is Edmund?'

'Just off to California. Looking for more work, he said.'

'Ah.' Maria looked serious but calm. She really had left her former self behind, full of eggshell-thin bravado in the face of despair. Her health seemed restored, too; nothing in that room matched the brilliancy of her looks. 'That's one of the things I've come to see you about.' She touched him on the arm, a beautiful woman certain of getting whatever she asked. It wasn't just her couture that was un-familiar; her manner had changed as well. 'You must give me Edmund's address, if you would.'

Everything was going to be all right, Digory thought, since Maria was no longer broken and unpredictable. It was only now, when she was an object of admiration again, that he felt free to pity what she'd suffered.

'But of course. What were the other things you wanted to talk about?'

'Thing, not things. One rather important topic, I'm afraid.' She looked away for a moment, like an orchestral soloist concentrating utterly between movements. 'Digory, I know you've been wretched, too.'

'Not compared to you.'

She made a dismissive gesture. Her speech had been rehearsed more times than she could remember. If she wanted to humour Digory, not meaning what she said, her words had to be so familiar that they were mere noises: novocaine for the brain.

'In the past I know I've asked too much. I've made demands that even you couldn't have met. Will you understand if I tell you that I can't bear to think of the awful things I've said and done? May I hope that you'll forgive me?'

As Maria listened to her own speech of self-humiliation, her voice was absolutely steady. The one thing she couldn't do was look him in the eye. In every other way she'd come armoured for ever against hurt.

He took both her hands in his. She really had done an excellent job of pulling herself together. If there was anything else behind what she'd said, Digory didn't notice. 'All I want,' he told her, 'is to see you look happy again.'

291

'Thank you, Digory. I knew you'd understand!'
She spoke with a rush, like someone who couldn't
wait to start her life a second time over. Gone was
the girl whose talk had been full of enthusiasms
and unexpected ideas Maria appeared set on remak-
ing herself, as a poised, determined woman who
would never again say a thing out of place.

But would she succeed? she asked herself privately. She might talk like an accomplished hy-
pocrite, but it was still costing her. Looking about
her, she recalled her first visit to this place, as a
child, new to America. How over — groomed and
compromised those people had looked. And how
well she now fitted in. As Digory helped her into
her ankle-length sable and escorted her out on to
the sidewalk, she steadied herself with the thought
of Edmund. Surely everything would be easier to
bear, once she'd rejoined him.

They waited under the awning outside the main
entrance, her arm in Digory's. A uniformed door-
man held an umbrella to shelter them from a snow-
laden wind; another blew a whistle to hail a taxi.
'Shall we share?' she asked. 'Where are you going?'

'I'm headed for Vermont. And you?', then, noticing that she had no luggage, 'Are you going directly
to California?'

'Why not?' A smile slid across her face – a real
one this time, specially for her.

'Not that I ever saw anyone on the Coast dressed
like you are.' Relieved that she wouldn't make any
more trouble, Digory was almost flippant, for him.

'I can always get something to wear once I'm there.' Shopping normally exasperated Maria, but now even that might be fun. The journey west was going to be like a first date, only infinitely better. This had to be a day that would help salvage her life.

All the way across America Maria kept the plane airborne by force of will. Or so it felt. Her anger at the loss of her children, that primed and loaded weapon, was something she'd figured how to hide. But her need for Edmund was as strong as ever. In the taxi from the airport she couldn't believe the Schwaab's ugly French Renaissance mansion would still be there as she remembered it. Surely it would have been replaced by a new condo. Or a hole in the ground.

But no. The house was there, and the same people were in residence. He was there, too.

'In the guest suite, Mrs Adams,' the butler told her, in the voice of the English Home Counties. 'One moment, if you would.' Unlike a lot of butlers in that part of town, he wasn't a resting actor, but a former headmaster from a private school in the Weald of Kent. He spoke Maria's name into a wall phone, then hung up.

'I understand that you know the way.'

She walked slowly up the stairs, then hesitated. Why wasn't he running to meet her? Maria was so overcome with expectation she didn't think of any ordinary reason, like being in the shower. Was he angry with her? Unforgiving, even? Would she be met with politeness and a hard stare? She broke into a run, along a marble corridor ornamented with a pair of settees of tubular chrome and pale blue suede. If their reunion was going to be unbearable she wanted it over with. At the door to the guest suite she knocked, then fumbled to turn the handle without waiting. Inside, a man's voice called out. He sounded almost unbearably glad.

'Come right in!'

She opened the door.

There was no one there. At least, not in the first room, a sitting area whose walls were hung with leopard skins. On the far side was the open door of a bedroom lined with mirrors. There must have been over a hundred of them. They were ranged at angles, like the facets of a gemstone.

He was waiting for her stark naked, his hair tousled and spiky. From the look he gave her, hands on hips, feet apart, this was one of his life's supreme moments. Certainly Zlotnick had the biggest hard-on he would ever know.

The rest of the daisy-chain briefly went on thrashing like an impaled earthworm. In every fourth mirror a pair of buttocks played peep-bo; in and out of view. There were only three people on the bed, but their reflections were so broken up that they looked like a multitude.

'Together again, by God!' exulted Zlotnick. Excitement made his voice as squeaky as chalk on a blackboard.

Not knowing what had happened, Edmund lifted his head from between the legs of one of the girls. The first thing he saw was his wife's face multiplied thirty times across the wall.

He couldn't believe he was here from choice. This time, Zlotnick hadn't had him seduced; it had been his own idea. The night of the party had seen him hogwhimpering drunk; it had been okay at the time, while he was still nine-tenths helpless, but in retrospect it had been appalling. By mid-afternoon next day, when his hangover was manageable, his memory had recovered, too. There'd been something horrible about finding himself nuzzled and fondled while half-conscious, like a broken-backed mouse being played with by a cat. At the thought of how he'd been used against his will he'd groaned aloud.

There'd been only one thing to do. The same again, but this time on his own initiative, not Zlotnick's.

Now, made foolish by despair, he scanned the wall of mirrors, as if one reflection of Maria's white face might be different – more bearable – than the others.

With the same expression as his, she looked back at one of his mass of images. He was St Sebastian stripped naked and bound, watching the first crossbow bolt being racheted in the bow, tight as the archer's strength could make it.

'What a piece of luck. For you, I mean. I'm sure we could fit you in. Or should I say, vice versa? Too bad Adams and I didn't know you'd be along to join our reunion.'

It took time for Maria to make sense of what Zlotnick said. Much longer to form words of her own. Staring at one of Edmund's shocked mirror-images, she whispered, 'Reunion?'

There was a noise of suppressed glee from Zlotnick. In an instant, her desperation was replaced by rage. It would be a very long time before she could think, Thank God I didn't have a weapon.

For the moment no more words came to her. Maria was twelve again and back on the atoll, a piously raised child with a nonexistent future. Still staring at one of the reflections of Edmund's ghastly face, she pointed at Zlotnick and said the first thing she could.

To everyone else the sounds she made were gibberish. – without realizing it, she had exclaimed aloud in the language of her childhood.

She turned to Zlotnick and repeated herself, in their language, 'They do say the fool returns to his folly, as the dog will always go back to his own vomit.'

She would remember little of what happened as she fled that room, that house, that city. The first detail to impress itself, so she could never quite be rid of it, was at the airport. Opening her handbag she found the catch sticky with what could only be sperm. Zlotnick had come on her.

The red-eye was mercifully unreal, taking her back over distant places she'd only just seen. Four hours since she'd looked down on their house outside Denver, now sunk in darkness on its mountain top. Nine hours since the airliner's shadow had wobbled across the icy surface of Lake Erie, in the other direction. And, as they banked into a clear sunrise over Long Island Sound, eleven hours since she'd left New York. As yesterday, the south end of Manhattan was a jumbled shape against a blindingly bright sea. It was as though she'd never been away.

On the flight up to Vermont, she dozed off. Sleep was no release, however, but a monster from the deep, dragging her down into a muddied, semi-feverish torpor. When the cabin light came on telling passengers to fasten their seat belts, she had to be shaken awake. She looked up at the stewardess in terror, not knowing where she was.

With consciousness came despair. Oh God, she was still alive. Worse, it was the beginning of another day. Maria couldn't believe she might be destined to spend years getting up each morning and dressing herself – for what?

Outside the airport the world was deep in new snow and pure as one's first day in heaven. Sundogs dazzled in a brilliant sky. Maria got into a cab with chains on its wheels and gave directions.

'Ain't no place here goes by that name,' the driver told her.

She struggled to understand. Of course. She'd

given the address of the Schwaab mansion in California.

But what was she doing here, if not reworking the events of the past few hours? On a long, straight road through a forest of pines she was beset by the same fantasies as yesterday. He wouldn't be at the house. A maddening rhyme ran through her head in time to the passing of the roadside telegraph poles. He will be there. He won't be there. He will; he won't. Might Digory have changed destinations at the airport? Or could she have misheard, when he'd said he was coming here?

As before, her fears were wrong. Digory was not only at home but upstairs in his room, having breakfast. She burst in without knocking.

'My dear girl! What on earth is the matter?'

He was mildly surprised at her clothes; she was still wearing the high-fashion-victim jewellery and silks of yesterday lunchtime. But the sight of Maria herself astonished him. With her hollow eyes and tumbled hair, she was changed utterly.

'Why didn't you go? Did you phone Edmund instead? Has he said something untoward – is that it?'

She shook her head, the grief rising in her anew.

'Have you had a falling out? Is there something I can do – something I can say to him – to make everything well again?'

'Oh, Digory! I did go! I've been all the way there and back.' She wept bitterly at last, clinging to him.

In all the world, who owed her the comfort of an embrace, if not her own father?

He held her very close, shushing her. She felt as if she'd be fractured by her own sobs.

A less experienced man might have been panicked by her tears. Digory was merely filled with anxious wonderment. He found tenderness rushing in on him, too. Even at the worst times, he'd rarely seen Maria like this; she'd usually been too proud. He sensed too that this time she wasn't going to make any inconvenient demand. Holding her head against his unshaven cheek, at length he said, 'Tell me what it is, if you like. Is it something I can put right for you?'

Maria could only break into fresh sobs. She barely managed to speak. 'No. Oh, no. Digory, help me! He's gone. He's lost. For ever!'

'What?' Seizing her by the arms, he looked in her face for an explanation. 'There hasn't been an accident?'

'Oh – no; no. We've separated. For always.'

'You can't be sure of that.' Digory was helpless with surprise. On his account, however, not hers. Good God, what was he doing with an erection at a time like this?

'I am, I am. Oh, Digory, I am. I can't bear it! Help me!' She was beseeching. 'Say you will. Please!'

'Of course I will.' He managed to keep his voice ordinary, even as she went down on her knees. Was he right? About what was going to happen? It was costing him the utmost in self-deception to pretend to himself that he didn't know. As she undid his robe and pulled it open, his face went blank with astonishment. At what she was about to do? Or because he hadn't stopped her?

By God, part of him was thinking, he'd been waiting for this long enough. No, no, another part said. He'd never imagined this; truly he hadn't. Not once, not even that time he'd caught sight of her as a child beggar with the Pacific wind sliding about them like a dry sea. That day when, in a single moment, he'd resolved to shape her as his own.

Believe it's not happening. There was still time. If it happened, quickly – now – right now – couldn't he still think he'd been caught unawares? ... Couldn't he?

As soon as she took him into her mouth, he forgot everything. Even as time began to spool senselessly out of him, he clung only to this endless instant. There was vacancy: he felt nothing; he thought nothing. No – wrong – a corner of his mind survived what they were doing. Tarry a while. Just one thing. An act like this . . . If he was confounding himself, it should have been his doing, not hers. What was a man if he only damned himself on someone else's initiative . . .?

Beneath his hands her head was silky and warm. He was standing above her in a parody of a priestly blessing, straining towards an ending he couldn't endure. The little depth became a thought, than everything as it bore down on him. At last it tore through him, leaving him as shaken as if he'd been in free fall.

Maria rose to her feet, still quivering from her bout of weeping. She ventured to meet his eyes. In his handsome face there was neither relief nor doubt. All he showed was shock; he looked unlike anything she'd ever seen. Even in the room lined with mirrors, now three thousand miles at her back.

She knew what was in his mind. He couldn't believe he'd done something so out of keeping with his public image, as a man without ordinary weakness. So much the better. She hadn't thought she was on her way to seduce him – she'd had no idea what it was she'd wanted. But now that it had happened, he was hers at last. If he wouldn't love her as a father, let him fear her power as a mistress.

And because they'd dared what they shouldn't, there was something else. He had to know there'd be more.

So did she.

Part III

CHAPTER
SIXTEEN

As the seasons revolved, Sarah Adams's disappearance and its aftermath left several objects behind.

The police file stayed open; it always does in such cases. Other items were either done away with or kept out of sight.

One of them was a letter from Maria to Edmund. 'Please don't write to me again. I couldn't bear it. If you must know how it is with me, I hope I never again lie down with a man I could love . . .' It was dated three months after their encounter in LA and postmarked Sydney. By then Maria had once again perfected her impersonation of a woman whom nothing could harm. She'd gone to Australia on business; in order to further her career as an art dealer she was setting up yet another new gallery. As an artist, she'd died with Sarah's disappearance. But as a saleswoman of others' work she was doing extraordinarily well. By coincidence, she'd travelled with Digory, who seemed to have reasons of his own for flying there.

Maria's letter was put away in an unmarked folder and stored in the office that took up the top floor of the riverside house in Chelsea. It was from this base that Edmund was setting up the first world-wide information system to help parents of missing children. In his own mind his wife's letter was also labelled Unfinished Business.

One document was carefully destroyed: a letter from Maria's gynaecologist, postmarked eighteen months later. To all appearances it was harmless, saying only that she was due for her annual check-up. Yet, not content with screwing it up, she set a match to it in a bedroom fireplace at the Rectory.

Thrust hastily out of sight, a copy of the satirical magazine *Quirk* announced that Digory must be having it away with someone else's wife. He had been seen sneaking back to his own suite in the small hours, at the George V Hotel in Paris. For the space of an evening it lay hidden among papers to do with his own Sarah Adams Memorial Fund, directed against poverty among children. Edmund had dropped in on him at his rooms in college, and somehow Digory was anxious for his son not to read about him.

Sealed in a dark place were several things Maris wanted to keep but not see. Over another three years her bank stored away every meaningless scrawl Sarah had done, as she'd tried to imitate a grown-up making a drawing. In the same vault lay

306

every sketch, photograph or painting Maria had made of her daughter, together with all the letters she'd ever received from Edmund.

Hidden more thoroughly than any of these were Maria's dealings with a certain bank in Liechtenstein. Zurich was all very well; but for handling seven-figure sums with discretion, the Duchy's banking system had the edge.

Things out of sight, destroyed or lost. But every one of them standing for something that would come alive in the end. This year, next year, sometime. Meanwhile Zlotnick had jetted back to England, obsessed with having himself knighted.

'So what's this doing here?'

Zlotnick was at his desk, seated on a tall swivel chair the size of a throne. Below him were the twenty other floors of Allied Consortia's British headquarters in Threadneedle Street. The windows of his office overlooked five million people, from the Thames estuary looping past the Isle of Dogs across the hazy Surrey uplands to the profile of Windsor Castle, twenty miles west.

From such a lofty point of view he wasn't to seeing things like the one on his desk.

Lalage didn't bother to give him a direct answer. 'You'd better look at it.' One of the reasons she'd been hired was because she sounded too superior to give a damn.

Zlotnick ignored everything else put out that morning for his attention. With a look of finicky

307

distaste he picked up a thin, grainy-textured copy of *Quirk* magazine.

'Well, hello again,' wrote their reporter 'Ratflack', of the Shitty Shitty Big Bang column on alleged City scandals.

> And now for something completely out of date. The about-to-be-terminated marriage of Allied Consortia's Chairman, laughing Jimmie Zlotnick, is such ancient news that no one from the Square Mile has even heard of it. The lady now departing from the life of our Jim is lissom former Filipino Mercedes Chavas. Despite evidence that the Zlotnick finances are not notably deficient, Mrs Z. leads an underfunded existence as an operative in an electronics factory in Swansea.
>
> How, we ask ourselves, has this alliance with the house of Zlotnick gone so long ignored? Our readers may not be a lightyear off target if they suspect a connection with jolly Jim's pursuit of the luscious Ginevra Devine, New York publishing's fairest, and daughter to the Republican Party's Senator of that ilk. Can it be that Ms Devine's charms take yet more lustre from the rumour that Daddy could be the party's next Vice-Presidential candidate? Watch this space in Jimmie's life.

'Fitchett and Maule,' ordered Zlotnick in quiet voice. They were the firm of lawyers his group's news-papers used in cases of libel. 'On the direct line.'

'Edward Fitchett's out of town,' Lalage said.

'I want him.'

'On Mustique.'

'Andrew Maule, then.'

'Ginevra will be pissed off, if it snowballs.'

'It's nothing to do with that end of things.'

Next door Crispin was eavesdropping. As Lalage came back in he remarked, 'I'd've thought it had everything to do with *la belle Devine sans merci*. Sure as hell I didn't know he'd been married. Not even,' lowering his voice, 'way back on the wrong side of the tracks.'

'Nor did I.'

Neither did Zlotnick.

'I want a retraction,' he announced on the phone to Andrew Maule. He spoke with the controlled annoyance of a busy man, whose attention shouldn't be making even a moment's detour past something so absurd.

'We assume, in that case,' came Maule's voice, 'that you're supported by documentation?'

'Good God,' Zlotnick exclaimed, 'do you think I'd waste even a day in court if I didn't know whether I'd been married?' And put the receiver down with the briefest farewell he could get away with. He knew better than to take up the time of the most expensive lawyer in Lincoln's Inn.

Unexpectedly, Zlotnick was forced to visit Maule's chambers in person. For discretion's sake, he wanted as few people as possible to know about their meeting. That afternoon he found himself walking into the traffic-free square overlooked by Fitchett and Maule's seventeenth-century premises at an impatient five miles an hour. Lalage accompanied him to carry his briefcase. Even when wanting to be invisible, Zlotnick didn't like to appear completely unimportant. Looking neither to right nor left, they scurried along, like police officers out to make a discreet arrest in a public place.

Andrew Maule received them in his white-panelled room on the first floor, with its view of the tennis court and trees of Lincoln's Inn Fields. Scanning Maule's desk, the first thing Zlotnick saw was the compromising letter he'd sent here this morning by courier. With a document as dodgy as this, he hadn't dared use anything as public as a Fax machine.

'Following receipt of this new document,' said Maule, 'I'm glad to say we've been able to open a new line of inquiry.' He was a youngish man with smooth hair and a high colour, rounded out by good living to look older than he was. 'I mean, of course, the letter from the solicitors representing the lady who styles herself your wife.'

As if to mark a new paragraph in what he was saying, he paused to bring another paper to the top of the pile on his desk. Through a window left open to admit the mild air of a greenhouse winter, the plop of tennis balls could be heard from the courts below.

Zlotnick waited, pulsating with frustration. Why

310

did a balls-up like this have to happen now? In a few weeks' time it wouldn't have mattered if he'd got his gong.

'I have to say,' Maule remarked, 'that it's the first time a case like this has come our way, though there are precedents.'

'Never mind the precedents. What about me?'

'Well, normally – if one can use such term as "normal" in these circumstances – the divorce, so-called, need never involve the party placed as you are now.'

'And how am I placed?' Zlotnick struggled to seem patient. He knew Andrew Maule never came straight to the point. Anxiously he reviewed Maule's connections with the Cabinet Ceremonial Office. Like anyone whose only talent was making contacts, Zlotnick carried a directory of such things in his head. Maule's partner's uncle was on the committee there who made recommendations for knightshoods, and two fellow-members had been at Marlborough with cousins of Edward Fitchett.

That was what he hated about England. All sewn up. It was for that reason that he wanted his K so badly. Get full citizenship in this country, and you were safe to despize anyone, anywhere.

Maule steepled his fingers. It wasn't a suitable gesture for a man with pudgy hands. On the evidence available to us, we can rest assured of your bachelor status. Independently, I mean, of your own assurances.'

Lalage, sitting in a far corner, could read Zlotnick's thoughts from behind. It wouldn't come cheap, being told any of this. Even if it was something he already knew.

'You may be flattered to learn that the lady has taken her time in dispensing with your name. It's four years now since she became registered as the wife of someone, shall we say' – he paused, turning over a piece of paper before him – 'not only with your name, but with your address and your date and place of birth.'

Zlotnick stared. Not at Maule so much as through him. His mind was running desperately in several directions at once. It wasn't the legal aspect of the case that troubled him, but the risk of publicity. Mindful of Maule's Downing Street contacts, he spoke as lightly as he could.

'Good newspaper copy, then.'

'I'd rather leave that to your judgement, professionally speaking. But you should have no problem getting a retraction from any paper that's printed this story so far.'

'This,' meaning the item in *Quirk*, 'is all there's been. I'd know otherwise.' Zlotnick spoke as much in hope as from certainty.

'Yes, well, I'd defer to you in judging public demand for a story of this kind.'

'What grounds would they claim for printing this?'

'Why, that they'd been deliberately deceived. Your name has evidently been used unlawfully, for the purpose of naturalization by marriage. It's one

312

more aspect of the trade in names and addresses, carried on without the consent of the people whose particulars are being sold. Most buyers – mail order firms and so forth – tend to be within the law. Only occasionally does a case like yours come to light.'

Zlotnick's closed face hid a riot of feelings. Revulsion, mainly. He had a manipulator's dread of being fingered without his knowledge or consent.

'Who did this? Is it someone I know?'

'We have particulars, if you'd like to see them.' Maule pushed another piece of paper across his desk. Among other information it bore the name Ferdinand Thwaite and an address in Bristol. Neither meant anything to Zlotnick, who said so.

'I thought as much. It's not usual, in such cases, for the perpetrator to be known to his victim.' Maule adjusted the documents already tidily laid out on his desk. 'We are prepared, if you like, to continue to act for you in this matter, both to obtain a retraction from *Quirk* magazine and to prosecute this Thwaite person.'

Now that Zlotnick's involvement seemed a mere accident, the last thing he wanted was a public proceeding. Not when the whole matter could be laid to rest. He got briskly to his feet and gave a smile of geniality bright enough to harm one's eyes.

'By all means let's do business with the people at *Quirk*' Behind him, Lalage also made ready to leave.

'Fair enough.' Maule shook hands over his desk. 'They can hardly withold a public retraction. Printed, dare I say, as large as you like.'

'Good Lord, no,' Zlotnick replied. It was half killing him, trying not to look as relieved as he felt. 'Who are we to shame such a valiant band of honest hacks? To give stick to any remaining practitioners of free speech in this once great country of ours? A private apology will be ample.'

'And Thawaite?'

Zlotnick waved his hand dismissively. Maule should understand that he was too generous a man to follow up such a small matter.

Afterwards, in private conversation with his partner, Andrew Maule asked, 'About Jimmie Zlotnick – remind me. Is one expected to know about that yacht of his?'

'The *Dominique*? The one that blew up?'

'Right.'

'No, No one is.'

'That's good. I was damned if I could remember whether one was supposed to commiserate.'

'Bit of a coincidence. What with this naturalization thing.'

'Is that what people say?'

'Certainly.'

'All of them or just a few?'

'Let's say, most of them.'

CHAPTER
SEVENTEEN

Bryan Hoskins, manager of Maria's London gallery, pushed open the heavy glass door of his workplace in Cork Street. He braced himself to seem pleased at the sight of Antonia, his subordinate and temporary replacement. She was almost beautiful to be true: long arms and legs, with dark hair sleek as a seal's. Inevitably, at nine on a Monday, she was already on the phone to one of her numberless Sloanie friends.

'Oh, spit. How frightfully dreary of you. I mean, we'll just have to talk again.'

'Anything exciting happen?' Pointedly Bryan raised his voice above hers.

Antonia swivelled her eyes across him without interrupting her conversation. She hadn't been his choice, and she didn't bother to hide her opinion of him as an irksome trog. Not only did he have a face like a pug and a scalp that looked as if he'd barbered it with a pair of horse clippers, but he gave instructions without the least sign of apology.

'Look, there's something here I've got to cope with,' she said into the phone, glaring at Bryan to show she meant him. 'Yah ... *Ciao.*' Turning to face him she announced, 'Not a thing.' What did you expect, anyway? her manner said.

He couldn't think why Maria had been so insistent on hiring the girl. Usually she chose each employee with the care she put into locating a new gallery. It was one reason why Bryan was still here in his thirties instead of striking out more boldly on his own, as a sculptor and critic. Few jobs offered both a decent salary and a workplace where everything ran as if newly oiled; he'd let himself be seduced.

On the way through to his office he noticed a new space on the wall.

'So the Arthur Boyd was sold?'

'What?'

'The drawing by Arthur Boyd,' indicating where something had been taken down.

'Oh, yah.'

'Why hasn't it been replaced?' He paused to glance at the label screwed to the wall. 'And what on earth is this about?'

'It was replaced. And there's nothing wrong with the label as far as I can see.'

Bryan stooped to read more closely. What was this?' '"Tohotaua at the spring"? "Paul Gauguin" ...?' He stood up sharply. 'But – my God, if we had something as valuable as this on our premises, do you think I wouldn't have known? What did replace the Boyd? And where is it now?'

'Oh, it was a real Gauguin. The man who collected it for the owner said so.'

Bryan stared at her in disbelief. The girl's interview had been a formality, he recalled. Antonia had assured him and Maria that the Post-Impressionists were really, really all right; also that lots of her friends would never think of working in any part of town but Mayfair. Afterwards Maria had murmured something about her being a goddaughter of Elizabeth Adams. 'My mother would have wanted me to give her a job,' she'd said, as if that justified everything.

'What man?' His whole body tightened in dismay.

'It's perfectly okay, you know. The owner rang personally, in advance. I suppose you imagine all art thieves do that.'

'It has been known.' He stormed into his office, wondering how sorry Maria would be if he got on with the rest of his life right now and resigned. Returning, he thrust a large opened book at Antonia. 'This?' He pointed at one of the illustrations. It showed a naked woman sitting with her feet in a pool, combing out her hair. The pool was overarched by a tree with tentacle-like branches whose shape was reflected in the swelling contours of the ground beneath and the limbs of the woman. Her hair seemed blown by a wind that left everything

317

else still. In the background, half-seen, a horse had lowered its head to drink.

Antonia gave it a glance. The first hint of defensiveness showed on her face. 'It could be.'

'So where's our record of it?'

'How should I know, if no one bothers to tell me about these things?'

'For God's sake! Maria must have told you.'

'Must she?'

'Yes, she damn well must. Especially if she gave you authority to take charge of something like this.' He slammed the book shut.

'Actually, she said nothing.'

'You mean you didn't call her when the Boyd was sold? As I'd instructed you?'

'Of course I called her.' Antonia was openly relieved at having an excuse to look hard done by. 'But it's hardly my fault if she didn't say anything about the bloody old paperwork.'

Bryan glared at her. 'Okay, just tell me: was it on Maria's say-so that the Gauguin went up on the wall?'

'Well, what do you imagine? I phone Maria, okay? She gave me the combination for the safe; then she told me to put the cheque in there and take out the new picture.'

'She must have said something else.'

'Actually, she did. She said she had every confidence in me. And she told me I was doing an excellent job.'

Behind a locked front door and lowered blinds they were joined by a member of Scotland Yard's Fine Art and Antiques Squad. Maria was there, too, just off a flight from Houston. She'd been in Dallas for the opening of an exhibition of nineteenth-century regional painters.

'I'm so sorry about this,' she said more than once to the man from the Yard, whose name was Gascoigne. 'Quite honestly, I've never had anything stolen before. I really am terribly sorry.' She looked jet-lagged.

Gascoigne seemed unfazed by what Bryan himself considered a monumental balls-up. 'So let's see who else has lost out,' he said conversationally while Maria was fetching the file he wanted. He was leafing through the catalogue raisonné that Bryan had earlier thrust at Antonia: sixty quids' worth of an Italian printer's finest wrapped around in the fierce deep colours of Gauguin's Tahitian period. 'You say this is your only photograph of the missing item?'

'So it seems,' Bryan confessed. He and Gascoigne were waiting around while Maria, helped by Antonia, were rummaging in the next room. Maria could be heard sighing with frustration as drawers were emptied and cupboards made untidy. Maybe she was as flaked as she sounded.

'I see this wasn't published this year.' Gascoigne looked like a backwoods landowner up in town for the day. Ultimate pinstripes and heavy cufflinks, with a furled umbrella and a short military moustache. Bryan wondered if chasing stolen artworks was his way of being a collector.

319

'Yes, but Maria says the entry we want is up to date.'

'Acknowledgements, then.' Holding the catalogue, Gascoigne adjusted its weight as he turned from the copyright page to the endmatter, which included current owners of Gauguin's work. He was about to read the entry there aloud, then thought better of it. Bryan reckoned he knew why.

'Has the owner been contacted personally?'

'Not yet. It was one of his PAs who confirmed that he'd never sent anyone here for the picture.' Looking over Gascoigne's elbow, Bryan wore the same ambiguous frown. The entry before them read, 'Tohotaua at the spring, Paul Gauguin, 1903, pencil, 21 × 30 cm. Collection of James Zlotnick, London.'

Without Maria there was little they could do meanwhile, except hang about. Gascoigne glanced around him at some of the other exhibits, then remarked, 'I gather you and your wife have just had three weeks in northern India.'

Bryan tried not to sound moodily ungracious. 'I'm glad I didn't know I was coming back to this.'

'I was up that way last April. Srinagar. Lake Dal. Fortunately those Mughal gardens are still worth seeing, if one's there at this time of year, don't you find? In summer the fountains and canals tend to be dead; they divert too much of the water into the rice fields. Of course the site at Achabal's okay the whole year round – Ah, Mrs Adams.'

Maria had come back, with an untidy file Bryan

320

had never seen before. 'I'm terribly sorry. I hadn't expected to keep you waiting like this. The fact is, our filing system is due for an overhaul, but I've been too busy to look into the merits of different databases.' She put down the file in front of Gascoigne with a vague air of apology. Behind her, Antonia looked lost and resentful at being upstaged by circumstances.

'I do hope what you need is there.' Maria peered anxiously at what she'd produced. Without comment, Gascoigne picked up a letter from Zlotnick saying that payment for the Gauguin was enclosed. It was dated three years back.

'If only I could get the knack of sleeping on aeroplanes. I'm sure it would help me cope better at times like this.'

Gascoigne went on looking through the file. Presumably he thought the politest thing he could do was to ignore Maria's distracted waffling.

Bryan observed her with surprise. Was this the first sign that she'd spread her empire too far? The Cork Street gallery was now one of over a dozen like it, world wide. In the last month alone she'd opened premises in Dusseldorf and Toronto. Maybe he wouldn't resign. If it wasn't too ignoble, perhaps he should take advantage of this crisis and hold her up for more control of the gallery, plus a thumping rise and the title of director.

Gascoigne turned the pages of the file, pausing frequently. His look of blandness faded to be replaced with incredulity. 'Is this what your client really paid?'

'I know; the price was surprising. But the previous owner simply told me he didn't want Mr Zlotnick to pay more than that.'

Passing the document back from Maria to Gascoigne, Bryan sneaked a look. All this had taken place before he'd joined the gallery. What he saw shook him. The sum paid by Zlotnick was a fifth of the picture's likely price at auction.

'Didn't you feel cheated,' Gascoigne asked Maria, 'if your client did you out of – what? – thirty thousand pounds' commission?'

Maria shrugged and gave an awkward smile, as if some answer might yet occur to her.

Gascoigne continued examining the file's contents. At length, still riffling, he said, 'There's no documentation here of the insurance. May I trouble you for a look at it?'

'Oh, I'm sure it must be there somewhere. If we'd put it anywhere else, Antonia and I would have found it.'

'I assure you, it's not here.'

Bryan was amazed at how mildly Gascoigne spoke, given the appalling possibility that suggested itself.

'Antonia,' Maria said, 'when you insured the Gauguin, did you file the papers somewhere else?'

'Me? Nobody asked me to handle any insurance. *Did* you, Bryan?' she asked, in her sweetest voice.

'Leave Bryan out of this,' commanded Maria, suddenly brisk. 'I'm terribly sorry,' she told Gascoigne. 'Worse than that, I'm embarrassed. I can't

322

believe that someone here hasn't insured the wretched picture.'

'I take it you know who'd be liable.' Gascoigne spoke with resigned politeness. In the unreal world of high art and the people who could afford it, he met this kind of incompetence more often than one might think.

'I'm afraid I do.' Maria looked pensive.

Thank God I'm covered, Bryan was thinking. All the same, his heart was going like a trip-hammer at the thought of how much money had been lost. He had to remind himself that for someone as rich as Maria even a blow like this couldn't count for much.

'There is just one thing,' she added, with a self-conscious laugh. 'Jimmie Zlotnick will be so satirical if I have to refund him the full value. I know he can't bear people who don't know how to organize their affairs. That does make me rather miserable.'

In his line of work Gascoigne was used to people taking their losses calmly. Put in Zlotnick's position, most of them couldn't wait to spend the insurance money. A stolen Hepplewhite chair would be cheerfully transformed into a modernized farmhouse in the Cevennes; an absconded piece of Meissen would become a month's charter of a boat in the Indian Ocean. A lot of them hadn't a clue about the value of what they owned anyway. Last week he'd had dealings with a widow living behind Harrods who'd been using a first-edition Audubon as a door-stop.

But Zlotnick was someone he couldn't figure.

The money paid out to him had evidently left him cold. Not so surprising, perhaps, for a man with a finger in so many pies. But there was something else.

'I suppose I'll, uh, give it to some worthy charity. You don't care to make a recommendation, do you?'

Zlotnick's mind was clearly busy elsewhere. Gascoigne had already noted that the man was concerned to avoid publicity. Instead of seeing him in the office suite above Threadneedle Street, Zlotnick had gone to the trouble of a meeting in his newly leased flat in Belgrave Square. In the overdraped drawing room they were each trying not to sink too far into an oversized sofa, like a couple of stage hands taking a break on a magnificent film set.

'Most registered charities are deserving, as far as I can tell. Drug rehabilitation gets less than most.'

Anyone would think Zlotnick wasn't clean. But the picture was quite lawfully his; no doubt on that score. The previous owners had been kosher, too. Gascoigne had recognized their names immediately. They were a married couple who mostly lived in Connecticut and who were among several of Maria Adams's clients with a taste for anonymity.

The picture wasn't a fake. And Maria's cheque to Zlotnick, for nine hundred grand, had also been the real thing.

So why was he behaving as though the money was hot?

'The poor old cokeheads, then,' said Zlotnick. His own dealer had been carefully phased out of his life some time ago. 'God knows, neither you nor I would care to live with a miniature improvised nappy shoved up each runny nostril.'

Zlotnick's real feelings had him torn in half. Maria had guessed right. The money mightn't mean very much to either of them; but to Zlotnick her own humiliation meant a very great deal indeed.

How he would have gloated. Normally, that was.

For of course he'd never owned a Gauguin. It was one thing to possess an ocean-going yacht or two without noticing them. But not a unique object like this. He never bought pictures, anyway; not seriously. The room where they sat now was newly furnished by a firm of designers who fixed everything, down to the silver-plated basket of glass grapes that dominated a vast side table varnished slick as ice.

For several days, ever since the article by those *Quirk* people, a seed of doubt had been swelling in his mind. Now it exploded into hideous full bloom.

He was being set up. Yes, but by whom? He'd humbled any number of employees in front of their subordinates, and robbed nearly as many of their pension. But he never shafted anyone whose helplessness didn't invite it. And it was unthinkable, to a man like Zlotnick, that anyone could harass him – him! – who had the taint of the victim themselves. Besides, what enemy could he have in common with Adams's wife?

325

Watching him, Gascoigne said, 'In the short term you may prefer to keep the money. I don't want to boast, but it's not impossible that the picture will be found.'

'What, er, measures do your people recommend, to track down such a thing?' All Zlotnick could really think of was getting this latest incident forgotten as quietly as possible.

'When something like this goes missing, there are several computerized indexes that could register it for you. *Search* magazine could offer you a good service; they've got a circulation list of at least two thousand, including, dare I say, most of the more circumspect receivers and informers.'

'Uh, right. If that doesn't work, how else might it turn up?'

'If the picture's been taken by amateurs, it could be found anywhere. Quite a few of them panic when they find they don't know what they're doing. We got a Rembrandt back once after it had been left in the Strand on one of those open-topped tourist buses. That one made headlines on both sides of the Atlantic. It was a family from Wisconsin who found it.'

'Priceless!' exclaimed Zlotnick with a dutiful smile. 'Look, um, seriously, I don't have too much time to spare on this. I have to say I'm not too keen on publicity either.' He tried looking jocose. 'An occupational disease among those of us who own the kind of goodies we're talking about.'

Gascoigne understood. He mightn't have worked

out what it was that Zlotnick was hiding from him. But the paranoia of rich collectors, however, was something he knew more about than most. 'That shouldn't be a problem. I'm not taking your loss lightly but there's really nothing special about it. I mean, except to you and Mrs Adams.'

'IT'S A PIC-NICK!' declared the *Daily Post*. Below, a lesser headline announced, 'Unknown thugs snatch million-pound art haul from heartbreak baby Sarah's grieving mum.'

> Disaster struck again for sexy multi-millionairess Maria Adams yesterday after thieves were found to have raided her exclusive picture gallery in Mayfair's Cork Street, haunt of big-time art lovers. A man posing as a friend of the owner made his getaway with this saucy picture by tearaway French artist Paul Gauguin – worth just ONE MILLION POUNDS. Some friend!
>
> Despair, too, for the picture's owner, reclusive media tycoon James Zlotnick, today mourning privately at his swanky Belgravia home for the masterpiece that meant so much to him.
>
> Tragedy has struck once before, in the lives of gorgeous Polynesian-born Maria and her husband, movie director Edmund Adams, whose films include *Hanging Loose*, starring movie legend Kathleen Fonda. A longed-for

visit to the fair turned to horror, five years back, when their daughter, baby Sarah, disappeared.

Interviewed in her luxury Chelsea home last night, Maria, 32, smiled bravely as she declared, 'I can't thank the *Daily Post* enough for coming over and letting the world know what a nightmare I'm living through. They have been brilliant. I just don't know what I'd have done without them.'

And apart from that?

Says Maria, 'There's only one thing I can say, isn't there? *Oh dear!*'

A photograph, some years out of date, showed Maria arriving with Edmund at a film premiere.

Everyone had run the story; the *Daily Post*'s article was the shortest there was. Most papers contrasted the missing sketch with a remarkably similar photograph of Maria. Bare-shouldered and barefoot, she was wearing a skimpy length of tropical-looking cotton. Her hair streamed loose. In every case the caption flogged her own South Seas connection to death and back again.

Several people were interested enough to read every version of the story that they could find. Alone on his mountain top in Colorado, Edmund marvelled that Maria should have agreed to such a corny piece of publicity. Her pose was as graceful as the girl's in the missing sketch, but everything else about her had been adjusted for the press. For God's

328

sake, she even had a white hibiscus tucked behind one ear. Her hair had been lacquered and tweaked, so that a strand fell seductively over one eye. Her garment was patterned with splashy white flowers, which looked striking enough in a grainy black-and-white photo. In the flesh it probably looked thoroughly tawdry. God alone knew what his wife's motive had been, but he had to admire her professionalism as a photographic subject.

Andrew Maule had also taken every paper the day the story was carried. As Zlotnick's solicitor, he couldn't help being embarrassed, over lunch that day, to hear how his client's name was being put about.

'There's nothing illegal about being undercharged,' announced his host at the Garrick. 'Even for a Gauguin as late as this one.'

Maule was being lunched by Max Blum, publisher-about-town, whose firm retained him as their libel lawyer.

'If it were,' Blum added, 'God help the book-buying public. Speaking as one of those who live to do what we can for the cause of good writing.' Blum's pomposity was legendary; some said he'd been in his twenties when he'd first begun pitching for the role of publishing's elder statesman. Others were only half in jest when they claimed his hair wasn't really white, but dyed that colour to point up a likeness to the elder Einstein.

'Even so,' remarked the feature writer making up the third of their party, 'someone will want to be seen investigating something now.' Unlike the Fleet Street stereotype, Kenneth Donaghue wasn't a grubby sot, but a neat, anonymous man from the lower reaches of a multinational conglomerate. 'Not the police, of course, but doesn't Zlotnick have hopes of this Honours List?'

Maule could hardly pretend to take no interest. He said, 'If he does, and he's right, they'd be looking into his finances anyway.'

'Ah!' Blum intoned. 'But may I turn your attention to the issue of the detonated yacht.' He always spoke as if chairing a meeting. Donaghue was there to discuss sub-rights in an important but boring political memoir. Maule suspected he himself had been invited because Max Blum couldn't bear to address fewer than two people.

Donaghue said, 'It's not against the law to be unlucky, either. The word among Zlotnick's own troops is that someone must have bombed the wrong boat.'

Loyal fellows, thought Maule, looking up from his langoustine bisque.

'Mere ill fortune may not be unlawful in itself,' announced Blum. 'That much I will concede. But it doesn't help when you're stalking a knighthood.'

Blum should know, Maule told himself. Next year, so the rumour went, it would be the publishing industry's turn for someone, but only one, to get his knighthood. For nearly a decade dear old Max – the windy bastard – had been jockeying to head the shortlist.

'Allow me to remind you what Dickens had to say.' Blum squared his shoulders, as if about to quote words of his own. '"Surely you know that all the greatest ornaments of England in knowledge, imagination, active humanity and improvement of every sort, are added to its nobility. This is the reason why titles will always last in the land!" Fine words, as I don't doubt you'll agree. But there's nothing there about being unfortunate.'

Three miles east of the Garrick, Dominique too was about to find Zlotnick interesting. At the moment that the wine waiter prepared to pour half an inch of Muscadet, estate-bottled by the proprietor, for Blum to taste, she was getting off a bus into the heavy traffic of Old Common Road on the border of Hackney and Bethnal Green. A copy of the *Sun* was wedged into her carrier, with an assortment of what she thought of as shopping. Nothing in her bag was chosen; it had all been picked up as the nearest thing to hand when no one else was looking. From a wholefood store in Islington she'd got a jar of Lark Rise fig and rhubarb compote, two lavender bags and a lone croissant. A supermarket in Holloway had yielded alphabet-shaped potato croquettes, a packet of dried beans and a furry blue elephant that nodded its head when you wound it up. Dominique had also been able to cram some liver into her pocket, where it sloshed bloodily about in its heat-sealed packet. Near the check-out – just for a laugh, there'd been so many people who could've noticed if they hadn't been so stupid – she'd nicked a book of nursery rhymes.

She walked down the exhaust – filled street towards the house where she was staying. Old Common Road was as pocky and made-over as anywhere in England. A used car lot, all plastic bunting stood on three sides of a Regency villa stripped of its portico and ironwork, like a former beauty without eyelashes or teeth. The street crossed a railway cutting, its banks a grey slurry of rubbish. On the other side a tall end house on a Victorian terrace bore an election poster saying, 'Don't Let Labour Take It All Away'. Just legible above the poster the painted lettering of an advertisement from sixty years ago read, 'Win Her Affection with an A1 Confection'. Further along the terrace the front of one house had been meticulously picked out in crimson, a brick at a time with the mortar in white; the window frames were turquoise. A Cypriot family lived there, homesick for the uninhibited colours of the eastern Mediterranean. Another house had fake stone cladding, and a latticed window in place of its bay. One was fenced off with corrugated iron and had a front garden crowded with spindly sycamores. It belonged to the council, who were too poor to keep it in repair.

Dominique passed the local shopping parade. There was a seventeenth-century brick house with Dutch gables, its ground floor knocked through to hold a garment factory. Next door was a butcher selling halal meat, who never had anything in the

332

window. The brightest-looking place was a cheap-and-cheerful shop called Vamoosh! where two healthy-looking women in smocks sold second-hand children's clothes and tried to publicize alternative medicine. The neighbourhood café had overhead neon lighting and customers who all seemed to be elderly Kurdish men. It stood next to an Asian news-paper shop open fourteen hours a day whose pro-prietor, with his sari-clad wife, had never been seen to smile. Beyond the shops were the chain-link fenc-ing and Portakabins of a primary school whose younger pupils had been sent home indefinitely for lack of staff.

The house where Dominique was staying stood in a yellow-brick Georgian terrace beginning to creep back up in the world. At one end, behind a scoured façade and bay trees in terracotta tubs, lived a consultant pediatrician from a grim nearby hospital with his GP wife. Dominique's house had cracked drains and a broken fanlight. Blankets were draped across the windows at each end of the double drawing room that was serving as a sleeping area, with mattresses laid on a lino floor. The house belonged to a firm of solicitors outside London who'd acquired it in part-payment of a debt and had more or less forgotten about it. For years now the main occupier, a mate of Dominique's boyfriend back in the West Midlands, hadn't been held up for rent by anyone.

In the basement Mrs Zlotnick was wiping down a wooden draining board with excruciating slowness.

Without acknowledging her mother, Dominique began unpacking her day's plunder. As she did so, Mrs Zlotnick caught sight of the book of nursery rhymes. 'Oh, that's nice,' she exclaimed, rubbing her spiky fingers up and down the cover. The skin over her knuckles was shiny and tight. 'I hope it didn't cost too much.' It was what she always said. Nineteen years on from when Maria had met her, in the dirty little house by Stinscombe Halt, Mrs Zlotnick had realized her potential for idiocy and gone ten-tenths gaga.

Dominique went on ignoring her. From the room where they slept there came the sound of a television.

'Turn that noise down!' Dominique yelled. Not understanding, her mother looked up with an expression both startled and slow. Mrs Zlotnick wore three layers of woollies, a shapeless skirt and ankle socks with slippers.

The television quietened. 'Mum,' came a child's voice. 'Can I have dinner in the kitchen?'

'You have it where I tell you.'

'I don't want it in the front room. There's shit in Grandma's bed.'

'Shit.' Raising her voice again, Dominique called, 'Wait and see what I tell you. You wait up there.'

'Mum?'

'Yes!'

'Mum?'

'What is it?'

'I want to go outside and play funerals.'

334

'What's she burying now, for God's sake?' muttered Dominique.

'Just till dinner.'

'All right. But don't come pestering me till I say.'

The child's footsteps faded. Dominique stood eating the health-food shop's croissant while glancing through the *Sun*. 'Difficult little sod. Don't know why I bothered in the first place.'

'Still, she's inherited Jimmie's looks, bless her. And who would've thought there'd be all that in the papers about his being a millionaire. Mrs Zlotnick's memory wasn't completely blown. Even now she made a household god of her eldest son.

Dominique went on turning the pages of the newspaper. She saw Maria's photograph, in a follow-up article on the robbery.

'Here's that woman again. I thought the papers had stopped writing about her, until the other day.' She put down the croissant so she could concentrate properly on what the *Sun* had to say. Frowning, she mastered the caption, then started in on the accompanying article. It was this story, in one form or another, that had brought her to London. Suddenly Jimmie had become more than one of her mother's boring preoccupations.

Beneath a lanky privet bush in the rubbish-choked back yard, the child went on playing alone. The funeral was for a kitten that Dominique had stolen from a pet shop and then allowed to die. As the child dug, with a silver-plated fish slice got from a West End store, she murmured a private commentary.

335

She had skinny arms with elbows as pointed as flints. Her tangled black hair hid the scabs of ringworm sores. She was seven years old, officially believed dead since babyhood. Maria's daughter.

CHAPTER
EIGHTEEN

Zlotnick's affairs were beginning to be noticed by officialdom. At first they were only the concern of a lowly clerical officer of the Inland Revenue. He was a man steadfastly working towards his pension of £15,759 a year including London weighting. But he was someone too for whom the size of every tax dodge was equally important, as a shark will chew up a flavourless life raft along with the tastier remains of its passengers. His place of work stood in a particularly dreary part of Pimlico, where in the eighteenth century there'd been a famous pleasure ground. Where formerly there'd been masked balls and firework displays, his office window now looked into a deep lavatory-tiled well between government buildings.

This man gave several days to his information on Zlotnick, working at a metal desk, standard issue for the grade, whose drawers clanged when opened.

At the end of that time, without comment to anyone, he reached for his out tray and placed a memo in it. He had to use both hands.

His summary, thick with reference numbers and initials of government bodies, made an exciting evening's reading for the twenty-five-year-old Cambridge graduate to whom he sent it. In her mews flat near World's End she sat up till three, scanning eagerly in her office/bedroom furnished with stripped old furniture newly re-upholstered. She went to bed with a whispered 'Tally-ho!' and a lustful smile of ambition. This should get her noticed in the department.

As the lastest revelations about Zlotnick landed on larger desks they got shorter. The two letters dictated by the Cambridge graduate were only a couple of paragraphs long. Each was accompanied by selected material from the original fat memo. The first of her letters went underground, into Whitehall's twenty-three miles of tunnels. Taking several complicated turns, it travelled beneath the Banqueting Hall, where Charles I had walked out of a first-floor window on to the executioner's scaffold; thence it passed under the foundations of the Cenotaph. At length it surfaced across the road from its starting point, to be placed near the top of the Ministry's hierarchy on the desk of Sir Geoffrey Peele. This was a desk that never had more than one document on it at a time, a monumental piece of mahogany with an embossed leather top the size of a flight deck. Sir Geoffrey's office was big, too;

you could have schooled a cavalry horse in it. The ceiling was coffered, the door was like a city gate, and the windows looked across Horse Guards' Parade to the trees and water of St James's Park.

When the time came for Sir Geoffrey to pass on what he knew about Zlotnick, the original information had been shortened even further. At the opera one night, standing unbuttoned in the lavatory, he found Zlotnick's name being mentioned to him by a colleague from the Cabinet Ceremonial Office.

Even at the Opera House the formality of black tie didn't always go with sharing a urinal, but the dignity of both men was equal to the occasion. Formerly Sir Geoffrey had put quite a bit of weight behind Zlotnick's advancement. Now, however, nothing could be easier than the way he murmured, 'Bit of a non-starter there. Something inconvenient brewing.' Adjusting his trousers he walked away. Enough said.

The second covering letter from the Cambridge graduate, Administrative Grade, travelled across town to a sorting office in Bloomsbury, then back again to the building next to its starting point in Whitehall. Its destination unknown to the writer herself, had been chosen several years before at the time she'd had nothing on her mind but undergraduate theatricals on a raft of punts by the garden of Queen's. Now at last it had arrived. At New Scotland yard, on the desk of an officer of the Fraud Squad.

Zlotnick looked hard at the photo his sister had sent him. His breakfast, served at one end of an empty table for twelve, grew cold. On the back of the snapshot was a message in Dominique's large, uneasy handwriting.

'It's been a long time Jimmie, To long. We have to meet. Your house, this evening, til tonite. Your sister.'

The photo looked recent. Since he'd last seen Dominique she'd evidently roughened at the edges even by her own standards. She and her mother were standing in what must have been an early Christmastide fairground. Behind them a couple of children were each being borne round and round in a model aircraft on the end of a boom. The two infants were hunched into winter clothes, the only pleasure-seekers in sight. They were overseen by a sullen man whose face looked like beef that had hung too long. Dominique wore a nylon quilted anorak, a short gathered skirt and high-heeled shoes. Her huge legs were much the same colour as the fairground barker's face, presumably from the cold. Beside her, Mrs Zlotnick looked lost and anxious to please.

Zlotnick went on staring at the photo. His face was pinched with anger and unease. The longer he looked, the more he noticed. There was something about the way his sister was jigging about for the camera and sticking out her tongue – had the picture been taken in the first place with the purpose of sending it to him? And knowing how her mind worked it was surely no accident that they'd posed in front of a roundabout. In which case . . . She was bound to be winding him up. Wasn't she? On the other hand, could either child be the Adams brat? It was impossible to know: one was muffled right up to the nostrils, the other had its back to the camera. Even if one of them was Adams's, Dominique might still only be posing with the child in view for the hell of it.

Or was she threatening him? Zlotnick put down the photo, deliberately steady. Every hair on his body seemed to prickle.

He was clean, and always had been. Now, as always, nobody could prove a thing. He didn't often think about Adams's child, but when he did his own innocence was usually all that entered his mind. Whether the infant was dead or alive, there was no reason for him to foresee any problem.

Or was there? Nothing had changed – and yet, irrationally, Zlotnick felt everything had, now that Dominique was threatening to reappear.

Occasionally he had wondered if the child was a piece of evidence that really shouldn't still be around, but such doubts had soon given way to his feeling of superiority at the huge mistake the Adams family had made. And continued to make, every day. A couple of years back there'd been a memorial service at Stinscombe Church – and now Adams was chasing everyone else's mislaid offspring the world over – when no one had died anyway.

Had he bought his self-satisfaction at too high a price?

Zlotnick didn't altogether hate Edmund Adams and his father. He just wanted his share of control over how they felt and thought. Until now it had been even more important to him than his own safety.

He put the photograph somewhere well out of sight and had himself driven to work. The day didn't drag; it passed in a blur of adrenalin. The prospect of combat always enlivened him.

Even so, when his doorbell rang that evening, he went to answer it with a feeling of confronting the most serious adversary he'd ever had.

'Nice,' said Dominique, stepping into the wide hall, with its gilt-framed mirrors and fresh flowers. 'I'm impressed.'

In a parody of politeness he indicated that she should come into the kitchen. He was damned if he wanted to treat her like a proper guest.

'Aren't you going to show me round?' she asked, peeking past the drawing room door. 'I think your house looks every so stylish.' Whatever she'd come for, there was a hint of gloating in her voice.

'Certainly,' said Zlotnick at his most contained. If correctness could kill, right now Dominique would have been fifteen stone of charred offal. 'Follow me, if you would.'

Briskly he made a perverse point of showing her every room in the flat, not excepting the slate-floored larders and the three lavatories. That done, they found themselves standing in the drawing room. Neither wanted to yield a tactical advantage by sitting down.

'How do you like my photo then? Nice, isn't it?'

'Of its kind I'm sure it's admirable.'

'Shows up the three of us really well.'

Zlotnick remembered the infant she'd had with her at Stinscombe Rectory. Pretending to misunderstand, he asked, 'And how is your little girl?'

'All right, now that you ask.' It was obvious she knew he was bluffing.

'You brought her with you once to Professor Adams's house.' Zlotnick didn't particularly want to sound conversational. Anything, though, to rile his sister, standing on his Aubusson in her pointed heels scuffed down to bare metal.

'That wasn't her.' Dominique glowered, contemptuous of his disadvantage.

'Sure – sure.' With a show of indifference he waited for what she had to say.

'Aren't you going to ask who she is, then?'

'Should I?'

'You know anyway, don't you?'

'If you say so.'

'I'd never had got stuck with another kid if it wasn't for you.'

Zlotnick seemed to think an answer was beneath him. Dominique said, 'Well, you know what you've got to do, don't you?'

'Indeed?'

'Don't think I haven't read about you in the papers.' From the moment she'd seen her brother's name in the *Sun*, Zlotnick had loomed much larger in her thoughts. She'd have been impressed enough to push him even harder if she'd seen him on television.

'That's nice for you.'

'So, now you're famous what are you going to do for us? Unless you want to be even more famous.'

He'd have preferred to die at the hands of a public torturer rather than look dismayed. 'That depends on what you're prepared to do for yourself.'

'I'm doing something right here and now, in case you hadn't noticed.'

Zlotnick tried to ignore her meaning. 'I can't see that you need my help if you want to sell the newspapers your own connection with the stolen picture. One of the tabloids might give you fifty pounds. On the other hand that sort of story goes stale sooner than you seem to realize.'

Dominique bristled, a big woman being triumphant. 'You needn't think you can fool me just like that!'

The thing was she was right, now even Sun-readers like his own family knew who he was. Suppressing the thought of worse things, Zlotnick pictured the headlines he'd get as a millionaire whose mother was living on the dole.

'I'll see what can be done.' He moved as if to show her out.

'Oh, no you don't! You've got to do something yourself – right now.'

Zlotnick turned on her, so violently that any other woman would have flinched. 'Look,' he hissed, 'what the hell do you expect me to be able to do?

344

Besides,' controlling himself enough to go on bluffing, 'you still haven't shown any real reason why I
should help you.'

'Oh, you've got to help, all right. I saw you watching when I took Sal away from you, off that, like,
merry-go-round. You needn't think I didn't clock you,
taking it all in. It was your fault anyway. All I
wanted was to give you a scare.'

With an effort of self-control he looked perfectly
indifferent as he took out his wallet and gave her five
twenties. 'This is all I've got on me.' It was the truth,
as it happened; these days he tended to carry almost
as little cash as a member of royalty. 'Now,' he said,
speaking purposefully, as if their encounter had been
his idea, 'I'll tell you what I *am* prepared to do for you.'

'Maria! What a surprise!'

'Jimmie! How amazing! How *are* you?'

Each of them pictured the other smiling into the
receiver till it hurt. Zlotnick figured Maria must be
within carshot of someone else.

'Oh, as the indifferent children of the earth.
Happy in that one isn't over-happy. On Fortune's
cap one is not the very button, it has to be said.'
One of the first lessons the young Zlotnick had
picked up from Edmund's friends was, when you've
nothing to say, don't keep quiet. Misquote Shakespeare instead. In secret he'd learned whole
speeches just for that purpose.

'How intriguing, Jimmie – or is it the way you
say it? What can I do for you?'

345

Zlotnick chuckled. 'That's for you to tell me . . .
No, seriously, it would be splendid if we could meet.
In the meantime – I hate to trouble you if you've
got people there . . .'

'No, no problem, really.'

'I need to see Digory. Do you think —?'

'But of course! At the first opportunity. When
would suit you?'

'In a couple of hours? If that's too soon, then —'

'No, that's fine.'

'Depending on the weather, of course. What's it
like down there?'

'Awful!' A cold spell had sheened the lanes
around Stinscombe with black ice. It was threatening to snow.

As if her least word were a delicious conspiracy
between them, he laughed. Maria pictured him
throwing his head back, the receiver to his ear.

'Good luck, then,' she said.

'Right! I'll be seeing you both.'

'I'll count on it. Byee.'

Driving west that evening in his hired silver BMW
735i, Zlotnick was rigid with repressed energy. He
responded the same way in desperation as in hope;
and today had to have been the worst of his life.

It just had to. Part of him refused to believe his
career might have peaked. On the other hand, why
this sensation of being carried towards the edge of
the world? How different things had been twenty-
four hours before. A bit too interesting for comfort,

sure, but he'd been confident of finding himself back in charge somehow.

On the motorway crossing the Chiltern Hills it started to snow. Flurries of wet flakes swooped endlessly out of the dark. Obsessively Zlotnick once more surveyed the events of recent days, trying to find some pattern of explanation that he could manipulate.

It had been the previous midnight when they'd burst into his flat. Warrant and all. As he drove, details of the raid kept seething to the surface of his mind like corpses from a shipwreck.

'You mean you can't explain these payments?' he'd been asked afterwards. They'd taken every piece of documentation in the place, had even searched the kitchen waste. Thank God he'd had the sense to get rid of the photo showing those two women in the bloody fairground.

'You're quite sure you don't want to explain this aspect of your affairs?'

The two men questioning him had seemed neither to accept nor disbelieve the little he could tell them. Most of the time he'd been silent with astonishment, his eyes sliding warily about in an expressionless face. To anyone who'd seen the evidence his response had had to seem like guilt.

Anonymous payments, undeclared. Made by telegraphic transfer into an account he used only when in the United Kingdom. Four years' worth of credits with the annual interest alone nearly worth six figures.

As Zlotnick drove his mind moved in circles, chaotically seeking connections where none existed. The dumb bint – as he inwardly styled his sister – could have been there too when the police arrived. Against all logic, Dominique and her lifelong unpredictability had started making Zlotnick uneasy to the point of superstition. So what if she had been? he thought, trying to shake some sense into himself. It would have been a perfectly legitimate-seeming encounter between brother and sister. They weren't interested in her, anyway.

'You've got to get us out of that dump.' All the way into Oxfordshire her angry voice haunted him nonetheless. The tail-lights of long-distance commuters sidled or whooshed past, haloed in a wet blur. It was Friday night and the exodus from London was swollen by people going down to their second·home for the weekend.

'What dump is that?'

'I'm not going to tell you that, am I?' Dominique had been too canny to give away her whereabouts prematurely.

In the end he'd been cornered into rehousing his mother and sister at an address of his own, a week-end cottage he'd recently bought in Northamptonshire. She'd wanted the keys in advance. They were her security against him, he realized: potential evidence in case he made a wrong move. 'You needn't think you can try anything sneaky. I know you.'

The venue for handing over the keys had been a

348

source of seemingly endless argument, as they'd baulked and haggled, he trying to lessen his loss of face, she determined to follow one victory with another, just to show him. 'So how do I contact you?' he'd finally asked, red in the face with humiliation and rage.

'At my friend's, of course.'

'Ah. Your friend.'

'You know. You must do. At Dave's.' She'd looked exasperated, as if this were something Zlotnick had been bound to know.

So he'd finally agreed to meet her at an address twenty-five miles beyond the cottage, in the devastated empty heart of Birmingham. There, in a call box on the corner of a half-demolished street of redbrick terraced houses, he'd had to make a prearranged phone call. Dominique had appeared across the road in a doorway, signalling elaborately. He couldn't think why she hadn't gone the whole way and hammed it up in a trenchcoat and shades.

Those two women. The raid.

His thoughts rebounded from one to the other, probing then flinching. The New Year's Honours list, so long an obsession, scarcely broke the surface of his mind. He couldn't bear to contemplate 'his' knighthood, lost to some other shitter now that the letters of notification would have gone out. Like a fatally sick man insisting he was healthy, Zlotnick simply suppressed the thought of it.

Numb with mingled indifference and shock, he recalled another thing that had recently gone awry.

The nubile Ginevra, his Republican almost-fiancée, had stopped taking his calls. Zlotnick's main response had been surprise at how convincing her secretary had sounded when lying about her whereabouts. It was a new experience, not having his calls returned. He'd never paid much attention when people had been telling smiling porkers on his own behalf.

Let the overweening slag go.

And her desertion could be the first of hundreds. On the screens of computer-based address files all over the world, his name was probably silently blinking out of existence.

The wipers clunked, pushing wedges of snow to and fro. West of Oxford the motorway was left behind. On sudden corners the headlights showed up stone villages whose buildings clustered against the highway as close as filings drawn to a magnet.

'You can't mean to charge me!' he'd exclaimed, in the first shock of seeing four plain-clothes men going through every drawer in his bedroom. What with, for God's sake? Tax evasion? Fraud? Impossible, both of them.

'You'll be apprised in due course, sir.' Shaken, Zlotnick had taken some moments to realize the man hadn't actually said 'cautioned'.

'Does this mean the UK tax authorities will freeze my account?'

'I don't doubt it.'

For two hours he'd loitered in his dressing gown, watching them search and feeling unable to sit

350

down anywhere in his own home. How soon would word of this be out among his corporate share-holders? Damn it, gossip was what made his world go round. And any moment now, gossip would begin to expand even the smallest rumour of his financial shakiness. He would have to do something to counter the effect of his mysterious credits as fast and as quietly as possible.

Lurking in the Belgrave Square flat next day, taking no calls, he let several hours pass as he wondered what to do. Mentally he held up each option in turn to see how it would look in the fierce light of his unlooked-for publicity. At length he began trying to make some calls.

But – what was this?'

Until he'd picked up the phone, it hadn't occurred to Zlotnick that he might be treated as he'd used others. For everything he himself had done, there'd always been some private, special justification. Acting triumphant. Dumping on people. Or spend-ing for the whole world to see and envy. But now that it was his turn to whiff of trouble, he could hardly believe how many meetings and long lunches had broken out among his acquaintance. No one was free to take his call.

Dusk had come. He'd had to decide something – anything. By now he'd been reduced to asking him-self questions that hadn't crossed his mind for years. Who was there who'd helped him when he'd had nothing? Whom did he know who'd once put their good name at risk by offering to be his patron? And

351

who in return had been so hard done by that they
dared not shun him for fear of looking like a bad
loser? Who was there who was too proud to risk
seeming vindictive towards him?

Even at a time like this, Zlotnick felt a grim relish
at such a paradox.

He'd called Digory's number.

In the Cotswolds it was snowing hard; Stinscombe
village was empty, an unused stage set. Waiting for
the traffic light on the bridge, Zlotnick's BMW was
the only car in sight.

The lane up to the Rectory was impassable; a
layer of ice had partly thawed, then frozen again.
Zlotnick gunned the engine, yelping aloud with frustration. He was at a pitch of anticipation where the
smallest hindrance seemed disastrous. The big car
rocked uselessly in a cloud of exhaust, its wheels
spinning. He left it and walked the rest of the way,
slipping on the dirty ice in his hand-made shoes.

The drive was snowed right over, the downstairs
windows dark. Zlotnick rang the bell. Buffeted by
nameless fears, his whole body cocked in readiness,
he waited. If he didn't succeed in charming the old
man, at least he'd die trying.

No one came. Had Adams's wife decoyed him to
an empty house? Snowflakes stung his face. He
stamped his soaking feet.

Even though he was there to ask a favour, they
couldn't expect him to stand around in a blizzard.
Prowling gingerly along a path nearly hidden by

new snow, he let himself in through the back lobby.

In the half-darkened hall he realized the place wasn't empty. From Maria's sitting room upstairs came the sound of voices. With prissy, purposeful tread, Zlotnick went to the foot of the stairs. Someone opened a door on the landing, and he got ready to look pleased to see them.

'Oh!' It was Maria, catching sight of him with a soft gasp of horror. Why was she staring at him like that? In an instant, seeing her tousled hair and hastily fastened robe, he thought he knew.

'Jimmie! So sorry not to be ready for you. I didn't think you'd make it so soon. I know it must look rude, but Digory will be around at any moment – I'm sure he will be!' Her face was aghast. A pulse ticked violently at the base of her throat.

Something close to the truth crossed his mind. He must have caught her fucking, but why her look of dismay? Smelling triumph without yet knowing why, Zlotnick pretended not to hear her properly. He ran up the stairs to where she was standing.

'I beg your pardon?' Grinning, he mimed deafness.

She stepped back from him, needlessly pulling her collar further closed. He could see she was very conscious of being naked under her robe.

'Look, Jimmie. I – I mean, we – I mean, I'll be with you in a moment, okay? Can you wait – please? – downstairs, right? – for five minutes? No longer than that, truly!'

She was whispering, afraid to raise her voice. Gloating, he advanced.

'I'm sorry?'

'No, Jimmie. I can't talk right now!'

'What was that? I didn't quite —'

'Please, not just this minute.'

'I'd hate to misunderstand you.'

'No, Jimmie – not now. Please!' She reopened the door to her sitting room a crack, as if hoping to slide out of sight through a three-inch opening. He put his foot in the gap and pushed.

'No – you mustn't!' She scrabbled helplessly to prevent him.

Zlotnick glanced into the room. What he saw left him rigid with surprise, then with satisfaction.

Against a background of firelight and untidy cushions, her father-in-law too had only just hurried into his robe. Awakened from a post-coital slumber while entwined around his mistress, Digory now wore the shocked expression of a man who'd had a limb accidentally ripped from its socket.

'No —!' Maria repeated, still pulling at the door in a pitiable effort at concealment.

Oh no you don't, Zlotnick thought. You can't make me pretend I've seen nothing. Sensing an undreamed-of advantage, he shoved her aside and held the door wide open, long enough to stare pointedly at Digory.

Maria couldn't look. Edmund's father, all humiliation and white hair.

From the beginning, it had been the risk to his

good name that had made their couplings so frantic. Digory had experienced every mating with her as though it had been the last one before sudden death. Now the pay-off had come, he was unmanned. In one poisonous dose, the unassailable Professor Adams was being fed a lifetime's shame.

Zlotnick looked his fill. He carefully shut the door again.

'Nobody knows but you.' Maria was almost inaudible, and wide-eyed with panic.

He gave her an unyielding stare, like someone probing the secrets of her home as a disagreeable official duty.

'Jimmie,' she ventured, in the voice of someone with nothing to lose, 'I know it's rude of us not to be ready for you. I appreciate how you must feel – truly I do. But we didn't mean it! I'll make amends – honestly I will. I'll do anything you like, if only you'll please – please! – be discreet!'

A slave to his own disdain, Zlotnick let her stew for a moment. Her ludicrous despair was too good to be true. Of course he'd let her bribe him, if that was what she wanted. One had a duty to make people pay for their errors if they were going to be as careless as this.

He named his price.

Maria ran to do his bidding. Coming back, still dishevelled and undressed, she endorsed a cheque for the amount he'd named, to be handed over at her own bank. 'I know how grateful Digory will be,' she said, trying to smile ingratiatingly, 'if you agree not to be too disappointed in us both.'

Zlotnick put the cheque in his wallet without answering. Who could tell how useful her money might be? In the short term it would certainly help to meet his sister's demands. Say what one would, the irony was irresistible. Who could have foreseen a chunk of the Adams fortune being spent like this – on keeping their brat in the style that he, Zlotnick, had once had to endure?

'Has the old man made a habit of shagging you?'

'Please, Jimmie! Don't be too hard on us. Try to see it from our point of view.'

'I think I'd hardly want to do that.'

Maria seemed not the notice the crudeness of Zlotnick's remark. She put her hand on his arm. 'I know how it must seem. But we're in love! You can't ask us to fight against something bigger than both of us.'

Wouldn't you know it! Zlotnick told himself. Trust Adams's wife to talk in cliché.

'So it isn't the first time you've entertained each other like this?'

'No, but —'

'In that case your esteemed father-in-law couldn't do better than to quote from your own doubtless well-used mouth. "As a dog returns to his vomit, so a fool returns to his folly."'

Once he'd gone, Maria waited a long time without moving. The emotions that had crowded her face were joined by others.

After some while more the door opened. Her

father-in-law shuffled out as if walking on ground glass. He was the ghost of himself, past, present and future – Digory as he might expect to be twenty years on.

'You permitted that encounter on purpose.' He sounded like an old, old man, husked of authority.

Maria said nothing. Her show of terror in front of Zlotnick had been at least half real, and staged on impulse. Even so, she was having to fight down her guilt as if it threatened her very life.

'May I ask —' His voice fractured into silence.

She'd known that what she'd just allowed to happen would be hard to bear, but not as fearful as this. Resolutely she said, 'Ask anything you like. It was you who always said the man was harmless.'

He was incredulous.

'Is that why you were so deliberately careless?' he cried. 'In order to say you'd told me so?'

'No! No, Digory – really it wasn't!'

Why hadn't she guessed it would be like this? Since childhood she'd wanted Digory's uncondi- tional love as her father, but all she'd gained was control over him as they'd hurtled together, on and on, down a tunnel of lust. Now he would never call her his dear girl again. Nor even describe her as the sweetest cunt in humankind. Wavering between yearning and anger, she'd only succeeded in adding one loss to another.

Nerving herself she said, 'You did do me wrong! You know you did! Why didn't you listen to me, before —'

357

'Before what?' Digory stared at her, bewildered. He still didn't imagine she bore him any serious grudge.

'Before Sarah was kidnapped.'

'Good God Almighty!' he shouted. 'Can't you understand? It was an accident! How was I to know? Tell me. How was I?'

Maria took fire from his own urgency. 'You could have listened,' she said, her voice coming thickly. 'You could! Even *you* could have faced your responsibilities to Sarah and me. Damn you, Digory, you could have paid some attention to the women and children in your household – just once!'

'And for that you've done this to me?' Digory looked at her, breathing hard. Seizing her by the hair, he dragged her close and tipped her face up to his. She struggled to step back as he kissed her, hard; it was meant to hurt and it did.

'Don't pretend you loved me! Not when you've used *this*' – thrusting his hand between her legs – 'as you have done!' He was frightened as well as angry, an old bull ousted for ever from control of his herd.

By an act of will she steadied herself to answer. 'I would have done anything for you, if you'd only loved me in the way you ought.' She pulled away, trying not to share his look of horror. 'I trusted you, Digory! For years I made myself believe you were treating me the way a proper father would. I wanted so much for you to be a good man – as good as you've told the whole world you are, with

358

your damned moneyed, posturing, white man's liberalism!'

He went on staring at her, dumb with amazement. Down the years the various women of his household might have got tetchy from time to time – his second wife had even stalked off empty-handed with another man, no explanations offered. But no one had ever faced him down like this.

'I'm sorry, Digory. No, I don't mean that. I'm not sorry. I'm broken-hearted, that's all. Bit by bit you broke my heart. You fancied yourself as more liberal-minded than anyone else on earth – but only while it cost you nothing more than money. And I didn't even want your money. I wanted you to take sides with me. Just as – as Elizabeth did, and would have gone on doing if she hadn't —'

It had been a mistake to mention Elizabeth, if Maria had meant to keep from weeping. At the memory of one loss too many, she fled, having silenced both Digory and herself.

His look of hunted disbelief followed her as she ran to shut herself away, frightened for them both. For years he'd dominated her against her will. Now, in moments, she'd broken him down into a frail old man. Henceforward, though, there would be a new oppressor in her life, one that she hadn't foreseen. Her conscience.

CHAPTER
NINETEEN

It was Dominique on the line.

'We need to meet again, Jimmie.'

Zlotnick had only just got back to town. 'I can't think what for,' he lied, trying to pass off unease as impatience.

'Oh yes you can. Mum and me can't be fobbed off.'

Being fobbed off, in Zlotnick's opinion, was the only thing his mother had ever done well. Not that he dared say so, even with his chest and legs suddenly prickling with rage. He was right to think the coon bint's cheque would be needed.

'Well?'

'Well what?'

'Are you going to do what you've to, or aren't you?'

'What in God's name is wrong with being put up in my own home?'

'This place is a dump.'

'I assume you can't possibly mean the house itself.' Zlotnick had been trying not to imagine what a few weeks of his family would do to this newly refurbished weekend retreat. A lot worse, no doubt, than saucepan-sized scorch marks on the four-hundred-year-old surface of his dining table.

'I hate this place you've sent us to. Supposing we didn't have the car? I bet you didn't even think of that, did you?'

Zlotnick bit down hard on his humiliation. 'Monday morning at ten thirty, then. Here.'

CHEQUE-MATE' was the headline in the *Daily Post*. 'BABY SARAH SNATCH MAN LOSES OUT AGAIN.

> Media mogul James Zlotnick was yesterday reeling from ANOTHER blow to his jet-setting lifestyle when the fortune – yes, folks, a whole FORTUNE – owed him by exotic South Seas lovely, art-dealer Maria Adams, couldn't be paid. The dud cheque was part of the money owed after thieves raided Maria's exclusive Mayfair gallery. Priceless masterpieces were stolen, including one owed by tycoon James, here seen sharing a party-time joke with Maria and blonde former fiancée, American heiress Ginevra Devine.

The photograph made both women's bare shoulders and long hair gleam in a way that real life never quite matched. Ginevra was wearing a balloon-sleeved gown worn so far off the shoulder that she was naked to the elbows; her half-exposed breasts were impressively cantilevered. Zlotnick and Maria were smiling hard enough for their faces to fall off.

> Ginevra, 26, was certainly ready to show what *she* was worth! But now it's Maria's turn to go bust. Our reporter watched, astonished, as her cheque, for FIFTY THOUSAND POUNDS bounced – all the way back from the bank.
>
> 'Say Maria, *I guess I didn't realize how hard my finances have been hit. This raid has been a terrible blow to my old friend Jimmie Zlotnick. But, believe me, my business has suffered dreadfully, too'.*

The *Daily Pest*, as its rivals sometimes described it wasn't noted for the accuracy of its reporting, but sometimes it came close enough to the facts.

You'd better leave me with something to fear, was Zlotnick's thought as he opened the door to Dominique. Why else should I go on humouring you?

She was twenty-four hours late. 'You weren't worried, were you, Jimmie?' she asked with a sly grin.

Zlotnick said nothing. In the last day and night he'd re-run every murderous thought he'd ever had.

'Anyway, people know you can't just snap your fingers and have them come running whenever you want.'

He led the way into the drawing room. 'Read this, please,' he said, holding out the article by the reporter Maria had planted behind him in the bank.

Dominique looked at it, then up at him. 'You can't expect me to be tricked by something like that. I know you're not poor all of a sudden. This house is full of stuff.' She pointed at random to a cigarette lighter set in a two-kilo lump of onyx.

With controlled violence he picked it up and thrust it dismissively into her hands. 'Take it. It'll keep you in groceries for at least five days.'

'Well, how about one of those?' she indicated a pair of wall-mounted light fittings. 'Those ones look valuable.' They had glided branched supports and a glittering superstructure of teardrop glass.

'Bring a van round. I'm serious. There's no money in my UK accounts. The authorities have frozen it.'

'Ah, but you've got lots of accounts abroad, haven't you? And Mum and me have got our standard of living to keep up.'

Zlotnick had resolved his answer in advance. 'Then you'll miss it all the more when I don't give you any more handouts.'

She laughed theatrically. 'And what about when I tell the papers all about you, and say how mean you've been?'

'No one would buy that, when you're living under my own roof for nothing.'

'You mightn't think that's very interesting but some people would, believe you me. After all – she paused for emphasis. 'There's Sal.'

'Out.' Zlotnick's voice was matter-of-fact, but in a way she should have feared.

'What?'

'Out of here.'

Seeing him move towards her, she dodged behind a sofa, still clutching the onyx cigarette lighter. 'Don't you dare lay a finger on me.' Dominique had seen this encounter in the movies and knew the right words.

Zlotnick's face was set hard. He made a rush at her. Clumsily she tried to hit him with the lump of onyx. He wrenched it away and delivered a punch to the side of her head that sent her skittering on to her hands and rump. Squealing with fury, she tried to run away. He got to the door first, however, and slammed it in front of her. There was an ineffectual flurry of kicks and slaps that mostly missed both of them. Concerned, Dominique did the only thing that would make him step back: she spat over his silk suit and custom-made shirt. Then she was gone.

Not only did Zlotnick change his clothes; he showered as well. He got dressed again, casual smart this time. There was no question of going through the motions today at the office, or at anywhere else in public view. There was no plan in his mind; merely a feeling that one would turn up somehow.

When the phone rang, he knew who it would be. He picked up the receiver braced to act, though he still had no idea how. Zlotnick was not prepared for a truce either, no matter what his sister was about to say.

'Yes?'

'Mum's been showing Sal some pictures. In the papers.' Dominique was using a public phone; in the background were crowds, including children, and musak. Probably she was in a motorway service station on the way back to the cottage in Northamptonshire. As an idea began to shape itself in Zlotnick's mind, it became more important, moment by moment, that he should have guessed her whereabouts correctly. He waited, wired as an athlete under starter's orders.

'Sal knows who you are. I'd be really careful if I was you. It'll be your fault if something bad happens. You were the one that got me into this. And it would only be for the good of the kid, know what I mean? Only, if I took things into my own hands, you'd have to worry about whether I'd like, implicate you . . .'

Earlier that morning in the kitchen of Dower Mill House, outside the village of Canons Thorpe, Mrs Zlotnick had been wheedling Sal.

'Go on pet. It won't hurt, just once . . .'

'Mum says I mustn't. You know she doesn't want us to shop round here.'

In Sal's life, Dominique was the father-figure, easily angered and often away from home. Any mothering came from Mrs Zlotnick. In winter, when Sal had had to find her own socks or go bare-legged, it was the old woman who'd say, ten times in an hour, how much better it would have been if only

Sal had had a hot breakfast. And in summer it was Mrs Zlotnick who'd try and nag the child to put on a nice warm coat, in case the weather suddenly changed and made her catch her death.

She had fastened now on the fact that Sal had a cold and a persistent cough. Mrs Zlotnick sensed that she was in unfamiliar surroundings. These days, too, she was less certain than ever which one of her family Sal was. It was all the more reassuring to her to be able to fuss over something familiar and undemanding like a child's runny nose.

'Go on,' she said conspiratorially, putting a ten penny piece in Sal's hand. 'You go out to the shops and get what you need.'

'That's not enough for asprin, Grandma.' Sal went into the quarry-tiled dining area next door and opened a drawer in an oak sideboard. Loose notes and coins were scattered on top of a pile of white damask napkins.

'Can I take plenty, please?' Since moving in some days ago, the three of them had been living on what they'd found there. They now lacked bread, cooking oil, teabags, milk, margerine, eggs, rubbish sacks, washing-up liquid, spare light bulbs, a batter for the TV remote control, clean bedlinen, toothpaste, elasto-plast, antiseptic, paper tissue, cleaning fluid for Mrs Zlotnick's dentures, geriatric nappies, lavatory paper and shampoo. The fridge freezer's cache of sole bonne femme and chicken tikka was gone, together with several helpings of Marks and Spencer's salmon en croute, cooked to a soggy dollop in the microwave.

366

'You're not making a mess of Jimmie's room, are you? I think you'd better come back in here, really I do.' They were living in the kitchen and one bedroom; Mrs Zlotnick because she was overawed by so much chintz and polished oak, Dominique from an instinct for self-protection, in case anyone in the lane took too much interest. Sal sighed to herself and went to get a door key; these days it wasn't safe to leave Grandma on her own without locking her in.

At the village shop, converted from a former smithy, she found her money wouldn't go as far as she'd expected. The prices were adjusted to the pockets of weekend commuters, ready to pay anything to avoid the ten-mile drive to a supermarket. Sal got asprin, tinned frankfruters and baked beans, resolving to put the rest of the cash back in the drawer.

At the checkout the shopkeeper pretended not to notice her appearance. He was a retired gas-showroom manager from Balham who clung to an idea of the countryside as inhabited only by nice people in muddy green wellies and flat caps. Under Sal's dirty bobble hat her hair was dull and tangled. Her nails were black, and a stye disfigured one eye. Seeing her step diffidently through his door, with its tinkling bell, his first thought was that gypsies must have turned up in the neighbourhood.

'You're not from round here, are you?'

Sal gave the answer she'd been taught several addresses back. 'We're on a visit to my gran.'

The shopkeeper counted out her change in silence. It mightn't be the child's fault that she looked and smelt as she did, but one had a duty to disapprove of the parents.

'Thank you,' said Sal meekly.

'That's all right,' the man replied, in a voice meant to show it was nothing of the kind. It was encounters like this that made the child cling to her supposed Grandma and strive to be sure of Dominique's approval.

With her carrier of tinned food banging against her thin legs, she hurried home through a village-scape very like Stinscombe, two counties away. The nearest house to Zlotnick's was a row of three cottages knocked into one. Its owner was a London-based copywriter who paid fifteen thousand a year just on fire insurance for his new thatch. Sal was anxious to get back; she knew how upset Grandma could be if she found she'd been locked in on her own. Month by month, the child had been sleeping further into the role of unpaid baby-sitter to the old woman. Nowadays, if she stayed out for too long, there was a risk that Grandma might have forgotten at first who Sal was.

In the kitchen of Dower Mill House, Mrs Zlotnick waited; but only a few moments. With no one but herself for company it took little time for her self-awareness to vanish like smoke. From some half-formed motive of obedience she went on sitting where she was in the kitchen, with its sticky brick floor and encrusted ceramic hob. She might have been uncertain who she was, but she knew that keeping out of the way was her job, these days.

As she sat several things were going on in her head; instead the rest of her too. Noises sounded from out of the gravel leading to the garage; it was Sal, returning, anxiously hurrying round to the back door. To the old woman, however, each footstep echoed through a disordered junction box of nerve-endings, conveying nothing but bewilderment. To her eyes, too, indoors and out had ceased to be; they were merely a mingled pattern of flat light and growing darkness.

The child came up the path and took out her door keys. Carefully, as though completing a difficult puzzle, she fitted it to the lock. All the while, Mrs Zlotnick sat motionless in her chair. Inside her chest something ripped and flapped like a loose sail; she couldn't move. A soundless cry poured out of her mouth.

Sal opened the back door and peered into the kitchen made dim by the wintry day. She'd been taught to watch herself out of doors, but given Dominique's temper and Mrs Zlotnick's idiocy home was a place of uncertainty, too.

Nothing was changed, including Grandma. Sal could see her staring at nothing; the old woman's shape was just a silhouette, but pin-points of daylight were reflected from her eyes. It struck Sal as odd that her Grandma didn't seem to mind gloom, since she was anxious about almost everything else.

Sal herself was terrified by darkness; alone at night she didn't dare turn over in bed for fear of seeing a dead person standing in the doorway, all falling to bits.

Not knowing that she'd come home to a corpse anyway, she turned on the light.

Mrs Zlotnick's joints had not yet turned rigid before someone else came into the house. Early in the afternoon her eldest son arrived, face to face with her after an absence of nearly a quarter-century. Entering the house, Jimmie Zlotnick gave the corpse a fraught glance and hurried past. He was conducting a search that left him no time for being distracted. Locking both doors, he was careful not to draw attention to himself by switching on any more lights, notwithstanding the darkness indoors. The winter's day was really no more than a six-hour twilight. It was raining, too, thank God: coming down in sheets. Anyone on foot would be walking about with their shoulders hunched and their eyes well down, with no time for his own doings.

He checked the windows were locked too, then he went to work on the place, taking each room apart one at a time. Cupboards were flung open, bedding was dragged clear of every mattress. He even kicked over the laundry baskets to make sure none of them could be hiding anything as heavy as a seven-year-old child.

Would Dominique try to stand between him and the Adams brat? Or would she pre-empt him in such a way that he'd be the one hauled in for questioning? Did she mean the threat she'd made when she'd phoned? Either way, it wasn't worth the risk of ignoring her.

At length it was obvious: there really was no-bobdy here. With his chest heaving from fear and urgency, Zlotnick surveyed the wreckage he'd left in the airing cupboard.

Now that he'd decided what to do, it seemed inevitable as well as right. So did his next destination. Leaving without another look in the direction of the corpse, he ran out through the rain to where his BMW was parked and set out again, for Birmingham.

'Maria, what's happening?'

Edmund flung a folded newspaper down in front of her. He looked uncertain, as if perhaps it should have been gauntlet instead. Maria glimpsed the photo of herself with Zlotnick and Ginevra.

'Ah,' she said, with a half-sigh.

'How on earth could you still owe him money?'

She went to close the door. They were in the drawing room at the Rectory, and she didn't want Digory within earshot. It was at his sudden, almost plaintive request that Edmund was there; they made an edgy party, as isolated as if the roomy old house were an ailing spacecraft.

'I didn't owe him.'

'So what does this mean? It's obvious that you set the article up. But why? God knows I realize

371

how little cause you have to like Jimmie Zlotnick but what on earth do you have to gain by this?'

'Shouldn't you ask what have I to lose?'

'I don't understand you.'

'Then let me explain,' Maria spoke calmly, but her seeming self-possession was the stillness at the centre of a great and terrible storm. Questioned by Edmund, one of the two greatest losses of her life, who could tell what she might say?

'After Sarah disappeared, neither of us knew what to do. You understand as well as I do how it is when you're trying to dodge something you can't bear. People might as well expect you to look dignified with your clothes on fire. You've done your best to adjust. And now I've done what I can too.'

'By hounding Jimmie Zlotnick? How can that help anyone.'

'How? You ask *me* how?' Maria's eyes darkened. She shrank back – not from her bewildered, reasonable husband, but from the spectre of her own feelings. 'Don't you see? It helps *me*! I've lost everything I cared about. Ever since I can remember my relatives were dying or dead, somewhere in exile. Right from the start – almost as soon as I'd learned to talk – I've had to be an adult. Sarah was to have had the childhood I'd never had; that much I'd promised myself. And all the poor little cow got was twenty-one months. Even if no reparations were due to me, do you think she isn't owed some revenge? For both of us – her and me – getting even is the only thing left.'

'By stopping a cheque? What good can that do?

372

Why can't you give up torturing yourself over a calamity that can't be helped?'

'Because that's what helps me,' she insisted. 'It helps me, and the memory of Sarah.'

He looked at her, saddened and weary. 'I don't know what to think.'

'Neither did I, while I tried to be reasonable and forget. And not make trouble for the sake of everyone about me. I admit it wouldn't have been much, stopping a cheque. But aren't you forgetting that it was made out to a man up to his mouth and nostrils in – what shall we call it? – compromise? Botheration? Public embarrassment?'

In an instant Edmund guessed what might be behind her angry elation. He paled. As well as most of his acquaintance, he knew what was being said in private about Zlotnick's financial affairs. His face changed as his understanding grew, rapid as ripples moving outward in a pool.

'You've been behind everything that's happened to him! You have, – haven't you?'

She found his expression of shock hard to face. To put off answering properly she said, 'He's got any number of enemies, besides me.'

'Yes – but how many of them are in a position to ignore what things cost, the way you or I can? That boat – how much was that, for God's sake?'

'Little enough, in the circumstances.'

'That painting – the Gauguin—'

'Only a sketch actually. Even if it was from the artist's later period.'

373

He ignored her faint attempt at a jest. 'All those payments you must have made, just to lay a trail to his door. They did come from you, didn't they?'

She nodded, sober but unshaken.

'But – good God, Maria – don't you have any doubts about whatever it is you've done? There've been men here from the Serious Crimes Division! Aren't you afraid of what could come out of this?'

'I haven't been afraid of anything for years.'

'And how much has it cost you? Millions?'

'What other use could I have for my money?'

He stared at her, aghast. At length he said, 'If you don't care what might happen to you, I do. Won't you tell me everything?'

Until now, Maria hadn't let herself realize how lonely the last five years had been. 'I can't wait!' she exclaimed, without thinking. Right away she found herself inwardly flinching. No – not every-thing.

There was still one secret she couldn't bear to tell. About Digory, newly aged.

Outside the room the phone rang. It was Dom-inique, calling from Birmingham.

CHAPTER
TWENTY

'Who are you looking for, love?'

Sal had been taught never, never talk to strangers. Not even women as ordinary as this one. She was being questioned in the street of back-to-backs, one side bulldozed to wasteland, where Dominique's man friend was staying.

But someone would have to help her.

'Please, which is Dave's house?'

'Dave who, do you mean?'

'I don't know,' said the child in a frightened voice. 'He lives in one of these houses.'

The woman, a matronly creature with frizzy hair, instinctively looked up and down the street for an explanation. She wore a velour leisure suit and a jacket in cheap black leather with batwing sleeves.

'Have you been looking long, then?' She tried not to appear shocked at Sal's bare ankles and filthy anorak. From the look of the kid, she wouldn't be surprised if she hadn't been sleeping rough. She was pale, too, and her breathing was harsh.

Sal nodded, trying not to cry. She wore an unfocused look of astonishment. It had been the shock on her face rather than her aimless dithering that had shown the woman she must be lost.

'I suppose you don't want to come into the house for a moment?'

The child came even closer to tears of fear and confusion. Going into strangers' homes was even more wicked than talking to them. 'No, thank you,' she said in a small voice.

'Well, you're sensible not to, really,' said the woman, understanding. 'Will you be all right waiting there for a moment . . .?'

Inside the house, where her father lived alone, the woman asked, 'You don't know anyone round here called Dave, do you, Dad?'

'Never heard of him.' The old man was watching *Win, Lose or Draw* in a room so full of upholstered furniture that the door wouldn't open properly.

'There's a kid looking for him.'

'What kid's that?' asked the old man sharply. He glanced up, as if a mob of steamers was already kicking in his front window.

'It's only a rather ill little girl —'

'Oh.' He turned his attention back to the quiz show.

'Only, if she's lost, I think maybe someone should know.' By 'someone' she meant the police.

'You do what you want,' he replied, without taking his eyes from the screen.

376

Outside, she said to Sal, 'You all right, then? . . . Good. I'm afraid my dad doesn't know your friend. But I'll just make a phone call for you.'

She hurried down the street towards where the call box stood, on the opposite pavement. Before she could cross over, she had to wait while a car went by.

The car pulled up next to where Sal was standing.

'What do you think you're doing here?'

It was Dominique, opening the driver's door. For once she sounded urgent as well as bullying. 'And just look at you!'

Reunited at last, Sal burst into hysterical tears. Dominique grabbed her by the arm. 'Get in the car.'

Sal neither resisted nor cooperated. She went on crying too violently to do anything but stand there and sob.

'Get in the bloody car!'

The woman came back up the street. 'Is she going to be all right?' she asked, torn between concern and not wanting to interfere.

'Oh, she'll be all right – now, for the last time, will you get in the car?'

'She ought to see a doctor, you know.'

Pitched on to the back seat of Dominique's Cortina, Sal sobbed with relief as if the rest of the world didn't exist.

'I know,' improvised Dominique. 'I've been ever so worried about her. I'm going to phone one now.'

Five doors up the street she rapped on the window. 'Dave! It's me . . . I said, it's me!'

On the pavement the woman lingered uncertainly. As soon as she saw which house Dominique had gone to, however, she decided to go home and not meddle. The child's mother had only shouted like that because she'd been worried; anyone could see that. And from what one heard you didn't want to get too involved with anyone from that house.

In an uncarpeted hallway with a payphone on the wall, Dominique set about making her call to the Rectory.

It was Digory who answered the phone.

'Who is that, please?' he asked, after he'd identified himself. Only a few days had passed since Zlotnick's calamitous appearance at the Rectory. Before Digory would have spoken in a tone of authority. Now he sounded brittle and querulous.

'I've got something for you,' came Dominique's voice.

Over the past five years Digory, along with the rest of his household, had been made to learn almost everything about hoaxers and opportunists. 'I doubt it,' he said.

'I'm trying to do you a favour, okay? I mean that.'

'If it's about the child, let me refer you to the police.'

'It's for your own benefit, you know. I want to make everything right for you. Why are you being so silly?'

'Do you think everyone here hasn't had this conversation before? And do you imagine that even now we couldn't distinguish the right child from any other?'

'You're not being very grateful, are you? The least you could do is show some, like, appreciation.'

'Is it?' Digory's tired voice was a desert of indifference. Glancing round the sitting room door Edmund, then Maria, also figured nothing now was being said.

'Oh, like that, is it?' You needn't think you can ignore me as easily as that.'

Digory rang off.

The only other thing Dominique did, before hurrying back out to the car, was to dial Zlotnick's number in Belgrave Square. Just to show him, she would have reversed the charges, but she didn't think there was that much time. Sure enough, there was no answer.

At no point that day had she stopped to think, Maybe *this* is what he'll do. But she ran, all the same, to get in the car without any more delay.

A man who was both young and old opened the door. He had slicked-back blond hair with dark roots and a neglected greying beard.

Zlotnick recognized him from his former visit to the house in Birmingham: Dominique's sometimes boyfriend Dave, by turns scaffolder, bouncer, professional kick-boxer and launderette manager. His current employer, the launderette-chain owner, also paid him as a promotor of illegal bare-knuckle fights mostly held in a derelict Victorian church nearby.

'Look, mate, do me a favour, would you? Confronted with this piece of low life, Zlotnick instinctively stepped part way back into the accent of his youth. 'Tell Dominique I need to see her.'

The other man eyed him without moving. 'They've gone.'

'Have they, begod? You wouldn't know where?'

Dave jerked his head at Zlotnick, meaning he should come into the hallway. It was almost dark inside. The narrow stairs were thickly crusted with cream paint on either side of a bare strip where a carpet had once been. Out of sight of the street, Dave said, 'You what?'

'I need to know where they've gone.'

'Oh yes?'

Understanding what was wanted of him, Zlotnick took out his wallet. 'The child was with her, did you say?'

'Yeah.'

'I've got something for them, you see.' With his wallet closed in his hand, Zlotnick waited to gauge Dave's response.

'It's all the same to me if you have.'

The man's sour indifference to Dominique was what Zlotnick had hoped for. Dave knew enough about her doings to guess that her brother was being milked for something, but no money had come his way, even so. 'I need it myself,' Dominique had told him, 'to give my little girl a good grounding in life.'

Without comment, Zlotnick counted out some

high-denomination notes. He rolled them up tight
before handing them over, as if the transaction were
an illegal one being made out on the street. With
the same expressionless face and furtive gestures,
Dave put the money in his jeans pocket.

Then he told Zlotnick what he'd overheard Dominique say on the phone.

Five minutes earlier Zlotnick's BMW had already
swooped past Dominique's rusty Ford Cortina on
the motorway. Even as they were both setting out
on a long-delayed rendezvous with destiny, they'd
been travelling in opposite directions and had failed
to see each other.

On the Cortina's back sea, Sal was feverish. 'I
want Grandma to sing *Neighbours* to me.' When
she'd been ill in the past, it had been the old woman
who'd held her in her arms or sat by Sal's bed, la-
la-ing theme tunes to *Dynasty* or from TV advertisements for Cinzano. 'The kitten's dead. I know because it looks like Grandma.'

Dominique said nothing. In a bright-eyed trance
of her own, she was driving as if to spite the whole
world.

In the Rectory at that moment, an eavesdropper
wouldn't have known to make of the low voices
from inside the drawing room door. by turns angry,
sad and triumphant, Maria was telling Edmund
every detail of her last four years and more. Except
to put an uneasy question from time to time, her

381

husband said nothing. She felt, after so much stoical silence, as if the words would pour out of her for ever.

In his study Digory sat quite still, unable to admit that Dominique's phone call had left him even more melancholy than before. Last night, teased by thoughts of self-destruction, he'd taken down his grandfather's Purdey from its place over the study door, as it were absent-mindedly. He'd meant to handle it as some kind of game, to show himself he couldn't really mean anything desperate. But it had been harder than he'd thought to put the gun away.

And today, for whatever reason, it would be harder yet. Feeling as much self-consciousness as despair – anyone might come in – he took it down and snapped open the breech.

South of Worcester, Dominique caught the notice of the police. Two patrolmen, driving over a motor-way bridge, saw her in the fast lane, obstinately refusing to give way to a Porsche.

'His engine'll be well knackered,' one of them remarked, assuming that only a man would drive in such a competitive way.

The patrol car stopped at its lookout site on the hard shoulder. Thirty miles to the north, Zlotnick was swooping after Dominique at twice the speed limit. Flashing and blaring his way past every other vehicle, he drove with his face set in a grimace of cold hatred and rage. She'd been right to sense that he'd be chasing her as if his car were a weapon of assault.

Only one vehicle was moving faster than the BMW. A red Lamborghini was being driven flat out on the same carriageway, for a bet, by a showroom assistant delivering it to his new owner. Joining the motorway at Worcester, it bombed past the patrol car two minutes ahead of Zlotnick.

'Hey, hey, hey,' murmured one of the cops. And away they went in pursuit.

Half an hour and one county later, anyone but Dominique might have been afraid. Slewing to a stop in Stinscombe village, the Cortina was at the back of a queue of vehicles waiting to cross the bridge. Behind the straight riverside stretch of Bridge Lane gave a view half a mile back. Turning into sight was a grey BMW.

The big car got to within a few lengths. In the driving mirror, as she muttered at the traffic light to change, Dominique could recognize her brother.

At that moment her view of him was blocked. The first of Manor Farm's thirty head of Frieesian cows was moving across the lane on the way out from milking, with almost hallucinatory slowness.

Zlotnick didn't hesitate. Swerving across the road, he drove the heavy car around the leading animal just in time. His offside wheel churned against the steep bank, then dropped back on to the tarmac with a thud.

At the bridge the light changed to green. Dominique watched the six cars in front of her as, one by one, their drivers got into gear. 'Move, you bastards! Come on! Sod you!'

One by one they went up on to the bridge, until the car in front of Dominique's Cortina had begun to move.

At the moment that Zlotnick's car got back on the road behind her, the light turned red.

Dominique ignored it. If she butted right up to the car in front, she'd make it before the oncoming traffic blocked her exit at the far end. By the time Zlotnick reached the traffic light, a Range Rover, a manure-spattered Mercedes and two horse boxes were bearing down on him. The horse boxes, built like removal vans, barely cleared the parapet on either side.

In the lane leading to the Rectory Dominique screeched to a crooked stop. The afternoon was darkening early; trees dipped before a soughing wind and stinging gusts of rain were clattering off the windscreen. At any moment the glare of Zlotnick's headlights would come probing up the hill.

Looking over her shoulder, Dominique wrenched open one of the rear doors. 'Out of there.'

'Where are we going now, Mum?'

For answer, Dominique dragged Sal out by the arm and slammed the rear door shut. She got back in the driver's seat. 'You can go in that house up there, if you want.'

'What's happening? I don't feel well.' Sal, shivering violently, started to weep.

'Never you mind what's happening.'

'I haven't been naughty. Really I haven't! Mum, what's happening?'

Dominique ignored her. A quick look in the driving mirror and she was away in a cloud of exhaust.

Sal ran after the Cortina's rear lights. The country dark terrified her. 'Mum! Mum! Wait! I'm sorry!' she shrieked, though she had no idea why she was being punished like this.

Surging up the lane, Zlotnick saw her ragged small figure in his headlights caught like a frightened rabbit. His lack of hesitation made him proud of himself. Not for one heartbeat did he doubt what he should do.

Inside the too-quiet house, Digory wondered if his hearing misled him. He got up, moving slowly.

Under the windblown trees Zlotnick registered that the lane was deserted; there were no witnesses. And the child had been officially thought dead for years.

He braked, so suddenly that the car bucked like a horse refusing a fence. Jumping out, he sprinted after her, leaving his door open to the rain.

Sal knew right away who this was. It was The Stranger, the person she'd been warned never to speak to. The Stranger could take many forms. He might look like a policeman. Or he could knock on the front door and pretend to be from the council. Whoever he seemed to be, all he wanted was to take her away and turn her into nothing. For years the thought of him creeping into the house had frightened her sleepless every bedtime. And now here he was, lunging at her wrists, trying to grab her by the hair, and all the while snarling, 'Fuck, shit, fuck!' as if to himself.

Sal screamed, a think high sound. 'Mum! Mum! Mummeeee!'

Within moments Zlotnick was as dishevelled as the semi-savage child struggling to escape his grasp. Sheets of rain had made his cashmere sweater sodden and plastered his hair flat. He muddied up to the knees. Minutes seemed to pass in the time the child fought against death like a wild animal; in fact she had only a few seconds' resistance in her. Zlotnick caught hold of her, recoiled as she scratched his face, stumbled and slipped after her, caught her again and finally got his hands around her throat.

On the far side of the house, Edmund asked Maria, 'What was that?'

'What?'

'I thought I heard the front door open.' He meant, on a night like this, why hasn't it been closed again?

Maria listened as he went to investigate. A snatch of someone's voice was audible over the sound of the wind. But there was no reason to think anything out of the ordinary was happening.

'What is this?'

Over his own noises of desperation, Zlotnick

386

heard a man's voice. Digory's tone would once have been commanding. Now he could only croak in astonishment at the murderous scuffle between Jimmie a strange child, lit by the car headlights.

'Jimmie . . .!'

Digory should have know better. Zlotnick was wrought to the point where he would dare anything. Taking the only course left, he threw himself into the car. The driver's door swung wildly as he accelerated from nought to fifty in four seconds.

Not a strange child.

The last things Digory knew were a roaring white light that gathered speed and size, and an unreverberating boom, loud as if his own backbone had turned to dynamite and gone off. A lid of darkness yanked him up into itself, then shut off the snarling sound that had closed with him. The car had smacked into him like a steak hammer into prime fillet, flinging him through the air in the attitude of a man relaxing in a deck chair – knees bent, wrists and ankles limp.

The child had gone, running into the wet darkness screaming for Dominique to come back and make everything all right. Zlotnick backed the car off, ready to accelerate after her. He was swearing in a voice quiet but deep, over and over.

'Fuck you. Fuck you. Fuck – aaaah!' He squealed with shock. There was a report as loud as one's eardrums being banged together, then half his windscreen was blasted away, exploding in sharp chunks of light over the car's interior.

387

It was Edmund, bawling at him in a transport of loathing. He held Digory's ancient Purdey trained on Zlotnick at close range.

'I'll kill you, motherfucker! I'll rip your fucking guts out!'

Despite the buffeting rain that smoked off the bonnet and slashed through the ruined windscreen, Zlotnick recognized his attacker. He scurried from the car, holding out his hands in a gesture of self-defence. 'Edmund! Thank God you're here! Look, old mate – there's been a terrible accident —'

Agog with seemingly unselfish concern, he turned between the barrel of the rifle and the shape caught in the hedge. Digory was suspended, head back and one knee raised. 'Can't you see? There's someone badly hurt here! You've got to let me get help!' Even now, bargaining for tolerance as never before,. Zlotnick didn't understand. The Adams family had just finished their career as unconditional liberals.

His words were drowned by Edmund howling with hate, all reason gone. 'I'm going to blow your head off, you cocksucker! I'll see you suffer!' Edmund's shoulders tightened as he aimed the gun. So did his trigger finger.

'Edmund! No! Please, no! Don't do it!'

What spared Zlotnick's life was Maria. Clinging to him while the household staff ran after her, she added her pleading to the two men's incoherent shouts of bloodlust and desperation.

Her husband was saved from committing a

felony. And Zlotnick was kept from meeting with an easy fate.

It was night rather than evening. Outside the Rectory gates there were men, vehicles and strong lights. Zlotnick had departed in handcuffs; Digory had been taken away by ambulance on a covered stretcher. All points of access to the lane were barred to the public, and the BMW, its door still open, was being cordoned off with fluorescent tape.

In his father's study, Edmund was being questioned while a constable stood on duty outside the door. He sat, the two police officers stood. The senior policeman, Superintendent Dysart, was a close neighbour and long-standing family friend. First names apart, however, this was no time for informality or even condolences; too much had to be explained. Edmund answered their questions well enough, for a man coming down hard from a thwarted killing jag. Responding as if for politeness's sake, he was calm but shaken, gazing inwards at himself with amazement.

In due course he mentioned that Digory had reported hearing what he thought was a child's voice outside. 'He'd taken one of the usual opportunist phone calls earlier. I think he was half expecting some kind of disturbance.'

An expression of heightened purpose showed on Dysart's face. He looked hard at Edmund.

'No one's mentioned a child before now.'

For an hour the police helicopter clattered to and fro working the valley. From the cockpit the beechwoods looked thin and unsdubstantial where the spotlight swept across their floor.

The chopper found nothing, but as Dysart and Edmund were leaving to complete Edmund's evidence at the police station, there was a phone call. Coming back into the hall afterwards Dysart said, 'Well, they've found somebody's child.' He paused to shrug on his coat. 'When I say they, I don't mean our people. The girl was found by someone from Fairmont. A bodyguard going off duty.' Fairmont House was the country residence of one of the royal princes.

Maria, who'd been waiting for him with Edmund while he took the call, said, 'Is the child old enough to be a witness?'

'She might have been, but by all accounts she's too ill. The man who spotted her caught sight of her feet trailing into the road as he was driving by. He thought at first he'd only seen a dead branch.' Dysart finished buttoning his coat before he added, 'Of course, you know what this means for one or other of you.'

Edmund scarcely bothered to nod. Someone would have to go through the formality of confirming that whoever the child was she wasn't Sarah.

'I can go,' Maria said. 'Right away, if you like.' It was late, but sleep was unimaginable. Especially with Digory's ghost newly present in the house.

'Wouldn't you rather wait until morning?' asked Edmund.

Dysart interrupted. 'I wish I could dress this up, but the child's condition is supposed to be critical. It may be a question of whether Maria would rather visit intensive care, or the morgue.'

The nurse whose shift on duty this was in intensive care finished changing the unknown child's IV. She was moving with the deliberation of someone used to being hurried; somebody's respiratory monitor, in the night-time shadows at the far end of the unit, had started bleeping again. Outside the doors to the rest of the hospital a uniformed policewoman sat waiting. At least she can do her job sitting down, thought the nurse. Going off duty shortly afterwards she would have said so, but for the sight of the unit's deputy matron approaching with a visitor.

Evidently the visitor was expected by the policewoman, who stood up as they approached. The deputy matron, looking serious as usual but otherwise expressionless, held the door open as Maria followed her to the nameless child's bedside.

Under the hospital sheet the girl's body looked insubstantial, as if it weighed no more than an insect's wing. Her face had a bluish tinge; she was so pale that it was hard to believe there was any life behind her unconscious features. Her fingernails were blue as well. Beside the bed, a respirator kept up a monotonous whisper.

The deputy matron, knowing who Maria was, had expected her to be calm, if not indifferent, so many years after she must have given up hope. Mistaking Maria's lack of comment, she considered it proper to make some remark before seeing her back to reception. It seemed wrong not to acknowledge somehow that her journey was bound to have been pointless.

'From the state this kid was in – I mean her clothes, not just her physical health – she's been neglected for years. She hasn't necessarily been wandering about, lost, for any time at all. The parents themselves could have dumped her; we've had one or two cases like that. She spoke in a whisper, watching the child as she did so. 'The doctor's prescribed tetracycline; it seems nothing else would be any better. Of course the problem with bronchio-pneumonia is the time you're forced to lose while altering the treatment in search of a drug that will work.'

Ever after, the deputy matron would blame herself for being unprofessional and making conversation when she should have been watching her visitor more closely. Seeing Maria step forward and slowly pull back the sheet, she exclaimed, 'You can't do that! Really, Mrs Adams —!'

The woman's astonishment grew at the sight of Maria's face. She'd seen women in labour looking like this: smitten dumb and glassy-eyed. Some people, in a crisis of pain, screamed as loud as they could; others found they couldn't move or speak, even to plead for relief. Maria held the sheet up, staring at the child's hospital-gowned body with blank eyes and parted lips. It seemed she'd crumble to dust as soon as move again. Even as Maria stared, made helpless by the discovery before her, she found herself registering everything with almost unnatural clarity. The edge of the sheet was laundered sharp as a butter knife. The deputy matron's eyes, frightened as well as astounded, had flecks of dark red.

Hours would pass before Maria could laugh or weep at what she saw. Meanwhile, deep in shock, all she could do was stare, while an inward voice cried out and over and over.

Help me. Help her. Please help.

CHAPTER
TWENTY-ONE

It was Dysart who took the call from the hospital. He listened for a moment, glancing involuntarily at Edmund as he did so. Then he passed the receiver across his desk. Maybe he should have got up and looked away, or left the room, for privacy's sake. As it was, while Edmund listened, Dysart found himself watching him, curious to know how a man might respond to something like this.

Maria's voice was anguished. 'Edmund! Edmund! Please! Come here quickly!' Dysart understood why there was no joy in her voice, but only grief; shortly Edmund would, too. Only now could she afford to realize how much had been lost to her over the years just ended.

Next to the death of President Kennedy, the discovery of little Sarah Adams was the item of news people would most remember hearing. Every television archive in the world was destined to file a print of Edmund breaking down on the hospital steps as he announced the finding of his daughter and confirmed her chance of a long-term recovery. For news editors everywhere, the kid's survival was the clincher; even given the other circumstances of the story, no one wanted a dud ending. At it was, this piece of footage was obviously a must for any roundup of the year's most momentous events.

The press were wild to know more about Dominique, too, following a deposition by Zlotnick. Was she pretty? Failing that, had she ever been photographed in the nude? Meanwhile Edmund's press secretary and her assistant noted how badly more than one head of government wanted to go on camera of a suitable opportunity with the child and both parents. 'So that they can look concerned, but somehow deserting all the credit,' she remarked, after fielding a particularly insistent call from a more high-powered version of herself.

At Digory's funeral Maria wept hysterically, supported at the graveside by Edmund and Sally. No one was surprised at her grief. As Professor Adams's adopted daughter, plucked from somewhere remote and underdeveloped, she was bound to feel she could never repay him.

No one guessed that she was consumed by remorse, at having let herself seduce him then humiliate him past cure.

Or almost no one. After the ceremony, the small group of mourners made their way out of Stinscombe churchyard past a sea of rain-soaked press photographers and private sightseers. In silence, Maria and Edmund drove on to the hospital, where Sarah's condition now left everyone warily hopeful. After Maria's outburst of weeping, things unsaid lay heavier than ever between them. But while she still leaked from the eyes and breathed with a shudder, Edmund hadn't the heart to speak. He felt as weary and as far from being happy as at any time in recent years. Hurrying into the hospital past another inevitable mob of onlookers, he nonetheless held her tightly by the hand. It was maybe a wishful gesture; certainly it was no less than people expected. Almost every news source had tried to upgrade the story by making them an ideal couple.

At Sarah's bedside, now in a private room, with the child deep in a drugged slumber, he felt the time had come for him to speak. Looking at Maria he said in a half-whisper, 'Next month, at the memorial service —'

'Yes?' Maria was calm once more, but guarded. In order to avoid her husband's eyes she bent her gaze on the unconscious child.

'I hope you'll let Digory's public reputation alone. Whatever you might think, or care to say, in private.'

She hesitated. For a moment he thought she hadn't heard him, watching the light rise and fall of their daughter's breathing. As she slept, ignorant of everything around her, Sarah could have been waiting to be born a second time.

Maria knew what Edmund really meant. If he hadn't suspected her affair with Digory before, he did now. This was his invitation to her to admit everything – now, while their mutual wounding of each other was overshadowed by more terrible things.

'Whatever they'll say about Digory, of course he'll deserve every word of praise. I did understand the good in him, truly I did.'

She'd meant to tell him everything, but now that the moment had come she couldn't bear to. It wasn't fear of her husband that silenced her, but dread of her own remorse.

Edmund was watching her intently. He made one more effort to discover the truth. 'I never did apologize, to your face, for the hurt I caused you.'

Maria looked embarrassed, then gestured at the sleeping child. 'None of that matters, now.' She found she was holding her breath, as if in anticipation. Both of them knew this was the moment that would decide the future of their marriage. With a hitch of fear in her voice she asked, 'You are going to let Sarah live with me, aren't you?'

'Good God, yes.'

'But – you wouldn't want to be separated from her again, yourself?'

'What do you think?'

'So what happens now?'

He went on looking at her, intent but uncertain. 'That depends on you.'

There were several days of drug-induced torpor before Sarah awoke fully.

When she did, Maria and Edmund were both at her bedside. Putting down a book, Maria suddenly noticed that the little girl was wide awake, staring at her very hard. She was looking too frightened even to move.

Maria tried to smile. 'Hello,' she said, hoping not to sound apprehensive herself. 'How do you feel, now that you're safely here?'

The child went on looking at her, rigid with fear.

'Don't you feel a bit better?' coaxed Edmund, visibly taken aback. 'We helped to find you, after you got lost,' he added.

Sarah mouthed something inaudible, tears springing to her eyes.

'What?' asked Maria, as gently as she could. 'What did you say?' She didn't even know what name to use.

'I want Mum,' whispered the child.

Neither of them could find anything to say. They'd been warned it might be like this. Now it was happening they were lost, unable to cope. 'I want my mum!' Sarah's sobs increased to a wail. 'Mum! Mum! Mummy!' she screamed.

Quickly Edmund did as they'd been advised, and rang for the nurse. The room resounded with the child's wails of terror as she went on calling out for someone – anyone – she knew to come and reassure her. As far as she was concerned, Edmund and Maria didn't exist. The only thing she wanted was for someone familiar to appear and make everything all right. The way it had been.

One evening a week later Andrew Maule was walking home through Lincoln's Inn Fields with an acquaintance from the firm of criminal lawyers on Zlotrick's case.

'Belgravia the blest, again,' said Maule. Zlotnick's imminent release on bail hadn't been anticipated everywhere, but in the Inns of Court it was taken for granted. Already a New York publishing house had offered a six-figure contract for his account of things as told to a ghost writer.

Striding briskly along, Bruce Tipp agreed. Tipp was a crop-headed man who worked out a lot. His colleagues never actually said that he looked like a villain, but they often told each other how he resembled a cop. 'It'll make that woman puke with rage, if it does come off.' Maria had given her own evidence in a state of false calm, steadied only by the belief that Zlotnick would be charged as he deserved.

'Just as well the sister's still AWOL,' Maule remarked. 'In the case of the old man, you might still be able to hold out for death by misadventure. But she could really stiff you on your claim that you were only returning the child at the first opportunity.' Maule spoke without irony, in addressing Tipp as if he were the client. The practice was widespread enough to be used even in moments of high seriousness.

'No problem. I've seen her photo. She's not only a dog; she's a pit bull terrier. No jury's going to convict on the evidence of someone who looks like that.'

'As to her general appearance, I'll concede that she'd be an asset to you. It would certainly help colour up accounts of your poverty-stricken childhood.' Stepping off the pavement outside the Sir John Soane Museum, Maule detoured round a group of widows on a cultural guided tour. 'Just as well, though, that you can't be shown to have killed your mother. And the marks on the child's neck needn't be yours.' A couple of women from the tour, doggedly recalling the prep they'd done on Hogarth's prints, looked up suddenly at the two men with their pin-striped waistcoats and unembarrassed voices. 'I know it would be as circumstantial as everything else, but one coincidence too many would've impressed any judge the wrong way.'

'Naw, I know we'll be lucky on this one. We may even come to trial before the Fraud Squad can get their finger out.'

'Who'll represent Adams, do you think?'

'Will he need someone heavy?'

'He should do. It looks as if some of us'll have a lot of unfinished business with the wife, too. She might have got away with everything, if only she hadn't stopped that cheque. As for Adams, I gather at the very least you're going to sue him as soon as you've been released.'

Unlike the forces of law, some people took a sniffier view of Zlotnick's charge sheet. On remand in a Victorian citadel of a gaol by a main railway out of London, he was being held under Section 43, for his own safety. If the other prisoners hadn't heard of him he might have bluffed it out, passing himself off in the exercise yard as an honest mugger or stick-up artist. As it was, he'd found himself in the nonces' wing, among rapists, child-murderers and bent coppers. Elsewhere in the gaol, his fellow-prisoners took a tolerant view of many things, starting with their own offences, but charges of attempting harm to a child had made him fair game on any terms. Reflecting the violent self-righteousness of prison sub-culture, the gutter press had insinuated as openly as they dared that Zlotnick was a monster and a fiend. Everyone about him knew that were he not under special protection within the prison, he would be more at risk than any man in the kingdom.

Lying on his bunk, Zlotnick waited for the last evening to end before he was due again in court. By God, he bloody well would get bail. The prison was always at its noisiest when everyone was being banged up for the night. Cell doors sounded off like distant artillery; walkways clanged; and orders were being given in voices pitched to drown out everything else. Zlotnick stared at the ceiling, rigid with impatience at one more night. Once free, he might have fallen out of sight as a leader of Allied Consortia. But he had new assets stacking up that should see him more than all right. In New York the East Sixties and Seventies were piled high with addresses where a dinner guest was more interesting for having faced down the right kind of rap.

People did like violence, so long as it couldn't be proved and it wore good clothes. Inwardly he grinned. Who would have thought the Adamses' patronage could have had this much mileage in it? And now that he knew the coon bint was behind everything, her pursuit of him would have been nothing compared to what he'd got lined up for her.

He didn't smell the smoke at first; instead he heard a large number of prisoners baying in response to it, a long way off. The prison had been built as a circle of spokes round a vast echoing hub: a giant wheel of misfortune which if stood on end would have reared up to the skies. At such a distance, could he be sure if the shouting was caused by the fear, jubilation or both? Zlotnick sat up on his bunk, soldier-straight, waiting to know if he should be concerned for himself.

The prison's switchboard operator was one of the first to realize the calamity that had overtaken the place. A riot had broken out — for some time, he couldn't work out where. Meanwhile prisoners were fleeing the violence, as well as members of staff. A part-time cookery teacher, about to go home for the night, found herself locked into her workplace with a warder and twenty pupils. On the phone the warder tried to insist on knowing when they'd be rescued. One prisoner, an eighteen-year-old on remand for credit-card fraud, wept as well as swore. Elsewhere a dozen panic-stricken men smashed a television room to flotsam in their attempts to barricade themselves in. 'Look, I'm telling you – you get us out of here quick!' shouted the least fazed of them down the phone at the operator. Next to the prison chapel, another group of men were crammed into the vestry, as uneasy as cattle in a badly driven truck. Every one of them watched the chaplain's face as he tried yet again to get through to the switchboard.

It didn't take long for the riot to spread almost everywhere. In a bottleneck near the refectory, at a pre-arranged signal, a warder had been hit on the head with a couple of batteries in a sock and his keys taken. The building's long vistas soon resonated with the sound of howling as a couple of hundred rioters smashed everything they could, including their own possessions.

Zlotnick didn't have long to wait, hiding behind his cell door. Four of them seized him, one by each limb. He was borne off down the walkway at a run, followed by a trail of other men sprinting behind with the urgency of medics at the scene of a crash. A series of ceilings revolved past him, seemingly without end. 'No – no – please – no! Please. I mean that – no – *please!*'

The din of chaos in the prison was so great they couldn't hear him anyway. Up one spiral iron staircase after another they heaved him, feet first. His head twisted violently as he cried out, nearly upside down.

Most of his abductors were in for life; they couldn't look forward to many chances to feel as

403

just and all-powerful as this, nor as close to real-life fame. It was almost like being a celebrity yourself, to lay hands on someone this well-known. By the time they'd shoved and carried him up four more floors, yowling at them to see things his way for a moment, Zlotnick had shat himself.

They dragged him out on to a night-time rooftop. Most of it had already been stripped to the bare timbers and its tiles reduced to shale. A week would pass before this part of the prison could be re-taken. A group of men, grunting with fervour, slashed and tore at his clothes while several others looked on in fascinated silence. Zlotnick was too far gone in terror to form words; all that came out of his mouth was a shrill whooping noise, over and over again.

When he was nearly naked, his remaining garments shredded down to the flapping edges of cuffs, and a belt, he was lashed to the roof by his arms and legs. Momentarily he managed to form words. 'Look out!' he cried wildly, as if there'd been a mistake. 'My feet are over the edge!'

Watching, the other prisoners on the roof saw one man lunge forward and make a small wound like a long red navel. Steam came from the vent in Zlotnick's abdomen as part of him was looped through a portable vice from the prison workshop.

The vice was screwed shut. Taking a step closer to the edge of the roof, the man looked over.

He let the vice fall.

CHAPTER
TWENTY-TWO

Slowly, a door to the future was creaking open. One day early in the year Sarah was sitting by the window of her hospital room. Outside, between grey trails of rain, the sky was brilliant enough to make you squint. In the hospital grounds a grove of winter-flowering cherry trees was misted with colour. Sarah, in her thick new dressing gown and fleece-lined slippers, was sitting up at a table. In front of her was a colouring book which illustrated the letters of the alphabet. She'd already gained six pounds in weight, and her hair, cut to a heavy bell shape around her delicate face, was now as glossy as Maria's. Day by day, with Maria or Edmund in attendance, she had inched away from despair, through resignation to indifference, to calm, then to the first stirrings of curiosity. As she recovered the beginnings of health, Maria saw in her an ever-increasing likeness to her own younger self.

Maria was sitting next to Sarah now, pretending to read a magazine and expecting sooner or later to be asked for help. With bursts of concentration during which nothing else counted, the little girl was colouring in her book's fancifully outlined acrobats, barber poles and candles, page by page. Almost as belatedly as her mother, Sarah had started learning to read.

Carefully she finished filling in pictures of the quail, quarterback, question mark, quilt and quotation marks. Maria waited, as instinct and the child psychiatrist on Sarah's case had dictated from the start. 'Don't reach out too fast for anything,' she and Edmund had been told. 'Affection, understanding – even attention; forget them until Sarah herself decides the time is right.'

'But how can we know when that is?' Edmund had asked. Sarah had still not been told any significant circumstances surrounding her admission to hospital. 'What if she ends up by blaming us for having held out on her longer than we should?'

The psychiatrist had looked thoughtful, but she hadn't hesitated. Edmund had been relieved to feel that he and Maria could trust her; he knew her already, from his work with Friends of Children in Peril. 'That's the lesser risk, Edmund, believe me. Let me describe how violently Sarah might reject you both if you're hasty in forcing your claim on her as her parents.' She had, too. He and Maria had left her office even more sobered than when they'd arrived.

Sarah tidily capped the red felt pen she'd used to fill in the giant outline of the question mark and looked at her handiwork.

'Tell me again how you and Edmund told the police helicopter to look for me.'

Maria was getting used to such questions, uttered without warning. Bit by bit, she was being nudged towards describing Sarah's immediate past – please God, in a way that would neither distress the child, nor make Maria herself into a liar. She repeated what she'd already said. It was a version of events contrived to raise as few further questions as possible.

'Tell me about going to school. Will I be able to stay for dinner?' At the same time that Sarah asked for the present to be explained, she was filling in a mental image of her future. Her method was much the same as with a real picture: details first, with the big spaces left empty. Maria gave an account of scenes from her own school life. She was careful only to mention unimportant things like how to make a noise with a straw in the bottom of the milk bottle, and vanilla ice cream with hot chocolate sauce.

'And will it be the school near where I used to live?'

'Do you mean the last place you lived in?' Maria was even more hell-bent than the police or the hospital psychiatrist in wanting to fill in the details of Sarah's last five years. Nothing was forthcoming from Dominique, even though she was at last in

407

police custody. She'd been arrested under another name only fifteen miles from Stinscombe, after getting into a fight with another member of the kitchen staff at a motorway service station. Obstinately she was holding to the story that it must have been her mother who'd run off with that baby. She was also threatening to sue at least one national newspaper for an item – admittedly false – saying that she'd once been a waitress in a topless cocktail bar.

Dominique's imprisonment would last for many years. Maria's only regret was that Zlotnick could no longer suffer the same fate.

Be grateful, she told herself. If he were alive he'd be as free as ever – and even more dangerous.

Sarah turned another page of her colouring book. 'Yes,' she said doubtfully. 'No. I don't know.'

'Tell me again about the places where you lived. There were lots, weren't there?'

'No, you tell me about when *you* were a little girl. Tell me about the storm that blew the houses away so that only the toilet bowls were left stuck to the ground.' Maria had been asked for some stories many times over. They'd become so ritualized that she wasn't allowed to alter one word.

'And now,' Sarah said, in due course, 'tell me about the time you were allowed to sleep on the beach at the seaside on your own.'

'It wasn't much fun. I mean,' Maria added quickly, 'it's not something that's going to happen to you.'

'But was it because your grandma had died?'

'Well, yes; I did have a grandma. And I suppose I wouldn't have been sleeping out of doors if she hadn't died.' Maria stole a careful look at her daughter. Suddenly she felt readier than ever to spill over with hope and dread. In their long conversations together, Sarah had flinched away from the subject of family relationships – hers or anyone's. Was this the moment to take a chance and probe her memory more closely?

· 'Do you want to know,' Maria ventured, 'about what's happened to – Dominique Zlotnick?'

Sarah hardly seemed to have heard. She'd picked up one of her pens and had started colouring in the outline of a rooster perched on the bonnet of a racing car. 'No. I want to hear about my grandma in heaven, and then I want to hear about how you went to live in a big house after your grandma died at the seaside.'

Marla told her, dwelling once again on the many expensive toys Digory and Elizabeth had bought her. She didn't mention how desolate she'd been on first arriving at the Rectory when bereavement, added to exile, had been made worse by years of insecurity.

'Is that what happens to many people whose grandma dies?'

'Not many, no.'

'But will it happen to me? Whose house will I go to?'

'Do you know whose house you'd like to go to?'

'Yes, I do.'

409

'Whose, then?'

'Guess.'

'Oh, I can't,' said Maria, trying to look as if any answer would be good enough to make her smile.

'Please guess!'

'If I shut my eyes and count to three, will you tell me anyway?'

'All right.'

Maria shut her eyes. Then, for the hundredth time, she counted her blessings.

One. She and Edmund were once more married to each other in spirit as well as in law. Tentatively, bound together by new fears for their child, they had become lovers again, and not just man and wife. Edmund would be here soon, to help keep Sarah company. Turn and turn about, one of them was with her for most of her waking day.

Two. A week ago yesterday, in response to some atrocious pun from Edmund, Sarah had laughed for the first time. Until then they'd scarcely seen her smile. Even the twelve-year-old Maria, left alone in New York and too frightened to go out, had looked more cheerful. Sarah's merriment, unforced as bird-song, had been a revelation. A first smile; a first embrace – who could tell what marvel might come next, even if there was no going back to recover what might have been?

And that left blessing number three. How could Maria have known that in this unimaginable way she would re-live her own infancy – let alone that she'd be blissfully grateful to do so? Years ago, waiting for Sarah to be born, she'd planned to give her a lifetime of untouched privilege. Now, after all that had befallen them, Maria was till going to give her daughter the childhood she herself had never had, but in a different way. Like Digory, she was mounting a rescue – one just as momentous as Digory's bungled attempt to change her own life.

All this passed through her mind in a silence as brief as the unfurling of an angel's wing. She opened her eyes.

'You didn't count.'

Maria counted, this time aloud. Then she waited for Sarah to speak.

'Now that I've got no grandma, will they let me go home with you?'